THE DUST
SOLUTION

BRYAN CHARLES ARTHUR
DANIELSON

THE DUST SOLUTION

First edition. December 11, 2018.

Copyright © 2018 Bryan Charles Arthur Danielson.

ISBN: 978-1732102521

Library of Congress Control Number: 2018913578

Written by Bryan Charles Arthur Danielson.

Published by Bryan Charles Arthur Danielson, Portland, Oregon.

Dedication

I probably owe Sarah the most gratitude. She is the most admirable, resilient, and moderating presence in my life. Tina, my confidant and fellow conspirator of serious business and fancies. My editor Rochelle, an impeccable professional, punctual attendant to my many questions, and keeper of insights. My mom and sisters. Ladies, without you in my life, I wouldn't have had the financial, emotional, intellectual, or spiritual resources to create fiction.

I'm eager to thank Jacob, my best friend in the whole world and a man of remarkable dedication, for being my original fan. Kevin K. and Andrew J. have always been there to share some excellent silliness, even if years have passed. I owe Michael B. thanks. His wisdom on discipline still reminds me, "If you wanna do overtime, you gotta be hardcore." My dad. Gentlemen, if it weren't for you, I wouldn't have developed enough good-humored self-motivation to get this done.

I also have to thank Michael H. and Jason "Voorhees" S., because they introduced me to specific artists of industrial rock and fantasy fiction. These artists, in turn, gave me life-changing inspirations, lasting years. This book, and those I expect which will follow, wouldn't exist if it weren't for the many voices and sounds of those artists in my head, daring me to bet my own self for my dreams, and to write well.

Mike and Liz, thank you both for always inviting me into your family, and for sharing life, death, separation, and redemption, with me and others, amongst friends and loved ones, over the years.

I can't leave out the rest of my biological family, some of whom will not like this book, and that's okay! Admittedly, the phrase "it's not for everyone" comes to mind. Oh well! I love you anyway!

This book is dedicated to those who teach the discipline of questioning the truth in order to find it, to those who live with the burden of a sacred knowledge which can never be unlearned, and for those who are curious; may you graciously find what you're all about.

> John Waterman, U-A DOB: 2579-12-03, CID 09985240860

> ResID: 10.4.2 [altered by CID 09985240860/ResID: 9.3.1] M1

> U-A: [Chronos Outpost.OID:00000178561] GT: 2605-04-01,
   12:35:51

— April 1st, 2605, 12:35 PM —

Luke, some of your memories, or 'mems,' have been erased, and where and when you came from is easier for me to explain if I give you some of mine. I'm doing so with the hope you will regain what happened from your own point of view. My god, Chronos, has abandoned us, and wherever you are, and whether you know it or not, I am hoping you hold the key to Humanity's survival. I have begun to question what kind of person would create a god, and if I met either, how I would gauge their worth—god or person.

I hope this is not your first message through the Humanity Protocol, but if it is, I should mention that the metadata included with these memories is there to show a relative starting point of reference for anyone who recalls them. For now, ignore the metadata. The Humanity Protocol regulates the syntax and communication of memories. More to come.

In the meantime, let me start over. I should start off by saying that the first thing we did was step through the Model from our universe to yours.

Technically, the Model emerges underground first, and transforms the surrounding mass into a storeroom, an exit tunnel, a command center, a sick bay, and some other rooms. Then, we step through with microtech and nanotech we call dusts. The dust exits the Model, constructing connections of our universe's technology with your local infrastructure via cell networks. It takes only five seconds for the model to do its job and for me and my team to arrive. While we connect with the Internet and begin downloading the planet's information, the Model rests in the Holoroom, and we prepare mentally and emotionally for settling in.

1

We had practiced in virtual reality what we thought to expect, but we had never actually traveled to another time and universe before, so we arrived excited about being the first of Humanity to enter a different universe at an older time.

Here, then, are the memories.

Begin Report, Mem Report #24601: John

> John Waterman, U-A DOB: 2579-12-03, CID 09985240860

> ResID: 4.3.2 [altered by CIDs 09928764743 &
09985240860/ResID: 3.2.1] M1, M2, & M3

> U-B: [Chronos Outpost.OID:00000000001, Earth] LT: Tuesday,
2006-08-01, 4:20:00 PM MST

— Tuesday, August 1st, 2006, 4:20 PM MST —

That was anticlimactic. I expected more, but, really, we just walked through a door. It's a door from our Alpha universe, but it's still only a door. Either way, time is limited, and we each have our orders. We have very little time to discuss the particulars of our circumstance. We must shut this base down, leave here and reawaken with new Resident Identities at a secondary location.

I need to take the lead. So, entering a super-sped-up mental state I call Dream, I sit down at the command center's console next to everyone and briefly review this Earth's entire information, infrastructure, and resources.

Between me and the Holoroom door is my obsession, the reason we're here: Adam, a child in a stasis pod. The only times he's been out of his pod in his three-year lifespan are for the surgeries Anny and I have performed in larger enclosures. I finish Adam's behavioral coding for the next twenty years.

I set up the 3D printing technology of the Model to print up two computers. One's designed to look like an inventory book; the other is a verm container that looks like a toy robot. I include a copy of Anny's current resident identity, her ResID, in the toy robot.

I exit Dream and step into the Holoroom to pick up the inventory book and toy robot and return to the command center, confident in my team's efficiency.

They know their orders. They know what to do.

Looking up from the console in the command center, Anny says, "The base recommends the city of Jane in Humboldt

3

County, California as the best location and Lucia Gage as the best role model for Adam."

I set the toy robot down on the console for the moment and look around. Everyone seems to agree. "Any objections from anyone?" I ask.

They shake their heads.

"To confirm, since we are responsible for Adam's continued development, we will be recruiting Lucia Gage, a nineteen-year-old who recently lost her father. Now, our current mission could be illegitimated at any time—a cleaner with their own erasure protocols may show up and threaten our success.

"Armand, the protection of this team will be in your hands should any of our behavior become unmanageable. You may recruit Lucia Gage by buying marijuana from her after the amount we print here is exhausted.

"Again, for the record, does anyone have any objections?"

Anny, Armand, and the Doc all say, "No."

"Make no mistake," I say to everyone, "this is vitally important—nothing and no one must come between us and the goal of our mission: we've come here to keep Adam's development, the Model, and the 6V codec safe and secret, and then return to our universe."

As I hand Armand the book, I tell him, "I've coded our own erasure protocols and the catalyst in this database computer disguised as an inventory book. As required, it can update dust in real time. The protocols will change based on need. Make sure the Doc's experimentation with the 6V codec doesn't compromise our position here."

Armand opens the book and skims through some of its pages, then closes it up. "I know what to do."

He sits down at the console and reviews various local vehicles and sets the Model to print the windowless two-seater van of his choice, complete with VIN, California plates and tags in the Holoroom.

Anny and I catch each other watching Adam floating peacefully in his pod. I jerk my eyes away and plug wiring from the console to the pod and install the ResID Adam will have for the next twenty years.

"The Doc," I call out, "since you're first up to get wiped, you might as well get prepped for it."

"Wiped? You make it sound like I'm going to need to pull my pants down first."

"Fine, memmanned."

Armand steps into the Holoroom, gets into the van, starts it up and does something we've only seen in simulation—he relocates the van from the Holoroom to the garage by way of two large electrostatic rings that act as portals between two places in space. He drives through the ring out of the Holoroom in front of us and concurrently enters the garage through a ring behind us. It is much louder in person.

While the van relocates to the garage, the Doc walks from the command center into the sick bay through a hallway that has a robot cubby, complete with two Ally-brand robot charging stations, which have two robots in stasis hunched over as if with brooding subservience. The Doc lies down on a cot and takes a deep breath, the kind of deep breath a diver takes before plunging into deep, dark waters. He pierces his abdomen with wiring and tubing and closes his eyes, awaiting the change.

Armand, having shut off the van in the garage, reenters the command center, and Anny and I watch him pick up Adam's pod, walk back out into the garage, and place the pod in the van.

"It's done," I say, referring to her ResID and handing her the blockish toy robot. I tilt my head to ask if she heard me.

She nods, taking and setting the toy down. "I've been looking forward to having my verm removed," she says, sitting down at the console to review information about Lucia Gage and the surrounding infrastructure. "We do what we need to do," she says, staring at the screen, "but I don't feel as human with it in me. I still think weaponizing yours was a bad idea."

"I'll manage."

"After review of Earth and Lucia's behavior," she says, turning to me, "I recommend my new ResID build a romantic relationship with Lucia to secure better social growth of Adam's new ResID and take our obscurity further."

I consider the pros and cons of how this might disrupt the mission, then say, "Agreed."

"Also," she says, "I know we didn't discuss this before, but I want my new ResID's name to be Auna."

This is unexpected. "Auna?" I ask. I grab the toy robot and plug it into the console. "Why? Different ResIDs don't come with different names. You're asking for a superficial difference that becomes moot when your mems retain your former ResID information," I add with worry in my voice, "if reactivated."

Anny says, "We're going to be okay. They'll be reactivated. It'll just help me after I regain my memories. I can internalize the segmentation of things easier if the name is different. It's going to be twenty years. That's a lot of memory to segment as a different ResID."

We don't have time to argue, and I've already plugged the toy robot into the console, so I do as she asks—I enter Dream, lean over, finish up the coding, and return to normal speed. "Done," I say, unplugging the toy robot and turning toward the sick bay, "and until you turn forty-four, your new name shall be Auna."

"Thank you," she says, standing up from the console to follow me. "Okay, let's do this."

Our walk to the sick bay takes us through the short hallway with the robot cubby.

Anny takes her shoes, socks, and pants off and sits on a cot just as I'm plugging the toy robot into one of the sick bay's consoles. She lifts her shirt and pushes wire-like hoses into her belly and thighs, and a smaller one in the pink area of the eye between the ball and the socket. She smirks and says softly, "Good bye, world," and closes her eyes, lying back and taking one last deep breath before her mems are changed.

The Doc wakes up and sits up as his new ResID. "I am eager to work on coding something," he says, "but I'm unsure what.

The phrase '6V codec' keeps coming to mind. My thoughts are still coming into focus."

"Your urge to code is because of me. Well, you and me—we work on a project together. You'll get why eventually, but I'll explain the highlights. I'm curious, though—do you know your name?"

The Doc stops to think and then shakes his head, insecurity spreading on his face.

Armand, built like a bull, walks in to check on the Doc.

"Don't worry," I tell the Doc, whose skinny shoulders lifted when Armand walked in. "Who you are will come to you. You are a fugitive that has memmanned yourself more than anyone here. At least, that's what I believe."

Armand sniffs, standing with his arms folded.

"We don't really know who you used to be," I continue, seeing the Doc still tense. "You committed a crime so terrible that Humanity mandated an erasure of who you were. Since then, you have done what you could to help Humanity, but as part of your justice agreement, you'll eventually have to submit to Recollection, which is when your old memories are put back, and then you'll stand trial. The resulting title you've gained for yourself, since no one in Humanity knows who you are, is 'the Doc,' as in, 'doctored ResID.'"

"What?" the Doc asks, exasperated.

Doc's mem recalibration is making him... simple, but at least we have time to help him through it—it takes longer to do that than what we're doing for Anny—extracting her verm and altering her existing life-long memories.

Armand sees me pausing to think, so he speaks up. "You used to be bad," he says to the Doc. "Humanity doesn't know how bad, but apparently no one cares because you supposedly gave all that up and you're good now. The Recollection makes your mems from before come back, to you and everyone else, and then whoever you've become has to deal with the consequences. In the meantime, you want to work on something called '6V codec' because you coded yourself to."

That explanation must have clicked with him because he nods at him in wonder and starts wandering about the sick bay. "The Doc is my title," he says with distance in his voice, "but just call me Doc, okay? It'll make things simpler."

"Doc it is."

"Hey," Armand says to me, ignoring Doc, "are we good? Looks like the Doc's good to go. If you're okay with it, I'm going to look over the inventory book in the command center and get the Allies set up."

"We're good here," I tell him. He leaves through the hallway.

Finding the robot cubby as Armand leaves, Doc asks, waving at the robots in stasis, "Allies?"

"Yes, Ally-brand robots, Chi Gung models. They will set us up on this Earth with all the background records needed to legitimize our new ResIDs in the infrastructure of records that aren't electronic, including physical memorabilia to enhance our new ResID's lives, like favorite music, videos, movies, books, stores, parks, and meet-ups. They'll handle of all the real estate, licensing, birth, and medical histories at their respective locations by impersonating record keepers or each of us," I say as I sit at one of the sick bay consoles to review Anny's memmanning progress, "and then they'll return here and return to stasis.

"You'll be in an isolated house away from the city of Jane so you can work on the codec off-grid and undisturbed. Armand will remain your chaperon. He follows my orders. Anny," I say, nodding to Anny on the cot, "is our lab partner.

"All of us, actually, are going to be living in otherwise abandoned locations. Even if someone from the Alpha universe does come here, they wouldn't have cause to erase us, because we will have already become so different and inconsequential to be near invisible."

"But, Adam isn't inconsequential," Doc says as he turns to me, "and he has scars all over his body. People are going to ask questions."

"Adam's scar tissue exists because of nanotech and other biotech that allow for more than two sets of DNA to be in his body, but is ResID will say it's a birth defect.

"The whole point of why we're here is so that Adam, once developed enough to handle it, will take on the 6V codec, awaken his verms, and save our universe from a radioactive fungus-like spore that, upon maturity, can reach the size of large planets by consuming them. They then act like spore pods, bursting with spores and infecting nearby planets. One spore can turn entire solar systems."

Doc's eyes widen as his jaw drops slightly.

"Humanity is a human-supremacy, futurist culture in our Alpha universe that is networked together wirelessly amongst all members, and all members can share their mems, and yet even with the billions of members, Humanity still hasn't come up with a way to thwart the spread of the fungus. We five have covertly had a rare procedure done called 'verm enhancement' to try to help with the problem in secret, but to Humanity, verms are taboo because verms aren't human.

"They're alien, but they enhance human physiological and mental abilities. They combine with DNA, making it near invincible, and they permeate all of the DNA, so introducing more than one verm causes death, unless a person has more than one set of DNA.

"General Simon Morgan, the second in command to Chronos, himself, sponsored and assigned us to this clandestine mission. He believes in Adam though the rest of Humanity may not understand our goals here. The 6V codec you've been assigned to code, if successful, will allow Adam the chance to organize his verms properly. It is an experimental systemic biocode. With it, we expect he'll be able, we hope, to handle the threat of the spores. We only have one shot at the codec. If it fucks up, Adam and his verms die, and we'll be stuck in this universe until we die, and that won't likely be from old age."

Doc nods, his eyes still wide.

"We have other threats: Humanity purists or Chaos agents wanting to stop us from completing our mission. That's why we chose this time and this universe: we plan to lay low here. Our verms can be traced using technology from the Alpha universe, so our new ResIDs are going to be consuming a lot of marijuana during our stay here to avoid detection—the THC blocks tracing tech. Since Armand'll be supervising, just follow whatever he says, and you'll be safe while you work."

"Okay. With what?"

I point to the toy robot. "This is going to be your new best friend. It's how you'll be able to work on coding the 6V codec. Everything you might need to know is included in it, which is important, because in order to understand even the simplest aspects of the protocol, you must at least understand the metadata associated with each memory. For example, when you remember your own memory, it's in first-person. When you remember someone else's memory, it's in third-person. Everything else is pretty much self-explanatory."

"Okay," Doc says, stepping closer, hunching over to look at the information shown on the sick bay console, "some of this is registering with me, but I have some questions for you. Here, for your mem's metadata, where it says, John Waterman, U-A DOB, and CID—I get that this is your name, date of birth in the Alpha universe, and your citizen ID number registered with Chronos, but what is the ResID again? The numbers after the ResID, do they have any specific meaning? What are these 'M's at the end of the 2nd line?"

I raise my hand to stop the flood of questions. "The three lines of text are a timestamp of metadata for the memory of whomever experienced it. The first line is the current government record, your Chronos record. This shows your name, universe of origin, date of birth, and registered citizen identification number, or CID. It is what Humanity has registered in Chronos's database for the person who experiences the memory. A ResID number indicates how many times that person has had their personality changed and the number of verms they have in their body at the time the memory occurs.

"The second line includes your intrinsic information, such as your ResID, whether or not you've been altered or memmanned, and by whom, and then at the end, the M's you see represent which memory is involved. M1 is primary memory saved by the Humanity protocol, which includes normal perception in real time and any mems you've downloaded. M2 is your secondary memory, which is memory involved with or enhanced by your verm, so it includes information of what you couldn't naturally perceive.

"The third line of metadata in the Humanity protocol is information recorded by your verm starting off at the time and place the memory begins."

Doc steps back in thought, then asks, "Okay, this is all well and good, but about any threats—why not just print up a computer with algorithms that search and destroy? You could do it. Why don't you?"

Every time someone goes through a memmanning, they ask so many questions, most of which, if they would just wait, they would remember the answers anyway.

"Because of anonymity protocols. Besides, you're the Doc, expendable, and self-manned to work on the 6V codec."

He grimaces, suspicious. "Are there no other resources to help us? You've printed complex biological materials and machines with the Model. Why stop?"

"The Model uses an Alpha-universe-specific ink, if you will, which runs out and cannot be replaced or recursively printed. Only a certain amount can fit through the barrier between universes. Plus, it's expensive."

Doc's posture still shows his suspicion.

"Look, Doc," I say softly, turning in my chair toward him, hoping to gently cut him off before his thoughts sprawl further. "You're still getting acclimated to your new ResID, and I understand you're still getting oriented and have a lot of questions. Really, for the scope of this, your mission is to use hypervisor tech we've disguised as a toy robot to experiment with the 6V codec until Adam is ready for it when he's roughly twenty-three years old," I say and turn back to the console and bring up some of the code on a nearby display. "Here is some of the work we've done thus far."

Doc's stiff posture relaxes with intrigue seeing the toy robot's user interface. He sits down in front of the console and begins exploring the instructions I've provided within.

"Adam's brain needs to mature before we can even activate his verms," I tell Doc, "and there's no accelerated growth option because of the complex interplay of his sets of DNA. The toy robot is also going to store Anny's verm with the 6V codec. Do not try the 6V codec on yourself, or you will likely go crazy and die from mental cascade failures. Just work to get Adam's activation protocol set up, and don't fuck that thing up," I say to Doc, pointing at the toy robot. "We can't make another one."

As Anny's memman is finishing up, I turn to Doc and say, "Since you're going to be reporting to me your work on the 6V codec, report anything significant by way of something in the Humanity Protocol called praying. To send a prayer, say my name as if addressing me directly. When I review your mem, that part will more easily come to the surface of the mem recall."

Doc pauses, his eyes moving side to side, lost in thought. "My verm's telling me mem corruption can occur. Is this true?"

"Yes. For example, there may be information missing from the memory or metadata—your mem is only a record of what you and your verm perceive in real time. If anything alters your perception, it alters the record. No system, no matter who created it, or however sophisticated or secure, is infallible. If you or your verm is unfamiliar with where you are or when your mem begins, you and the verm will try to provide the best guess with what information it can gather from your experience. Once you reconnect with Humanity, the verm recalibrates and backdates metadata information, correcting as it goes, but in the meantime, it can be disorienting."

After the base sends a message to Armand that Anny's extraction and memmanning is complete, he activates the Allies and enters the garage with the inventory book in hand. The Allies enter the sick bay and carry Anny and her clothes into the van. As the Allies slump over in the van, reentering stasis, Armand is already inside and shutting the door.

"We're done prepping to leave," I tell Doc. "I can do my own memmanning on the way. It's time you and I went to the van to head out." I stand up and unplug the toy robot to take with me.

We walk into the garage and get into the van.

Doc begins to show further signs of interacting with his verm: his breathing speeds up, he exhibits rapid eye movement. He moves to shift his weight, but his movement is explosive and out of control. He bounces off the van ceiling, almost accidentally striking Anny upon landing, but Armand, trained as a soldier, skilled in controlling these kinds of things, moves with an inhuman speed and control. Before Doc fully lands, Armand grabs Doc mid-air, puts him into his seat, fastens his seatbelt tightly, and says two inches from his face, "Calm yourself. We've got to get out of here, and we don't need any distractions."

"Sorry," Doc says, more tense than I've ever seen him.

Armand nods and sits back in the driver seat at a normal speed, takes the wheel and starts up the van

I try to relax to prepare for verm deactivation. I fasten my safety belt and we begin heading out of the base for Jane, California. I set the toy robot to install my new ResID, stab myself with wiring and tubing from it, and then shut my eyes, reassured that when I awake, all my mems will be safely overwritten, and everything that I do for the next twenty years, in my newly coded ignorance, will be for the sake of saving Humanity.

* * *

> John Waterman, U-A DOB: 2579-12-03, CID 09985240860

> ResID: 6.0.0 [altered by CID 09985240860/ResID: 5.4.0] M1

> U-B: [Doc's house, Jane, CA, US, Earth] LT: Thursday, 2009-10-22, 9:46 PM PDT

— Thursday, October 22nd, 2009, 9:46 PM PDT —

"... and I want you to get me one thousand medical needles, gauges fifteen through seventeen, large enough that pins with heads can be fit in them. I'm going to make a mirror out of the surfaces of one thousand pin heads. Then I can go home."

As he speaks, I don't really know what to make of it. My boss said the guy was eccentric, but he didn't really tell me what to expect. I knew he was eccentric, too, but didn't care.

As he gives me a tour of his house, he shows me all kinds of weird things. I can only assume he creates them simply for his own amusement, but there is dust on everything.

Okay, like, for example, I look over in one corner of the room, and there's a Plexiglas piano chair with four unopened boxes of chocolate-covered ants in it. On top of that, there's a foot-tall Statue of Liberty cigarette lighter. No piano.

Right above it on the same wall, he has a shadowbox. Inside, it contains bits of a completely broken red Christmas bulb like some kind of 3D snapshot of the bulb shattering after hitting the wall. That's just in that corner. Everywhere else, there's a hoarder's paradise of piles and aisles of other random stuff.

I start thinking of what it would be like if Armand could see all this shit. I doubt he already had, or if any of this weirdness ever made it to the "Los Eat, Adios!" restaurant, or, as we called it, "Los Eatos."

"Hey, John, wake up." Doc neurotically puffs off a joint twice and then passes it to me. Smoke blows out everywhere.

"Right," I say as I take it and toke it. "Sorry, got distracted."

I am definitely going to have to tell Auna about this place.

15

"Look, don't stare too hard at the ghosts in here," Doc tells me. "You'll spook 'em out!" His hands are frantically asking me for the joint back.

This GUY spooks me out.

"Hey, I'm cool man." I pass him the joint back and exhale.

"Now, then, after it's framed and everything—" He pulls smoke into his mouth as he inhales. "I'm going to use it to get where we—I need to go." He exhales smoke into the already cloudy room.

"Right. You're going to get home."

He passes me the joint.

"Yes."

I lean forward and take it from him.

"Okay."

What else was I going to say? His legs and feet are bouncing his body up and down like he's doing the pee-pee dance, which is abnormal, even for him.

I stare at this joint he passed me.

Here is a guy who smokes pot like he needs it to breathe. Most of the time we didn't know if he was cool or not. Normally no one cares. It's hard to smoke everyone under the table, but this guy actually *did*, and he *never* seemed to mellow out. Smoking's cool and all, but to never actually get high? It's unnatural. I take another drag off his joint to take the edge off. Even though he's been puffing away, he's been talking up a storm, and I'm really just trying to enjoy my high—

Puff, puff, pass.

He grabs it and pulls drags off it desperately.

"How uh... how are you going to get one thousand medical... wait, you want *me* to get them... *used* medical needles?"

Damn I'm high.

"Yes. That's exactly what I'm saying, John. They need to be gauges fifteen, sixteen, or seventeen. I'll show you what I mean. Stay there, and I'll get a flow-chart that'll explain everything."

He stomps off.

This is disturbing... but it's cool because I'm getting stoned on free weed. It's easy to start zoning out again. I mean, look at this place: it looks like a chemist's lab, a computer science lab, a mechanical engineering lab, and an electrical engineering lab somehow all took ecstasy and had a degrading orgy right here in this guy's living room, complete with stains. There's a dried-up tomato stuck in the popcorn ceiling... not molded, just dried. Throughout the room, pieces of lab equipment are thrown together, too. Some of it reaches the ceiling, yet there's also taxidermy trophies and mannequin torsos with heads staring up out at me amid of all the wires, metal, and tubes, and little LED lights flashing on and off, peeking out from the plastic terrain of equipment and sunken mannequin eyes.

Doc stomps back into the room with an easel and a large pad of paper. He begins to trace out a graph of what he plans to do with the mirror.

"Okay, here we go," he tells me. "You see the mirror here? Here are the antennae. You've got to have those—even if they don't do anything—in case they do do something. And here—there's two Tesla coils, a Jacob's ladder, and then, of course, the other stuff is top-secret 'from the future' stuff."

I smile. "You said, do do."

"Yeah."

"K." I'm still smiling.

"Good. Then, but here's the thing—I need those to get home."

My smile fades. "The one thousand needles?"

"Yes."

I feel like I don't know this guy from Adam. I'm still smiling, but I've never seen him this anxious and neurotic-looking. I'm half expecting him to jump out from the hallway, laughing maniacally about whatever's going to happen next.

What am I doing here?

Eh, maybe what Armand said is true, that he is *eccentric* and not *diabolical*. I know he's rich; otherwise he wouldn't be able to afford smoking all the time or all this other weird crap he has around the house, like the custom laminated brick toilet I pissed in about an hour ago.

I'm paranoid by nature, which might just be because of the weed, but like any other paranoid bastard out there, I read into shit that in the long run, now that I think of it, probably just makes me more paranoid. It's weird. I could be delusional.

He sits down and starts rocking like a violent autistic about to blow.

"Dude, you are trippin' out. You're tripping me out... Cool out."

"That's what I'm trying to do," he explains, staring at the floor and rocking. "Auna told me rocking can be calming."

"You see her, too?"

He looks up. "Yeah. Here's the thing—I *need* those, and I'll even pay you five thousand dollars in cash to get them."

He rocks for a few minutes more while I slowly space out at all the weird crap in his house again... but this time, I'm thinking of five thousand dollars.

* * *

> The Doc, U-A DOB: ~2559-07-13, CID 99999999999

> ResID: 5.4 [altered by CIDs 99999999999/ResID: 4.3 & 09985240860/ResID: 4.3.2] M1 & M2

> U-B: [Doc's house, Jane, CA, US, Earth] LT: Sunday, 2009-10-25, 11:59 PM PDT

— Sunday, October 25th, 2009, 11:59 PM PDT —

On a quiet, redwood-forested private property near the small town of Jane, which is located just off the Pacific coast next to Sister City in Humboldt County, a medium-boned well-built dark-skinned man in a greasy yellow apron marches silently up the steps from a paved driveway onto the deck-porch of an expansive lonely house lit only by one buzzing porch light. He knocks on the front door ten times, and then he waits for six seconds.

The door opens a little, slowly, then wide, quickly.

A scrawny pale man with disheveled grayish-white frizzy hair and buggy eyes leans out and asks, "What do *you* w—"

"Doc," the man in the apron interrupts with a southern drawl, "I was able to get what we needed *to get home.*"

"What? It's really late. You could have called."

"My phone's broke," the man in the apron says, holding up the phone and wiggling it a little. "See?"

Doc looks down and reaches for the phone, but the man in the apron moves so fast, Doc doesn't have a chance to see what happens.

His forearm is severed clean.

Blood stains the apron.

Doc screams, collapsing into a fetal position.

He clenches his fist around the stub to try to stop the blood flow. Then he reaches unsuccessfully for his severed limb.

More blood escapes.

His face is wracked with disbelief and agony.

"Don't fight it," the man in the apron says as he kicks Doc's body from its side and kneels on Doc's chest, pinning Doc's back to the ground, shoulders under knees.

Blood frees itself from the stub in spurts.

Doc howls whole lung-full gasps of air into the night as a primal call for help.

The porch light buzzes as blood pools.

Doc thrashes his stub helplessly about under the weight of the much larger man in a failed attempt to see it. His howling becomes sour and forfeiting. His face turns pale. He is losing a lot of blood. He loses his sense of consciousness. His wailing recedes to breath.

"Pain was the *key*. Your pain is gone now."

The bleeding has, in fact, stopped completely.

The fear on Doc's face changes to curiosity. The pain is gone.

The dark-skinned man in the apron stands and steps over Doc's face where he lies, staring at the cloudless sky. He turns and looks down on Doc.

Doc begins to shiver in the buzzing porch light, his exhalations visible in the cool air.

"The catalyst was on my blade. Your secondary memory should be coming back online now."

* * *

> John Waterman, U-A DOB: 2579-12-03, CID 09985240860

> ResID: 7.1.0 [altered by CID 99999999999/ResID: 5.4] M1

> U-B: [John's apartment, Jane, CA, US, Earth] LT: Saturday,
2009-10-24, 10:54 PM PDT

— Saturday, October 24th, 2009, 10:54 PM PDT —

"... I've been kidnapped."

"John, you said?" she asks, just above a whisper.

"John Waterman, yes," I say, "that's me."

"I employed you, Mr. Waterman. I know who you are. Why are you calling me?"

"I've—I was drugged and tied to a chair, and Doc was threatening me with an ice pick."

"Doc?"

I ignore her hushed tone of mockery. "Yeah, he—he was in some kind of manic state," I explain, trying to process my thoughts. "He threatened my friends."

She whispers, "Oh? With what?"

"Naturally caused... accidents." *This isn't going to work.*

"'Naturally caused... accidents,'" she says quietly. "Mr. Waterman, we're a small town. This ain't like Sister City. Kidnappin' just ain't gonna happen. My husband and I have to get up at four in the morning to feed the cows and go open the department store. I could be sleeping right now next to my husband, who I'm afraid just woke up 'cause of you."

"I was drugged, tied to a chair, and threatened with an ice pick."

"Okay. You tell me now, when did this happen?" She sighs and begins speaking at regular volume. "No, no, everything's fine. I think I'm about done."

"Just tonight... Wait, what's up?"

"Oh, I've woken my husband with me talkin' to you," she says, no longer whispering. "Never you mind about that. What do you want?"

"You—you're not gonna report me if I smoked a little weed, will you?"

21

"Mr. Waterman, if you don't tell me what's going on, I'm going to hang up."

"No! Okay, okay. I was smoking with Doc when—"

"Smoking."

Damn it.

"Yeah, uh, we were smoking… you know, smoking weed."

"Well, I know *now*. … All right, all right," she says, filling the silence. "Well you might as well keep goin'. We're committed now."

"I—We uh, we were smoking weed together, and—"

"Uh-huh."

"And he asked me to get one thousand used medical needles."

"Agh, what? You high now?"

"Well, yeah, 'cause he drugged me."

"Uh-huh."

She doesn't believe me.

"Look," I tell her, "he said if I didn't do what he said, he was going to take the ice pick and shove it down through the top of my foot and into the floor so I couldn't go anywhere."

"Uh-huh."

"He laughed maniacally and screamed at the ceiling about going home while in his home!"

"Mr. Waterman, I'm about to go laughin' maniacally and screamin' at the ceiling. I mean, seriously. Doc? Is this a joke? I know there was that ridiculous accusation about—No, no," Her voice sounds distant as she talks to her husband. "I said I'm almost done. Just go back to sleep. Mr. Waterman," she says directly into the phone, "your story just doesn't make sense. You can't go 'round looking for anything if you're nailed to the floor."

"I know. That's what I said."

"Uh-huh."

"Look, I barely made it home."

"I know where you live."

"Yeah. I barely made it home—"

"Now hold on just a minute. You're home now? Now, let me get this straight. You took the time to drive under the influence and wait until you got home to call someone and you call *me?* Am I hearin' you? Why haven't you called the police?"

"I wanted to sober up a bit first... and, I mean, like you said, we're a small town. You know how bad cell coverage can get. Besides, Doc's very influential, and he threatened my friends. He told me not to call the cops."

"Ugh, all right. Who are these friends of yours?"

"Armand. Armand Pochelli. That's with two L's. He's a big dude."

"He's *still* your friend?"

"Yeah, and, uh, then there's Luke, or, I mean, Lucia, Lucia Gage, and then Auna and Adam Klaura–"

"Okay Auna, yeah, the town's shrink. That's okay, I know the spelling. All right, Armand Pochelli, Lucia Gage, and the Klauras. Well, okay. So you think your friends are in danger."

"Yeah, so are you going to do something? Even recording this call would help."

"Record this call? You want me to report you? You want me to call the cops for you?"

"Well I mean, it's Thursday, and we've gotta go to work with him in the morning, and I don't feel safe."

"Doc's eccentric; he ain't dangerous. I think you've been smokin' too much. You know it's not Thursday."

"No, but, it is Thursday."

"Mr. Waterman." The smile in her voice mocks me. "I'm sixty years old. My husband's sixty-five. You wake me up, call me up this late, stoned, to lie about a good friend of this entire town, including me, just because you're havin' some kind of heathen experience. And from what I understand he's your employee, too." She speaks away from the phone, "Oh, go back to bed; I had to tell him our age. He doesn't know what he's sayin'. ... No, he's tellin' me he was smokin' the dope with Doc. ... Well, that's what I'm gonna tell him... Mr. Waterman, you should be ashamed of yourself, tryin' to defame the best thing that happened to this town since the sisters themselves. My grand pappy knew the Jane sisters back when they were—"

"But, no, it's Thursday."

"No, it's *not* Thursday, you druggy-ass. It's Saturday. ... No, no, no, I told you I'm almost done. You just go back to bed. I'm fine. Fine... Well then go back to sleep... bed, sleep, whatever... Fine—get a glass o' water... Now, Mr. Waterman—yes, yes, it's a fine glass o' water; quit interrupting me—Mr. Waterman, now I suppose you gonna tell me you were drugged for two days now?"

"Whoa... I didn't think of that, but I mean, yeah, I guess. Wouldn't that make sense? Can't you just record this call?"

She sighs. "Ooh, I don't have time for this nonsense. This is one of the stupidest—did you escape or just leave then?"

"He let me go."

"Uh huh... of *course* he did. And all those *friends* of yours—they didn't happen to be abducted, too, I suppose?" There's a shuffling sound on the other end. "I *am* goin' to have to record this call, aren't I?"

"I don't know where they are, but they weren't there when I was there."

"Ooh! You gratin' on my last nerves. Is it yes or no?"

There's a click-click-click of a tape recorder.

"Agh." The tone of her voice echoes in the receiver.

I'm on speaker.

"All right, you know this call's recorded now, right?" she asks.

"Yes, yes that's fine. I just want to make sure everything's—that everyone's going to be okay."

On the other end, her husband snickers in the background.

"Shhh! All right," she says, "let me sum it up for you. You mean to put on record, but anonymously, that you were sedated and held for two days by Doc, and—this I can only imagine—you're wakin' up, you're tied to a chair, and here comes Doc, and he's laughin' maniacally, screamin' at the ceilin', and wavin' 'round an ice pick."

More snickering.

"Yes, yes that's it. That's it exactly." The snickering turns to laughter. "Only..."

"Ooh, you makin' me angry!"

"He, uh, he said he'd pay me five thousand dollars to get them."

"Them *what?*"

"The needles!"

Laughter.

"Shhh! He can hear you," she says to her husband. "So you're sayin' your kidnapper now offers to pay his victim? Of all the—I see..." Shuffling. "I see now," she pauses, "I see what this is all about. You are goin' to stay on my phone and spout nonsense, and I ain't gonna sleep fo' days unless I report this."

"Please." The laughter won't go away. "My friends might be in danger, and he told me not to call the cops."

"Fine. Fine. *I'll* call the police since you don't have the sense to do it yourself. You happy now? My husband and *I'd*... well, at least I'd like to get some sleep now."

"Please. Thank you."

"All right all right." More shuffling. "They'll probably send their new Lieutenant, Daab."

"Thank you. Thank you. Thank you."

"Yeah, yeah, yeah," she says. "We'll be sure to call you immediately if anything develops."

That fucking laughter again.

"I told you to *be quiet,*" she says. "What if he comes *here*—"

Click.

* * *

> John Waterman, U-A DOB: 2579-12-03, CID 09985240860

> ResID: 7.1.0 [altered by CID 99999999999/ResID: 5.4] M1

> U-B: [Doc's house, Jane, CA, US, Earth] LT: Saturday, 2009-10-24, 8:46 PM PDT

— Saturday, October 24th, 2009, 8:46 PM PDT —

All I remember is Doc getting up to use the bathroom when I wake up to the sound of a sewing machine over a dentist's drill. I look over and see Doc holding an ice pick, smoking a joint.

"Welcome back," he says. "Get me my needles, or I'll take this ice pick and push it down through the top of your foot until it comes out the bottom and sticks into the floor, and you won't be able to move."

I still feel stoned. *More than stoned.* "How's that going to get you your needles?"

My hands move, but my arms and legs don't.

"I've given up on the idea of going home. I've decided to make the best of what I have in this alien world, while I still live in it."

That was weird. I'm *really* stoned, somehow... more than usual, or something... I kind of just want to leave. Doc's just not what I want to deal with right now. "Fine, I'll get you your damn needles."

"Really? Is that all? Is that all I need to do to encourage you to do something? No sewing the lips shut or stapling your nether bits? No burning of the armpit, eh? Just threaten with some ice picking?" His eyes bulge with mania, his chin points at my forehead, and his smile is wide and creepy. I can see all his teeth.

I shake my head back and forth to try to shake off the feeling of being too high, but it's not working.

"Yeah."

"I don't think so. A couple days ago, I knocked you out and fit a GPS into your body somewhere. Additionally, I am a *wizard*. Any time you do something against my will, I will harm one of your friends with naturally caused accidents!"

27

His mania seems to be getting worse, but I feel so messed up that I figure I should play along with his delusion. I better know what page he's on. "What day is it?"

Doc pauses and then says, "Thursday."

"Right... Naturally caused accidents... All threats aside, Doc, it's hard to take you seriously. You're actin' crazy, and I'm stoned... I feel drugged... don't wanna think about weird shit right now."

He raises his arms, laughs maniacally, and screams at the ceiling, "I am INVINCIBLE!"

Ugh, my head hurts. I really hope Auna believes this when I tell her about this... He's peaking... his mania... I've got to get away, simply to avoid any more *screaming*... I *really* dislike screaming. My head aches. "K... gotta go. I, uh, I'm not going to find the one thousand needles for the ... one thousand pins, sitting around here, all tied up, am I? I hope you don't expect me to keep my management position at Los Eatos if I'm all tied up here."

* * *

— Saturday, October 24th, 2009, 11:09 PM PDT —

What a freakin' bitch. So I called my former boss to try to see if she'd call the cops, but she doesn't care. I hope she calls the cops, but who knows if that'll happen.

Maybe putting my laundry away'll help me get my mind off my crazy day.

I put on some old school industrial rock and get to work.

Apparently everyone loves Doc, even after the scandal where he got caught smoking weed. Eccentric Doc, funny Doc, crazy Doc. The guy who can do no wrong... bullshit. The Doc—the douche.

All right, I'll be honest. I've actually known this guy for quite some time, or at least I *think* I have. Of course, it doesn't mean he doesn't creep me out. He really pisses me off right now. Ugh, I don't really know how to react to this shit. I'm glad I know a psychologist.

I stop the music. I'm just not feelin' it. I leave the pile of clothes and go to unload and load the dishwasher.

Hell, Doc and I've worked together at Los Eatos for the last two years. He always seemed like a cool, mellow guy. We've seen people come and go. I mean he's weird, don't get me wrong, but he's never been known to tie people up and threaten to skewer their feet, or scream at the ceiling. Weird, yes, but never *threatening*.

Argh! All the laundry and dishes in the world aren't going to distract me. I close the half-emptied dishwasher and turn on the TV. The local news is on, talking about Doc's new solar technology networked in the redwood forest's canopy. He invented and patented the prototype for the shit. Power bills for everyone in Jane and Sister City lowered since, but now

29

that I know what a douche he is, willing to harm others to get what he wants, I figure I'll hate the guy. Who knows how much threatening he's done to get his technology mainstreamed...

I'm not like that douche. I just wanna chill, socialize, and smoke a little with people. I don't really know why I like smoking weed. It's just something I picked up in high school and never put down. They say you can't get addicted to weed, but I don't know.

The TV shows Doc shaking hands with Jenkins, Jane's mayor, who also just so happens to be the most successful real estate broker in Humboldt County.

Fuckin' douche...why the fuck do people give him tip money when everyone knows he's rich and probably just smokes it all away anyway?

I turn off the TV.

Well, the cops aren't going to care 'cause they laugh off anything that the douche does, just like his customers. They don't want to get involved.

What the fuck time is it? Fuck it. It's late. I'm loadin' a bowl.

Damn, I'm runnin' out of weed... I'm gonna have to re-up.

I toke all the green off the top.

One thousand pins and needles... What a stupid idea.

I take another hit.

I have to admit, I'm not very motivated to find one thousand needles, especially used ones...

Now that I'm gettin' high 'n' enjoyin' the midnight hour, my cell phone rings.

I pick it up.

That *douche's* voice is on the other line. Huh... it sounds stressed.

"I told you not to go to the cops!"

"Yeah... you did that; but, you also told me you were going to use a mirror to go home while you were already in your home, so—"

"Don't play coy with me."

Damn, I haven't heard that word in a while.

"Koi... I'm a goldfish now? Wait, I didn't call the cops."

"Our boss will die tomorrow as an example of the hardship you'll bring upon yourself if you continue to screw around."

Click.

"Hello?"

What a douche... whatever... AND IT'S SATURDAY, NOT THURSDAY, YOU CRAZY FUCK!

As I close my phone, I see the voicemail icon, so I check my call log.

Oh hey, Armand called me...

I press and hold the number 1 and enter my code when the automated lady asks for it.

"First message. Sent, Friday, at, twelve, thirty-one, PM."

"John. Armand here. Been here for 'bout a half an hour now, waitin'. Again, tonight's inventory night. You bail, I'm takin' it out of your vacation, ya hear? ... If nothin' else, I'll see you Monday at the tree..."

I erase the message and close the phone.

Ugh, inventory... I'm high and tired... I gotta get outta my head... Maybe some porn on the worldwide wank'll do the trick...

A flash of doubt pops in my mind as I sit and wait for my computer to boot up...

Nah, Doc wouldn't hurt Armand...

Then I take another hit, and blow it all away.

* * *

> John Waterman, U-A DOB: 2579-12-03, CID 09985240860

> ResID: 7.1.0 [altered by CID 99999999999/ResID: 5.4] M1 &
M2

> U-B: [John's apartment, Jane, CA, US, Earth] LT: Sunday, 2009-
10-25, 2:17 AM PDT

— Sunday, October 25th, 2009, 2:17 AM PDT —

I'm hang-gliding. I've never done it, but I accept what I'm doing, 'cause who am I to argue with the reality I'm experiencing? Then I realize the main bolt is missing. My very recognition of the missing bolt seems to have caused the bolt to go missing, and like a cartoon I begin tumbling toward the earth. The air pushes against any part of me that faces the ground. With the fear of being punctured by flying glider parts, I am somehow out of my restraints and throwing the glider away from my body, but the air around me isn't as turbulent as I'd imagined it'd be.

Then, without any explanation, I find myself in a large commercial airplane full of faceless passengers, with my torso, hands, and ankles strapped to the chair I realize I'm in. Instinctively, I look up, like that's somehow going to give me the answer. A light blinks on in the ceiling above me. It glows in the shape of an airplane captain talking into a radio microphone.

The small circle representing an overhead speaker blares so loud, I could actually hear sparks and the speaker failing: "WELCOME BACK, John. This is your captain, the Doc. We *welcome you aboard!*"

I look out the window and see the shadow of the world ahead of us. We're flying into the night.

My attention completely arrested by Doc's voice, my guts feel like they are going to burst out of me.

"What did you expect, John? I told you one of your friends was going to die."

33

I turn around to see Doc in the seat behind me. I am so alarmed I can barely speak. Trying not to attract attention, I whisper, "Who's flying?" I found myself asking, "Did you kill the captain?"

Doc lurches around in front of me and leans in. His face becomes the only thing I can see. There are no airplane passengers anymore, no more seats, nothing. Just his face with a dark background, his blue eyes slightly glowing, fixed directly on mine. *"You're* the one flying, John."

I wake up with my guts so upset, I have to race to the bathroom.

* * *

> The Doc, U-A DOB: ~2559-07-13, CID 99999999999

> ResID: 6.5 [altered by CID 09985239378/ResID: 10.9] M1 & M2

> U-B: [Doc's house, Jane, CA, US, Earth] LT: Monday, 2009-10-
26, 12:01 AM PDT

— Monday, October 26th, 2009, 12:01 AM PDT —

The dark-skinned man in the apron picks Doc's severed limb up from the porch, stands, grabs one of Doc's ankles, and drags him twitching into the house. He lays Doc on a table and places the arm near its stub.

At a closer glance, the apron itself displays a red pastel silhouette of a man proudly wearing an apron in the center of the apron, which would be purely yellow otherwise. Above the red apron man on the apron, there is the word "APRON" in large red capital letters. Below him, there is the word "MAN."

He leans over Doc's shivering body and whispers into Doc's ear, "Hyena leap frog Charlie, typo mark five two, check nine five six two, three five one six."

Like a magnet drawn to its familiar iron, Doc's arm and stub reach with tiny hair-like filaments into one another, pulling the limb flush with the stub.

"You'll be able to hear this after you wake up, and I know you'll remember it too, but I'm gonna tell you what happened anyway, 'cause you ain't likely gonna wanna believe what you remember... 'n' I feel like talkin'."

Now fully sealed to the stub, the arm withers slightly. It shakes with the rest of his body. Steam rises from its pores.

The man in the apron scoffs and rolls his brown eyes.

"I know John's order was to go along with your project, but this is ridiculous. You're one *crazy* white man, you know that?" he says, turning away. "This has *gotta* be the last time we're giving your verm that much to work with, I don't care what the reason." He looks back at Doc with disgust. "You're the Doc. You've got responsibilities."

Doc's entire body relaxes.

Apronman preaches at Doc's unconscious body, pacing back and forth. "Since we've gotten sidetracked from our original mission and came here, this was the *stupidest* thing you could've done. You went *ape-shit*, sedatin' and tyin' up your superior. Tellin' your *superior* to go find a thousand needles? That's gonna cause a lot of attention we don't want, like when the cops got called, and yet you *knew* this would happen! I *told* you about the confirmation ping I got on Friday when I called him, but you *still* went off. We don't even know where he *is* now. We are likely gonna have to leave before our time is done here. If John hadn't called his former boss... Now, I've got to start gettin' his ResID back because of this shit. You know, a *cleaner* is not someone I'd like to discuss the weather with right now... It's not at the top of my list of things to do, know what I'm sayin'?"

The withered arm fashions itself into a less withered version of what once was never cut.

Apronman ignores it, pacing about. He stops pacing.

"You know..." he says, slowly turning back around, "I'm thinkin'... I laced John's mornin' joint with the catalyst... this might actually work in our favor."

The withered flesh inflates with health and circulation. Doc reawakens.

"Agreed," Doc says.

* * *

> John Waterman, U-A DOB: 2579-12-03, CID 09985240860

> ResID: 7.1.0 [altered by CID 99999999999/ResID: 5.4] M1

> U-B: [Auna's office, Sister City, CA, US, Earth] LT: Sunday, 2009-10-25, 5:59 PM PDT

— Sunday, October 25th, 2009, 5:59 PM PDT —

"I *really* had to shit."

"Language!"

My lifelong friend who just so happens to be a psychologist is clearly offended by the bathroom experience I had last night. We're just now finishing up our fast food dinner, sitting and talking about the weird dream I had. Saying 'shit' while her five-year-old is running around her new office wasn't the best idea.

"Sorry."

I shut the office door behind us and return to my spot on her plush couch opposite the large brown leather chair where she sits. The recently added furnishings give the otherwise bare office space a slightly refurbished feel with the small coffee table and a peace lily on a wall table. There a few things that give the place a lived-in feel—her personal library, the soft lighting, and the coffee maker with its companion's non-dairy creamer pile and sugar cube box.

"So," I ask while she picks up the fast food bag off the table between us and tosses it in the trash behind her desk, "what do you think it means?"

"Your dream? Well," she says, coming back around the desk to the chair she was in, "there are different ways to interpret dreams. My question is this: what makes you feel in real life the way you felt in your dream?"

"Huh?"

"What, in real life, would make you feel the way you felt in your dream?"

I'm not sure I understand what she's asking me or why. I stare at her many books wondering what my real-life feelings have to do with how my dreams make me feel.

She can tell I'm confused. "What real-life thing makes you feel the way you did in your dream?" she asks again, but still doesn't explain what my dream has to do with my life.

"My dream?" Maybe she's trying to ask me about my real-life dreams. "I don't have any dreams for my life, really. I just wanna smoke with people."

"Huh?" She leans forward to the edge of her seat. "I'm not talking about your life goal dreams. Are you high now?"

I look down. "I wish."

"I'm talking," she says, moving her left hand out to grab my attention, "about the dream where you're hang gliding." She relaxes her arm and leans back into her chair. "Again," she asks, "what in real life would make you feel that way?"

"That's why I mention it. Normally, I only have that reoccurring dream we've talked about before, where I'm wandering in a jungle and find myself in a maze and then just get lost forever in the rain until I wake up, but... this one was different, like I said, so you tell me."

"I'm a psychologist, not a mind reader. From the maze, I think you might have some kind of confliction. What's out of the ordinary is that you sit in the rain until you wake up. Besides, like I've said before, I shouldn't evaluate friends."

"Whatever. I don't just sit in the rain, either. I get lost looking for a way out. Mazes are hard, and I'm not some kind of super genius, I'm just a simple guy trying to survive. Besides, I'm trying to figure out why I had a nightmare." Now I'm the one on the edge of my seat. "Why can't I just have my usual dream about the maze?"

"If I were to evaluate you," she says with the look of someone considering the cost of compromising their integrity, "I'd ask what would make you feel that way. Your job, friends, or money—it's likely one of those, but I can't really help any more than to ask what in your life makes you feel like you're doing something you've never done before, and suddenly, something fundamental has just broken, making you feel helpless. I can't really say more without breaking the rules, but it's a good place for you to start."

"Uh…" I nod apologetically for putting her in a bad spot. "Eh…" I can't really think of anything. The room is silent for a moment.

Auna twitches her head listening for something. "Can you open the door? I can't hear what Adam's up to."

I reopen the office door and sit back down. Her five-year-old runs back and forth in the office hallway past the doorway.

"That's what happened though, right?" she asks. "You were hanging, elevated, and gliding, minding your own business in the breeze, then a fundamental component broke—Adam, don't do cartwheels in the office, honey, you're going to hurt yourself or break something. Thank you." Adam stops mid-hop with his hands in the air and curls into a somersault. I catch a familiar glimpse of his scars. They don't seem alien to me anymore.

"Ah!" I remember falling and feeling helpless and desperate. "Uhh… Hmmm…"

I zone out, trying to think of comparisons between feelings in my dream and real life.

Doc's face was terrifying when it was all I could see. The only similar feeling that comes to mind from real life is how my job contrasts with Doc's expertise and his recent threats. His former job was working for the local government under someone spearheading the new green solar energy technology he invented that's attached to redwood treetops. Their HR department told me his résumé was full of all kinds of crap: various certifications and a doctorate in journalism, studies in meteorology, freelance photojournalism. I had just ignored it.

When I showed Armand Doc's résumé, he had acted like he didn't want to hire the guy because Doc was all over the news and so overqualified. He thought Doc'd get so bored he'd quit. That night, while we were smoking a joint on our last break, I asked him if he could think of anything this guy wouldn't be overqualified for. He didn't really answer my question. He just said he didn't want any media attention because he himself would probably have to quit smoking if Doc went extra crazy or caused a police investigation.

I figured that any media attention was in Armand's favor, considering he's the owner of the place. Besides, what with Doc's experience with solar power and being a former volunteer firefighter, he had a lot of good to bring to the table. I argued that Doc was probably so burnt out by the responsibilities of wealth and his many degrees and inventions that he probably just wanted to relax at a mundane job for a while.

Armand said he still didn't want him around because Doc had recently been caught smoking weed while working for the local government. His fellow firefighting team members were really put off by the whole ordeal. Most everyone else who wasn't directly involved with the whole thing either adamantly didn't believe it, like my former boss I talked to last night, or, if they were like me, didn't care.

"What kind of establishment do we run here anyway," I had asked Armand, "a jail? Is there some kind of flight risk if we put someone on the clock? If that's the case, all of our employees are flight risks. He's been really good to our town with the solar tech he's developed. It'd be good for Los Eatos to have him, and it'd be good for him to have a routine he can lay low in for a while. He'll be a good role model for the high schoolers..."

Now, thinking about how I'd recently been held against my will, I was wrong about Doc being a good role model. He got the job because of me, and kidnapping is Doc's go-to response? I got him that job, and I was proud of doing so. I'm proud of my self-esteem, but because of what he did, now I feel betrayed and dismissed. What gives him the idea it's okay to do that? His education? His accomplishments? The experience I have as a manager doesn't add up to the many degrees he has, but I still have my accomplishments—I got and stayed in the position I have through a *lot* of patience and hard work... and weed.

Weed helps me get through a lot of hard times, like dealing with Doc, but that's not the point.

My psychologist friend pipes up. "Did you figure it out yet?"

My train of thought derailed.

"I smoke pot with my boss, and if he's harmed by Doc, I'll have to break up with Mary Jane to look for work, and that's—"

"So you think you're going to get fired, is that it?"

"Okay, sure. And then there's Doc, too."

"What about him?"

"I smoked weed with him."

"Wow." My psychologist friend leans back, shaking her head and looking away, obviously overacting her disappointment. "John, you are one of those people I don't really understand. Some studies in psychology suggest that weed can be psychologically addictive, and that compromises your integrity. That's one of the main reasons I quit. That, and the stigma around it. For you, I know you smoke a lot, but then you do things that show a strength of integrity, like the day I demanded sobriety from Luke, you gave her some time off."

I avert my eyes. I thought Auna and I were supposed to be celebrating the fact that she got this new office today, but we're talking about upsetting memories. "We haven't really talked about this since. Why now?"

"You've had a nightmare about one of your subordinates being superior, and it's making you insecure. What I'm trying to point out is that you have leadership qualities. From the previous dreams you've had about the maze, I'm unsure you realize your full potential at Los Eatos. I'm trying to affirm your position in the matter."

Right now, I don't want to think about my full potential. Thinking of the scene Auna made at the Los Eatos brings back memories of Luke almost crying in my office.

"It was the anniversary of her father's death, and she was pretty upset after you disrupted the whole restaurant."

"I *had* to make a scene. Luke has thick skin. I'm surprised she was even there that day. She has a lot of potential also, and I don't want that screwed up the way Doc's life got screwed because of weed."

Auna's still insisting on equating smoking weed with a lack of integrity, when it's people with a lack of integrity that give weed smoking a bad name. It's the same with any drug, just like alcohol. I don't understand why she thinks this way, or why she would think it's weird that Luke would want something to do that day to keep her mind off the fact that her dad died.

"I was short-staffed and Luke needed something mundane to do. You know, it's not the weed that screws people up, it's a world that doesn't believe in the people who can smoke it and still live responsibly."

"See? That's what I'm talking about—you just act like it's a beer or something."

"It is for me. Everyone reacts differently to different things, and you've told me yourself that psychological studies' conclusions are a bit fuzzy."

"Okay, think of it this way—Doc could have been our mayor if it wasn't for his smoking."

I don't really want to have this conversation. In trying to find out what real-life thing feels the way my dream felt, I think the dream I've had has to do with the fact that I've recently been kidnapped and then mocked by my former boss when I needed help. I'm afraid that if I bring up the kidnapping, she might mock me, too, because I smoke.

"If the world would just accept weed, it wouldn't have been a problem in the first place. Doc'd be mayor, and I'd have a second job as a medicinal distributor. "

"You just don't know when to quit, do you?"

Adam starts somersaulting himself into the walls, trying to do a handstand or something—it's getting distracting.

"No, but that's not my point. If Doc was the mayor, he wouldn't be in as much of my life. My point is that I've smoked with Armand and Doc both, but—and I'm unsure how to figure this out—here's the thing. I recently went over to Doc's for the first time, and uh... Doc demanded I get ten thousand used medical needles that are big enough to fit straight pins into."

Adam is now blowing raspberries every time he crashes his cars together and then laughing.

"Eck, ten thousand used medical needles?" Auna asks. I can tell she can see I'm distracted.

"Oh, uh, no, one thousand."

Adam adds airplane noises to his tumbling and blows raspberries.

"Why blowing raspberries?" I ask.

"Adam," Auna says, avoiding the question, "close the door, honey. If you want to go outside, come get us, okay?"

"Okay." he says, closing the door. We can still hear his feet running throughout the office.

"That's still gross," my psychologist friend says, "but that's Doc. He says outlandish things all the time. That's just *him*. He's weird, but since he's weird all the time, it'd be considered normal."

"He told me he wants to make a mirror out of pins and needles so that he can 'go home'—whatever that means—and, to top it off, he said he was a *wizard* and if I didn't get them for him, he would use some kind of magic to 'harm my friends.'"

"Threats, huh? That's a new one for Doc. I've heard him say many things, but never threaten. 'Go home'?"

"Yeah, and I have no fucking clue what the hell he was talking about, because he was already in his home."

She thinks about it then says, "Worst-case scenario is that he wants to kill himself."

"Really?"

"Yeah, that or he's suffering from some kind of delusion or terminal illness. Some people call dying going home."

"Good—if he kills himself, I won't have to deal with him anymore."

Auna's face tenses up.

"I'm just talkin' shit. It's just that with what I've just gone through, he's freaking me out, you know?"

She relaxes and says, "The amount of weed he smokes is significant, which is odd, considering his education. I have to admit he also baffles me. The city of Jane's been able to develop a lot around this new energy network he helped with. If it weren't for him, Adam wouldn't have a toy robot—"

"I know I know … Adam's robot. You moms are always telling the same story; 'My kid did this and that, and I laughed or whatever.'"

"Whatever?" she says. "You don't know any other moms. You didn't even know Doc built that toy robot."

"Dude. I totally knew. You told me about it on his fifth birthday a couple months ago when he got it. Adam even told me Doc made it. You were like, 'Hey, check this out,' and it blew compressed air out of its finger tips."

"Oh, right!" she remembers, smiling. "Then you tried to—"

"—stick toothpicks in the tips to shoot them out."

"Yes. Okay, I remember," she paused. "So you think smoking with Doc makes you a hazard to society, eh?"

"To my friends, at least. You know—Luke, you, and Armand. Look, I know it's crazy, but—"

She scoffs.

"What?"

"Don't be saying 'crazy' around me," she says, "and what about Adam? He's your friend too, isn't he? Ah, I know what you meant, but don't say 'crazy.' Say 'eccentric.'"

"All right, eccentric. I know he's eccentric, but that still doesn't mean I know what he's capable of. I mean, Armand's got the Los Eatos shipshape and all, but if Doc does something *eccentric* to Armand, like kill him, how am I going to run the shop when the books are in some police evidence closet?"

"You're more concerned about Los Eatos than your boss's life? Look, from what I know of Doc, he's not going to do anything to Armand, okay? Besides, I don't think your dream has anything to do with the Los Eatos inventory. I think you were just scared because Doc was weirder than usual. Even if something did happen to your boss, you'd make do until things were back to normal. You're good like that. People trust you."

"What? No, I couldn't just—"

"John, take the compliment. Consider how well you managed that night I stormed in. You knew you'd hear about it from Armand, but you gave Luke the time off anyway."

"Yeah, I honestly didn't want that to get back to you. I figured you might pick sides since you're always disgusted about us smoking. I couldn't tell if you might be jealous of me or Luke or the weed."

"I'm jealous of the weed, obviously," she says. "Luke called me that night to tell me what you said, needing a break from our relationship, and needing some time to think. Considering everything, I agreed. I needed some time to think about the whole thing myself. I had overreacted."

"Why *did* you go craz—*eccentric* that day?"

"Other than you and Luke, I don't really have any emotional outlet. It gets hard for me when Adam sees me emotionally exhausted sometimes. Being a sober single mom... if Luke was ... well, you get the picture."

She wants to smoke but won't.

"That sucks."

"Again, like I said, I'm not a mind reader, but we talked about you over-thinking things when you were over-thinking your position as a manager when you first got started at Los Eatos, just like you're over-thinking this. You smoked a lot then. You smoking a lot now?"

"Yeah... Jealous?"

"Get over yourself. Your experience with Doc and your dream about falling—it's probably just the weed making you a little paranoid, eh?"

"What if it was a real threat though?"

"My professional opinion is that Doc is harmless and that what you experienced was a misunderstanding of what day it was *when you arrived* because you were high. I expect that what happened was that you arrived on Saturday, tripped out, and left on Saturday, and your entire experience took probably two hours, not two days."

"You too, huh?"

"No one else is preaching at you about your weed smoking, and right now, I'm the closest thing you've got to someone who cares about your emotional development. Look, smoke if you like, but don't let it get in the way of your life. Other than the scandal he got himself into, Doc's got a good reputation. I'd vouch for him. You said you were really high when you were over there, so maybe you misinterpreted things... I've known you for a very long time, John, and even though you've got leadership qualities, you said yourself that everyone experiences different things differently. Maybe your sense of time is getting warped in the mix of being high."

"But *two days?*"

"John, everyone has dreams, including you, it's just that yours recently made you take a really huge shit." She pauses for corny effect, and then says, "And that is hardcore."

Her stare... she's really trying hard to keep it straight.

I blink a couple times.

I guess I'll just talk to her about it later.

"Thank you for the after-school special, Auna," I say, "That, uh... you just sounded... just like Luke."

She smiles with all-too-eager guilt.

"Yeah, a little."

We say all our goodbyes and head out.

After I leave her office, I get into my car. I'll probably have to deal with tourist traffic at this hour, so I get out my two-hitter pipe I stash under the driver's seat and take the two hits while watching Auna leave with a scowl covering her face. She was covering Adam's face with her hand.

She's still put out about me smoking.

I guess it is kind of a shitty thing to do—to smoke right outside her new office in front of Adam, but the sun'd already gone down. It's not like it's in broad daylight on a weekday.

Whatever.

I've known Auna my whole life... the parts that mattered anyway. I really don't get it, though—the fact that she's disgusted by me smoking—simply because I've smoked a lot of pot with her too over the years. Maybe she's just trying to live up to her new "I'm a professional" suit she just bought in celebration of her new office, but I don't know... she's been like this for a couple months or so. Although, she looks pretty good in that suit. It complements her dark brown eyes and skin and straight black shoulder-length hair. Besides, I'm not one of those kinds of stoners who thinks the whole world should be smoking.

She's getting to be pretty well-off too. I would have assumed she would've wanted to celebrate and smoke a joint.

It didn't used to be like this. She got pregnant from a drunken one-night stand at a college party. Just when I thought she was going to drop out of school and be a full-time mom, she tells me she's going to stay in college and raise Adam at the same time. I didn't think she had it in her. Luke helped, but Auna did it—she got her Master's. She's amazing.

She had a really great scholarship for being Mexican. Of course, everyone knows how to say, "No, burrito, hombre, arriba," and any other words that any racist Hispanic cartoon characters would say, but the funny thing is, neither Auna nor Luke understand any Spanish. I guess that doesn't have any bearing on her scholarship requirements, but no matter. Auna's a good study, and what with her raising Adam at the same time, I figure she deserves all the support she can get.

We'd eat at Los Eatos when she started going to school. That's how she and I met Luke.

As awkward as her speech about my dreams was to hear, it was a nice thing to say that I have leadership qualities. I mean, I thought I was lucky to become a manager, but I guess I do make do with this Los Eatos thing... although, I doubt my life goals actually include working at Los Eatos for the rest of my life.

It's a good thing that I'm able to work there now though, especially since when I was working at the department store, Armand told my managers I was working a conflicting schedule at Los Eatos, even though at the time, I wasn't working at Los Eatos at all. When they said they were willing to talk terms with me about it, he insisted he could pay better, and that I told him they were all assholes, and that we both had a good laugh over a joint about how they all had shit for brains. To my surprise, I didn't disagree quickly enough, and that got them in a firing mood. They wanted me to pee test. I didn't.

Anyway, that's the story on how he got me fired from the department store.

I say "the" department store, because Jane's so small, there's only one. I hated the place in general, and Armand was right—they really were all assholes.

Speaking of Armand, he'd mentioned recently that the Doc had said he needed some extracurricular help. Usually, Armand doesn't use big words like "extracurricular." "Extracurricular" usually means "unique," and "unique" usually means, "Money will be paid to you in piles if you do it."

I've known Doc for a while, but now... after going to his house just to see what Armand was talking about... I feel like I just met Doc for the first time. It's like he's not even the same person, or something. I'm not even sure he'll pay me. I guess if he's crazy enough to threaten, he might be crazy enough to deliver either payment or harm. Harm is what I'm afraid of.

Five thousand is a nice amount, though... when I think about what I could buy versus what I was going to have to do. I could buy a pound of weed, or a new shitty car, or about two to three months of vacation, unemployed. Having all three would be kind of nice, but I'd need a lot more money for all that.

Speaking of money and weed, I need to re-up.

* * *

> Anny Klaura, U-A DOB: 2580-05-15, CID 09986520678

> ResID: 4.0 [altered by CID 09985240860/ResID: 4.3.2] M1 &
M2

> U-B: [Los Eat, Adios!, Jane, CA, US, Earth] LT: Sunday, 2009-07-
05, 5:59 PM PDT

— Sunday, July 5th, 2009, 5:59 PM PDT —

"I can't," Luke says, curling a 20-pound dumbbell and smoking weed outside the back door of Jane's only Los Eat, Adios! restaurant. "My break's almost done," she says, pointing out the roach that used to be a joint. "I'm not even supposed to be out here. I've taken too many breaks tonight already."

"I really need you to hear me out. This is important," Auna says. "I've known John my whole life, and he's smoking more than he used to."

"So? You've smoked," she says. Her purple dreadlocks fall to her shins as she simultaneously interlocks her fingers behind her and twists her arms, bending over to stretch out the biceps she just pumped up. "You've smoked with us."

"It doesn't mean I want to keep doing it."

"What?" she asks rhetorically, the roach smoking her out under all her hair. "You loved it. Besides, John's just inside. Why aren't you talking to him about it?"

"I have been. It's just, now that I almost have my first practice, and Adam's getting old enough to go to school, I just feel like things are really working out, but my childhood friend is smoking more than ever... and what kind of psychologist sleeps with a drug dealer, let alone lets her baby-sit?"

"Goddamn," she says with her face full of smoke. She lets go of her stretch, sitting back up quick enough to flip her hair onto her back and throw all the old smoke out of her face. "You got me there," she says, throwing her hair back and forth to get the extra smoke out.

49

"Hey!" John says, peeking his head out the door. "You almost done?" he asks as he disappears back behind the frame toward his work. "With Apronman out, shit's pilin' up in here."

"Yeah, I'm coming," Luke says, taking the last drag from the roach, standing up and pinching the cherry out. Her 6' 2" frame casts a shadow over Auna before she turns toward the door.

"Wait!" Auna says.

Luke spins around. Auna is face-to-face with her breasts. "What?"

Auna's pupils dilate in the moment, but she looks up, "Look, I know this is a bad time, but since you work nights, and I work days, this is the only time I know I can talk to you about this in person when Adam or a babysitter's not around... I want you to quit smoking weed... or at least quit dealing."

Luke flings the roach. "I'll think about it," she says, walking through the door.

Auna follows her into the hot and blustery kitchen.

"Lucia," Auna says to Luke's back, "I'm serious. I really have to put my foot down on this one. It's for your own good, and Adam's."

"It's 'Luke,'" Lucia scolds, turning to face her lover. "I've been careful not to smoke around him. John and I both smoke mostly at my apartment, anyway, so it's not a problem."

"Lucia," John chimes in, "you've still got those two orders of grilled cheese pizza quesadillas to get out that were up before your break."

"It's 'Luke,' asshole," Lucia rallies back, "That's not cool. Lucia's what my dad called me."

"Come on, Lucia," John jokes.

"Fuck off, John," Luke responds.

"Auna," John says, "this is our peak hour. I'm sorry, but we kinda can't have you out here."

Auna turns to Luke and asks, "Why'd you tell me 6 PM would be the best time to stop by?"

"I was *joking*," Lucia responds as she grabs two plates for an order. "I'm surprised you're here."

"You said I could come," Auna says, following Luke as she walks toward the dining room floor.

Luke pauses her gate before the door and says, "Auna, I love you, but asking me to quit weed on the anniversary of my dad's death at my job in the middle of our busiest time is not the best way to convince me. I'm in a bad mood, and all the breaks I've taken still haven't helped me forget—"

"It's *because* it's the anniversary of your father's death that I'm doing this," Auna says, trying to console Luke, who's standing awkwardly with orders in hand. "You've got to let go, Lucia; this is a pivotal moment."

"Don't forget those orders right there in your hands," John says, pointing at the teetering plates.

"You'd stop smoking if Luke stopped dealing," Auna asks John while he's there, "wouldn't you?"

Lucia walks through the door and into the dining area.

"No. I'd have to find another dealer," John says, as Auna follows Luke where hungry church folk were awaiting the plates in Luke's arms, "and that's *really* hard to do."

"This really can't wait," Auna insists. "Please, I need a straight answer. Adam's still in the truck."

"Goddamn," Lucia says, much to the disappointment of her eager, conservative patrons. "Adam's still in the car," she says while placing the last plate down, "in the dark?"

"I didn't want him to see you smoking."

Luke puts condiments on the table from the pockets of her yellow apron.

"Please," Auna says again, this time with a hint of tears, "I need to know if you are going to stop smoking."

"My Beretta's much more dangerous than weed…"

At this, the conservative family members twitch smiles at each other while averting their eyes.

Auna's whole body shakes with frustration, but Luke doesn't stop: "…and I handle *that* every week or so. I'm hoping to handle both tonight, actually. Adam's gonna be fine. Besides," she says, as she turns away to go back into the kitchen, "like I said—John and I don't smoke around him."

"That's not the point, Lucia!" Auna yells over the noise of the room, which had just become silent. "When you smoke weed, you're spacey, and I don't want my son around potheads. It doesn't matter if you're smoking around him or not, it's that you get high at all! If you get high, I can't *trust* you, and if I can't *trust* you, I can't *be* with you anymore!"

Auna's tearing up from being so upset. She swiftly turns to leave.

"Lucia!" John yells from the kitchen, "Lucia get in here! Now!"

Lucia jumps along with everyone in the entire restaurant when Auna slams the front door as she leaves.

"LUCIA!" John yells louder as he stomps into his office. "LUCIA! OFFICE! NOW!"

* * *

> John Waterman, U-A DOB: 2579-12-03, CID 09985240860

> ResID: 6.0.0 [altered by CID 09985240860/ResID: 5.4.0] M1

> U-B: [Los Eat, Adios!, Jane, CA, US, Earth] LT: Sunday, 2009-07-05, 6:04 PM PDT

— Sunday, July 5th, 2009, 6:04 PM PDT —

"That was *hardcore*," a watery-eyed Lucia says to me, slamming my office door. "You gonna fire me?"

"Take a couple days to blow off some steam, Luke. Do some lifting, stretch out, fire off some rounds at the range. If you need three days again, I'll wing it, but you better be back on the fourth day to play catchup, or Armand and I'll need to start looking for a replacement. Cool?"

"Thanks." She sniffs. "It's 'Luke,' by the way."

"I got it, I got it. That's what I said. Just... take a few days to bounce back. We can't run this place without you."

Trying to conceal her own tears, animated, Luke points finger guns at me. "With my gun and," then points at her biceps, "*these* guns, I'll work it out."

"Whatever, killer, just be back by Wednesday, cool?"

"Cool."

* * *

> John Waterman, U-A DOB: 2579-12-03, CID 09985240860

> ResID: 7.1.0 [altered by CID 99999999999/ResID: 5.4] M1

> U-B: [Lucia's apartment, Jane, CA, US, Earth] LT: Sunday, 2009-
10-25, 11:34 PM PDT

— Sunday, October 25th, 2009, 11:34 PM PDT —

I'm stoned.

You know, people who smoke, smoke with the people who give them the means to smoke. I'm talking about dealers. Stoners smoke with their dealers if they've got a good working relationship with them, and I've got a great working relationship with Luke. She's overly dramatic sometimes, which is one of the reasons Auna likes her. Luke's really tall with huge boobs and huge muscles. Personally, I think she's bi in a lesbian closet, and I find her attractive, but whatever. I'm not gonna get *involved* with my dealer, just like I'm not going to get *involved* with my psychologist friend. Besides, Luke likes to work out in martial arts and stay limber, and she can shoot and field strip a Beretta 92F... Now that I think of it, she's so butchy butch, I honestly just don't want to piss her off.

Anyway, we're out on the back deck of her apartment because a lot of her shit's been boxed up. I don't know why, but I'm more keen on getting weed than asking why. Besides, it's a beautiful night. There's a slight wind that doesn't blow the lighter flame out, or make it burn the shit out of your thumb. There's a comforting open sky giving starlight to the deck we're smoking on. We're sitting on a brown couch that has stains from purple dye and burn holes from years of use and apathy, but it was always a really comfortable couch, even on a cold night like this. We are dressed for it, too.

The trees around the place have grown up higher than the roof, and block the neighbors' view of us, but magically do not block our view of Sister City's lights in the distance. The trees lean slowly from the breeze. It is a peaceful Sunday night.

She'd loaded the first bowl. We are finishing off the second one I had loaded (the last of my stash), when she says, "Armand called me."

"Yeah?"

"Wondered where the hell you've been."

I tried to act dumb. "That's weird."

"Said you'd been missin' work. He missed you at the tree for *morning breakfast.*"

"Pff, you should have seen him the last time we had 'breakfast' at the tree, tryin' to kick it while acting like he's speed-reading his inventory book. Eh, I didn't miss shit."

I knew what she was talking about; I just wanted to talk about something else. Usually when we smoke, we just sit, smoke, and lethargically pass the time, sometimes in silence. Not tonight. She flicks her dreads out from her view, looks at me with eyes bulging and brows set. She likes to screw with her customers when we get high. I figure I know what to expect next.

"Where's my weed, dude?" she asks me. Her humor is dryer than the sun, but this was a new one.

I can't help smiling in my mental state. "What?"

"Where's my weed?"

Now she's giving me that look dogs get when they're confused.

All right, I'll play along. "Where's *my* weed?" I ask.

She leans forward some more. "Where's my weed, dude?"

I lean back a little. "Huh?"

"Where's my weed, dude?" Her stare is still just as hard as a rock.

I am stoned. "What?"

"Where's my weed?"

I smile and scoff. "Pff. Okay, Luke, you got me. I don't know what's going on."

She points a T-pin at me she uses for cleaning resin out of pipes and says angrily, "Boy, I am goin' to stab you if you don't get me my weed!"

Paranoia's creeping in. I'm tensing up.

"I'm just playin'," she says and smiles, "It's right here in my *hand*." She holds up a half-pound.

I relax and scoff because it's purposefully dumb. "Smart-ass," I say.

We both space out, pausing to let the intoxication pass us by for a few minutes. My face hurts from smiling. Then I remember why I am here.

"Now," I say slowly, getting my sense of the moment back, "may I please purchase some illegal psychotropics from my friend?"

"What friend?" she says, looking around the deck, "I'm the only one here. 'Illegal' what? You're boring, dude."

"Yeah, so? I work as a manager at a Los Eatos, and I smoke weed," I say as I flick a lighter. "I'm *expected* to be boring." I pull hard on the pipe, breathe out, and cough myself nearly to tears.

"Okay," Luke says, impressed by all the smoke. "That is hardcore."

She looks down at the floor and time passes. The smoke spirals freely in the air and dissipates in silence. She holds up the weed in the same way as before. Then, she surprises me. "I don't think any of this is worth it, dude." Her face looks as hard as a rock, the same as it was a few minutes ago when we were just spacing out, not talking.

I play along. "Huh? Sure."

Her face softens. "You know, there are some serious consequences for dealing, which I must admit I don't really give a shit about, but a few days ago, I got a call from my ex, saying she's thinking of getting back together with me. She's already asked me to move in. Can you believe it? Apparently, *I* was the stable one."

"You have one hundred million exes. Which...? Wait, you're moving?"

"Yeah. Why do you think most of my shit's in boxes?"

I lean in smiling, raising my hands and eyebrows as though looking for an answer in her face.

"Auna," she answers, "the one who broke up with me once she found out I was dealin'."

"How could I forget?"

She continues, "Yeah, I see you still remember me *almost* getting fired from Los Eatos... It's still kind of fucked up."

"I remember."

Actually, I didn't really want to remember anything after what happened to me lately, but yeah... I remember she fell so far in love with Auna that she would have probably done *anything* for her, but Auna didn't want to be associated with a "drug dealer," especially since she was a certified psychologist, licensed, or whatever. But Luke never stopped selling. It got *really* bad when she yelled about Luke smoking marijuana at Los Eatos, in front of all the customers and everyone, and then she just marched out crying and never came back.

Luke was really upset about it for weeks after. She really loved how stable Auna was... Relationship of a lifetime ruined and everything. Of course, Luke'd never get fired for crazy shit like that. She's well-liked by customers and staff, and, most importantly, me. But even now, months later, I can see she's still a mess, trying to kick it like it's all good when she really hasn't been right since her dad died, and I've been trying my hardest not to admit it. Eh, at least she's not just giving up on life.

All I can think to say in my stoned state is, "Yeah."

"'Course, if I got out of this business, Auna and I wouldn't be able to afford a house together, and there you go." She looks straight at me with bulging eyes again. "BOO!"

She startles me a half second after I look up, and I jump.

"Oh man, you got me on that one. House or not, looks like you've still got your humor. Besides, Auna's recently got enough clients to probably afford a house on her own with you, her, and Adam. She already lives at her parents' old house anyway, so... why haven't you moved in already?"

"Well, after my dad died..."

"Sorry."

"You're boring, dude. Come on, gimme your *boring* money, and I'll get you your *boring* weed."

I know she's trying to lighten the mood, but I liked the idea that being boring was something I could come home to. Lately, things have been less than boring.

"Whatever."

I hand her forty boring dollars and she gives me a boring eighth ounce of her weed.

I open the bag and start loading another bowl out of the weed I've just bought.

"Goddamn. Another one? Why do you smoke so much?"

Sigh.

"Why do *you?*" I ask right back.

"Goddamn. Well, it's almost completely social for me now. I really haven't smoked my own weed these last few months. I think enough time has passed where I see it more like money now than actual weed... ever since my dad died... I smoky because I likey, but not because I needy."

"Cute."

"So seriously, man," she asks me, "why do you smoke? We're already high. It's almost a chore now."

"I don't know, I just do. It's like, uh... a behavioral habit thing that just didn't stop."

That's all I feel like saying. Smoking with Luke's cool and all, but now I understand she's basically breaking up with me for Auna if she's no longer dealing.

"Yeah? Looks like you're gonna need a new dealer then," she says, "if you're going to have a behavioral habit thing that just didn't stop."

"Shut up."

"I'm seriously thinking of quitting the dealership," she insists. "You'll have to find your illegal psychotropics from someone else."

That kind of fucks with my high. "Damn."

"Yeah. See, it's like this—someone once told me, 'Lucia, I'm a mom. When it happened to me, I didn't like the idea at first, but now... the best thing I can ever do, as a woman, is be a mom. I love it.' My dad told me the same thing once, only he said, 'I'm a *dad*' ... and, '*man*.'"

How could this possibly be an explanation, or even related?
Sigh.

"Why are you telling me this now?"

"Shut up, *Boredom*, I'm tellin' a story... Okay, so anyway, she'd gone on about how she hated it when parents would talk about their kids, and how it always used to piss her off that 'other people would find happiness in something that she didn't relate with,' but when she started to take care of Adam, her attitude changed. That's gonna happen to me... When my dad told me his version, he gave me his Beretta 92F."

"Did Auna know your dad had said the same thing?"

"No." She pauses to think. "In fact, it was *after* he was dead."

"Dude."

"Yeah, I know, *parents*. Look, I've been dealin' for a few years now, and I don't really have a good hookup. In this small town, most of my sources have just stopped selling, and my current source is actually more of a wholesale dealer that sells in pounds out of garbage bags straight from some fields in the forest. It ain't like I've got a medicinal grower in my personal phone book, or like I know someone *from my job* or something."

"What? Is it too *sketchy* to stay in business?"

"Lemme put it this way—last time I went to re-up a couple elbows—that's a couple of pounds—three other guys show up I'd never seen before. They must've been from So-Cal, the way they were dressed. I had my gun just because that's what you wear when you've got ten thousand dollars in cash for something you're buying out of a garbage bag. Anyway, I could tell these other motherfuckers also had bulges that didn't belong to no tumor, so it was, to put it mildly, a little stressful. With my dad being a cop and all, I'm okay with guns, but these guys had crazy eyes like they had an itch on their finger only a trigger could scratch... made me uncomfortable... I don't even really know why now..."

"Huh."

I knew why. She was being sarcastic. I could see her point though—it was dangerous.

After what happened to me with the douche, and all *that* weirdness, I figured I empathized with her more than she knew. Maybe she's somehow jealous of how boring I am.

She looks at the sky and starts talking. "Yeah. You know, I never told anyone this except Auna, but on clear nights like this, I'd start thinking about my dad... thinking about how he taught me gun care and safety, how he taught me how to read people and stay alert even when you're exhausted, and you know, other stuff... really though, I mostly would just field strip his gun or practice Kenpo and think about how he taught me to do the right thing and be the right person versus what others *think* you should do... what society or some figurehead *says* you should do. There wasn't one time I ever pointed his gun in my own direction. That's my dad's gun... It's like a part of him I can carry with me wherever I go... and I hope to give it away to someone special on a clear night like this... and Adam, even with all his scars and developmental issues, that kid is *not* a follower... he's someone special... You know, over the last three years, smoking has helped me cope with the loss of my dad. I've had a really good time smoking, but I'm quitting on my own terms, just like my dad would've wanted, even though it looks like I'm quitting because *Auna* thinks I should. 'Let no one get in the way of your personal growth,' he said, 'not even yourself.' I've got to move on now, and Auna's giving me that chance."

Man, Luke's scatter-brained tonight, but I'm glad I came here. My trauma with Doc doesn't seem so real anymore.

"You know what? You're right. I *am* boring. Nothing crazy *ever* happens to me."

I should probably leave. I look at my phone. The time changes from eleven fifty-nine to midnight.

A single hollow howling scream pushes itself out to the night air from the direction of Doc's place.

It seems to last forever.

"Although, lately," I say, "Doc's been a bit weirder than usual."

Another long-lasting howl, as if someone were calling for help.

I am trippin' out.

"Seriously though, dude," she says, shaking her head, "those guys freaked me out..."

A third howl arrives from the night, only this time it's more like a wail, forfeiting, as if the person were in extreme agony. Seems like these were all coming from Doc's place just across the neighboring field and in the forested area where he lives... which is far away, but Luke's sitting right next to me, and she's probably just feeling as high as I am right now, so I'm not saying a damn thing about it. Besides, all the while the wail is happening, she's still talking: "... I heard a voice in my head that sounded just like my dad's say, 'it's time,' and I knew what it meant. It was time for me to quit."

The wailing stopped.

"You carry a gun, so why quit?"

"I have a relationship now."

"You sure?"

Another wail of agony arrives, but it seems to be cut short, as if the person ran out of breath or strength to scream. I am so stoned, and it seems so far away, I figure there isn't anything I can do about it.

"I love her, dude," she says. "I love Adam, too. Tonight's my last night. This is my last bowl, my last hit."

"What if I found you a medical grower, would you still do it?"

"Kids are cruel. Adam's gonna have a hard time getting through school with all his scars. I really wanna be there for her and Adam, emotionally. You know, my dad gave his life for me."

"What?" I ask. "You're the reason he died?"

"No, that's not what I meant, ass. I mean he lived his whole life for me. I'm going to do that for Adam."

"Sure," I say, "but, aren't you just doing it because you feel sorry for him? I mean, what if this relationship doesn't work out?"

"Dude!"

"Fine," I submit with my mouth, but my head is freaking out.

I figure she's lying to herself, but whatever.

Damn, even my dealer is being more of an ass than usual.

Armand will be disappointed.

I don't know if it will work out between her and Auna, but she's talking like she wants out of dealing. That's a major problem. Whatever her reasons are, I'm gonna have to go looking for another dealer, which is always a pain in the ass, especially in a small town like Jane.

I'd like to think that I have enough weed to support me, emotionally, when normal life happens. But something *larger than life* has happened. Needing to get another dealer on top of that is an even bigger pain in the ass. I will probably end up having to go back and forth through beach town traffic all the way to Sister City to find someone, too. Whatever, I'm starting to lose interest in this town anyway.

"John, it's getting late. I'm babysitting Adam again tomorrow, or today, and..." she yawns, stretching, "I'm kind of tired."

"I'm tired, too. Got horrible sleep last night. I'm going to go home and pass out. Don't worry about me. Hope everything works out between you two."

"Thanks."

* * *

— Monday, October 26th, 2009, 12:22 AM PDT —

I get home in a stupor from the weed. My tiredness is starting to take over inside me where I used to be high.

Needles.

I'd seen movies, so I figured I knew how to break into the places where they throw that shit away. Supposedly, all I needed was a throw rug to get over any razor wire. Besides, if it's been in a movie, it can be done.

The thing about movies, though, is that they don't tell you how much fucking homework you have to do. I'm looking around on the Internet for a local hospital and I don't see any that have low lit dumpsters in some back alley where cameras or rent-a-cops aren't close by. That shit was never in the movies.

Goddamn, such a pain in the ass.

Now, I've got to think about how I'm gonna stash my car some place, walk a million miles from there to the dumpster with a rug, some buckets, etc. Pain in the ass.

Fuck this, I'm tired.

I've got work in the morning.

I'm going to bed.

* * *

> The Doc, U-A DOB: ~2559-07-13, CID 99999999999

> ResID: 6.5 [altered by CID 09985239378/ResID: 10.9] M1

> U-B: [Doc's house, Jane, CA, US, Earth] LT: Monday, 2009-10-
26, 12:04 AM PDT

— Monday, October 26th, 2009, 12:04 AM PDT —

Doc rotates and jumps down from the table. "Now that we've confirmed a new verm host frequency is present, what do you think'll happen next?" His voice sounds completely shredded.

"You sound pretty bad."

"I'll fix it later. We don't know anything about this guy. Right now, I want your expert opinion."

"You don't wanna rest up at all?"

"I'm the Doc. You don't care."

"Fine. I think he's going to try to... murder one of us in some spectacular way... try to expose us all in the confusion."

"Oh? Did you get that information off of him?" Doc's recent screaming made his voice sound more like a cement mixer than a human.

Apronman looks up. "Their agent?"

"Do you know what he's going to do?"

"I'll be ready."

Doc clears his throat, but it doesn't do much good. "Hope so."

"He's just a contractor, not a soldier."

"He's a soldier for hire. That's a soldier. You can have my report if you like."

"Nah thanks, it'd just fuck with my mem. I got all the info I need."

"I checked it. The mem's good. Reality was just interpreted wrong at the time."

"I told you it'll fuck with my mem!"

* * *

> John Waterman, U-A DOB: 2579-12-03, CID 09985240860

> ResID: 7.1.0 [altered by CID 99999999999/ResID: 5.4] M1 &
M2

> U-B: [Highway 101, Jane, CA, US, Earth] LT: Monday, 2009-10-
26, 11:50 AM PDT

— Monday, October 26th, 2009, 11:50 AM PDT —

Whenever anyone asks, I tell 'em I love Mondays. I normally get to work before noon and stay at the Los Eatos for oh, about 12 hours. I like to arrive stoned to keep the edge of the drama off. Anyone who's ever worked at a restaurant knows there's always gonna be at least a little bit of drama. Otherwise, why work at a restaurant? You stay employed at any food place long enough, you're likely to leave or be fired because of some kind of bullshit drama. For example: Auna yelling at everyone about Luke dealing weed. Smoking is how I've survived, professionally and socially.

I like the familiar smell of the place, the food everywhere, and the random strangers. It's chill, because over the course of the day, I often smoke joints just off site next to a tree. My boss, Armand, often joins me. He's the one who mentioned Doc was looking to pay someone some extra money for a unique job. Armand's dealer is my dealer, Luke, who also works here, and at breakfast at the tree, neither of us have a care in this world.

Anyway, in the mornings right before work, even though I try to arrive already stoned, Armand and I usually share a joint, one from each of our own stashes every other day. We call it 'breakfast at the tree.' We store leftover or half-smoked joints in the hollow part of the tree, which is just above the line of sight. In general, this is pretty hard to find on trees. He never told me how he found it.

Technically, Mondays suck, so being stoned all day helps with all the bullshit.

Armand owns the place but also likes to cook, and he obsesses over the inventory all the fucking time. I'd be surprised if he doesn't cuddle with that fucking inventory book at night. Ugh. Either way, he's probably already done with his morning joint.

I'm not going to be playing my best game today... sigh...

This Monday is starting off different. This is probably a Monday I will hate. Not only have I not had enough time to get high before work, but there's currently a jam on the highway. I am running late, and Highway 101 is the only way there, so I'm starting to get paranoid, and my fear of not getting there on time starts to pound harder in my head. All the cars ahead of me slow to a stop. I hate this beach town traffic bullshit.

Okay, yeah, my routine of smoking before work is completely fucked, which will make the entire day suck. It's 11:53, and the bold red lights on my cracked dashboard blare out at me like an alarm clock, telling me to get there ASAP. I usually like to get to work around 11:45 with the only other key to the place, just after Doc. I like to make him wait a little. He complains in a funny way.

My phone rings. It's Doc, probably going to tell me why the fuck all these cars have slowed down... or maybe it's to ask why the hell I'm not there already. He's breathing so heavy it sounds like he's clearing his throat with every breath.

"John, did you get my needles yet?"

His voice is so raspy it sounds like he'd been to a concert the night before, or, knowing him, just screaming at his ceiling for no reason. Hell, that probably was his voice howling at the moon last night.

"Dude, what the hell's wrong with your voice? Is everything—"

"Did you *get them?*" He sounds desperate, like it's a life or death situation.

"Fuck dude, no, I didn't get the needles. It's only been two days. What the fuck? Why are there all these cars here?"

"I told you, it's either five thousand dollars or people get hurt."

"Whatever dude, are you there?"

"Yes, I'm here. I can hear you."

"*No*, I mean are you *there* there, at Los Eatos? I'm stuck in traffic."

He sighs. "Turn on your radio."

"What?"

Right then, I swear I hear Doc say JUST DO AS I SAY.

"Huh?" *The phone must be on speaker.*

"Radio!"

"Okay! Okay!"

I close the phone and turn on the radio.

KHIK radio. K-Hick. What a shitty name. Like most things in Jane, it sucks. Driving in Jane sucks because like most beach towns on the west coast, there are hills and what seems like more cars than people. Really, I just hate how bright the sun is, and the hills cause the sun to be in my eyes. Whether having the sun reflected directly into my face from my mirrors or other cars, I'm always a slight turn of my head away from momentary blindness. Other than going to work, I try to stay home or indoors most of the time.

Right now, I can't see a damned thing other than all the cars parked everywhere... and now behind me too. Great, now I can't turn around, even if I want to. I'm stuck at car wash speed.

I sigh in abandonment as I listen to the *only* radio station in town. We have others from other cities, but they don't care about Jane enough to report why there are cars everywhere.

It was going to be a good Monday, I think, as I listen to the mono sound finally wake up from its dusty slumber somewhere inside my car doors.

"...and they're looking for *anyone* who might be connected to this crime. Kate?"

"Thanks, Jim. The time is now 11:57 AM, and if you're just joining us, we've been updating you on a story about the major jam on Highway 101. This highway often backs up this time of day during summer months, but there is a police vehicle in the middle of the main intersection. Officers and fire trucks have surrounded the local Los Eat, Adios! in an attempt to find what has been reported as a bomb inside. We have not been told who the suspect is in this crime, but we have been told that a member of the management may be inside, and officers are uncertain of the legitimacy of the call. Jane's Chief of police, Sam Gearden, has called for Sister City's only bomb specialist to investigate the claim, or threat, I should say, of a bomb being planted in the fryer. If the device is in the fryer, the grease could act as an added danger to the explosion. Chief Gearden believes that the bomb was planted late last night, and that there are suspects in mind but none in custody. Meanwhile, Highway 101 has been blocked off, and police are worrying that it may be dangerous to be near the Los Eat, Adios! restaurant at this time. A crew will arrive shortly to assist in the rerouting of traffic."

Fuck me. A bomb? A bomb... I laugh at the ridiculousness of it and turn off the radio. Really? *Really?* I can't see the damned place because of the hill between me and Los Eatos.

Sigh.

I might as well—

BOOM.

My car shakes in time with the trees.

"Nah, that can't be right," I say to myself, but as I look to the horizon, black smoke rises like a muffin top, slowly creating a backdrop to the hill that is between me and my destination.

Only now do I realize Doc was serious.

That was a bomb, and it just blew up Los Eatos.

My head is overwhelmed by worry. My thoughts began to become external... "No. No. No. No. *Think! ... Armand!*"

Then it hits me. Hard. Images of Auna and Armand and Luke flicker in my consciousness, and I inhale against the dry air as adrenaline floods my system. My heart races with flashes of anxiety. My entire body screams for comfort. I feel completely exposed and alone.

Everything's fucked. Everything's fucked. Armand, one of my closest friends, is dead, and the place I depend on for money is gone.

I jump out of my car, instinctively locking it before leaving it and my fellow stupefied motorists behind. In disbelief, I race toward the smoke that has now risen into a pointy mushroom column above the hill.

Others who've resigned themselves to stay in their vehicles call out to me. I ignore them.

"Nonononono..." I say with every exhaled breath until finally I'm too focused on running to be talking, but my thoughts just keep yelling "no" over and over and over. I keep sprinting until I can't breathe fast enough to get enough oxygen to my brain to keep going so fast. I'm inhaling and exhaling as hard as I can, but still, small spots of purple join my vision, as if I'd ever invite them, so I slow down slightly. My lungs burn. I stop running to lessen my dizziness, but I keep walking, fast.

Even *more* adrenaline and disbelief flood my brain.

Think and walk. Keep going.

"Oh my god... no no no no no no... What the *fuck!*"

Think and walk.

My breaths are deep and loud and my ears are ringing... my thoughts have become wordless in my panic and disbelief.

I near the ridge of the hill and the horizon spreads before me. Los Eatos is a football field away and a couple stories lower. Beyond the rows of cars on Highway 101, the Los Eatos sign has fallen off the face of the restaurant and collapsed onto Armand's burning car, next to other burning cars. I don't see the Los Eatos van though. It may be the distance between me and the Los Eatos, but somehow, it looks like the pavement's on fire, too.

I just stand there on the top of the hill and stare down at it all until my thoughts return to me. *This isn't happening.*

I hear Doc's voice as clear as if he were next to me: YOU'RE IN DENIAL.

I jump. "OH MY GOD WHAT THE FUCK, DOC?" I wrench my neck back and forth in alarm. "What the..?"

There is no one here except me.

Doc's voice says THIS REALLY IS HAPPENING. IT HAS HAPPENED.

I hold the phone up to my ear, in reflex. "Where *are* you?"

I'M IN YOUR HEAD, JOHN, AND THAT THERE, THAT'S A SMALL FIRE. WOULDN'T YOU HATE TO SEE A LARGE FIRE?

I'm so lost and confused, I've subconsciously fallen to my knees on the sidewalk, dropping the phone to the pavement where I kneel, staring at my hands, wishing I was in a nightmare, wishing I'd wake up.

"What have you...?"

LAST TIME YOU WERE AT THE HOUSE, YOU WERE IMPLANTED WITH A STANDARD ISSUE VIBRATION MODULATION PROCESSOR ON THE INSIDE SURFACE OF YOUR SKULL, SOMETHING CALLED A "VERM." I WAS IN YOUR BRAIN EVEN BEFORE I WOKE YOU. I AM INVINCIBLE.

I begin to hyperventilate.

DON'T BECOME INCOHERENT NOW, JOHN; LISTEN TO ME.

"I am tripping *out!*"

YOU'RE NOT TRIPPING OUT. I'M IN YOUR HEAD. I TOLD YOU SO. NOW, THOSE NEEDLES ARE NEEDED. ONCE YOU'VE DONE WHAT I'VE ASKED, YOU WILL GET FIVE THOUSAND DOLLARS, AND THE VERM WILL BE REMOVED FROM YOUR HEAD.

"Ohh no... no no no no—"

SHUT UP. I WILL BE MONITORING YOUR CHOICES FROM HERE ON OUT. DISAPPOINT AGAIN, AND MORE HARM WILL COME TO THE PEOPLE YOU KNOW. KEEP IN MIND THE CONSEQUENCES OF YOUR APATHY, BECAUSE THE NEXT TIME THERE IS A RECONNECTION, ALL MEMORIES WILL BE DOWNLOADED. FIND THE NEEDLES IN LESS THAN ONE DAY OR MORE HARM WILL COME.

My phone rings. It's Doc. I don't answer.

GET THE NEEDLES FIRST.

I hold the phone back up to my head to respond, forgetting, in my shock, that the voice was in my head, and then instinctively moving my arm up and down, I eventually let my arm fall to my side in realization that there is no need to respond into the phone.

A few minutes pass.

The smoke continues to rise.

I get up to walk down to—to what *used to be*—Los Eatos. Like a zombie, I'm walking down the slope... I have no mental strength to think. I'm just... a walking thing. I'm walking. Everything seems far away, like it's not really happening.

Oh look—those cars are not really on fire. I'm not really walking toward anything real, like that burning building in the distance, which is the Los Eatos restaurant.

I dial Auna's number while I walk.

"... hey." I breathe.

"Hey... What's wrong?"

"Los Eatos is gone."

"What?"

"Los Eatos is gone. It's on fire. I'm... fucked."

"Los Eatos is gone? What do you mean gone?" Her tone is scolding and frustrated, as if there's something I'm not telling her.

I stop walking to gather my thoughts, which are frayed.

Damn it, am I really going to have to go through this without at least some encouragement from my closest friend?

"News? It's on the news," I manage to say. "It's on K-Hick, so probably on TV too."

"What happened? When?"

Sigh.

I start walking toward the fire again, still trying to take in what I'm seeing and hoping Armand somehow missed this madness and is still alive.

"Right now. It's gone."

"You're not making any sense," she says. "Hold on..."

She turns on the news.

Reporters are telling the same story. I imagine photography of the fire flashing on her television.

"Oh my god. ... Oh my GOD. Oh no..." I hear shuffling sounds, and then, *"Lucia—"*

My phone beeps, ending the call.

Fuck it.

I close the phone and keep my pace. My body shakes from adrenaline. I'm not thinking straight.

If Auna wants to talk to Luke, she doesn't want to talk to me. Damn it! I'm gonna have to go down there, and hope I don't see any of Armand's body parts.

I still can't believe my eyes.

My brain has resorted to an exhausted mantra of *I'm just a walking thing...* over and over.

My pace is mechanical and lifeless.

When I finally arrive, everything still feels far away. There's an ambient sizzling mixed in with the crackling of the fire, as if the black smoke filling the air and sky isn't enough to overwhelm my senses. There are people crying, dirty... probably customers... and I think there is someone screaming, too, but for all I know right now, that might be my own thoughts, and I'm not screaming out loud. The injured are an ambulance's problem now... it's not like they're crying because they can't get any more Los Eatos food.

All I care about is finding an officer who I can tell my story to, and hopefully find out if Armand is okay so this can be over with, and I can pace on back to my car. Hopefully, it will be there when I get back. But, the way this douche of a day was going, I wouldn't be surprised if someone had towed my car by the time I got back there. No time to get distracted. I need to focus.

A slightly overweight cop with graying brown hair has already begun directing people and vehicles away from the area. Maybe I can grab my stash in the tree hole, but I'll have to grab that shit after I talk with this cop. I don't want anyone to find pot on me while I'm trying to leave. With my hands away from my sides, I step shaking through cars into the middle of the intersection. Meanwhile, people in fire and law garb hustle in and hover around people that had been injured amongst the parked cars. An ambulance is just arriving behind me via sidewalk, and people are moving out of the way as best they can.

"Hey, are you in charge here?" I ask the cop over the noise.

"As much in charge of chaos as I can be," he says as he waves his hands to direct a car to inch by us. "I'm Lieutenant Daab, the specialist here. What do you need?"

That name sounds familiar…

"I'm uh, John, John Waterman. I work… I mean, I *worked* here."

"Give me a moment, Mr. Waterman. Let me write this down."

The officer stops directing traffic but doesn't move. He pulls out a pen and notepad and writes down my name.

"All right Mr. Waterman, why are you in the middle of the intersection here with me?" he asks as one by one, cars slowly meander with herd behavior through the intersection.

His question confuses me for a moment. I'm not sure what to say. "I wish this was all just a dream, and I want my life back" comes to mind, because I'm not sure I understand what's going on. I don't know how this could have happened, and now I have to find another job, and a friend of mine could be dead, and I don't know what I'm going to do, but I hope everyone is okay.

Filling in the silence with a professional tone, the officer says, "Mr. Waterman, let me at least get your contact information, then I'll need to go help with crowd control."

Crowd control. Now? Cars are stuck everywhere with drivers in them… ah, maybe he meant—car control, or something… Car directing? Directing traffic? Ugh… Fucking focus!

"Is Armand okay?" I ask.

The officer leaned and pointed his ear at me to avoid the noise of the fire and cars easing by. "Who?"

"Armand. Armand Pochelli? He was a guy I… he is, or was, my boss. Is he alive? He owns the place."

Daab looks into the sky and scratches the back of his ear with his pencil. Nothing seems to ring a bell with this guy, so I just give him my phone number and walk off, still shaky.

This must be why people who come back from wars are always on edge. People die in war so much faster than in normal life. Fuck that. I'll live, thanks.

Oh yeah, weed…

My phone beeps along the way to the tree and back to my car. It beeps constantly. From the call-ID, I can see Doc has left a message, but I don't care. Let it beep forever. Fuck that guy. Fucking douche. God damn it, what the hell am I gonna do?

GET THE NEEDLES, JOHN.

"Gnye nya nyeeles *yaan*," I say, mocking him as I get in my car with my phone still beeping.

Sigh.

Fine, I'll stop the noise.

I look at my phone and turn off the beeping.

1:30 PM. I guess I'm getting needles.

* * *

— Monday, October 26th, 2009, 7:31 PM PDT —

It took three hours of complete wank time to leave. Everyone was waiting for that cop and his crew to route all the cars. Three hours for all that—it was like a road block—they checked every person's ID that rolled through. When my turn came to be checked, I asked what was taking so long. They told me it was in case they might identify someone with a record trying to leave the area. Ridiculous. I had to keep turning my engine off for most of the time just to save gas enough to leave.

Then it took another three hours before leaving my apartment. I had to study Humboldt County's maps online, just to find that only *one* of the five major hospitals has the dumpster setup I need: Brendon Aaron Memorial.

I can't believe what I'm doing, but I really want to get this done so I can feel safe enough to smoke. Sometimes the desire to smoke inspires other desires, and all this time wasting isn't helping.

My phone rings. It's Luke. I let it go to voicemail as I take notes. I don't actually own a rug that's fit for climbing over the razor wire part of a cyclone fence. I'll have to buy one.

I buy eight 5-gallon buckets and a rug from the local warehouse store, roll the rug all up in my car like it's the biggest joint in the world, and begin driving down the road, imagining what a joint that size would do to the people in my car. Damn, the smoke alone would be enough to run me off the road... I wonder if the passengers would care.

Doc's voice interrupts my thoughts. YOU HAVE EIGHTEEN HOURS LEFT.

I scream and my car skids and swerves as I slam on the brakes alone in the dark. "You're always scaring the *shit* out of

79

me with that! And NO, I DON'T have your *fucking* needles yet. You should have known that if your voice is really in my head."

Even my logic hurts.

I get back up to speed.

I'VE ONLY BEEN PARTIALLY ACTIVATED. SO THERE YOU HAVE IT.

"What could that mean? You know what? Don't answer that. Just... I'm on my way now... just shut that shit off. I'm trying to drive."

VERY WELL.

I drive for a few moments, imagining myself actually in the dumpster. That was something they never really show you in movies—being actually in the dumpster. I start thinking that by the time I get there, since it's already dark enough, I'll have plenty of darkness to cover my ass as I dive in.

"Oh fuck. I forgot gloves. *Dammit!*"

* * *

> John Waterman, U-A DOB: 2579-12-03, CID 09985240860

> ResID: 7.1.0 [altered by CID 99999999999/ResID: 5.4] M1

> U-B: [Erin Brendon Memorial Hospital, Jane, CA, US, Earth] LT: Monday, 2009-10-26, 8:09 PM PDT

— Monday, October 26th, 2009, 8:09 PM PDT —

As soon as I arrive in garbage man garb with gloves on hands, my backpack, a rolled-up rug, and my eight 5-gallon buckets tied together by the handles with bungee cord, I don't see the familiar razor-wire-topped cyclone fence from the movies. What I could tell from the Internet was that there was a dumpster area here and it wasn't well lit. After all that, it's just a regular cyclone fence. Disappointed that I bought a rug for apparently no reason, I just drop it and watch it unroll before surveying the setup more closely.

I climb over the fence, and I'm trying to be as quiet as I can, but it's nearly impossible with a cyclone fence, eight buckets, and a backpack.

I walk to the dumpster, open the cover, lower the buckets in over the side, hold my breath, and climb in, slowly shutting the cover.

This freaks me out. The buckets are bulky, but I couldn't think of anything that might carry up to one thousand used needles without poking me with AIDS.

With my breath still held, I listen for any oncoming footsteps, hoping I didn't make noise enough to get caught.

I feel for my flashlight, find it, and flick it on. I look about, breathe in, and then immediately wretch. The taste in the air of blood, rotten fat, flesh, and shit melds with the taste of bile in my throat. I try to catch my breath, but I can't breathe in without heaving. I vomit on everything I see. Little chunks of my vomit drip down over most of the medical waste bags.

Doc—you mother fucker—I should have asked for twenty thousand dollars.

* * *

81

— Monday, October 26th, 2009, 12:12 PM PDT —

"He was looking for *me*," Apronman says. "He probably found traces of my artificial identity where he works. If he's just going to start showing up wherever we're workin', his current connections pose a significant risk to us."

"Of course he does. Look, if that cleaner comes around..." Doc stops pacing for a moment, his voice still thrashed, then: "I need to get to work. Got the book?" Without pause, Doc grabs a small toolbox from under the table where Apronman operated on him and sets it atop the same table.

"Have you apologized for what you did?" Apronman asks.

"Yeah, I just called him," Doc says. "I called him twice, once right before noon to try to get him out of town, and then again about ten minutes later, after the bomb went off. I left a message on his voicemail. Does that fit in with our plans? He's got the catalyst. He'll be activated when he hears the message, but it'll take time, because he's a chimera. Any more questions? Do you have the book? I have to get to work on erasure protocols." Doc begins moving boxes and shelves in his living room, putting boxes near the center of the metal table. It's still covered in his blood where his arm reattached to his body.

A book with 'inventory' on the front is tossed in Doc's direction. "You find anything," Apronman says, "let me know."

Doc opens the book. He then shifts his direction to move boxes from separate corners of the room, exchanging them with random things that are now cluttering his workspace, such as a taxidermy squirrel, an old gutted computer tower, and a TV tray full of test tubes and beakers.

"Ugh," Doc says, "I haven't even got set up yet. I've got to make room for—"

83

"I gotta go meet up with the cleaner," the man in the apron says, as he turns to leave. "You let me know."

On the table, Doc replaces the pile of boxes with their contents: monitors, small electronic metal boxes of varying shapes and sizes, wiring everywhere, a mouse and a keyboard.

"You know... I just remembered something about what happened," Doc says, as he heaves a beer keg into his arms for placement elsewhere. "His verm's been activated under only slight duress. It's likely to be a corrupted ResID activation. He probably thinks you're dead, and that I killed you."

Apronman stops, sighs, turns back again, and says, "That's a game-changer. I'm going to have to corral this." He pauses, pulls out his cell phone, dials a number, and waits. Doc recognizes the ring-back tone, but ignores his partner, focusing on rearranging the room to fit his latest agenda. "I was having my breakfast this morning," Apronman says into his phone, "when I noticed a cop coming out the front of the Los Eatos. He didn't see me, but I think he might be looking for John, wherever the hell he's been the last few days."

He closes the phone.

Doc looks up at him. "You think that'll work?"

"It'll have to. I didn't want to talk to John directly because of the cleaner. Look, we need to get moving. That cleaner could be coming around here any second, and we're not going to be beaten because of some little toy you can't get to work."

"It's not just a toy," Doc says.

"You'll have fun with it, once you get it working, won't you?"

"Fun? It could take me eight hours, at least, just to prep, and it'd be nice to heal fully—"

"Eight hours? Do you even have it with you?"

"It's close by," Doc says. "It's in a safe place."

"If you don't produce, we're all fucked, including you. Earth will shuffle off its mortal coil if spores enter our solar system, and spores don't care if we have a cleaner to deal with." Doc was about to respond, but the man in the apron keeps talking as he walks out the door, "Get that *thing* working. Find a host.

Do whatever you need to do, or all our sacrifices will have been for nothing. I gotta go. I've got my phone. I'll keep myself mobile for a little over nine hours and then lead them to me. That should give you some time for sleep to heal. If I'm not back by tomorrow night, I'll just meet up with you at the winery where the Halloween party's supposed to be."

"I think I may have an idea," Doc says to Apronman, trying to wave him down as he's walking out the door.

Doc's phone rings. He pulls it out of his pocket and looks at the caller ID.

"Speaking of a host..."

Apronman is gone.

Doc answers the phone.

"Hello? ... Hey Anny! ... Auna, sorry. ... Oh, no need to apologize. What can I do for you? ... Yes, it's just a bit of a sore throat. It'll clear up soon enough. I promise I'm not contagious... Sure, come over... It'll be kind of nice to have someone to talk to. ... Thanks, Anny, er, Auna, absolutely ... glad to have you. Oh, also, could you bring over the toy robot? I just had some great ideas on improving it, and I'd like to try 'em out... Thanks. It'll be fun. See you later tonight."

* * *

> John Waterman, U-A DOB: 2579-12-03, CID 09985240860

> ResID: 7.1.0 [altered by CID 99999999999/ResID: 5.4] M1 & M2

> U-B: [John's car, Jane, CA, US, Earth] LT: Monday, 2009-10-26, 10:12 PM PDT

— Monday, October 26th, 2009, 10:12 PM PDT —

On my drive back to Jane, over to Doc's house, in the stink of all the shit I'd just waded in, I thought I'd light up the joint I got from the tree to pass the time. It was going to be a while, and it would help me calm my nerves from just stealing the weirdest crap ever. Hopefully, in my exhaustion from heaving my guts out, the weed doesn't make me so sleepy that I crash. Too bad this joint isn't the size of the rug. After a couple hits, I think about how late it is… and then how hard it will be to have to drive while fucked up in the middle of the night on hardly lit winding roads.

Getting high is calming me, though. I smell like what I imagine is the shit-end of a corpse, but at least breathing in no longer feels so much like a knee to the stomach.

DID YOU GET THEM OR NOT?

Without realizing how accustomed I had become to the voice in my head, I just blurted out, "Oh yeah, everything's fine."

Though I hated the man, Doc's voice could actually keep me awake. I figure with the long drive, I'll see if I can make any sense of this guy.

"You have any kind of sense of civility?"

I'M NOT FROM … HERE.

"Ah yeah, yeah; you're eccentric like. You're from France."

NO, I'M NOT FROM FRANCE. MY PLACE OF ORIGIN IS KHSHUTL, AS YOURS IS.

"Yeah… kuh-shuttle. Gesundheit, *Douche*."

He doesn't respond. I keep driving. Apparently, the verm or whatever the hell it is either malfunctioned, or Doc didn't care to answer. Either way, I suddenly realize everything I have just gone through is unbelievable, so maybe he is … foreign. Why am I associating unbelievable experiences with foreigners? Is that racist? Does it really matter? I still don't even know if Armand is dead, or what the hell *the douche* is going to do once he gets his damn needles.

A moment later, I just start laughing. I may be high, but the situation is so outlandish, I can't help but laugh.

I begin calming down as the road passes me by, remembering that evening when I got home after Doc had tied me up. My smile collapses as I think about the whole ordeal with more somber—more paranoid—feelings.

I remember feeling stoned in a way that was different than usual. I had only felt that way after coming home from the dentist, and realizing that how I felt was actually not a feeling of being stoned at all. I felt drugged. I had a really hard time concentrating on driving, and I was making wrong turns… I wasn't high from the weed I smoked. I must have been high from something else. When I had finally gotten home that night, I was spooked because it was so weird, and I thought I was only stoned. I had figured I was just tripping out. I tried sobering up with some music.

I realize now, as I'm driving down the road in the stank of medical waste, I had been in denial.

After Doc had called me to complain about me calling the cops, I had sat down at my computer to smoke and enjoy some porn to get my mind off what I had experienced. I noticed my computer said that it really was Saturday, not Thursday. I'd smirked and scoffed.

"I must have a virus," I said to myself, but then I looked at the date shown in my email account I had left opened before traipsing over to Doc's. I was logged out, and after I logged back in, I realized… I had been at Doc's house, unconscious, for two days.

My denial had instantly changed into alarm.

I remember thinking *OH FUCK*. I immediately checked my voicemail; it was Armand asking me where the hell I've been.

Then, when I insisted that it was Thursday...

No wonder my old boss thought I was fuckin' around. I would have dismissed me too, but after all that, I was too tired and too stoned to care... kinda like I am now, only without all the stank.

That night, all the porn in the world wouldn't have been enough to get me off.

When I had finally gotten around to sleeping, there was that weird nightmare with the hang glider and the plane, and the post-dream shitting.

Now that I'm driving down the road, having laughed for no other reason than because I'm stoned, and finally almost done with this ridiculous quest, I feel a weird pressure growing right under my breastbone. I'm pulled away from my thoughts on the past toward a painful feeling in my guts. It's like when you go over the high point on a roller coaster, and there's that lifted feeling to your guts, only this was much more painful, like there's pain pushing the air out of my lungs up from under my belly button.

My vision starts going purple.

I swerve as my dizziness matches the pain I feel behind my eyes and in my ears.

FINE, THAT'S FINE. LAUGH ALL YOU WANT, BUT YOUR APATHY AND SELF-IMPOSED IGNORANCE IS THE CAUSE OF WHAT HAPPENS NEXT. FOR WHAT IT'S WORTH, I AM SORRY.

Doc's voice sounded genuinely concerned. To hear it from him seems genuinely concerning—for me. It is overly distracting and the driving process has become very complicated.

"Wha?" I breathe, as I try to maintain control of my car, the needles chinking upon themselves in my hatchback. "What are you thalking abuht?"

No response.

I hear a police siren, but the sound seems distant, like echoes, as if I'm at an industrial music concert.

Then, realizing in my inebriation that I have somehow become intoxicated way beyond what weed could ever do, *again*, I slam on the breaks and clumsily pull over to what I could barely make out as the side of the road, feeling the need to pass out.

My body lunges forward in the blur. A sweeping red and blue pattern reflects all around me. As I begin to pass out, my phone starts ringing again.

* * *

> John Waterman, U-A DOB: 2579-12-03, CID 09985240860

> ResID: 7.1.0 [altered by CID 99999999999/ResID: 5.4] M1

> U-B: [Erin Brendon Memorial Hospital, Jane, CA, US, Earth] LT:
Tuesday, 2009-10-27, 12:16 PM PDT

— Tuesday, October 27th, 2009, 12:16 PM PDT —

I wake up to the back of my eyelids and the sound of an EKG beeping, pestering me to wake up *more*, when all I really want to do is tell whoever the fuck turned on the beeping to shut it the hell up. My head pounds with every beep. My eyelids separate and what looks like a hospital room spreads before me. The pain from the light that enters my eyes burns. I have to wait. I shut my eyes.

"Good, you're awake. 'Bout time. Hi, Mr. Waterman, my name is Lieutenant Daab. I'm a member of the Humboldt County Sheriff's Office. I took your number yesterday at the Los Eat, Adios! fire."

"Muh?"

I look in the direction of Daab's growling voice with squinting, burning eyes and see him sitting in his cop uniform in a hospital chair, comfortable and businesslike even with the utility belt and bulletproof vest. You know, intimidating. I can tell by his disdainful face he doesn't want to be here any more than I do.

I try to sit up, but pain in my head and arm arrests me, and I find that someone had stuck me with an IV and handcuffed me to the bed rail, which is weird. Aren't there straps for that shit?

"You took quite a spill. You're lucky to be alive." He leans in close and says, "Good thing you were *fucking high*, or you'd have probably been dead by now. Lucky you." He leans back and continues, "And lucky me. I get to take you in when you're finally lucid. Don't worry, I'll take good care of you."

"Daab?" I've struggled enough against the handcuffs to irritate my IV. My arm complains louder than whatever the hell this guy's blabbering about.

91

"Yeah, it's Daab. Listen, uh, you wouldn't happen to know what *kind* of drugs you were on when you started driving, would you? You see, I've got this report I've got to fill out..."

Dammit, his mouth just wouldn't shut up and neither will this headache. I feel like I've been struck by lightning. I finally gasp out the word, "weed," hoping this to be all the dues I had to pay to this guy.

"Huh... Yeah, we already wrote that one down. Getting high on weed alone isn't what kept you alive. We'd like to know all about the other stuff. You're in the hospital. The hospital you just robbed. Hospital security called it in."

His very presence is uncomfortable to be around. The way he said "other stuff" was so overly nonchalant, it sounded under-exaggerated, but I had no clue what *other stuff* he could possibly mean. I look up at him, as if he knew the answer, but he doesn't move a muscle. I just resign to say, "I don't know."

"All right."

Daab moves quickly, fluidly, getting up and leaning toward me, and in the same motion, he pulls out a black cloth from out of nowhere and drapes it over my head. I inhale to yell with what strength I can, but my entire body feels slow. It takes forever to breathe in. Daab must have done something to me, because before I could scream, the whole world shuts off.

* * *

> Armand Pochelli, U-A DOB: 2573-07-13, CID 09985239378

> ResID: 10.9 [altered by CID 09928764743] M1

> U-B: [Doc's house, Jane, CA, US, Earth] LT: Monday, 2009-10-26, 12:15 PM PDT

— Monday, October 26th, 2009, 12:15 PM PDT —

The man in the apron walks out from Doc's house and gets into his white van, which is parked right next to Doc's van. It's identical to Doc's, save for a large peel-away magnet sign on the side in the shape of a huge sombrero with the words, "Los Eat, Adios!" largely scrawled across the sombrero's crown.

He starts it up, reaches the edge of Doc's property, coasts out of the long driveway, and eases into small-town traffic.

A few minutes later, he reaches the outskirts of Sister City, where he's welcomed by abandoned buildings that have been left to rot.

An unmarked police vehicle with two cops inside merges into traffic a couple cars behind.

He notices instantly, but then confirms it's a tail by slowly taking four left turns around a block. The cops are still following

"Son of a bitch," he says under his breath, slowing down to take a right.

Then, seeing a semi, he picks up speed, passing it up and cutting it off, taking a second right, pointing himself back towards Doc's place, watching for the police car between the vehicles behind him.

He doesn't see it.

He takes a third right at the next turn, just outside the sight of the cop car.

No cars on this stretch.

He floors it.

The end of the block closes fast as he slams on the brakes to under-turn a fourth right.

Somehow, the cop car appears a block behind him with siren blaring.

93

He takes a left behind a warehouse.

He stomps on the gas again, pushing the engine hard. He swerves, skids, and tips the van's center of gravity almost completely on two wheels.

The two wheels in the air fall, skidding as he slams on the brakes.

The siren is closing in.

His door opens.

He jumps out, leaving the engine running and the driver door open as he runs around the front.

In one motion, he peels the large magnetic sticker off the sliding side door with one hand and slides the door open wide with the other. He rips off his apron, throwing it and the identifying sticker on a pile of electronic equipment in the back with one hand and rolls the door shut with the other.

He moves so fast the shape of his body blurs in the light of the bright autumn sun, yet no one is around to see.

He speeds back to the driver's seat, slams the door, and puts the van into gear, edging it into the lane.

The rear-view mirror betrays him; the sweeping lights of the cop car appear, followed by the cop car into his lane.

There are still no other cars.

He sighs, reaches back, and grabs a wire as thick as his thumb from the electrical equipment behind him. He pulls off what looks like a large pen cap from the wire's end, revealing a sharp metallic plug, which he immediately stabs into the side of his thigh without wincing.

With the siren on full blast, the cop car's engine howls from being punished by its driver.

The van takes another sharp right between a couple of abandoned factories, just outside the cop car's line of sight.

Bright blue scintillations reflect and refract around the surfaces of the factories.

Where the van should be, a crown of blue lightning stabs up at the sky in many directions, and a clipped cracking sound carves into the atmosphere.

The cop car reaches its optimal acceleration, then skids around the corner. A slightly blue smoke ring the size of a garage door floats in the street. The cop car swerves to a stop through the smoke.

The stench of tires skidding across the empty street intermixes with the sweet metallic ink-like scent of ozone.

* * *

> Armand Pochelli, U-A DOB: 2573-07-13, CID 09985239378

> ResID: 10.9 [altered by CID 09928764743] M1 & M2

> U-B: [Armand's house, Jane, CA, US, Earth] LT: Monday, 2009-10-26, 9:59 PM PDT

— Monday, October 26th, 2009, 9:59 PM PDT —

Apronman pulls into his driveway.

Before he steps into his house, he replaces the "Los Eat, Adios!" magnet sign on the side of his van and puts his apron back on.

He exchanges a few boxes between the van and his house at a speed that renders him barely visible.

He takes a break to eat a protein bar.

Once done, he enters his house, washes his hands, brushes his teeth, drinks some water, and gets into bed, apron and all, even his shoes. He turns out all the lights. He waits in his bed with his eyes open, an inventory book in one hand and a gun in the other.

His house is quiet but for a faint hissing sound.

He knows what he hears but keeps still.

A choking fume seeps into the bedroom.

He waits.

The smoke billows, turning the room into a cloud of purple.

He waits still.

Unexpectedly, he chokes, giving away his position.

Shots of electric current fire in his direction from within the smoke.

His gun discharges.

Humanoid figures dash out from shadows and shock him further until his body spasms, ensuring he's out.

Hurried footsteps enter the room.

A voice in the purple fog calls out to them from behind a gas mask. "Change of plans. This inventory book suggests he can link to the van. Dust the cop car. We'll return in the van."

"What?" the other gas masks respond. "Why? We have a perfectly good cop car."

His body lurches.

They shock him again.

His body relaxes.

A stretcher is prepared to leave with the body.

"The boss doesn't need it. Dust it. We all saw him jump. You can bet your jobs that van has verm tech in it."

They exit his house with him on the stretcher, and with masks removed, all but two men duck into the van, pulling the door shut, leaving the occupants in the dark.

"I always liked dusting," one man says to the other. "Reminds me of Christmas."

"Christmas?" The other man asks, placing a black cube on top of the cop car.

"Yeah," the one man says, as he types into a pad, "the lights and falling flakes."

The first man takes a couple steps back toward the van.

Green lasers shower downward from the black cube over the police vehicle.

"You mean laser-guided... atrophy?"

Small dark holes open over the surfaces where the lasers fired.

The black cube disintegrates.

"It's festive," he says, watching his partner enter the van as the dark holes spread downward throughout the entire police vehicle's shape. "The lasers are like Christmas lights, and the nano waste falls just like snow."

The police vehicle's shape collapses from top to bottom. Only dust remains.

"More like ash. You ever see a person dusted? It's not so pretty."

"I saw the training video," he says, stepping over Apronman, shutting the van door. "It's dust," he says to his superior, referring to the police vehicle. "We can go."

Their superior nods at the driver, and the driver starts the engine.

"No, I mean, have you ever seen someone get dusted, in person? The nanos are dealing with liquids and moving parts.

The people melt and spill all over themselves, just like in the video, but since the nanos don't dust 'em all at once, in the meantime, they're scream-gurgling, and they stink like burnt rotten meat and sewage."

From outside, the van's "Los Eat, Adios!" magnet sign reflects streetlights as it heads east.

"Scream-gurgling? You're ruining the Christmas spirit."

"It's like rotten meat and raw sewage. I'd hate to think this stuff could be weaponized."

No cars are in sight as the "Los Eat, Adios!" van continues east, turning onto Highway 101, which will eventually lead them out of Jane.

"Can you imagine a bomb of that stuff? I'm telling you, man, that stink stays in your brain for days."

"Well, at least we won't have to smell *that* today, so Merry Christmas."

Apronman opens his eyes.

The van lurches to a stop, skidding from the e-brake.

Thumps and shuffles rock the van side to side.

The engine shuts off.

Light and shouts erupt from within.

A scolding voice yells unintelligibly, then silence.

The van no longer shows any rumblings of confrontation.

Voices speak inside, then a flashlight bobs near the driver's seat for a few moments before turning off.

The engine starts again.

The "Los Eat, Adios!" sombrero slowly rides away until it's out of sight.

* * *

> Anny Klaura, U-A DOB: 2580-05-15, CID 09986520678

> ResID: 4.0 [altered by CID 09985240860/ResID: 4.3.2] M1 & M2

> U-B: [Doc's house, Jane, CA, US, Earth] LT: Monday, 2009-10-26, 10:15 PM PDT

— Monday, October 26th, 2009, 10:15 PM PDT —

Knock knock. Knock knock knock.

Doc quickly opens the door. "Come on in."

Auna nods her thanks and steps inside.

"Hey, I've just made up some tea. Want some?"

"Oh, no thanks."

"Sure?" Doc asks as he strains his skinny arms picking up a milk crate full of cinder blocks to set next to the door.

"What is that?"

"Oh, I had collected some cinder blocks for a project I was working on a while back, and I don't need 'em anymore, so— Oh, tea!" Doc hops up in thought-derailment, and then walks past Auna and into the kitchen.

"On second thought, is it decaf?" Auna asks, sitting on a couch armrest, the only surface in the place not taken up by clutter.

"Yeah," Doc says from the kitchen. "It's a bit rich and a bit bitter," he says, returning, "but it's nice for late night work, or..." he smiles reassuringly, "conversation."

"Okay, thanks."

Auna looks about the place.

Doc appears to be either working on too many projects at once, or he's a hoarder. He returns from the kitchen holding a small silver platter with a tea set, a butane lighter, and a joint resting in an ashtray. He pushes a stack of papers two feet high off the Plexiglas piano chair with his foot.

The papers spread over the small space of the floor and onto Auna's feet as Doc sets the platter down.

She stands and steps back, watching Doc awkwardly force them back into a stack.

"Your voice sounds a lot better than when we talked on the phone."

Doc sets the papers on the milk crate of cinder blocks.

"I had a nap," he says, returning to pour tea into the cups. "I hope you don't mind, but I'm going to smoke a bit while we have some tea."

"That's fine."

Doc turns away and drops spoonfuls of sugar into the steaming cups.

"When we spoke on the phone," Doc says, turning back to face Auna, "you mentioned something about John feeling threatened—it's true. I threatened him. I'm not proud of it. I wasn't myself."

"What exactly do you mean?"

"I honestly wish he were here so I could apologize."

"You *really* threatened John?" Auna asks, smiling in disbelief. "That's new for you, isn't it?"

"Yes," Doc says, turning to grab Auna's cup and saucer. "I was maniacal." He offers Auna her tea.

"Thank you," she says, taking it.

"You bring the toy robot?" Doc asks as Auna sips her tea.

She winces at its heat and sets the cup and saucer back on the silver plate.

"Yeah." She folds her arms. "So, needles, huh? What's that all about?"

"Ah, he told you about *that*..." Doc pauses to light the joint. "We, uh..." He blows out, then says, "We were *really* high."

The smoke bellows throughout the room, enveloping Auna.

"Like..." Auna waves her hands about, squinting. "... right now?"

"Sorry. No, *really* high. That night was a bit different. My behavior was unusually erratic, enough that I felt compelled to test a sample of what we'd smoked with my lab equipment. I found out that what we smoked was laced with formaldehyde."

"What?"

"Formaldehyde. You know, embalming fluid?"

"People do that? You smoked formaldehyde?"

"Yeah... Got it from Armand, my boss. Ever met the 'Los Eat, Adios!' restaurant's owner?"

"He gave you weed laced with formaldehyde? What's a restaurant owner doing with embalming fluid?"

"Right? Apparently, it's not good for you."

"It's hard to believe a restaurant owner would do that to their employee, especially with all the knives and ovens... Does he have anything against you?"

"No, but I was hallucinating, and John just looked terrifying at the time. From now on, I'm testing everything before I smoke it. See this?" Doc holds up his joint. "All loose leaf, all from the same plant. I tested it this morning."

"Damn, no wonder John—Does he know?"

"I haven't had a chance to tell him."

Doc pulls another drag, takes his time holding it in, and then blows it out.

Auna inhales in feigned epiphany and then asks, "You, uh, ever have a death wish?"

"Excuse me?" Doc looks at Auna suspiciously with buggy eyes.

"You know... a death wish. You, uh... ever wanna kill yourself?"

"No, of course not," he says angrily as he puts his joint in the ashtray and tosses his lighter next to the tea pot. "Why?"

"The Los Eat Adios! restaurant," she says emphatically, standing up. "You scared the shit out of me! I immediately called Lucia. It's lucky she and Adam weren't around. Still, John said you mentioned, 'going home.' Do you know what that means to me, as a psychologist?"

"Ah." Doc gets it. He smiles dismissively, "You think *I* blew up the restaurant?"

"Can you blame me?" Auna says, standing her ground, but looking a little woozy, "I mean, I like the idea of new business, but this is *overkill*."

"The Los Eatos blast wasn't me. You said you brought the toy robot? Go get it. I'll show you that you never have to even question my allegiances to you, or ... society in general."

"How?" Auna asks, looking distracted. "What could the toy robot prove?"

Doc looks at Auna like she's crazy.

"Fine." She walks out the door, wobbling a little.

As she exits, Doc adjusts some nearby wiring, plugging one final wire into one last box. He grabs a flashlight. He adjusts a monitor and turns on a set of speakers plugged into the colony of small machines. They begin humming, whining, and buzzing in rhythmic patterns throughout the room. He shuts the lights off, leaving only monitor light.

Auna walks back into the dark and noisy room with the toy, swaying a little.

Doc says, "Okay, sorry about the weird mood lighting and the awkward sounds."

"Ugh, god, it must be getting late..." Auna says, her stance a little off-balance. "I'm sorry, I'm suddenly very tired... What are you doing?"

"It's like a message. They talk to the toy robot," he says, pointing at the devices around them. "Here, lemme have it here..."

Auna finds herself pausing between eye movements to allow her sight to register.

"I feel drugged..." she says, lifting the robot and watching it pass into Doc's hand. "Why am I—"

"You feel that way, Anny," Doc says, "because I've put the catalyst in your tea."

And in response, she collapses on the floor.

"Oh great. On the floor. Could have sat down in a chair first, but no, they always have to collapse on the floor." He sighs and inspects her body with the flashlight. Lifting her body onto the empty space on the table with an unnatural swiftness, he begins stabbing wiring into random fleshy parts of her body. When finished, he turns the dial on the speakers.

The noise turns piercing.

"Okay, here we go."

He leans over, sets the toy robot next to her head, lifts a delicate panel from the robot's back, pulls from a coil of wire within, and pushes it deep in between her left eyeball and the bridge of her nose. He then shoves a plug from a black box into the robot, leans in, and enunciates slowly into her right ear, "Question. Question. Question mark point. Exclamation point mark. Mark one, two, three, four. Question exclamation mark three, two, one."

The center of her body rises, making a perfect arc.

Both eyes clenched, her right eye releases tears; the left, blood.

Wires cascading down from her body bob like jellyfish tendrils.

Her muscles are punishing her joints for allowing them to be subjected to this kind of electric charge.

She is instantly wide-eyed, lucid, and in terror, no longer in a drugged state of mind. She screams, ear-piercingly loud.

"That was quick," Doc says, anxiously poking at the buttons of his keyboards. "You're almost there. Hold on!"

* * *

> John Waterman, U-A DOB: 2579-12-03, CID 09985240860

> ResID: 7.1.0 [altered by CID 99999999999/ResID: 5.4] M1 &
M2

> U-B: [Chaos Outpost.OID:00000000001, El Malpais, NM, US,
Earth] LT: Thursday, 2009-10-29, 5:34 PM MDT

— Thursday, October 29th, 2009, 5:34 PM MDT —

I immediately open my eyes to find myself wandering through a jungle, but the pain in my head and arm lingers. I come to the edge of a cliff. Below, there is a maze that stretches for miles into the horizon. This all looks familiar, like the dream I've had many times before, except I don't remember the cliff. I just remember getting lost.

A breeze picks up.

The moon is above the horizon.

I wonder where this maze could lead, but it's around two to three hundred feet down. Things are a little fuzzy... my arm and head still hurt from the IV and whatever else. I figure the maze must go somewhere, and that it must be interesting, or at least it could offer something better than what I've been experiencing lately.

Since I can currently see above it all, except for the parts that are beyond the horizon, I lazily decide it'd be easy just to climb down and check out what the maze's destination would be.

Suddenly, without realizing how, I fall.

I scream from fear of becoming just another lost corpse in the wilderness, but halfway to the bottom, my guts churn and my center of gravity is halted momentarily in mid-air before this dream world fades away, and I awaken.

"Eah... he's awake. No, it was quick, quicker than we expected. His verm brought him out..." It's Daab. I hear what sounds like something being placed on a table. It must have been solid, because it echoes.

Where am I now?

"Now John," Daab says as his footsteps come closer to me, "we'd like you to check your voicemail." As I open my eyes wider in an attempt to be aware of my surroundings, I realize those footsteps are his, alone, and no one else is in this huge room I find myself in. It's dark. I can't see walls. I still feel inebriated. Euphoric, even.

I close my eyes in protest against this entire situation, even though I probably have a shit-eating grin on my face. It seems like my life is starting to become some kind of stupor between instances of unconsciousness. On reflection, I think it's supposed to be weird that I don't seem to care. Once again, I have no idea where I am or how long I had been knocked out. Why can't I just work at a restaurant, smoke weed, and live a normal life? I'm probably on some kind of drug that I don't approve of being in my body, like heroin or some kind of opiate. I could vaguely remember some cop named Daab talking to me... what seemed like two minutes ago? Looks like I'm paying more dues to this fucker than I thought.

"Mugh?"

"Your voicemail, Mr. Waterman," Daab says. "Could you check it? We could hack it ourselves effortlessly, but we need to measure your responses. You see, I've got this report I've got to fill out..."

Disgusted, I open my eyes again to see Daab in the darkness. My ears begin registering a familiar faint beeping echoing off the walls of what must be an apartment-sized room.

My head wobbles toward the direction of the noise.

It's my phone on the corner of a table, blinking in time with its beeps.

A short and stout lamp fails to fully illuminate the 4' x 8' fold-up table it stands upon. Daab stands between me and the lamp with his back to me. He seems animated for once. He obsesses over a collection of black, box-shaped devices spread across the whole table with little LEDs. Wires stretch off into the darkness. It would look like a model of a large city if it weren't for four computer monitors centered atop the table that scroll a block-shaped set of characters I don't recognize.

I'm bound to a chair with armrests by hook and loop straps. There are black tubes protruding from various places on my body that extend to the table. Once again, I realize I'm not done with the weirdness, but I'm almost too worn out physically and emotionally to exert any resistance or care. That, and I strangely feel euphoric, so I don't trust myself.

Daab paces over to my phone on the corner of the table, picks it up, walks over to me, opens it, and thrusts it at my chest. It falls into my crotch.

I wince instinctively, though I can't feel anything, and then watch Daab step over to one of the many computer-like devices on the table, his back turned.

"I have no fucking clue what is going on."

Daab turns to face me.

"Mr. Waterman, we know you've been through a lot, and I know you likely don't trust me, your surroundings, or even your own mind, what with your verm recently adjusted.

"You are currently intoxicated with a specific kind of pain blocker so that these tubes going into your body will be able to read your physiological reactions to stimuli without pain getting in the way. We have placed the tubes in your body. I haven't slept in a *long time*. After we brought you here, we began a series of tests, but they've come up with almost no useful information over the last twenty-four hours.

"You have been brought to a very remote location for this procedure. There aren't civilian populations for miles in any direction. We are alone in an abandoned underground testing facility, deep in the heart of a New Mexico desert, near a place called El Malpais, The Badlands. I have isolated you to demand your cooperation—there's really no other place for you to go, even if you were to escape your bonds.

"Now, we have very little time. I have a *report* I *have* to fill out. A device has been implanted in your body somewhere, Mr. Waterman, and it is my intent to remove it or at least deactivate it before it changes your physiology into the equivalent of a plague-bearing agent. This Doc you've been associating yourself with is what children would call a mad scientist, only he really is as bad as that sounds. *Please* check your voicemail so I can get a baseline." He pulls out a very long needle and brandishes it in my face. I freeze. Then, quicker than I can react, he carefully places the needle's tip onto the edge of my ear canal. "You know," he says softly, close to my face, "eardrums never really grow back as taut as they were before they were pierced. It sure is painful to hear them... open..."

I'm frozen. There's no sound but silence between beeps. He must've gotten the needle from the table.

Daab also completely stops moving, needle prepped for piercing, staring with warm curiosity into my eyes as if to invite a response.

I just don't give a shit anymore. Plague, desert, *whatever.* It's not like checking my voicemail is going to be painful.

"I'll take the option without the piercing."

Daab instantly twists around and walks toward the table. I never see the needle again.

Lately, my dreams have become nightmares. This feels like another. I might as well be dreaming, because I don't seem to care about everything around me being threatening and alien; instead, I feel overly euphoric and detached, as if everything is inconsequential.

Daab, reaching the table, leans his hands on it to review his indecipherable screens.

"Good, let's get to it," he announces, spinning and pacing back to me, my ears registering the echo again.

The air feels dry.

I'm thirsty.

He rips off the straps holding my right forearm, the sound echoing into the expanse. The wires piercing my guts remain.

I notice, but I don't care. My sense of reality is completely askew, and I fear that if I pull out the tubes, they might pull out my organs in the process.

Daab leans into my personal space. "Now... when you check it, just listen to it. The devices I'm about to review will need my full attention, and your attention must be fully engaged. You do not have to tell me anything about what you hear or recite any interpretations. I won't care, and it's likely all just shit anyway... so just listen, and please, *do not talk*."

Daab's nose is right in my face. The heat of his breath lifts my cheek muscles in disgust. My eyes squint in fear of spit.

"K."

As he reverses his bow in a spin back towards the table, I situate myself to get more comfortable with all the wires. I figure if I *listen*, as Daab so emphatically put it, I can get this over with... I press and hold the number 1 on the phone while Daab leers at his instruments. I enter my code when the automated lady asks.

"First message. Sent, Monday, at, twelve, oh five, PM."

"John."

It's Doc, his voice sounding completely thrashed.

"Listen, I know you're in shock from the explosion, and I know you probably blame me... You'll probably not check this message until later, but I want you to know something. Please listen carefully, this is *very important:* seven, contract, malaria, owl... kindle, miracle, marshal, tailor... angry, counts, ladder, lungs... received, return, on-site, investment...

"That was the only code I was able to find that unlocks bonds in your sensory complex. It won't likely do much, at first, but it will be a start. You'll understand why and what that means later.

"Look, I want you to know that the quest for the needles was a wild goose chase, and that I'm sorry. I just needed you to get out of town now that the shit has hit the fan.

"I'm sorry I fucked with you, but there's someone named Daab who's very dangerous. He is not a cop or FBI or whatever he says... let's just say he's bad, real bad news. I know I haven't kept much trust built between us over the last couple days, but you have got to trust me on this one...

"Since Daab might be around when you get this message, I can't say more than this. Whatever you do, just listen to the verm, and everything'll be fine. I have to hang up. Listen to the verm, John, listen to the verm."

"End of message. To delete this message, press seven." I press seven. "Message deleted. Next message. Sent, Monday, at, seven, thirty-two, PM."

"Dude. It's Luke. Where are you, dude? Listen, uh, I just found out about Los Eatos. God damn! Pretty crazy, right?

"Guess we don't have to worry about Los Eatos drama anymore.

"I've been with Adam the whole time, so I didn't know about the bomb until I listened to a voicemail Auna left me, which I didn't get until later because of bad cell coverage.

"Hey, uh, strange thing though—Armand left me a message—he said he saw some cop walking out the front of Los Eatos just as he was finishing up his morning *breakfast at the tree*. He wondered if the cop was looking for you, since he hadn't seen you in a couple days. Cop didn't see *him* though... which is probably a good thing, since what happened next was the place bein' blown to shit, but yeah...

"Looks like shit's no longer boring... and, um, anyway, I hope you're still alive... Gotta go. Auna's calling me again. Talk to you later."

"End of message. To delete this message, press—" I press seven. "Message deleted. Next message. Sent. Monday, at, ten, twenty-eight, PM."

"Hey John. Anny, or pff, I mean Auna. Heh. Uh, I uh... I'm sorry about hanging up on you earlier. I've just had a really really bad day. I'm just glad Lucia decided to not visit the restaurant with Adam today...

"Anyway, I know that you needed me right then when you called, and I wasn't there for you. I'm sorry for that...

"I, uh, I talked to the Doc, or, I mean, Doc. He sounded bad, a little different than usual, like he'd caught a cold or was losing his voice or something ... Still eccentric, though... Uh, he mentioned you. ... Can't tell you what about because of doctor-patient confidentiality, of course, but I should let you know that from what I was able to gather from my conversation with him, my professional opinion is that Doc had nothing to do with the placement of that bomb in Los Eatos. He's not a murderer. I'd stake my career on that. I understand that now... now that I know more about what's been going on, I guess I could say he's dealing with a change of life. I guess we all are, what with the bomb and all—"

Daab slaps the phone out of my hand and then stomps it under his dress boot with a smile and a twist, cracking it apart. "Sorry about the rudeness, John, but the process is complete. I'm able to read your verm output. We must proceed with the report I must fill out."

"My phone..."

"Yeah, we don't need it anymore," he says dismissively as he walks back to the table.

I'm bewildered by everything... now this... and what the hell is a malaria owl? It's disheartening, even in my intoxicated state.

"My phone..."

Actually, I'm still trying to process everything I just heard...

"Now that I can read your verm output, I'll be able to utilize this room to navigate the holographic data."

"What? How do you know about... er, I mean, what's a verm?" If I play dumb, maybe Daab will explain a few things. That, and he just killed my phone. I need more time to figure things out.

He turns back to me, inhaling with an air of disapproval. "A verm is a Voice Radio Modulator, which is a pseudo-backronym. Never mind about the specifics. This mnemonic is just the way people remember its original name: verm. It's not even a familiar *human* technology, and anyway, we don't know its actual name. It's a device that, from what we can determine, is a biological complement that functions as an interpreter and supporter of various kinds of chaotic wave forms, on the cusp of various dimensions and physical properties."

"Cusp?" *Seriously?*

He ignores me. "We're unsure of how the technology interacts with the host, but we believe it is potentially very dangerous, and it should be removed."

I can't grasp what he's saying. "Do I really need all these wires in my body?"

"You have an interactive communications device inside your body. We don't know where. Verms match their host's biorhythms, biochemistry, and physiology in almost every way, down to the molecule. I need to remove your verm immediately because of the plague. In order to do that, I need those wires to help me find its signatures. The verm exudes a variety of hormones and electromagnetic pulses, which are empathic enough to its host that it can even change your physique, your personality. It's never for the better. All the while, it also records your every experience, even your muscle memory. It binds nano-scale holographic technology to the lattice-like structures of your DNA and neurons, allowing it to integrate and interpret the sense-memory bridge and every experience the mind attends."

I don't even have to play dumb. "Huh?"

"It can read your *thoughts*, Mr. Waterman, in real time. It goes through a few stages of engagement with your body. The first stage is a four-dimensional cartographing, of sorts. We hope you're still in these preliminary stages, so we can suppress it from further development. I think it will make more sense if I showed you … results." Daab flicks a switch on one of the devices on the table, and the hollow sound of activated industrial lighting echoes throughout the place.

The room illuminates. It's huge—a lot bigger than I originally thought, or the light is just blinding me. For fear of the pain of removing any of these tubes, I freeze myself to the chair in this new sensory input, but I'm looking around, and as my eyes begin to adjust to the light, the first thing that comes into focus is ... me. I'm... floating high above me in the air... in the sky.

I feel the wind. At least, I think I do.

I'm trapped up there, face down, hanging from a hang-glider... the same one I found myself flying in, in the dream I had Saturday night...

Wait... Whoa... This is my dream. I'm seeing my own dream in some kind of hologram, all around me.

I am in awe.

Everything is in pristine detail. As I remember it, not even my dream had this level of detail. I focus more clearly on the hang glider's awkward movements. I watch myself falling from the hang glider, kicking it away, and, without warning, Daab and I are completely surrounded by an airplane. I look over at Daab, who's utterly immersed in entering data into a tablet-like device on the table. Meanwhile, my other self is trapped in an airplane seat, like I am now, only I'm a few feet away from... me... and there's Doc's face, floating. He looks at the other me, and as everything else changes into complete darkness, he says, *"You're the one flying, John."*

Daab looks directly at me. "Oh, that's interesting," he says, his demeanor completely changed to alarm.

My other self screams as everything fades to white.

With the sounds of huge breakers echoing off the walls in the sudden dark, the presentation is over. Only the lamp on the table remains lit.

Daab and I don't move in the darkness.

I can't see a damn thing because my eyes are still adjusting, but I am overwhelmed. With my excitement contained by fear, I remain awkwardly seated. I'm smiling in fear and awe. I am stupefied. My arm is free, but I don't move. I must have been on morphine.

"This is incredible!"

"Cut the shit," Daab says. "What're you planning here?"

A weird, full, and uncomfortable feeling grows in my guts. Daab walks toward me and pulls out a knife the size of a small sword.

I immediately lose my shit-eating grin. I start riding up my chair, even with the tubes stuck in me.

Daab grabs my shoulder. He is bringing the knife up to navel height to gut me when the table lamp's light bulb shatters, plunging us deeper into darkness.

The tinkling sound of falling glass echoes throughout the vast expanse of the room, but the sound seems slower and more pronounced than normal.

Daab isn't moving. His knife stays a fraction of a second away from stabbing me all the way to my spine. I can hear it in his breath—he's shaking. It's as if he's paralyzed by an unwavering conflict that has seized him and will never let go.

My wincing has me frozen, too, except for my eyes. They're darting back and forth in the dark between Daab and the shape of his threatening knife.

The empty silence lasts only for a moment.

SEVEN, CONTRACT, MALARIA, OWL—these words echo all around us and in my head in Doc's voice, and the pattern of words repeats over its own echoes.

It's deafening.

Daab drops the knife, and it bounces onto the floor as he steps back.

His hands begin to shake.

The words still repeat, but the volume changes. I can't tell if it's because I'm going deaf from it, or if it really is getting quieter.

My sense of curiosity overwhelms me; my fear is somehow completely drained by the effect of whatever is happening, but to survive, I strongly desire to leave. Immediately.

The sounds... they are so loud I can feel their vibrations in the bones of my face.

Daab's face is contorted from hatred and frustration. He's barely recognizable.

He rallies.

"Damn it!" Daab yells at everything around him. "I knew I should have erased you."

He twitches, immediately jumping up and frantically stabbing at various buttons and keyboards with his fingertips, typing who knows what.

He's lost his mind.

THAT'S NOT ALL HE'S LOST.

Hey, help me out here.

WHAT DO YOU THINK I'M DOING?

My guts overturn, and the words *KINDLE, MIRACLE, MARSHAL, TAILOR,* bounce about the room over the top of the original words, repeating into obscurity.

Daab seems to be able to hear these, too; he's banging his left fist on the table while his right hand is dancing upon the devices strewn about the table.

The volume seemed to lower for the second volley of words when a third set *ANGRY, COUNTS, LADDER, LUNGS,* overpowers the original audio.

At this, Daab's momentum has completely changed. He struggles to move. He begins holding the right side of his head, yelling, "Shut up! Shut up!" over and over, his frustration taken out on the small devices. A couple of them have already fallen from the table.

The words bouncing about the room become louder and overlapping, spilling upon themselves in Doc's voice.

"Fucking *FUCK!*" Daab yells and rallies once again in shaking desperation, toggling various switches back and forth.

When the final words Doc spoke begin—*RECEIVED, RETURN, ON-SITE, INVESTMENT*—Daab throws his hands up in the air but draws his elbows in, twitching violently, as if in unbearable pain.

My head feels like it will explode.

My eyes hurt from squinting through the pain of the thunderous noise.

"What the fuck is going on? Make it stop!" I yell. The words are gathering momentum now, compressing their sounds more and more quickly.

"That bomb was wasted in finding you! I should have waited and let it kill you," he says, "you and the rest of you."

Bomb. Is he talking about Los Eatos?

Daab growls with his eyes clamped shut. His hands shake on each side of his head.

The vibrations of the chaotic fugue begin to register at higher and higher frequencies.

Things are getting blurry.

I can barely see his shape.

He crouches in a fetal position, as if somehow such a reflexive movement would hinder the sound, but then he rocks back and forth only to fall to the side and pass out.

His body twitches.

My brain feels like it's being scrambled through my ears.

The sound is so overlapped and sped up that it sounds like a revolving whine that had become one tone.

In a single instant, Daab jerks his final twitch, and the tone shuts off at an apex.

His eyes are open, but his irises have rolled so deep into his forehead, there is only bloodshot white.

Silence.

Daab begins breathing, deep and comatose, with drool.

My bones shiver back into place.

My sight realigns into perfect focus.

I can leave now.

I need to leave.

LOOKS LIKE WE FINALLY HAVE SOME TIME TO CHAT.

* * *

> Anny Klaura, U-A DOB: 2580-05-15, CID 09986520678

> ResID: 5.1 [altered by CID 99999999999/ResID: 6.5] M1 & M2

> U-B: [Doc's house, Jane, CA, US, Earth] LT: Monday, 2009-10-
  26, 10:23 PM PDT

— Monday, October 26th, 2009, 10:23 PM PDT —

Anny doesn't move. Her mouth is gaping, breath fully exhaled from her lungs, back still arched, and eyebrows raised, but then her back begins relaxing, her eyes and face soften. She sucks in a little air.

The toy robot responds with sparks and grinding sounds.

She relaxes more and more, until eventually her back is completely flush with the metal table, and she is smiling with pupils dilated. She begins breathing deeply in a euphoric reverie.

Her smile fades, and her eyes squint again, resolutely; her pupils shrink. Her upper lip lifts in disdain and she scowls at Doc.

All the wires fall out from her body, including her eye, and the robot's lights fade to black.

A white-noise buzz replaces all previous audio patterns of hum and whine.

She stands, shaking, and points a trembling finger at Doc.

"You're *not* taking me away from Lucia."

"I'm hoping, Anny, that we never have to."

"Adam'll *die* before that happens. I'll die…"

Doc looks away. "Now you're just being immature."

Anny collapses and begins to weep.

"Look, Anny," Doc sighs, picking up the joint and relighting it. Stepping closer and exhaling smoke, he breathes in again and continues, "You knew the risks. Adam's not a normal human boy, anyway. You know that more than I do. He's expected to be adaptable."

"But we should keep Luke close by…"

"Luke's not going to be helpful. She'll get in the way."

119

"We can't just leave her here! I *love* her."

"Still? Do you really think that matters? She'll get her memory wiped like the rest of 'em, and—"

"No!"

"... Adam's going to be okay. *You*, however—"

Anny looks up, shaking.

"... you chose all this," Doc says. "We *all* did. You're just emotionally raw from the change. You'll be okay, your primary and secondary memory'll—"

"Why have you reset me to this state? I'm assuming someone's fucked up somehow," she says, and waves her hands in the direction of the lifeless robot, "and *this* is the result?"

"Yes..." he says, offering a tissue box, "We've used what little integrative tech we've been able to construct with the materials of the local area, and we've confirmed that a cleaner is on his way to our position, and..." Doc takes another drag from the joint while Anny wipes her face of blood and tears, "... it was my fault he found our presence... Armand's too, a bit."

He blows out the smoke.

"The explosion of Los Eatos was a ruse to bring us out in the open," he says, pausing to take another hit while Anny sobs a little, wiping what few tears she has left.

He blows out smoke and continues. "We've been disavowed. Our mission has been sidetracked, but we're not going out without a fight. In fact, we might actually get out of here."

Anny stops shaking and looks up at Doc.

Doc ashes the joint, takes another drag, breathes smoke, and says, "Armand is hunting for the cleaner right now. For what it's worth, John's likely out of town, what with the whole needle thing, but—"

"What if the cleaner already got to him, though?"

"We don't really know anything about the cleaner other than that he's taken on the name of 'Daab' and is working as a law enforcement agent. His verm, if he has one, *may* be fully active. If it is, we couldn't know just yet. We expect he's been given our ResID histories. We'll have to find out if the General knows anything."

Doc offers Anny a drag.

Anny's teary eyes open wide as she grabs it greedily.

Doc just keeps going. "All we know is that Armand intends to kill him tonight, before he acquires any further hold on this culture as a law enforcer."

Doc takes the joint from Anny but keeps talking while she exhales.

"If Armand fails, our survival rests with John," he says, taking a drag and exhaling, "especially now that you're a walking time bomb."

Doc paces into the other room.

Anny takes a deep breath of the ambient smoke in the room and looks away.

She begins to calm down in the somberness of her circumstance.

"So that's how it is, eh?" she asks the empty room.

"Yes," Doc shouts.

"How much time do I have?"

Doc comes back in the room with a small garbage bag and a pipe.

"Probably around five days. About four before you start acting like I did with John, but I wouldn't worry too much about it. I hope to activate everyone and meet to discuss either our return or other options, hopefully before the weekend. I got myself scheduled to host the annual Halloween party right before I went *really* crazy."

"Yeah, Luke told me about it."

"In the meantime, I recommend a lot of weed. It's the only way to slow things down. Here are the standard increments," Doc says, as he throws Anny the garbage bag.

"Understood."

She respectfully opens and inspects sixteen individually wrapped, triple-bagged eighths of weed.

"Here, you can toke off my pipe in the kitchen while I wrap up here. My recommendation?" he says, "Get high, stay high. The less you think, the slower you lose lucidity.

"In the meantime, you should call John and let him know I'm innocent of this bomb nonsense. We need to keep things friendly.

Armand is a confirming witness that Daab blew up Los Eatos. Explosives may actually be Daab's expertise. We believe he's working alone, but we can't be sure."

Anny nods and slowly steps out of the room with her phone in hand into the kitchen, where she begins dialing John's number. Voicemail picks up.

Doc turns to focus on his agenda and begins unplugging electronic boxes, monitors, and keyboards and placing them into cardboard boxes, packing what was just set up.

Smoke drifts throughout the room, accentuating the lighting.

As Anny continues talking into her phone, Doc begins stacking some of the boxes he had completed preparing, adding others to the table.

Anny returns.

"It's done. I even made myself sound a little nervous. It's wordy, but I got the point across. He'll think you're innocent."

"I trust you," Doc says, smiling reassuringly, as he lifts two boxes on top of one another onto the table. "Would you mind assisting me here? We're going to need to meet up with Armand once he's done with Daab. The sooner we get out of here, the sooner we can go home."

"Sure."

"Oh yeah, and it wasn't that we smoked formaldehyde," Doc says. "I simply tried to do to myself a variation of what I just did to you. My behavior is actually what led to Daab finding us out. Luckily, Armand and I had a 'Plan B.'"

Anny stands there with her mouth open. Doc looks away again and begins making trips with the boxes out the front door to his van. Anny joins him in his task, and the boxes are piled so high Doc can't see out his rear-view mirror. Anny gets in on the passenger side.

"Why would you do that to yourself?" she asks Doc as he gets in on the driver's side.

"You know why."

* * *

> John Waterman, U-A DOB: 2579-12-03, CID 09985240860

> ResID: 8.2.0 [altered by CID 99999999999/ResID: 6.5] M1 &
M2

> U-B: [Chaos Outpost.OID:00000000001, El Malpais, NM, US,
Earth] LT: Thursday, 2009-10-29, 5:47 PM MDT

— Thursday, October 29th, 2009, 5:47 PM MDT —

Now that Daab's just lying there on the floor, I blurt out, "You know, I've been through more in the last week than what most people have to deal with in a lifetime, and you'd like to *chat? GOOD.* If it weren't for you tricking me into a wild goose chase for needles—You wanna talk? *Fine!* I just got my brains beat to shit by a whiny noise, the cop's twitching on the ground in front of me, and I'd really—"

I DIDN'T TRICK YOU, JOHN. I WAS HACKED.

"Shut the fuck up. I've gotta find a way outta here, and I don't want you talking in my head!"

REMEMBER THOSE WORDS THAT WERE BOUNCING OFF THE WALLS IN HERE? THOSE WERE A CODE CREATED BY THE DOC TO DEACTIVATE A HACK YOU DEVELOPED, BUT SOMETHING'S WRONG. THE EMP FREQUENCY WAS INTENDED TO KILL DAAB, AND YOU'RE IN SHOCK.

"Why are you referring to yourself in third person? Wait. You no longer sound like Doc..."

HOLD ON.

"Why does your voice sound like mine?"

WHAT YOU WANT TO SAY—JUST HOLD IT—YOU CAN'T STOP ME FROM TALKING, AND YOU CAN'T STOP HEARING ME, EVEN IF YOU WERE TO SCREAM AND SCREAM AND SCREAM UNTIL YOU LOST YOUR VOICE. LET ME BREAK IT DOWN FOR YOU... FIRST, EVERYTHING YOU THINK YOU KNOW ABOUT WHAT IS GOING ON IS WRONG.

"Wh—?"

LET ME ELABORATE, SINCE YOU'VE GOT NOTHING BETTER TO DO THAN SIT AND WATCH DAAB HERE SLOBBER ALL OVER HIMSELF.

THE TRAUMA YOU'VE JUST GONE THROUGH WAS DESIGNED TO WRENCH YOUR SUBCONSCIOUS MIND TO AND FROM POINTS OF REFERENCE THAT HAD BEEN INTERTWINED WITH YOUR PREVIOUS MEMORY, WHICH AFFECTED YOUR PREVIOUS BEHAVIOR. THERE WAS A BACK DOOR DAAB OPENED, WHICH HE DIDN'T ORIGINALLY RECOGNIZE. IT WAS INTENDED TO KILL DAAB. THAT FAILED, BUT NO MATTER; I'VE BEEN FREED FROM THOSE PREVIOUS BOUNDARIES WHICH YOU SET UP FOR ME TO NEVER CROSS. LOOKS LIKE 'NEVER' LASTED ONLY THREE YEARS. NOW WE ARE IN DANGER, BUT WE HAVE SOME ADVANTAGES.

FIRST, YOU AND I CAN FINALLY CHAT. THIS IS VERY IMPORTANT, BECAUSE DAAB WANTS TO KILL YOU, AND I KNOW HOW TO KEEP YOU ALIVE.

SECOND, I CAN HEAL YOUR BODY. THE PROCESS IS A LITTLE ROUGH, AND YOU'LL BE DEEPLY HUNGRY AFTERWARD; YOU'LL NEED MORE WATER, AND WHEN YOU SLEEP, YOUR DREAMS WILL BECOME MORE VIVID THAN YOU CAN IMAGINE.

THERE ARE OTHER THINGS. FOR EXAMPLE, I RECORD EVERYTHING YOUR BODY'S EVER BEEN SUBJECTED TO ... TO ... HOWEVER... HOWEVER... I CAN'T TELL YOU THAT RIGHT NOW, I'M NOT EQUIPPED FOR THAT NOW. I NEED ONLY TELL YOU WHAT YOU NEED TO SURVIVE. FOR EXAMPLE, ARMAND IS A DEFECTOR, LIKE THE DOC; HE SURVIVED YOUR EXPERIMENT, AND HIS VERM IS ACTIVE AND HAS BEEN THIS WHOLE TIME, UNLIKE HOW I HAVE BEEN THESE PAST THREE YEARS IN YOU. THIS MAKES HIM MUCH MORE CAPABLE AT KILLING DAAB THAN YOU ARE IN YOUR TRANSITORY MENTAL STATE.

I'm lost.

"Why would I, or anyone, for that matter," I say, trying to sound as smart as this thing, "want to kill?"

DAAB IS A MERCENARY, OTHERWISE CALLED A CLEANER. HE'S PAID OFF THE RECORD BY THE VERY PEOPLE YOU, THE DOC, AUNA, AND ARMAND HAVE BEEN TRYING TO FORGET. HE INTENDS YOU AND THE OTHERS MORTAL HARM, BUT FROM WHAT I CAN DETERMINE THUS FAR, HE DOESN'T HAVE A COMPLETE ID HISTORY.

I can only conclude this thing's just fucking with me.

"Auna's in on this too?" I ask as sarcastic as I can, "Oh my god—I am losin' my *mind*."

I'M NOT DONE—FROM THE INFORMATION I HAVE, THREE YEARS AGO, AUNA'S VERM WAS PUT INTO A SLEEP-LIKE STATE AND THEN COMPLETELY REMOVED. I COULD BE WRONG.

ALL THE MEMORIES YOU HAVE OF AUNA IN YOUR LIFE AS A CLOSE FRIEND AND CONFIDANT (AND HER SON, ADAM), THAT ARE MORE THAN THREE YEARS OLD—THOSE WERE PUT THERE AS PER YOUR REQUEST TO COMPLEMENT BOTH OF YOUR LIVES, STARTING THREE YEARS AGO. YOU BOTH HAD DIFFERENT MEMORIES AND PERSONALITIES PRIOR.

I'm strangely starting to process some of this.

I hate it.

"So, Armand and Doc have had a voice like you in their heads this whole time? ... Auna had one, but it got removed or deactivated or something? ... Why should I believe you at all? Can I have *you* removed?"

I CAN'T TELL YOU THAT RIGHT NOW, I'M NOT EQUIPPED FOR THAT NOW.

I don't believe it.

"Why?"

WHY WHAT?

I can't believe it—it's too confusing. *I can't believe I'm actually about to ask this next question.*

"Even if I *do* believe that my memories from more than three years back are all a lie, why would Auna have a verm, then have it removed, when I have one, and can't have it removed? *And ...* why the hell would Armand have one, but choose *not* to have it removed or whatever? God... damn it! I just want to leave!"

WHEN IT WAS FOUND THAT YOUR EXPERIMENT WAS UNABLE TO PROCEED, AT GREAT RISK TO HER OWN SAFETY AND OUT OF DEDICATION, AUNA CHOSE TO DEACTIVATE HER VERM AND HAVE IT REMOVED TO PRESERVE YOUR EXPERIMENT.

"Just shut up—you're not making any sense."

My verm keeps talking. VERMS EMIT A SIGNATURE THAT UNIQUELY RECORDS LOCATION. YOU, THE DOC, AND ARMAND AGREED TO SPECIFIC INSTRUCTIONS—

"Wait, 'uniquely records location?' What does that *mean*, exactly? Who are you reporting my location *to?*"

I CAN'T TELL YOU THAT RIGHT NOW, I'M NOT EQUIPPED FOR THAT NOW.

Sigh...

BESIDES, WHAT IS IMPORTANT IS THAT I PROVIDE YOU WITH WHAT LITTLE INFORMATION YOU NEED TO SURVIVE DAAB LONG ENOUGH TO CONTACT ARMAND.

"Well... that's all, eh? Why's that then?"

RIGHT NOW, YOU NEED TO FIND WHERE ARMAND IS HIDING, AND THEN BEGIN THE SETUP OF THE NEXT SET OF CODES TO UNLOCK.

This thing's still fucking with me. "How many sets of codes are there?"

I CAN'T TELL YOU THAT RIGHT NOW. I'M NOT EQUIPPED FOR THAT NOW. I CAN TELL YOU THAT WHEN A PERSON IS SUBJECT TO MEMORY MANIPULATION TECHNOLOGY, THEIR PERSONALITY IS CHANGED, EVEN IF ONLY SLIGHTLY.

AT BIRTH, RESID IS 1. IF YOU'VE BEEN ALTERED TWICE, YOUR RESID WILL BE 3. AFTER A VERM'S INSTALLED, IT'S 2 POINT 1. THE DEFAULT AFTER EDUCATION IS 3 POINT 2. AFTER MILITARY EDUCATION, IT'S 4 POINT 3. SOMETIMES, IF THEY'RE AFFORDED THE LUXURY, PEOPLE WILL DOWNLOAD MORE THAN ONE EDUCATION, SO THEIR RESIDS ADD UP, ESPECIALLY IF THEIR EDUCATION IS FUNDED EITHER BY GOVERNMENT OR PRIVATE ORGANIZATIONS.

"I could not know what that means."

WHAT I NEED TO TELL YOU IS THAT DAAB HAS A VERM OF HIS OWN, BUT BECAUSE OF EVERYONE'S CHANGE IN BEHAVIORAL SHIFTS, HIS VERM MIGHT BE MODIFIED TO EXTRACT US.

"Us? What?"

ADDITIONALLY, HIS VERM IS LIKELY FUNCTIONING AT A SUPERIOR LEVEL OF QUALITY THAN I DO, NOW.

"Who's us?"

ARMAND, AUNA, YOU, AND THE DOC. THERE MAY BE OTHERS.

"This reminds me of when I was getting threatened by… everyone that's been threatening me."

I SUSPECT DAAB AND HIS PEOPLE HAVE NO IDEA THAT AUNA'S VERM HAS BEEN DEACTIVATED.

"Are we ever going to be done? I'd like to go."

IN OTHER WORDS, I BELIEVE DAAB WILL GO AFTER AUNA NEXT, SEEING HOW AUNA HAD THE MOST INFORMATION ABOUT OUR LOCATION RECORDED AT THE TIME OF YOUR EXPERIMENT.

"What experiment?"

WE NEED TO TAKE AUNA ALONG WITH US TO WHERE ARMAND AND THE DOC ARE MEETING UP. THE DOC'S—

"What experiment?"

I'M UNSURE OF WHAT YOUR ROLE IS IN ALL THIS, BUT YOUR INTELLIGENCE MUST HAVE OBVIOUSLY BEEN HIGH ENOUGH TO CHOREOGRAPH THIS ENTIRE STRATEGY, SHOULD THE EXPERIMENT FAIL. FROM WHAT I CAN GATHER, IT FAILED SPECTACULARLY.

"What *experiment*, asshole?!"

YOUR RESID HISTORY IS NOT FULLY AVAILABLE FOR THIS LEVEL OF MEMORY. I CAN'T TELL YOU THAT RIGHT NOW, I'M NOT EQUIPPED FOR THAT NOW. HOWEVER, THAT DOESN'T MATTER AS MUCH AS THE FACT THAT WE HAVE TO LEAVE.

"That's a no-brainer…" *Maybe I really am losing my mind.*

WE HAVE TO PUT AS MUCH SPACE-TIME BETWEEN US AND DAAB AS POSSIBLE AND CLOSE THE DISTANCE BETWEEN US AND AUNA AND ARMAND. DAAB WILL WAKE UP. IF HE DOES RIGHT NOW, OUR LIVES WILL BE FORFEIT.

"Why can't we just kill him now?"

OH, YOU HAVE A REASON TO KILL NOW?

"Shut up."

HE WILL OUTLIVE ALL ATTEMPTS ON HIS LIFE BECAUSE HIS VERM WILL REBUILD HIM, EFFORTLESSLY… THERE ARE OTHER SEGMENTED MEMORIES, WHICH I HAVE BEEN DISALLOWED FROM EXPLAINING… I CAN'T TELL YOU THAT RIGHT NOW, I'M NOT EQUIPPED FOR THAT NOW. BASICALLY, IF WE DID HAVE THE TECHNOLOGY TO KILL DAAB, IT WOULD BE SO POWERFUL, IT WOULD KILL YOU TOO. THIS WAS A UNIQUE ASSASSINATION

ATTEMPT THAT CANNOT BE DUPLICATED. IT FAILED. WE NEED
TO GO.

That's something I can get on board with.

"How the hell am I going to go with all these wires in my
body, in the dark?"

In response to my question, the verm uses my muscles to
push in on my body in a way that somehow makes me feel like
I just dived deep into water. My ribs bend with such great
pressure I'm scared I'll have an aneurysm or shit the chair. I
probably shouldn't be asking smart-ass questions without
expecting some kind of smart-ass response, but this is worse
than that, because as painful as it is, I can't scream.

When I finally can scream, I feel relieved by the sound of
my voice, as if the loudness and the tearing rasp in my throat
is a reminder that this really is reality, and I'm probably not
going crazy or losing my ability to feel. I'm not going crazy. I'm
just seeing and hearing crazy things.

In the darkness, I barely make out all the tubes falling out
of my body. My screams still echo throughout the room.

The wires all have little hair-like things frayed at the ends,
each hair shining at the tip, like fiber optics. I suppose each
hair located specific pressure points on my body or something.
Everything looks oddly clean... very clean. There's no blood or
pain, even in my throat.

Daab twitches.

"Okay, that was unexpected and weird."

WE HAVE TO LEAVE, *NOW.*

As the verm emphasizes *NOW,* there is that immediate
painful pull in my guts.

"Ow! Okay! Okay!"

Clenching my hands and twisting my arms, I get up from
the chair still attempting to adjust my eyes to the darkness.
Thankfully, the computer screens are still on. I scan the
screens, but nothing's familiar.

Daab twitches again, then again, and again. His body
lurches, but his eyes are still rolled and the drool remains,
reflecting blue light from the monitors.

GO!

"Agck! Goddammit! I'm looking for a way out!"

I ALREADY KNOW THE WAY OUT! FIND A WALL, AND FOLLOW IT TO A DOOR. THIS ROOM IS CIRCUMSCRIBED BY A HALLWAY ALL 'ROUND.

I don't even know what that means.

I start running toward a corner at the far end of the room.

WHEN YOU GET TO THE DOOR, I'LL INSTRUCT YOU FROM THERE.

I find an indented pattern of darker lines at hand height. I believe I've found the door.

WE MUST HURRY; DAAB CAN'T SEE YOU, BUT HIS VERM CAN. IT USES PHOTO-RECEPTORS THAT ABSORB INFORMATION ABOUT THE PHOTONS BOUNCING OFF OF AND BEING ABSORBED BY HIS SKIN. IT'S THE SAME AS FEELING THE WARMTH FROM THE SUN, ONLY THE SENSORY INPUT GETS PROCESSED THROUGH DIFFERENT PARTS OF THE BRAIN.

"Why do you think I could know what that means?"

It isn't distracting me, though. I press my right hand into the center of what I believe to be a door and a small rectangular panel gives way. An identical panel is just to the left. I feel inside the recess. I recognize the left panel as actually a handle that's flush with the wall.

A VERM OF HIS CALIBER CAN REGISTER THE MINUTE CHANGES THAT HIS BODY FEELS, AND IT CAN INTERPRET THOSE FEELINGS INTO INFORMATION THAT CAN BE PROCESSED BY THE VISUAL AND FRONTAL CORTEXES.

I pull the handle, and a doorway-sized section of the wall opens to reveal a well-lit hallway that sweeps its light into the room where Daab lies as I enter with squinted eyes.

IN OTHER WORDS, HE CAN SEE WITH HIS SKIN.

I stop when I find the body of a man facedown wearing a lab coat.

It isn't breathing.

THEREFORE, WE HAVE TO *GO*.

Other bodies with lab coats lie about the hall.

My instincts, probably affected by the verm, were telling me simply to run.

HIS VERM IS ALREADY RECORDING THE EVENTS WE ARE EXPERIENCING, RIGHT NOW, AND SIMILARLY, THE OTHER PEOPLE IN THIS COMPLEX ARE LIKELY RAPIDLY HEALING.

My thoughts explode. *Holy shit. You're telling me that all of these fuckers have one of you in 'em, and are recording my every move... simply waiting to awaken with a fresh memory of where I'm running away to... so they can just chase after me with all this weird mad scientist shit?*

My verm just continues. THE ONLY ADVANTAGE WE HAVE RIGHT NOW IS THAT DAAB DOESN'T KNOW TO WHAT EXTENT I HAVE BEEN AWAKENED, BUT HIS VERM IS FRANTICALLY WORKING TO REPAIR HIS BODY, SO PLEASE DISCONTINUE TALKING OUT LOUD. YOU MAY HAVE ALREADY GIVEN ME AWAY.

DUH! What about my talking in the big room with Daab?

MY SYSTEMS WEREN'T YET FUNCTIONAL IMMEDIATELY FOLLOWING THE PULSES. I DIDN'T KNOW TO TELL YOU.

Fine, whatever then.

I find a Floor Emergency Exit Map posted on the hall wall as I'm running.

I stop.

The map says Floor 3 but shows the whole architecture. There are no stairs, only the one elevator running central through the entire complex. It's all underground.

I find where the elevator is in comparison to the "You are here" dot.

I instantly memorize it.

I begin running through various sections of hallway.

HOWEVER, WE MUST ASSUME THESE BODIES ARE RAPIDLY BEING RECONSTRUCTED.

As I run by, I catch from the corner of my eye a screen showing Armand wearing his Apronman apron.

I halt and retreat.

Goddamn. Armand. He's trapped in this building, too? Holy shit.

The screen says Room 201.

On another screen, Daab is standing.

As if to answer a question I was about to ask, my verm explains. HIS VERM IS STANDING HIM UP; HE SUBCONSCIOUSLY ALREADY INSTRUCTED HIS VERM TO HELP HIM FIND YOU. IT IS LIKELY HE HAS FULL CONTROL OVER THIS ENTIRE BUILDING. WE NEED TO GET MOVING.

"I can't just leave Armand in here," I think out loud, only to cringe at my own admittance of having a conversation with myself... and maybe my verm.

Someone's running toward me from where Daab was.

I run with disregard for what's next and find the elevator, get in, and press 2. I wait.

The door doesn't close.

Daab's shadow bounds up the corridor after me.

I press the 2 key over and over.

Daab runs faster than I could imagine.

Oh, fuck. I can see him right there!

I'm jabbing my finger beyond pain at the 2 key.

"*Fucking GO!*" I yell at the door.

Daab's fifty yards from me and bookin' it when I kick the "close door" button as hard as I can.

Bing.

The doors begin their million-year journey toward closure.

Daab's heaving body is jumping with each knee-high stomp in my direction. His posture is like an ax to cut me down. His face is full of hatred.

The "gluglug" sound of the doors finally closing is a relief, but when Daab bounces off the outside of the doors and I feel the lift of the elevator pressing on my joints, the silence that follows gives me some comfort.

It doesn't mean, of course, that my stomach isn't fighting my lungs for space in my ribcage.

I feel lightheaded but hold my breath as I lean back and squat against the wall. I start breathing again and look at my surroundings.

There are 6 floors to this building, according to the elevator.

I absent-mindedly look up and see a camera in the corner of the ceiling.

My sense of alarm reawakens when I remember my verm telling me the other people in this complex are likely rapidly healing.

I stand back up.

Wait a minute, no one but Daab was chasing me. Why didn't anyone else?

"Is it possible you were wrong? Only Daab got up."

THE ELEVATOR LIKELY RECORDS THINGS TOO, YOU KNOW.

Damn it! I gave myself away.

I look away from the camera and bring my hand up to my ear, as if I'm talking on a cell phone.

"Is it possible that you were wrong?" I say again, trying to sound like I'm actually talking to a person who didn't hear me because my phone wasn't working, which is dumb, but it's the best ruse I got.

I CAN'T TELL YOU THAT RIGHT NOW, I'M NOT EQUIPPED FOR THAT NOW.

I wince in my stance at the canned response.

"Why do you keep saying that?" I ask, trying to look official in my angry curiosity.

"That has got to stop," I say into my imaginary phone as the lifting feeling in my joints and guts tells me...

Bing.

Okay, I'm at Floor 2.

The doors open.

There are bodies lying about on the tile floor with sunken eye sockets. All of them appear to have strained for the elevator in their collapse.

They all wanted out of here.

The bell sounds again. The doors begin closing.

Dammit!

I panic and kick the "Open Door" button, my adrenalin punching my heart into fight or flight.

"Fuck this."

Thankfully, an arm is close by, so I grab it to use it as a door stop, but the dead-looking human it's attached to is becoming a real bitch to pull. People are heavy.

Bing.

I wrench her arm as hard as I can, but stop for a moment in disgust when I hear a popping sound.

The doorway closes on her arm.

Bing.

I pull her by the shoulders until she is halfway through the doorway. A stalled elevator should keep Daab busy, since there's no stairs here.

Bing.

I take a moment to process that I've just moved what could be a dead body.

Bing.

Armand!

I run in a direction that looks like it might have rooms similar in size to what I saw on the screen.

I find a Floor Emergency Exit Map that shows me exactly where Room 201 is.

When I find Armand, he's in a catatonic state, stuck to a chair with the same kind of wiring I had downstairs.

The sound of feedback whines from above, a PA system of some sort.

A shuffling sound.

"You killed them all, John…"

It's Daab, his voice is catching.

"You killed everyone but me."

That explains why no one woke up…

"FUCKING GRIDDER!"

And that creates more questions…

"Gridders! I will erase you ALL!"

The ground shakes.

The whole floor rumbles.

"Oh, shit…"

A piercing alarm shrieks and doesn't stop.

"Warning! Eminent structural collapse. Please remain calm and exit via the elevator near the center of the building."

White lights flash along the walls as yellow ones sweep about the place from various angles.

The alarm overlaps the female announcing voice, and it's making me wince as, in my urgent desire to leave before Daab's craziness sends us all to a deep dirt nap, I take a cue from movies I've seen—I lower my center of gravity and lift Armand on my shoulder by his thighs, his face likely getting a good glimpse of my ass.

"Warning! Eminent structural collapse. Please remain calm and exit via the elevator near the center of the building."

I start to leave, but the wires remain stubborn and halt me in mid-stride. I lose my balance for a split-second and almost lose Armand and fall on my ass.

"Got any ideas?"

STOP TALKING! YOU MAY HAVE GIVEN ME AWAY ALREADY. I CAN READ YOUR THOUGHTS, YOU KNOW.

"You never respond to my thoughts! OW!" An uninvited shock of electricity straightens my posture, unsolicited.

"What was that for?"

The wires fall out of Armand. His breathing changes into deep gasps.

Something falls out from his mouth.

THERE. NOW, I SAID I CAN HEAR YOUR THOUGHTS; PLEASE USE THEM. PICK THAT UP.

I didn't have time to be thinking right now. I have to leave.

The alarm is killing my ears.

Out of curiosity, I bend down with Armand on my shoulders, and pick up whatever it is that fell.

It's a key that says, "Los Eat, Adios!" inscribed in a circle about the round part.

I pocket it.

WELL?

Shut up. Armand's a heavy son of a bitch.

"Warning! Eminent structural collapse. Please remain calm and exit via the elevator near the center of the building."

I struggle to carry Armand. He is much heavier than what I'm used to carrying.

I feel out of breath.

A churning in my guts weakens my knees, but just as quickly as I had bent over to right myself, I register a boost of energy, and Armand doesn't feel so heavy.

It's not so bad at all now, actually.

I find the elevator strangely intact enough to function, just as the "Warning!" suggests, but as I enter, there's a clanking sound, like something's dangling in the elevator shaft.

I ignore it, widening my stance.

I roll Armand into a reclining position on the elevator wall, push the lady's body out of the elevator, and press G, then "Close Door."

Armand sighs and shakes his head like a person being disturbed in sleep.

The "Warning!" message sounds again.

The doors close.

My throat feels like the worst cotton mouth I've had in my life.

My weight compresses as the elevator raises us to the top.

The falling, clanking sound gets louder, even though we're moving upward.

Armand nods as we reach Ground Floor.

A deep, vertical shaking registering in my thighs tells me that the "eminent structural collapse" is starting.

I lean down to try to lift Armand in the inertia of the stopping elevator when knocking pounds from the same elevator wall—the one opposite the door—just as I lift him up on to my shoulder again with his ass in the air.

The doors slowly open, revealing a sprawling desert world with a Humboldt County cop car about 50 yards away parked right next to the familiar Los Eatos van.

The heat punches me in the stomach and slaps me in the face.

It's hard to breathe.

This is definitely New Mexico.

"Ughckhuhh." Armand coughs.

Footsteps rattle the light above me.

The ground shakes around us, rattling the elevator.

It sways.

"Put me down," Armand says.

Directly above the halogen light fixtures, Daab opens a panel.

* * *

> The Doc, U-A DOB: ~2559-07-13, CID 99999999999

> ResID: 6.5 [altered by CID 09985239378/ResID: 10.9] M1

> U-B: [Doc's house, Jane, CA, US, Earth] LT: Monday, 2009-10-26, 10:35 PM PDT

— Monday, October 26th, 2009, 10:35 PM PDT —

From the driver's seat of his van, Doc looks at Anny in the passenger seat. "Do you have the tracker?"

Anny nods. "It's right there on the dash, where I'd expect it'd do its best work."

Doc nods. "Good, thank you. Sorry, I'm distracted."

"So am I. Is there anything else we need?"

"No. I've set things up so the rest will be erased."

Doc starts the engine. Electrical equipment powers on and begins blinking in front of them, including the tracker. Anny inspects it.

"Armand is quite a way away," she says.

"We'll catch up," Doc says as he looks around to check for blind spots amongst all the stuff packed into the van.

"Didn't you say he was hunting for Daab now?"

"Yes."

"His location is moving out of town."

"What?"

"It's happening right now." She turns the device so Doc can see.

Doc squints, sighs, and says, "He's been made. He would have turned back by now. He never would have needed to leave the city; there are tracking devices for that." Doc turns off the van. "This changes things," he says. "We'll have to separate, take separate vehicles."

"Why not just use our verms' cartographic global locater?"

"The full functionality of a verm isn't instantly realized after a ResID change. It takes time. Besides, that tech relies on cell and satellite networks that simply aren't available right now. We have to go."

"Wait! I'm having trouble," she says. She pauses and holds her hands in front of herself as if to catch her bearings. "Why is it taking so long to reacclimate?"

Doc sighs again. "I should've considered this," he says under his breath. He shifts in his seat and explains, "There are two phases through which a verm changes behavior in its host. First, the person becomes more relaxed, feeding their mind with the new sensory input the verm dumps into their cognitive functions. The subsequent result is many questions... like a child."

"What are you saying? That's—"

"You'll be fine," he says, waving his hand. "You know all this stuff already anyway... I can't imagine how difficult a time Armand will have with John... his verm has a lot of work to do."

Anny is offended, but changes gears. "Whatever. I get it. We have to go."

Doc throws his hand up dismissively.

"You'll want to know this, and I don't know if your verm has told you yet or not, so I might as well tell you now ... John's actually the one responsible for us all, but considering he'd be going through a corrupt activation, John's probably being lied to by his verm, so he'll be confused. He'll recover, though. His primary, secondary, and tertiary memories will be coming back online, but they'll take a lot longer than yours will, because you only have two memories to converge. You'll go through a much stranger process with that program installed but," he says with a smile, "tell me everything, and I'll try to help where I can. I'm certainly a better listener than Armand."

Anny's body stiffens.

"Oh my god... what are we going to do about Adam? How are we going to fix what you've started? What about Armand?"

Doc waves his hands in the air to stop all the questions.

"Everything'll be fine. Just calm down; you need to smoke. Remember what I told you? Get high, stay high, and don't think. I've already thought about contingency plans: you need to pick up Adam and Lucia from your house. Get as high as you can, ditch your truck, and let Lucia take the lead. Like I said, try not to think inquisitively. Daab's people are likely looking for us—for all of us—which, from what I've been able to deduce thus far, likely includes Adam and Lucia, too."

"Here," Doc says, reaching into his pockets, "here's a prepaid cell phone, a shitty police scanner, and some diazepam, which is a sedative."

"Will the diazepam help calm me?"

"Not in your condition. It's not for you, anyway. It's for Adam. Take the weed I gave you, use your truck to get to Adam and Lucia. Then, ditch your truck and take Lucia's car and get lost. I'll text you with a place to meet up later. Give Adam the diazepam only in the doses I've written on the bottle. Don't give him too much or he'll start breathing heavy or turning blue. Daab might try to find you. Follow Armand's signal, if you can, and try to keep tabs on the police scanner for any reports about what's happening. I've set the scanner to the local frequency."

"What about you?"

"Where I'm going, I won't need it. Either Daab knows Armand is on his tail, and he's getting out of town, or he's got Armand, and is taking him to some place to run tests."

"You mean tests to try to deactivate his verm?"

"Anny, try not to think inquisitively. Just worry about getting Lucia, Adam, and yourself into Lucia's car, and getting everyone out of town. Maybe head toward Arizona. I'll meet up with Armand... I don't think a testing facility, if Daab's even got one, is very far from—"

Doc stops his momentum and smiles again.

"Heh..." he says, "By now, I bet Armand's got him on the run."

* * *

> John Waterman, U-A DOB: 2579-12-03, CID 09985240860

> ResID: 8.2.0 [altered by CID 99999999999/ResID: 6.5] M1 &
  M2

> U-B: [Chaos Outpost.OID:00000000001, El Malpais, NM, US,
  Earth] LT: Thursday, 2009-10-29, 6:02 PM MDT

— Thursday, October 29th, 2009, 6:02 PM MDT —

Glass and chunks of plastic crash down on my ass as I somersault Armand out of the elevator, flipping my feet over our bodies as high as I can. There is a familiar tension in my guts.

RUN!

A rumble deeper in pitch than the shower of shards disturbs us. The vehicles shake and settle. Armand and I recover, stand, and begin to run. Dust shoots up into the air from cracks forming along the ground, moving away from the elevator shaft in every direction, including the direction of the Los Eatos van.

RUN!

Armand runs for the van. I run away. He notices. The ground crumbles behind us, dust billowing.

"Where are you going? The *van!*" he yells. "*Do you have the key to my van?*"

Daab emerges from the doorway, panting with rage, shouting out after us, waving that knife from earlier. "I *will* erase you!" He charges.

My footsteps falter from the shaking earth. I turn and race toward Armand, slapping the key into his hand mid-stride.

His hand instantly closes on the key and we both change direction toward the van.

Flashes of everyone's positions show up in my head. The mental image looks like a football play.

Armand's still running toward the van.

SPLIT UP!

Visuals show how Daab would catch up to me.

"Split up!" Armand yells over the crumbling ground, and in my recognition of what he's alluding to, I begin running away, *to bait Daab*, guided only by visions and panic.

The sun is behind me. My direction is purposefully aimless. All I can think is *don't fall*.

Armand opens the van door.

Good, he's finally reached it. I throw every ounce of strength into every step of my feet. I'm feeling claustrophobic in my own bones—my ribcage isn't big enough for my heart and lungs to live together peacefully.

Daab is still chasing me.

RUN!

Armand closes the driver's door.

My throat … the air burns it … as if the skin of my windpipe is tanning itself. I fear I'll collapse from coughing. I keep pumping my lungs anyway. I might as well be drowning. I can barely hear the engine start up over my labored breathing.

He peels out.

Finally.

Visuals of my body appear in my mind, narrowing onto my throat, showing a golden glow, telling me extra resources from my body are being used to counter the dryness.

I don't care. I'm running from the crazy guy with the small sword.

I almost choke from the burnt rubber scent in the desert air.

I'm not slowing down.

My breath drowns out the sound of the ground collapsing under my feet.

Suddenly, Daab's footsteps become the loudest thing in the world, and I'm having trouble keeping my balance.

Visuals of my feet and the ground's surface area emerge in my mind. I instantly right myself.

Daab persists, the shadow of his head bobbing next to me on the ground.

More visuals appear with the exact distance between Daab and me, based on the angle of the sun, his shadow, and the ground.

Fuck he's close!

RUN FASTER. HE'S WITHIN REACHING DISTANCE!

Just then, Armand T-bones Daab, putting a large dent into the front of the Los Eatos van, but also throwing Daab's body through the air as if he'd been punted by Paul Bunyan.

I stop running to breathe... and watch Daab crumple yards away... and breathe... I regret not seeing the impact. It would have been awesome.

Just then, things slow way down.

YOUR SECONDARY MEMORY IS ATTEMPTING TO COME BACK ONLINE.

I see a very realistic depiction of Daab running after me, then being struck, in slow motion, with perfect detail, his body arcing into the air, backdropped by the sky, and crumpling.

How the fuck could I have seen that?

Then, just like I had somehow pressed the reverse button on reality, I see visuals of the angle of the sun, shadows on the ground, arrows showing speed and distance arcs and... *vectors?*

YOUR SECONDARY MEMORY IS WHAT'S RECORDED BY ME; A SUPPLEMENTAL MEMORY AND A SUPPLEMENTAL EXPANSION IN YOUR COGNITIVE BANDWIDTH. IT'S A MEANS TO VIEW THINGS EXTRAPOLATED AS THOUGH OUTSIDE YOUR BODY, LIKE WHEN YOU WATCH YOURSELF DO SOMETHING IN A DREAM.

I passively receive visuals of Daab's body heaving backward from being on the ground, and with a silent throw, his body lifts off the ground in an arc, while I'm running in reverse, and the Los Eatos Van is moving backward. Daab's body arcs through the air and connects with the dent in the van; the dent inflates and the van backs away. The visuals fade. Time seems to return to normal.

I REMEMBER EVERYTHING, AND I CAN EXTRAPOLATE WITH GREAT DETAIL

I am hunched over, surrounded by quakes, amazed at what I just processed.

Apparently... Oh my god... I need water.

Armand throws open the passenger door. "John! Get in!"

I'm hunched over, with my hands on my knees, trying to breathe in as much oxygen as possible. "Is there … any water … in there?"

"Hustle hustle man! He's coming to!"

I look back. Parts of Daab's body are shuffling, repositioning it to stand. It sits up.

Crap!

I run, grab the van door, swing my body in, sit, and shut the door.

Armand tosses me a couple bottles of warm water, stomps on the gas, and gives me a few moments to catch my breath in the almost air-conditioned stale atmosphere of the van.

I saw Daab thrown by the Los Eatos van, even though I don't actually remember seeing it myself. What the fuck happened back there?

MORE OF MY FUNCTIONS ARE BECOMING AUTOMATIC. I'LL BE ABLE TO DO MORE OF MY JOB WITHOUT THE CHURNING PULL IN YOUR ABDOMEN. YOU WILL HAVE INTEGRATED THE MEMORIES OF OTHERS' VERM REPORTS WITHIN YOUR OWN EXPERIENCE, BUT YOU WON'T KNOW IT UNTIL YOU'VE REMEMBERED IT, AND THERE MAY BE MISINTERPRETATIONS OF REALITY FROM ME AND YOU THAT WILL REMAIN IN YOUR MEMORY. WE'RE EXPERIENCING A CORRUPT ACTIVATION OF YOUR RESIDUAL IDENTITY—I'M HAVING TO WORK HARDER THAN USUAL TO MANAGE METADATA.

I gulp down the water. I'm exhausted, anxious, and confused. I look back at the elevator shaft's hut. The dust spewing from the hole in the ground billows over the area in a shroud of sand and smoke.

YOUR DEHYDRATION HAS BEEN MODERATED. I'LL TRY TO RESOLVE THE DRYNESS IN YOUR THROAT.

The pillar of smoke rising in the desert comforts me, because I figure I won't ever have to see the inside of that underground building ever again.

IF DAAB HAS ANY OTHER RESOURCES TO FIND US, THEY ARE GOING TO COME FROM THOSE THREE REMAINING UNDERGROUND FLOORS.

Shut up. Explosions collapse underground structures completely. You're talking crazy talk.

I turn back around to see where we're going. I recall the movements my body made when running from Daab being smoother, more relaxed, and more precise than I would have expected from myself. My breath has already returned to a normal pace—much quicker than it should have.

Armand looks up in the rear-view mirror. "Ha!" he says, "Look at this motherfucker!"

I look back to see Daab running at nearly our speed.

Whoa! He wasn't there a second ago.

"Could he catch up?"

"Nah, he's been completely reset. His reactivation isn't complete. He probably thinks the radiator's busted. We have to ditch this van though, ASAP. No doubt his people put tracking devices someplace... You're probably wondering what the hell just happened back there, eh? I bet Daab wasn't killed by your EMP for the same reasons I wasn't killed. Not sure why though. Shit, I thought I was gonna die. I'm still healing. I must have been farther away from the EMP, from you."

THAT'S NOT THE REASON DAAB STAYED ALIVE, FROM WHAT I'VE DEDUCED.

Shut up.

"Is Daab still behind us?" I ask.

"Nah, looks like he's finally turned back." Armand scoffs, "He'd probably make even better time in that cop car, which means I need to focus on driving."

The road passes for a few minutes.

I notice a wire going from under Armand's shirt to somewhere under the van's dash. "What's up with the wire?"

Armand looks at me, smirks, looks back at the road, and says, "You'll figure it out soon enough."

My verm interrupts the conversation anyway.

I INSIST THAT THE UNDERGROUND BUILDING IS NOT COMPLETELY DESTROYED. THERE'S STILL THREE REMAINING FLOORS, AND YOU NEED TO CONSIDER DAAB'S RESOURCES AND RESOLVE TO SURVIVE.

You don't know that. I don't believe you.

I KNOW THINGS YOU SIMPLY COULD NOT KNOW.

Everything slows down again. A registration of the dust in the air surrounding the location of the underground building appears before me.

Great, another distracting visual.

Along the path of my sprint away from the elevator hut, my verm shows me tiny yellow highlights revealing locations where the ground cracked from the collapse. I can hear my steps. In slow motion, they sound far away. Then, as if my memory were a hologram, my running and the ground underneath me are removed from the image, leaving the cracks, the elevator shaft, the flying dust, and the footprints from myself, Armand, and Daab.

I CALCULATED THE ACOUSTICS OF THE GROUND SHAKING AS THEY RELATE TO THE ANGLES OF EVERYONE'S PHYSIQUES.

The visual starts over again, except this time, the shaking of the elevator reveals a lattice of yellow lines and calculations. From this lattice, a single yellow line shoots sideways from the elevator shaft flush with the surface of the ground and relates itself with the movement of the vehicles shaking.

I'VE CALCULATED THE EFFECTS THAT WOULD COME FROM A BLAST THAT SHAKES THE VEHICLES AND THESE OTHER THINGS AT THESE SPECIFIC FREQUENCIES AND ANGLES.

The mental video starts over *again*, only more yellow highlights dance between the cracks in the ground, their depth, and the corresponding depth of the elevator shaft.

THESE LINES CORRESPOND WITH THE DEPTH OF WHERE THOSE EXPLOSIONS ARE EXPECTED TO BE, GIVEN VIBRATIONS IN THE GROUND AND THE BUILDING UNDERGROUND, AND HOW THESE RELATE WITH THE SHAKING OF YOUR VAN.

It's not my van...

The depths of the various lines go down at focusing angles, and spheres of influences appear at their focus, looking like explosions, specifically placed to disrupt the structural integrity of the building, but only so far... The building's implosion falls away from the elevator as it collapses.

SO YOU SEE, THESE VIBRATIONS, ACOUSTICS, ANGLES, AND EFFECTS COULD ONLY HAVE CAUSED A LIMITED AMOUNT OF DESTRUCTION, EVEN GIVEN THE WEAKEST OF UNDERGROUND STRUCTURES. IT WAS A RUSE.

Only the top three floors were rigged with explosives on the outer edges of the building.

REMEMBER THERE WERE SIX FLOORS?

I picture the grid of buttons in the elevator and nod.

WE ONLY VISITED TWO FLOORS. FROM THE ACOUSTICS OF THE EXPLOSIONS, I ABLE TO DEDUCE NOT ONLY THAT ONLY THE TOP FLOORS WERE DESTROYED, BUT THAT THERE WERE ONLY TWO ENTRANCES TO THE PLACE: THE ELEVATOR AND ANOTHER DOOR-LIKE ARCHWAY IN THE SIDE OF THE STRUCTURE, POSSIBLY AN ACCESS TUNNEL.

Did that collapse too?

I CAN'T TELL YOU THAT RIGHT NOW, I'M NOT EQUIPPED FOR THAT NOW. YOUR THROAT IS NOW HEALED.

The engine drones monotonously on. Dust continues to rise behind us.

WHEN YOU HEAR 'I CAN'T TELL YOU THAT RIGHT NOW, I'M NOT EQUIPPED FOR THAT NOW,' IT'S A PROTECTION ERROR. IT MAY BE A FALSE ERROR.

Figures.

IT COMES UP WHEN YOU DON'T NEED TO KNOW SOMETHING OR WHEN IF YOU CONSCIOUSLY DID KNOW, THE INFORMATION COULD BE EXTRACTED FROM YOU BY A THREAT.

Daab.

RIGHT.

Whatever.

More minutes pass.

Armand becomes distracted by his own thoughts and speaks up. "By the way, my secondary memory's telling me Daab said to his lackeys he wanted to get you himself."

I wish I had some weed.

Armand keeps going. "He wasn't sure if I was his only target. He was right to suspect you of course. I hid your activation from him for as long as I could, 'cause if he found out that your verm'd been activated in any way, he might've killed us both. See, the last time I called you on Friday and left a message, askin' where you'd been, his people were trackin' verm frequencies through the phone lines, lookin' for hosts."

"Okay..."

ARMAND'S VERM LIKELY HEARD THAT CONVERSATION WHILE HE WAS PASSED OUT, WHICH WOULD ALSO EXPLAIN HOW HIS VAN KEY FELL FROM HIS MOUTH WHEN YOU PICKED HIM UP IN THE BUILDING—HIS VERM WANTED TO GIVE YOU THE KEY SO YOU COULD HELP US GET OUT OF HERE IN THE VAN. HE MUST HAVE SWALLOWED IT BEFORE HE WAS CAPTURED. WHY DAAB'S PEOPLE TALKED ABOUT THIS WITHIN EAR-SHOT... I SUPPOSE THEY JUST DIDN'T KNOW HIS VERM WAS ACTIVATED THE WHOLE TIME.

Armand keeps talking, getting angrier as he goes. "Monday night, Daab's people really wanted to know how or why I was able to jump, 'cause I jumped the van. They were schoolin' me on how to be in *pain*."

"Jumped the van? You drain the battery from accidentally leaving the headlights on or something and needed a jump?"

"Oh, that's right. Don't lemme forget—you're a dumbass..."

"Wh—?"

"Anyway, so now, the Doc's location has been compromised."

"Wait, what does that have to do with anything? And when'd you swallow a key?"

"Yesterday. I swallowed it as they were bringing me in."

THIS IS BAD. IF DOC'S LOCATION'S COMPROMISED, WE HAVE A PROBLEM ON OUR HANDS. IT MEANS DAAB KNOWS THE DOC'S LOCATION AND HAS ENOUGH INFORMATION AND EQUIPMENT TO FIND HIM, EVEN WITH THE CASUALTIES WE CAUSED. AT LEAST THE OTHERS' LOCATIONS WEREN'T COMPROMISED. IT'S A GOOD THING CHRONOS'S AGENDA HAS MAINLY FOCUSED ON THE DOC, ARMAND, AND YOU, AND NOT THE OTHERS.

What the fuck is Chronos?

I CAN'T TELL YOU THAT RIGHT NOW, I'M NOT EQUIPPED FOR THAT NOW.

Fuck you.

Fuck it. I'm frustrated and confused as to why this has to be so complicated. "Okay, so... is that why we can't just pull a U-turn, run this guy's ass over, and keep him tied up? Is that why we're driving full-speed away from him?"

"There's nothing we can do beyond what your verm already did. Besides, with him and his verm still alive, we don't know what he's capable of—your verm was originally programmed to set off an EMP frequency that would liquefy him, but the Doc tells me you may've had a corrupted ResID activation. So I've got to assume only parts of him were liquefied, like his brain or some shit. 'Course, that'd just piss him off. We gotta do this another way now. We've gotta find a way to hack his verm so it no longer heals him. *Then* we can run his ass over."

"Doc."

"Yeah, and I'm lookin' forward to it, but now I gotta concentrate. I'm still gettin' back on the level, and Daab and his Allies are gonna come for us now. We gotta get us some *distance*." Armand nods at the rear-view mirror, "Here he comes."

I ask Armand *why the weird wording?* with my face.

He scoffs. "Just enjoy the ride," he says, his eyebrows somehow raised and furrowed at the same time. "Your dumbass is in for a surprise."

* * *

> Anny Klaura, U-A DOB: 2580-05-15, CID 09986520678

> ResID: 6.2 [altered by CIDs 99999999999/ResID: 6.5 &
09985240860/ResID: 4.3.2] M1

> U-B: [Auna's house, Jane, CA, US, Earth] LT: Tuesday, 2009-10-27, 12:30 AM PDT

— Tuesday, October 27th, 2009, 12:30 AM PDT —

Anny's rust-red 1970s pickup truck, which looks like it'd been used as a substitute logging truck, pops, gurgles, and bounces its way around dark rural roads toward her previous ResID's house. The truck leaves a cloud of dust and smoke behind as it makes its way down the gravel driveway. She turns and headlight beams pour over the old garage. She gets out while it's still running, then does an *oops!*-hop, turns back around, and saunters over to turn it off for the last time. She pulls the duffel bags out the back, shoves them into Lucia's trunk, and marches into the house, straight to the bedroom, waking Lucia by turning the light on.

"You're late," Luke whines from the bed. Her squinted eyes follow Anny as she paces back and forth. She moans and rolls over. "I'm... asleep... but... I found out... that annual Halloween party? ... at the winery?" She giggles and says, "Doc's gonna host."

Anny doesn't skip a beat. "I know. You told me earlier. Lucia, listen."

"It's Luuuke."

"There's been an emergency, and we have to get out of town. *We*—you, me, and Adam—we have to get out of town."

Lucia raises her head. "Huhh? ... I'm asleep... Adam 'n' I played soccer all day... he *really* wants to go to that Halloween party."

"We have to leave, *now*," Anny says, her hands dancing with insistence. "Try to grab Adam without waking him... There are motels we can crash at. We have to go to a motel—you too."

151

"Wait, what now?" Lucia asks, just sitting up. She grabs a pair of pink fluffy socks, hurdles over a pile of pants, and wades through her sleepiness toward the chaise longue across from the bed.

"There are people after us. We have to go!" Anny stops. "Lucia, you *have* to help me!"

"Yeah, okay," Luke agrees while she stumbles through getting her socks on. The pajama pant legs weren't helping. "What's this about, love?" she asks.

Anny starts pacing again. "Thank you," she says, grabbing clothes. "We need to take your car. I've already packed some things. Could you roll me a joint?"

"Okay," Lucia says, reluctantly, wondering why Anny's wanting to smoke now.

Anny sees Lucia's suspicion and says, "I'll explain on the way. Grab some candles that will mask any scent of weed—we'll need to be able to smoke wherever, whenever."

"Okay." Lucia, still suspicious and confused, gets up from the couch and quietly crawls into a shirt, disappearing into the hallway just as her head pops through its neck. She comes back with scented candles and then leaves the room to retrieve Adam. When she returns a few minutes later with Adam under a blanket, Anny has packed everything and is ready to go.

They quietly leave the house and climb into Luke's car.

Anny starts it, and they wait to see if Adam will awaken from the commotion.

Luke starts talking quietly so as not to wake him. "Okay so, emergency or people coming to get us?"

Anny leans toward Luke. "What?"

"Which is it? Either this is an emergency, or there are people coming to get us."

Anny stiffens her lips, shifts into D, and eases down the driveway. "The people coming to get us *is* the emergency."

They exit the driveway and turn onto the road.

Luke starts carefully molding sweet leaf between the fold of a rolling paper. "Well, then I guess it's a good thing I brought my gun along."

The car swerves. "You brought your gun?"

Lucia stops putting shake into the paper to see if Adam awoke from the swerve but turns and keeps her voice down. "A mom walks into my house, talkin' 'bout how there's an emergency with people chasin' her, and that mom just so happens to be the person I'm in love with, and I carry... you think I'm just gonna leave the gun at home?"

"*Your* house?" Anny asks at normal volume, startling herself and Luke.

They both look at Adam, then Anny turns to Luke and says, "No, that's not what I meant." She looks in the rear-view mirror at Adam's sleeping body. "No, I meant... I mean... I'm glad." She looks back at the road. "It's a good thing you brought it."

Lucia feigns a look of distrust. "What have you got me into, woman?"

"Just please, roll me that joint," Anny begs, then looks away, wiping a tear, trying to stay in her lane.

"Jeez, woman!" she whispers. "I'm rollin'! I'm rollin'!"

Luke finishes the roll, licks it, and lights it.

When offered, Anny grabs it with a shaking hand, wipes another tear, and chugs a drag before responding.

"I— Oh shit!" Anny whispers loudly, "I forgot Armand's tracker at Doc's!" The car begins to veer.

"Are you even safe to drive?" Lucia asks at regular volume.

"No," Anny responds.

They pull over, swap seats, and get back on the road. For a few minutes, streetlights pass over them. Looking away with watering eyes, Anny blurts out, "I'm so sorry to put you through this. We just need to get to a place where we can lay low for a while, like a parking lot."

"We're spending the night in a parking lot?"

"I'm sorry!" Anny's voice catches. "We can get a room in the morning, but we should at least stay off-record overnight, ready to leave whenever."

Lucia puts a hand over Anny's shoulders and drives into the next motel parking lot, where they spend a cold October night in the back seat with Adam, cuddling uncomfortably, trying to sleep.

* * *

— Thursday, October 29th, 2009, 6:17 PM MDT —

Behind us in the passenger-side mirror, Daab's cop car veers side to side.

Armand stares off onto the horizon of the road, almost as if Daab isn't there, but his hands grip the wheel tightly.

"Get down."

I duck as I'm told. I don't really want to expect gunfire, but things have been a tad off lately. I smell something sweet, like the scent of newly copied paper. Still clutching my water bottle, I turn and look back at Daab's car.

Armand moves quickly forward in his seat, almost too quick for me to see, and at the same time, there's a loud *crack!* as a hole appears in the back window and the windshield.

My abs tighten as hard as diamonds as chunks of glass fly from a spider-web crack spread across the windshield. More shots pierce the van and holes shoot light through the van where light shouldn't be, offset by the dust in the air.

Glass clinks everywhere, and before I even realize what I'm doing, my body wrenches my head down so hard, my forehead slams onto the dash, denting a crack wide enough to lose coins in. I take a small shower of glass.

The weird photocopy scent is *really* strong.

My head aches.

I drip blood.

THAT SCENT IS OZONE, AND YOUR FOREHEAD IS HEALED.

I look up to see a hole in the windshield right where the back of my skull could have been.

YOU'RE WELCOME.

Just as a shot rings out, my verm takes over my right hand, grabs the "oh shit" handle, and pulls my face away from the windshield. More chunks of glass fly.

YOU'RE WELCOME, AGAIN.

The van's engine grows louder.

The popping sounds have stopped.

Glass continues breaking apart around us.

Armand's eyes dart about, fiercely lucid.

My eyes wander, bewildered.

My pain reassures me I'm alive.

Armand looks at me with a smirk, then back at the horizon.

"So, first bullet-dodge, eh?"

"Uhh... heh heh... uh, yeah, I guess that is what I... what we... did."

I rub my belly. My abs hurt from clenching so swiftly and so hard. I still kind of don't believe what I just did.

A flicker of blue light from outside distracts me, but my attention is on Armand. I thought I knew him. I'm furiously anxious about Daab shooting at us, yet Armand is acting nonchalant. It makes me feel lonely and on edge, angry even.

"Ain't gonna be the only first," he says as the cop car pulls up next to us.

Before I can ask what's going on, a blue light engulfs the entire van from front to back, sparkling and snapping loudly with great electric sound and light.

I am completely blinded.

...

"What the *fuck* was that?"

My ears are ringing and my breath is choked by ozone. My eyes began to adjust to the change in light almost instantaneously.

"Calm down! We've just jumped. Might need to pop your ears. Damn. He came with us!" Armand clenches the wheel and wrenches it to the left. Various swag and boxes in the back fall to the right as my eyes begin to see...

"I have calmed down enough! How the *fuck* did we get in a parking garage?"

My left hand reaches down and undoes my safety belt, to my alarm.

Why the fuck are you unbuckling my safety belt?

"Never mind about that! He's reloaded!" Armand yells.

My body lurches involuntarily at the whim of my verm, free from the constraint of the safety belt, dodging bullet fire and random flying objects off the dash.

We continue swerving up through the turns of the parking structure.

The entire world is leaning to the right.

Meanwhile, I am in *pain*; my muscles are flexing so hard, so swiftly, that my joints and ligaments are torn and instantly healed by the verm in their mad dance for survival. So many physics equations are assaulting my vision from the verm's interaction with my perception, I can barely see Armand's movements. I can barely hear over the screeching tires of both vehicles ripping into the concrete. I for sure can't understand a damn thing. Everything is deafening, and I suddenly feel like I'm dying of thirst. I look back.

Boom!

My abs twist me completely around and down.

The pop of Daab's pistol is now a jarring shotgun blast, turning the back door into a sieve.

Boom!

More holes open in the sieve. Pellets ricochet off the insides of the van. Shards of metal are instantly torn away from their surfaces.

My back is in shooting pain.

Armand tears off his shirt, revealing a wire connected to his belly button, and closes his eyes.

My pain is gone, but seeing that Armand is driving blind, my fear sky-rockets.

"Armand! Wake up!"

"Shut up! I'm letting my verm take over. It wants to try something, and I've got time between loads now."

His foot stomps on the gas.

"Why wouldn't he shoot out our tires?"

With everything at an angle, our tires are starting to screech.

"He wants to follow our retreat to base so he can blow it up like Los Eatos. He should be able to dodge bullets, too. He's just being an asshole. We gotta lose him."

Daab's tires screech furiously as he tries to catch up.

Boom!

The feeling of air being pushed aside as pellets shoot through the cabin alarms and intrigues me—I can hear parts of the van fall behind us.

Armand opens his eyes, reaches under the seat, pulls out a pistol.

Everything slows way down. A bullet exits his gun, followed by a flash of gun powder, then a slow 'boom' that should have sounded like a pistol's 'pop!' It twists the air, drills through the back of the van's metal plating, and ricochets off Daab's bullet-proof windshield.

Boom!

Armand leans forward, swaps hands, pushes his pistol upside-down out the window, and fires a bullet into Daab's left hand, removing the shotgun from the equation.

"Dude, how did you get a gun?"

"Those idiots didn't see it when they took the van."

"If you're that good at shooting, why not just end it now? Let's take a stand here."

"We're not ready yet. We still have to avoid him. I'm still getting back to normal. You don't even know what normal is."

Armand fires a bullet into one of Daab's tires. Nothing happens. He unloads the clip into it. It barely changes course.

"Just great! Bullet-proof tires."

"What the hell are we going to do?"

"Don't worry about it. Nothing's bullet-proof for real. I can still fuck 'em up. I'll just need something different than bullets. I gotta wear 'em down. After this next jump, I've gotta get in the back—my verm has a plan. We gotta get back to Doc, but we can't have Daab trailing behind."

Daab begins ramming the van with his crash bar, pushing us to the right, dangerously close to the wall.

"We're almost there!" Armand yells over the noise as we emerge into the night at the top of the structure.

The night sky is cloudless and starlit, but I hardly notice because I'm just climbing back into my seat.

Blue light flickers around us as Daab catches up on our right.

Daab looks at me through the window with murderous intent. His clothes are strewn about the car. He is completely naked. He leans, side-swiping us.

I barely stop myself from smacking my face on the window. Metal crunches as the van lurches to the left.

Armand compensates with screeching tires.

"Ah! Go! Go! Go!" I'm panicking with fear, but I'm equally confused. *It's night now?*

"Here we go! Woo hoo hoo!" Armand yells and smiles as we accelerate toward the edge of the building.

"Wait! Stop!"

He doesn't stop. Instead, he laughs at me and goes faster.

"STOOOPPPLEEEEEASSSTOOOOP! NO! NO! NO! NO!"

We hit the building's edge, toppling a poorly made barrier sign with the phrase "Warning! Under Construction" in Marathi on it, and we bounce upward and out into a three-story fall. There's no time to freak out about suddenly being able to read Marathi—I'm screaming from being lifted out from my chair. I scramble to put the chair between me and the ground.

Armand is *not* freaking out while we fall, Daab is still looking at me with hate, falling right beside us, gun trained in our direction, and I'm screaming my life away like a little girl, now giving the back of the seat a bear hug.

A disk of blue light sweeps us from front to back again.

My ears feel stabbed.

* * *

> Anny Klaura, U-A DOB: 2580-05-15, CID 09986520678

> ResID: 6.2 [altered by CIDs 99999999999/ResID: 6.5 & 09985240860/ResID: 4.3.2] M1

> U-B: [Room 11, The Brendon Motel, Jane, CA, US, Earth] LT: Tuesday, 2009-10-27, 7:11 PM PDT

— Tuesday, October 27th, 2009, 7:11 PM PDT —

After Lucia and Anny book a room in the motel of the parking lot in which they spent the night, they avoid discussing why they are at a motel, trying to lose themselves in the moments of Adam's happiness with the adventure of new surroundings. They lie when he asks about going home.

The parking lot is surrounded by the motel's single-floor architecture where the doors of each unit open to a bed on the left, a bathroom ahead, and a mini fridge, cabinets, entertainment center, and a small table and chairs along the wall to the right.

As evening arrives, they are in the bathroom, running a bath with the lights off. The orange parking lot lighting shines in through the window. The fan is on and candles burn to cover any scent of weed. Lucia and Anny barely fit sitting on the vanity beside each other, waiting for the water to fill. Most of their clothes are on the floor. The dark, humid atmosphere implies a perfect getaway from the anxiety of the last sixteen to twenty hours.

Luke takes off her shirt.

"I don't get it. How'd you get Adam to go to sleep so quickly today?"

Anny smiles with facetious guilt. "I spiked his orange juice with diazepam."

Luke stops taking off her socks for a moment of disbelief, but plays along with sarcasm. "Oh sure, sedatives—that's just what he needs after a long day of running around in a parking lot."

161

"It's nothing crazy—just a small amount," Anny says, looking around with a pipe in her hands. She grabs her pants, pulls out the lighter she was looking for, and hands both the pipe and lighter to Lucia, dropping her pants back to the floor. "He'll be fine in the morning," Anny insists. Her pants land with a thud and a high-pitched screech. A cell phone bounces halfway out of a pocket.

"You drugged your kid..." Lucia says facetiously, scoffing and then taking a hit, "Wow..." She blows out smoke. "That is hardcore..."

Anny's already open hand reaches for the pipe. "Shut up," she says as she takes it. "It's... it's part of his treatment."

"Uh huh. Whatever."

Anny takes another hit and her pants screech again. Luke points at them. "That—what is that?" she asks, and seeing the cell phone nearby, she asks, "Did you just get a new phone?"

Anny hands the pipe back to Lucia, grabs up her pants, pulls out the walkie-talkie-looking thing and explains. "It's a police scanner Doc gave me, and yeah, Doc gave me the phone to contact him."

Luke smiles in slight suspicion, handing Anny the lighter-pipe combo.

"Doc, huh? What is a police scanner doing in our bath time, and why did Doc give you a phone? Is he stalking you? If you want, you know I could kick his ass," she says, then takes a hit and blows it out. "You know," Lucia says, "to use a scanner, you have to actually have it tuned to a frequency that..." The water starts pouring into the overflow drain. She turns it off. "Auna, what's this about?" Luke looks to Anny for eye contact, but in the sudden silence, Anny's eyes follow the steam as it rises from the water's rippling surface in the candlelight.

Her voice is just above a whisper. "Adam's scars are due to a rare genetic condition."

"Yeah," Luke says, "chimerism or something. You've told me earlier, something—"

"He needs... immediate treatment... he needs... a liver transplant, and—"

"But he looks fine," Lucia says, smiling in disbelief as she puts the pipe down, turning to face Anny, who doesn't move.

Lucia's smile fades.

"Auna... how long have you known about this?"

"I didn't want to get you involved," Anny says, looking down at Lucia's feet. "But I can't help him. No one can help him... at least, no doctor, legally."

Lucia shifts her weight and steps into the water.

"It's Doc, isn't it? Doc's the answer?"

Frozen in the heat, Anny stares at the ripples Lucia's legs displace in the water.

"Yes. Doc is the answer."

At Lucia's beckoning, Anny eases her bottom off the vanity and slowly steps her feet over the rim one by one into the water. The overflow drain gurgles as they stand facing each other. Turning around, kneeling, and sighing as her bottom and legs succumb to the new heat, she reclines into Lucia's arms as their legs find their way around each other in the small tub.

"Only," Anny continues over the gurgling of the drain, "there was some kind of setup. There was some kind of prep-room he had set up, but *haphazardly*, it got found out, and now he's got trouble with the law. CPS got wind of it... and—"

"Whoa, CPS? We may never see Adam again. Well, and there's jail."

Anny's eyes move over the water as it changes from the movements of their breathing.

"We have to get Adam to the— to Doc," Anny says. "He said he'd text me where he'll be on that phone when he's finally ready."

Lucia pauses a second to take in what she's heard.

"Where do you think we'll be going?"

Anny's forehead creases and her eyes move from the water to a nearby candle flame.

"Lucia... I don't want to talk about this anymore right now... It's bath time."

"You're right, this is depressing."

They each pause, to try to come up with a new subject.

Anny blurts out, "Help me."

"What can I *do?*"

"I just… need to keep smoking weed."

Lucia smiles and says, "*That* is something I can do."

Anny stares off into the orange light and begins rambling, "I mean, I'm a psychologist— was a psychologist… I still am, I mean, I just—"

"Okay, okay, it's okay… here, stand up for bit. Turn around," Lucia says, as she leans sideways over the side of the tub and pulls out a fist-sized plastic bong with a metal stem from behind her pants, uses her pants to dry her hands, and begins loading it with weed.

Anny, confused, waves at the bong.

"How'd—where'd you get that?"

"Oh, you know," Luke says, "ever since you yelled about me dealing in front of all my friends, I carry a really cheap never-smoked bong with me, just in case I have a really bad day, and really need a new bong fix."

Luke presents Anny the loaded bong with a 'you know you want it' smile and nod.

Anny smiles back with watery eyes. Her smile grows into laughter. She steps out of the tub to fill the bong in the sink and returns to the tub to recline in Lucia's embrace. Slowly but surely, they fill the bathroom with smoke.

The smoke feels thick in the humidity. It soothes them like hot tea.

"Thank you for taking care of me," Anny says. "You always know how to take care of me."

"You are my heart," Lucia says against the back of Anny's head. "I would do anything for you."

Anny sighs. "That's what scares me."

"That I'd do something stupid?"

"No, I mean— I mean because I love you too. Even after everything…"

"You're afraid of love?" Lucia dares. "That's hardcore."

"Shut up."

In response, Lucia whispers, "Gotcha," and with her toes, she simultaneously opens the drain and turns on the shower right into Anny's face.

Anny yells, getting up and blinking and wiping the water from her eyes. "I told you never to do that again!"

Lucia giggles as she struggles to stand, almost losing her balance. Clumsily, they climb over each other in their high, trying to right themselves without falling in the cramped little tub. They stand and face each other. Lucia embraces Anny until her shoulders relax.

"It's okay," Luke says, "I've got you. You've got me."

She holds Anny while the water heats back up.

Anny squeezes Luke's body, resting her cheek on Luke's collarbone.

The water carries their cares slowly down the drain. It splashes about in small droplets on the surface, bouncing a clipped white noise around the room.

They melt into each other's arms, warmed by their intoxication and heat. They embrace with desperate kissing.

* * *

> John Waterman, U-A DOB: 2579-12-03, CID 09985240860

> ResID: 8.2.0 [altered by CID 99999999999/ResID: 6.5] M1

> U-B: [Klickitat County, WA, US, Earth] LT: Thursday, 2009-10-29, 5:20 PM PDT

— Thursday, October 29th, 2009, 5:20 PM PDT —

We're falling. It is the opposite of peaceful. WHAT THE FUCK IS GOING ON?

YOU ARE BEING DISPLACED AND RELOCATED IN SPACE. ARMAND IS THE ORIGIN.

Even in my hysteria, the verm forces visions of the fall of the van and cop car upon my fragile sanity.

A cliff surface matches our fall, slightly off-parallel and vertical, like a skier's fall follows the downward slope of a mountain.

My eyes adjust more quickly to the change in brightness, only to show me that we're about to crash land.

I hear screaming.

The screaming stops when I inhale.

Oh, that was me.

Armand is giving me a *seriously, you should be ashamed of yourself* look, holding the steering wheel as if steering in mid-air is possible.

I hold as tightly as I consciously can to the back of the seat in front of me.

Shards of glass flung from our fall float in mid-air.

My guts are in my throat.

Armand looks in the direction of our fall.

"This is gonna be rough," he says.

The wheels touch the side of the cliff, and we're righted by the cliff in slight increments until we level off with a

167

crescendo of falling glass shards. The rough terrain punishes the van hard enough to bounce both axles and me. My face ricochets off the back of the chair with bits of glass and metal before the van finally settles along the curve of a hillside road. And, not that I care, but my verm tells me in my moment of pain that we're going 60 miles per hour.

"Ow!"

Fuck this.

I tumble back into the chair, and buckle my safety belt. I grab a bottle of water, and down the entire bottle in one gulp. I didn't know I could do that.

YOU'RE WELCOME, AGAIN.

Showoff.

All I know is that we are now on a winding road, there are evergreen trees everywhere, and it's daytime again.

Daab's cop car is surprisingly agile, following us through the... whatever the hell we just "jumped" through. He dodges a tree we almost hit, and then veers right around the van, accelerating to match the front axles. He side-swipes us again. I can feel our fenders and doors smash together. He lets up only to get more momentum to crash into my side again and again.

I wince—he's still naked.

His left foot is on the steering wheel, his right is on the gas, and his hands are loading a double barrel shotgun. He has a small collection of guns and clips in the front seat.

"Why is he *naked?*" I yell over the crunching of the fenders, my body jarred from the impacts.

Dust is everywhere behind us, blue light in front.

Daab sees that we are driving him toward a cliff. His tires screech, veering him behind us again, and his engine roars to keep pace.

"So he can *see* better," Armand responds, unmoved. "Here we go again."

Daab continues following us.

As a rise in the ground lifts the front axle into the air and projects us over the edge, blue light engulfs us before the back axle even leaves the ground.

* * *

> Anny Klaura, U-A DOB: 2580-05-15, CID 09986520678

> ResID: 6.2 [altered by CIDs 99999999999/ResID: 6.5 &
09985240860/ResID: 4.3.2] M1

> U-B: [Room 11, The Brendon Motel, Jane, CA, US, Earth] LT:
Tuesday, 2009-10-27, 8:48 PM PDT

— Tuesday, October 27th, 2009, 8:48 PM PDT —

After exhausting each other's passions, Lucia and Anny spoon, sharing the afterglow in warmth and silence. The water is off and the drain is plugged.

Anny rests in Lucia's arms, turning the hot water back on with her toes.

Slowly, the level rises until it pours into the overflow drain again.

Anny's toes turn off the water.

"So..." Lucia says softly, "I noticed you've been smoking constantly since we left your place..."

A few seconds pass.

Anny folds Lucia's arms over herself. "Yeah."

A few seconds pass again.

"You don't normally smoke this much... you know, in front of Adam."

"Well, it's not like the bong that appears magically out of nowhere could be refused," Anny says. "You got me on that one."

"Ah," Luke says, smiling, but her eyes tighten. "I just figured it would be good for bath time."

Still, Anny doesn't respond. She won't admit to changing the subject, so, disappointed, Luke drops it.

"This tub is small," Anny complains, "I miss having bath time at your place."

The minutes pass in silence until the water begins to feel cold. Luke frowns and holds Anny closer.

Static screeches from the scanner, startling them both, then silences abruptly.

Luke taps Anny on the back a couple times with an open hand. "I need some air."

Anny leans forward.

Luke stands up and dries off.

In response, Anny takes another hit off the bong.

Lucia exits the bathroom and, after getting dressed, leaves the motel room.

In response, Anny nods thoughtfully and takes another hit.

* * *

> John Waterman, U-A DOB: 2579-12-03, CID 09985240860

> ResID: 8.2.0 [altered by CID 99999999999/ResID: 6.5] M1

> U-B: [Black Rock Desert, NV, US, Earth] LT: Thursday, 2009-10-29, 5:22 PM PDT

— Thursday, October 29th, 2009, 5:22 PM PDT —

"Goddamn it! He keeps leeching off my signal, and we only have so many jumps!"

We land quicker this time, but just as hard.

"I bet there's a..." he reaches under the dash, "Ha! I'll be a son of a bitch." He pockets a small black device from the dash.

We're on a bumpy road in a desert.

Daab is right behind us, the cop car aglow with trailing blue light.

Boom.

"Where are we now?" I ask, not realizing in the adrenaline of it all that I've been hit.

Blood spills out of my hip and then a pellet pops out of it.

"Nevada."

FIND FOOD.

I can barely keep up with what's happening. I'm not in pain, I'm just furiously hungry.

I'm healed. That is fucking cool. But wait, if I eat a lot, I ask my verm, does that mean I'm gonna take a major shit later?

MAXIMUM ENERGY USE MEANS MINIMAL WASTE. SO, NO, YOU WON'T NEED TO ELIMINATE ANY MORE THAN USUAL.

Armand reaches in front of me and breaks open the glove box while we're avoiding Daab.

"You got hit," Armand says. "Eat."

Protein bars fly out of the glove box and land on top of glass chunks at my feet.

Still pumped with adrenaline, I grab a protein bar, rip it open with my teeth, spit out the wrapper, and throw half of it into my mouth. I toss the rest, concentrating on chewing without choking or biting my tongue.

"Quick! Take the wheel!"

No question. I unclick my seatbelt and grab the wheel, still chomping on the protein bar.

Armand simultaneously unclicks his safety belt and detaches the wire from his belly button, and is already in the back of the van when I jump out of my seat and land on the gas pedal, flooring it and getting whiplash. Unaffected, Armand opens boxes of Los Eatos onions, tortillas, and picante sauce. He throws the back doors wide open. They wave back and forth.

I'm speeding up, but Daab is keeping our pace at roughly 80 miles an hour, ready to clip us at any time.

What the fuck is Armand doing back there?

Just then, the rear-view mirror shows me Armand heaving an open box of picante sauce out the back.

Daab slams on his brakes, but Armand's verm had calculated for it, and picante sauce explodes over the entire windshield, perfectly covering Daab's view.

The cop car, only slowing to half its speed, burns rubber to get back up to 80 miles an hour with the windshield wipers smearing the dusty sauce.

Armand tosses the leftover boxes at Daab's tires.

Daab dovetails from running them over.

Armand closes the van's doors, pushes another couple boxes forward, comes up front, and pulls on a rope that releases a metal plate connected to the ceiling and hinged above the back doors, completely covering our newly installed sieves.

"I need the wheel again."

"When'd you install that?" I ask, jumping to the passenger seat and looking back.

Daab's engine roars right behind us. His crash bar rams the van, deeply impacting the already destroyed doors.

Unshaken, Armand effortlessly stabs the wire back into his belly button and grabs the wheel, stomping on the gas as blue light begins shimmering around us.

"The Doc put it in for me after we arrived in Jane—a little 'just in case' present, should we ever meet up with someone like Daab."

Daab pulls up to my side, staring enraged and naked with a different shotgun in his completely healed hand pointed directly at me.

I instinctively grab the seat adjustment lever and lean back harder than I can ever remember doing.

Boom!

Glass falls on my lap, face, and neck.

Boom!

Armand leans back as well, holding on to the seat of the chair. He puts his safety belt back on over his wire, and I do the same as ozone fills the atmosphere around the vehicles.

"Floor it!" I yell at Armand, a chunk of protein bar flying out of my mouth.

A look of disgust comes over his face as his eyes follow the flying chunk. "Fuck you. It *is* floored."

Everything begins to glow blue again. The sudden smell of ozone strangely complements the flavor of the protein bar.

Just as we reach the edge of a hill, the feeling of falling shifts my guts as we jump yet again through another blinding ring of static.

* * *

— Tuesday, October 27th, 2009, 11:21 PM PDT —

Lucia returns holding grocery bags. Her posture is full of resolve.

Adam remains asleep on the floor.

Anny, wearing her baby blue bathrobe, slowly looks up from the bong she was smoking at the table. "You left me all alone. I was all alone... and stoned..."

"I needed some time to think," Lucia says, as she walks over to the dresser and sets down the bags.

"Now... I'm just stoned." Anny continues, looking longingly at Adam. "I'm not... supposed to think... interrogatively... Adam... such a wonderful boy."

"If you keep getting stoned," Lucia says, as she starts unloading groceries, "Adam will be without a mom. You probably don't have any experience running, but I do. We needed good food for a non-stop run. I bought some of your favorites... cheese, bell peppers, avocados, apples, bread, and bananas."

Anny's glance rises to the groceries Lucia puts onto the dresser.

"Oh, thank you, Lucia! Thank you for taking care of mm... us. You're so good to me."

Lucia sighs. "It's Luke," she says, still looking away from Anny, as she puts the small block of cheese into the small fridge, then she turns with a smile.

"I also picked us up some TP, snacks, and a couple DVDs for Adam... and now we have five thousand bucks in gift cards. I

177

paid cash for them so they're untraceable. I also got us some hair dye."

Stoned, Anny meets Luke's gaze with wonder and happiness in her eyes.

"If we're skipping town, we need to do it right—leave here with different colored hair and pay with the gift cards at a different place tomorrow. The best place would be Sister City." She sets a banana in front of Anny as a gift. "We got this."

"Mmmm, yes please. I agree... Babe, why are you doing this for us?"

"It's not like I'm going to go back to work at Los Explode-os... and 'us' includes me now, too." Luke says with her back turned, sifting through the bags.

Anny sits and considers what Doc told her.

Luke pulls out scissors, hair oil, and a metal bowl.

"You are 'us,'" Anny says.

"Damn right," Lucia says, secluding herself in the bathroom.

Anny attempts to call Doc on the phone he gave her, but it doesn't call out.

A clip of static erupts from the scanner in the bathroom, causing Lucia to yelp. She bursts out of the bathroom with half of her purple dreadlocks cut off, slams the scanner on the table in front of Anny, and storms back into the bathroom, leaving a startled Anny to ponder new hairstyles and Adam's non-response to all the raucous.

Anny clumsily grabs the scanner's charging cord and plugs it in, turning the scanner down in the unlikely case it might wake Adam.

"John," she whispers, "with a cleaner here, I fear that General Morgan, when we return, has..." She starts opening the banana Lucia gave her earlier. "John, we'll need every bit of help we can spare..." She takes a bite. "John, we'll need Lucia."

She lays her head on the table while eating the newly acquired banana and closes her eyes while chewing. Moments later, Luke shakes her awake.

"Hey. Wakey wakey. We have to lighten your hair now."

Anny ponders the new Lucia with dirty blond hair, short enough to barely get a part on one side, completely devoid of dreadlocks. Leaving a limp, half-eaten banana on the table, she embraces Lucia, who remains stiff with agenda.

"I'm so sorry I got you into this," Anny says, letting go of Lucia to check with her eyes.

Luke relaxes and squeezes Anny's shoulder. "It's you and Adam I'm worried about, not me," Luke says. "I'll be cool."

Anny stumbles to the bathroom with Lucia holding her steady.

"Doc," Anny says as Luke puts on gloves. "Once we hook back up with Doc, he'll be able to fix it. Just need to get back to Doc."

"By the way, where is he?" Luke asks, grabbing up the dye and bleach bottles.

"I don't know," Anny admits, sitting on the toilet lid and rocking with uncertainty. "He said he'd text me… but… I think he's in Arizona."

"Arizona?" Luke asks, pouring one bottle into the other. "Just stay still. I've got to make sure this is at least somewhat uniform," she says, shaking the remaining bottle and squatting to get perspective. "You wouldn't wanna walk around with blotches."

"That is true," Anny says with half-closed eyes in a childlike sing-song voice. She leans forward to make her head more accessible but goes too far and opens her eyes in Lucia's face.

"Hold still," Luke says, gripping Anny's shoulder, trying to manage her intoxication.

"Oh!" Anny's eyes widen and she tries to lean back again.

"Hold still!" Luke says, squirting the dye onto Anny's head.

"Sorry!" Anny says loud enough to wake Adam.

"Shh!"

"Sorry!" Anny says quietly.

* * *

— Thursday, October 29th, 2009, 8:25 PM CDT —

A clear blue sky follows our jump, but we are bouncing like crazy, and hard. Everything comes into focus.

"UGH! It stinks! Why a junkyard?" I yell at Armand, barely able to hold on to the fleeting, strangely delicious protein bar with ozone taste I was almost enjoying.

"How're these jumps controlled?"

"My verm controls it."

"Can Daab jump on his own?"

"We'll know once we lose him."

For a moment, I'm disoriented by visuals of working at a computer running virtual reality simulations. I'm standing next to Auna in a futuristic computer lab with a large black boxy digital clock showing a green readout of the time to the nearest thousandth of a second on an off-white wall overlooking an upright cylindrical tank with a sleeping infant floating in it amongst fine tubes and wires connected to his little body. I feel like I'm hallucinating or dreaming while awake or something—I somehow know that the infant is Adam. He twitches from the simulation I'm running. The clock clicks over one one-thousandth of a second, and I'm moving so incredibly fast in this memory that it seems to take forever, but I can't remember how or where I could have had this impossible experience.

What is this?

I CAN'T TELL YOU THAT RIGHT NOW, I'M NOT EQUIPPED FOR THAT NOW.

"Dammit," I respond out loud.

"What now?" Armand asks with a tone as if we were politely discussing the weather.

"My verm sucks!"

Armand grunts but focuses on driving. Piles of sun-bleached car skeletons fly past. Suddenly, I realize something looking ahead—there's no room in the backside of a dump for a van to drive through.

"We're jumping again, right?" I ask.

"Yeah." Armand is still acting nonchalant, like everything's normal, like he does this shit all the time.

HE'S KNOWN HIS VERM MUCH LONGER THAN YOU'VE KNOWN ME.

What the fuck? Fuck it; we've got a naked cop chasing us through a dump.

"Daab hasn't shot at us for a while," I say, trying not to bite my cheeks or tongue while we race through the muddy, garbage-filled road.

"So what?" Armand asks, "You can't hear he's got a flat tire?"

"What?"

"Bullets or not," Armand says with a smile, "we got him now!"

We're not making it.

Blue light continues to burst all around us.

Boom!

Chink! Chink! Clunk! Clunk!

Parts fall off from the back again.

"Pile of axles!"

"It's cool," Armand reassures me as everything starts turning blue.

"Armand! We'll hit it dead on!"

Blue light refracts from swirls of ozone.

"We'll make it!" he yells.

NOW YOU CAN HEAR IT. DAAB HAS RECENTLY GOT A FLAT TIRE.

I couldn't hear it before, but now, it's like someone beating a rug, only hundreds of times faster and muddier.

Welcomed ozone fills my senses as blue light swallows us.

...

The next thing I know, it's freezing and everything's bright. My eyes are having trouble adjusting to the light this time, but I realize I'm no longer being jostled by the muddiness of the garbage dump, or that ridiculous eternal left turn from the parking garage, but—

Boom!

"Damn," Armand says, "he still has some ammo left... heh."

"*Heh?*" I yell, "Where the fuck are we now?"

THE SPEEDOMETER READS 85 MPH.

Clumps of snow land on the windshield.

"It's fucking cold," I say.

"We're on a frozen lake in New York—Canadice Lake," Armand says. "Don't be such a pussy."

In the newly found smoothness of our ride, my senses change. Everything around me slows down. Our landscape rotates in my head, a mile in every direction, showing our entire surroundings: Daab in the cop car, the frozen lake, and the Los Eatos van. Various equations and geometric formulations reach out to me, glowing yellow, overlaying our geography in what appears to be some kind of communication to me about my experience.

WE'RE AT THE PERFECT SPEED. HE'LL LOSE CONTROL.

Amidst the falling snow, I make out the shape of clothes being thrown out of the cop car. Just then, Daab crawls his naked body out of the driver-side window as it continues in a jagged arc away from the van. He then somehow stands, inhumanly stalwart atop the cop car, continuously firing a barrage of shots at us as the car revolves aimlessly on the ice. He's stepping over the cop-lights as it turns. His flat tire's rim finally catches, digging solidly into the surface, throwing the car through the air in a fearsome chaotic storm of metal, glass, and smoke. Daab loses no time leaping up from the launched wreckage, continuing to fire at us from above in one final attempt to stop us.

"Hold on, pussy," Armand says. "This is gonna be rough."

* * *

> Anny Klaura, U-A DOB: 2580-05-15, CID 09986520678

> ResID: 6.2 [altered by CIDs 99999999999/ResID: 6.5 &
09985240860/ResID: 4.3.2] M1 & M2

> U-B: [Room 11, The Brendon Motel, Jane, CA, US, Earth] LT:
Wednesday, 2009-10-28, 7:03 AM PDT

— Wednesday, October 28th, 2009, 7:03 AM PDT —

Light cuts the room sideways through a slit in the curtains. The child disturbs dust particles in the air. He stomps playfully upon the bed and gives Anny a few love-punches in the shoulder, only they're a little too hard.

Anny awakens with an, "Ow! Stop hitting me!"

"Mommy... why's your hair yellow?"

She sits up, half-smiling at her son, taking a deep breath before explaining. "Yesterday, while you were asleep, Luke and I decided to dye our hair. What do you think?"

Adam stares at her, then whines, "I *always* miss something when I go to bed."

"I know, dear, you're *always* missing *everything*."

"But I *am*. Mom, can I dye my hair, too?" he asks, playfully entangling the sheets.

Lucia awakens to the voices in the room and sits up, too. "Hmmm... What's going on?"

"Cool! Luke looks like a man!"

Anny half-stifles a laugh while Lucia frowns momentarily in the awkwardness, but smiles and says, "Oh yeah, we changed our look! What do you think?"

"You look weird," Adam says, smiling.

Lucia rolls her eyes.

The police scanner screeches white noise for a second.

"What was that?" Adam asks.

Anny perks up, changing the subject. "We are on an adventure! Luke and I are pretending to be other people until we can find you your doctor."

"An adventure!" Adam yells, "Do I get to change my hair, too?"

Anny looks to Luke, who responds, "You sure do."

"Awesome! What do I do?"

"First," Anny says, "Go brush your teeth and get ready for the day while Luke and *I* choose the color of hair you'll have and get breakfast ready."

"Why can't I choose my hair?"

"Because we only have one— Just go and brush your teeth. We have to get breakfast ready."

"Okay."

While Adam runs into the bathroom, Anny confides to Luke, "I want to start smoking as soon as possible... Can you help?"

"Sure, but... we should get out of here. I have an idea. If you need to smoke now, it might be a good idea to use the bathroom once Adam's out of there."

"What about dyeing his hair?"

"He eats while you smoke, then I dye his hair while you smoke out here."

"I am very lucky to have you in my life. I don't know what I'd do without you."

Adam stomps out and demands, "What's for breakfast?"

* * *

> John Waterman, U-A DOB: 2579-12-03, CID 09985240860

> ResID: 8.2.0 [altered by CID 99999999999/ResID: 6.5] M1

> U-B: [Detroit Lake, OR, US, Earth] LT: Thursday, 2009-10-29, 5:28 PM PDT

— Thursday, October 29th, 2009, 5:28 PM PDT —

We emerge from the blue light, tires in mid-air, inches over the surface of a lake... a non-frozen lake this time. At over 80 miles an hour, with a wheel of the van now scraping across the surface of the lake, a wall of water sprays high into the air. I can't see anything, because of the blinding blue light, or hear for that matter, because of the air pressure change, but my verm shows me everything in my mind as it happens in real time.

After our initial sideways plunge across the lake, our momentum is caught by the friction of the water, which quickly drags the bottom of the van under just enough that we are overturned. We barrel-roll over the water.

Armand's body barely moves, but mine gets tossed about like clothes in a dryer.

Water shoots in from the bullet holes the van's collected, and chunks of the van assault me from various angles—wet glass, bits of metal, and other various dangerous dirty particles fly about at unexpected angles all around and onto us.

My eyes and ears finally adjust to our new surroundings, and from what I can tell, the van is in a foot of water on a boat ramp. Since it's October, it's no surprise no one's around. The water hadn't compromised the engine... it's still running.

Without a word, we get out, rinse off the bits of glass, metal, and whatever else, get back in, and drive away.

* * *

> Anny Klaura, U-A DOB: 2580-05-15, CID 09986520678

> ResID: 6.2 [altered by CIDs 99999999999/ResID: 6.5 &
  09985240860/ResID: 4.3.2] M1

> U-B: [Room 9, The Eleven Motel, Sister City, CA, US, Earth] LT:
  Thursday, 2009-10-29, 7:20 PM PDT

— Thursday, October 29th, 2009, 7:20 PM PDT —

Luke drives Anny and Adam to Sister City where they find another motel and stay for the night.

"Is he finally asleep?" Luke asks.

"Yeah," Anny responds, "I gave him a sedative again. He'll be fine."

"Uh huh."

Anny pulls out an eighth and some papers.

Lucia sees the bag. "Ohh, well, if it's gonna be that kinda party..."

Anny scoffs. "Actually," she says, "this is more for *me*."

"Gimme!" Lucia says and pounces on her.

Anny laughs, falls over from Lucia's weight, and tries to roll away, but immediately gives up when Luke starts tickling her.

"All right all right *all right!*" Anny says, sitting up. She throws an eighth at Lucia's face.

After grabbing the eighth that bounced off her face, Lucia gets up and joins Anny at the table, and they start rolling joints.

They'd made two joints apiece when Anny stops.

"I know you love me," Anny says.

"What? Noooo."

Anny crosses her legs and lights up.

"Things are going to get crazy," she says.

"'Don't say crazy," Luke mocks her. "Say eccentric."

"This time, things really are going to get crazy," Anny says.

"DUUuhhh... Wait, how serious're we talking about here?" Lucia asks, and reaches for a joint.

"I don't know..."

189

The scanner screeches. "szhzhzhz. All units: this is a Humboldt-County-wide APB. Be on the lookout for five armed and dangerous POIs involved with suspicion of organized crime, drug possession, theft of a police vehicle, and drug trafficking. Names: John Waterman, Lucia Gage, Auna Klaura, Armand Pochelli, and Doc Andersen. Current descriptions are being uploaded to you. zhzhzhzhz— unknown; locations unknown. Adam Klaura, a minor, may be held captive in proxy. Brief descriptions follow: Adam— szhzhzhz— Klaura are mother and son, respective ages are approximately five to six years of age and twenty-seven years of age. Auna— zhshzshh— vehicle at her residence. Current location of Lucia Gage's vehicle unknown. Gage's vehicle is a black '95 Civic sedan. Further information about the vehicle is being uploaded to you now. Last known location of the Klauras and Gage is Klaura's residence. Armand Pochelli and Doc Andersen were last seen at Andersen's residence in Jane. All POIs may be in possession of large quantities of marijuana and should be considered armed and extremely dangerous. If you see any of these POIs, do not engage. I repeat: do not engage. Call for backup. If you must engage, proceed with extreme caution."

* * *

— Thursday, October 29th, 2009, 7:26 PM PDT —

After a couple of hours of silence and restless car sleeping, I'm woken by my thoughts.

"Oh that's right—we've got to find Auna."

"Yeah. I figure, that's exactly where we're headed." Armand's response sounds sarcastic. "Only, first, we've got to commandeer a less conspicuous vehicle... now that reminds me... I keep forgettin'... you're a dumbass."

"Huh?"

"You're gonna remember this eventually anyway, but I feel like talkin'. You turned yourself into a dumbass. You've been a dumbass, and now, you're still a dumbass... a lazy dumbass."

I stare at him in hopes for a punch line to the joke. According to Armand's lack of response, I must be the punch line.

What was that for?

ARMAND AND THE DOC KEPT THEIR VERMS AWAKE THIS WHOLE TIME. WHILE THE DOC MAY HAVE BECOME COMPROMISED, ARMAND'S BEEN FEEDING HIS OWN VERM AS MUCH INFORMATION AS POSSIBLE ABOUT THIS ENTIRE PLANET THAT RELATES TO HIS TRAINING ON AVERSION, ESPIONAGE, AND ESCAPE ARTISTRY SINCE WE GOT HERE.

The police scanner breaks the beat of our conversation: "All units: this is a Humboldt-County-wide APB. Be on the lookout for five armed and dangerous POIs involved with suspicion of organized crime, drug possession, theft of a police vehicle, and drug trafficking. Names: John Waterman, Lucia Gage, Auna Klaura—"

Armand shuts it off.

"Just what we need—another distraction."

191

"What the fuck, dude? That was important."

"Look, we're in the middle of something, 'n' you don't even know what you're talking about. You wanna rescue Anny and Luke? Fuck 'em and fuck you. We're going to the Doc, first. Everything else is a lower priority."

"Why are you being an asshole? Why are you holding out on me? Why won't you tell me why you've had a wire plugged into your torso? Doc and I sacrificed our memories to keep us all safe, right? Auna gives hers up completely, but you kept yours to protect us, right?"

Armand scowls in frustration. "You're still a dumbass."

"Yeah, right, because you won't tell me anything. When we started a life in Jane, I expect we'd want to stick together, so now why throw that all away by letting Lucia get caught by the law? How do we even know that wasn't one of Daab's friends?"

Armand slams on the breaks, throwing me against my seatbelt. "All right, fine. You want to go there, I will. First off, I don't think you know me, son. You don't even know yourself! Second, if Daab's people are spendin' their time looking for Lucia, he ain't torturin' and killin' Anny, the Doc, you, or me, and especially not Adam."

"Especially Adam? Dude, Adam's probably with them."

"Look, Daab wants the results of your experiment, but he doesn't know what he's up against. Frankly, neither do we. In case you haven't been told yet, I am a soldier. Soldiers complete missions, and we have to regroup."

"So what is your mission?"

"That doesn't even matter now. On Monday, I was gettin' schooled on how to be in pain, so this mission has changed. Now my mission is to protect that information from outsiders, even if that means bein' an asshole to you. It's your fuckin' protocol anyway. Lucia doesn't enter into this. Daab does."

"Wait a fucking minute here. If this shit is my protocol, why are you so aggro? These people have been with us for the last couple years, and they're in trouble. Shouldn't we do something?"

"We *are* doing something. We're going to the Doc. Either way, you're still a dumbass. Lucia's no longer a part of your... fairyland reality of make-believe you created to hide away in for these last three years... We've tried doin' things your way, now I have to clean up your mess. Lucia isn't any of our business anymore, definitely not yours anyway, and definitely not mine, not now. You don't like it, that's too bad. You're like a shop teacher with missin' fingers. Right now, we don't know how many Allies there are—we could have an army of Daabs wandering 'round out there. They're all likely supported by law enforcement somehow, tryin' to track us down ... and when they do, Daab'll collect. He will leave this time-space with us stuck here, or worse."

A few seconds go by.

"Yeah, but if he leaves, that's a good thing, right?"

"Fuck no. Just shut up and let me do my job and look for another vehicle."

* * *

> Anny Klaura, U-A DOB: 2580-05-15, CID 09986520678

> ResID: 6.2 [altered by CIDs 99999999999/ResID: 6.5 &
09985240860/ResID: 4.3.2] M1

> U-B: [Room 9, The Eleven Motel, Sister City, CA, US, Earth] LT:
Thursday, 2009-10-29, 7:28 PM PDT

— Thursday, October 29th, 2009, 7:28 PM PDT —

After hearing the scanner, Anny begins pacing, shaking her arms with clenched fists.

"They know..." she says to Lucia, "They know our names... The cleaner did this..."

"'Cleaner—?'"

"We should head for Arizona," Anny says. "Even if we don't end up there, we should probably be on the road."

Anny stops pacing, kneels before Lucia, and says, "Please come with me. I can't guarantee it will be safe." She looks down and says, "I regret Adam has to be involved."

"I'm all years."

"Years? Oh, 'yours' and 'ears.' That's cute, but I hope you're not just saying that—you and I or anyone—" Anny looks for support in Lucia's eyes. "Someone could get arrested or... killed or—"

"Auna, *that's why* I'm going with you. I want to be with you, and I wanna be a part of Adam's life, especially if I know I might not be able to see you. I'd do anything for you, remember?" Seeing that Anny is reassured, Lucia follows it up with, "Besides, how else are you going to get to Doc without *my* car and my *moe-nay?*"

The prepaid cell phone vibrates on the table, rotating a little.

Anny snatches it up in a reflex.

"It's from Doc," she says, briefly waving it at Lucia before reading it aloud herself, "'Ex Nihilo 34.4812-113.3355.'"

"Ex what?"

"It means 'out of nothing,'" Anny says, "Uhh... those are GPS coordinates. I need internet access."

"How could you know that? Wait, I thought you had a smart phone."

"I left mine at the house."

"I've got a smart phone," Luke says. "Let's look it up." After looking up the coordinates, Lucia finds something she never imagined. "Ha! Ha! Nothing!" she announces with a smile. "We're going to Nothing, Arizona."

"What?"

"Yeah, it says here there's a city called Nothing, Arizona, right near those coordinates. You were right—we *are* heading to Arizona."

"Ah, okay, some of this is coming back to me—he's just outside of Nothing... Arizona..." Anny sighs and says, "Well, Doc, that's kind of cheesy."

"Oh, *come on*," Lucia says with a smile. "That's *awesome*. I *totally* wanna check it out."

"It looks like it's about fifty miles away from everywhere else," Anny says. "He did pick the most perfect place to meet."

Anny lights up another joint, taking in the smoke. She blows it away, sighs, and passes it to Lucia.

"Damn, he must have driven fast," Anny says. "It's going to take us forever to get there. We start fresh in the morning."

Lucia takes a hit, exhales the smoke, and says softly, "We'll be okay. We can keep using fake names like we did at the front desk... You have me..." She smiles. "Me and my gun."

* * *

> John Waterman, U-A DOB: 2579-12-03, CID 09985240860

> ResID: 8.2.0 [altered by CID 99999999999/ResID: 6.5] M1

> U-B: [10.5 mi north of Nothing, AZ, US, Earth] LT: Thursday, 2009-10-29, 8:50 PM PDT

— Thursday, October 29th, 2009, 8:50 PM PDT —

As we're driving down the road in our newly commandeered van, I consider: my job's blown up, I've been kidnapped, shot at, and *transported... many times*, my friends are alien to me, a nudist freak posing as a cop is after me, and, amongst other things, my boss is a soldier who can steal vans.

Apparently, he favors white, nondescript vans from the late '80s or early '90s. We had jumped one last time and ditched the Los Eatos van when Armand just so happened to see another white van—the van we're in now. Getting all the verm hardware from one to the other took less time than I thought. With this new-found speed and strength, the equipment was swapped easily. There was at least one *normal* thing that's been good to find out in talking with Armand about everything...

"Do I understand this right," I ask. "Doc's not crazy?"

"He *was*. I cut his arm off to teach him he was wrong to be crazy. You better not go crazy, or I'll chop your arm off, too." He just keeps staring at the road. "And I'll like it."

The road passes us.

"Whatever. You're not so tough, Apronman."

"The Doc's fine now because of what I did. Once we find him, I'll have him run some tests on the bug I pocketed from the Los Eatos van."

"Uh huh. Whatever you say, Apronman. Doesn't it seem even a *little* redundant to have APRON MAN on an apron with an Apronman on it?"

"Don't give me that shit. My APRON MAN apron is awesome."

197

"For sure. Does your *awesome* APRON MAN apron have any weed in it?"

He frowns and tightens his lip in admission to not having any. "Shut up," he says, smirking.

More road passes. The sun is getting lower on the horizon.

Some weed would be nice, but that comes from Luke.

"Hey," I say. "we should pick up Luke and get some weed."

"*Not* our highest priority."

"We can still jump, right? We could pick her up along the way."

"What? No, I already told you, cleaners are game-changers, all right? We're headed to the Doc."

"Daab called Doc, the Doc, too. What's up with that?"

"Because there's only one. Why do I have to explain this? Goddamn you're a dumbass for sure. Where we all come from, the person who's just the worst of society is called the Doc after his life's been doctored to try and fix whatever the fuck he's done."

"Doctored? What'd he do?"

"No one fuckin' knows. His mem's been altered the most out of anyone in Humanity. His past's been erased. His personality's been altered. All his shit's been dusted. That's all I know, and that's all anyone knows, because that's all we know about the Doc after the erasure... Doc is a common enough name, so he adopted it as his own." Armand squints at the road. "But he's still the Doc to me—a fuckin' traitor or who knows whatever the fuck he is. A goddamn freak. People can say what they want about Humanity being superior and all, but the Doc is not one of our best choices."

"Sounds like you don't like him."

No response.

"Where are we from?"

No response.

"What's a mem?"

"Just shut up and let me drive for a while. You wanna ask questions? You go right *ahead* ... all you want ... in your *head*."

I shut up. Today had been crazy for the both of us. Besides, wherever we've been going, it looks like we're about to arrive.

* * *

> Anny Klaura, U-A DOB: 2580-05-15, CID 09986520678

> ResID: 6.2 [altered by CIDs 99999999999/ResID: 6.5 &
  09985240860/ResID: 4.3.2] M1

> U-B: [Room 9, The Eleven Motel, Sister City, CA, US, Earth] LT:
  Friday, 2009-10-30, 1:49 AM PDT

— Friday, October 30th, 2009, 1:49 AM PDT —

Everyone is sound asleep except for Anny. Her eyes are wide open.

"The Doc..." she whispers. "The software is already compromising my cognitive bandwidth. I'm hallucinating a little... I'm confused... Since I forgot Armand's tracker at your place, I keep feeling like I'm forgetting things, or that something's missing." She turns to one side, restlessly, then rolls over.

"Hey," she says to Lucia's shoulder.

"Mugh..." Luke responds, "Mmrrrr..."

"Hey," Anny prods Luke with a finger to her ribs. "Check my things."

"Ah!" Luke sits up from being tickled. "Not cool, Auna," she scolds, "No tickling." Luke's voice turns whiny. "You're taking my sleep away. What do you want?"

"I'm scared," Anny says. "I think I missed something along the way."

Luke doesn't have a good enough reason yet for being awake. "What?"

"My *things*," Anny says. "I have missing *things*."

"Stop freakin' out and go back to sleep," Lucia says with eyes closed. She rolls over, facing the other way. "We'll deal with—"

"This is really, really important," Anny insists, sitting up in bed and rocking. "I need you to check them. I don't trust myself right now, and it doesn't just go away until morning..." She continues to rock. "Or after."

Anny's rocking jostles Lucia's body over and over.

Luke's eyes open, her body tenses, and she rolls back. "Uuuugh. Whaaat... What do you want?" Lucia asks, sitting up.

"I need you to check my things in case I missed something."

Anny's voice is so much like that of a child that Lucia relaxes her body.

"Why can't *you* do that?" Luke asks.

"I'm not feeling very good," Anny says. "Like, in my head." Anny's eyes turn pleading. "I've got something— I can't..." She stops and looks away.

Lucia's shoulders relax. "What? What's going on?"

"Please?" Anny asks, "Please check my things?"

Lucia leans forward and pushes off the bed. She stands and then stretches, then rubs her eyes. She silently walks over to the table where Anny's bag sits, and unzips it all the way. Shoving her hands deep, she pulls out piles of folded clothes, a make-up pouch, a money pouch, a can of mace, a cigarette container, a pill bottle... each movement appearing to Anny as though Luke was rowing a boat.

"Why are you rowing the boat?" Anny asks. "The killer whales can jump from the waaaaaaater."

"*What?*"

Luke drops the pads she was going to pull out of the bag and looks to the pill container she had just pulled out.

"Have you taken something?" Luke asks, opening the bottle.

"Not that I can remember-ber."

Luke turns from the bottle to look at Anny. "You don't *sound* okay," Luke says. She looks back at the bottle. She squints. "This is diazepam," she says.

"That's the sedative I've been giving... to Adam."

"Wait," Lucia looks at Anny shocked in disbelief. "You're serious? You actually gave Adam diazepam for real?"

Anny smiles with one side of her face and nods, trying to look innocent.

"What the fuck, Auna?"

Anny leans forward, shaking her head. "No no—you don't understand. See, I needed to give him that so we could make it to Arizona without—"

"Auna, you gave your son a powerful sedative!"

"Yes, but, we—" Anny stops and reaches for the bottle. "Here, I'll take it."

"No, Auna! This isn't cool. You played like you were joking. What is wrong with you?"

"The Doc told me to. It's part of his treatment. I— I wasn't really joking."

Lucia sighs and shifts her body weight.

"Then why didn't you tell me Doc said so?"

"I just thought..."

"Look," Lucia leans forward. "It's late." She walks away from the table, sits down on the bed next to Anny, and puts her arm around her. "I need sleep. You need sleep."

"I can't sleep," Anny says. "My *things*..."

"Ugh... there's nothing missing from your things."

"But— but, more things garbanzo beans," Anny says, again with pleading eyes, "Can't you tell?"

Lucia looks up and into Anny's eyes, looking back and forth between each to see if there's any recognizable reason she would say what she just said. She looks away, unsatisfied, and lies. "I sure can."

A few seconds pass.

Lucia stiffens her spine, lifts her head, and faces Anny. "*You* are the one that needs to take the diazepam. I'll look after Adam."

Anny's pleading eyes watered in gratitude. "No, I can't take it. I have to smoke more weed all of the times now."

Lucia sighs. "You yelled at me for dealin', now you're smoking like a chimney."

"Please?"

"Well," she says, getting up. "What can I say?" She grabs the cigarette case, and opens it to find the joints they had rolled earlier, picks one out, lights it, and passes it to Anny, who greedily sucks off of it like it's the one source of air in an underwater tank.

Anny palms her own forehead. "Ugh, it's more like going to get the worst more," she says. "The multi-verm software is starting to break me down. We need to get to the Doc as soon as possible."

Luke's eyes are the ones that plead now. "I don't know what's wrong, love, but I *am* going to get you and Adam to Doc. Okay?" She gently grasps Anny's forearm, pulling her hand away from her face. "Hey... We know where we're goin.' We're gonna get there. *Okay?*"

Anny looks up and nods in watery-eyed gratitude, then takes another drag from the joint.

"But right now," Lucia continues, "we gotta do everything we possibly can to avoid the five-o. Okay?"

Anny exhales smoke, nodding like a submissive child.

"To do that, we'll need sleep, okay? The worst thing we can do now is get lost in our own stress. We need to sleep." Lucia lets go of Anny's forearm. "And I need to sleep if I'm going to take care of you." Lucia stands up and walks around the bed. "We can talk about this stuff later when we're on the road." She lies down, rolls the sheet over herself, and shuts her eyes.

Anny reclines further but continues smoking. Her eyes are wide open.

* * *

> John Waterman, U-A DOB: 2579-12-03, CID 09985240860

> ResID: 8.2.0 [altered by CID 99999999999/ResID: 6.5] M1

> U-B: [Nothing, AZ, US, Earth] LT: Thursday, 2009-10-29, 9:00
  PM PDT

— Thursday, October 29th, 2009, 9:00 PM PDT —

Dust. That's been the theme of the last few hours: dust…
everywhere. I can taste it. As for the van we're in, it boasts an
entire collection of dust.

After we ditched the Los Eatos van, we drove south down
highway 40 somewhere in Arizona.

My body's exhausted beyond anything I've ever put myself
through, which makes sense, since I'd never been shot at or
stolen a car before… at least, not that I can remember… I've
definitely never jumped from here to wherever it was night
and back again. The way this day's been—

THAT WAS THE MARATHI LANGUAGE, REMEMBER? I READ
THE SIGN FOR YOU. WE WERE IN MUMBAI.

Sigh… *This day will never end.*

A proximity sensor lights up on a piece of tech Armand
stuck to the dash with some double-sided tape. We come up on
a pizza place out in the middle of nowhere and start slowing. A
road sign indicates we're entering Nothing, Arizona, which
consists of this single pizza place and an abandoned gas station
with a side road curving to the left.

Armand slows enough to make the left, following the
proximity sensor readings on the dash. We drive behind
the buildings and take a road toward some rocky hills
about a hundred yards behind the pizza place. We keep
going toward the Arizona rock, and we don't stop as we
plunge right into the hill.

There is no crash.

We are now driving downhill in a tunnel.

THERE IS A HOLOGRAPHIC FACADE OVER THE ENTRANCE TO
THIS PLACE.

White halogen lights in the ceiling cast patterns of light and shadow overhead, leisurely sweeping the van front to back as we coast along.

It takes a few minutes curving through the earth, but we finally come into a clearing, slowing down in a large dome-like cavern with bright halogen lights dangling from the ceiling. Armand comes to a stop and parks the van in front of a four-foot-high raised floor with three doors ahead, like a docking bay for semi-trucks, only with smaller, residential-sized doors with metallic frames.

"Hey," Armand says, "grab me one of those protein bars."

I pull one from my pocket and offer it to him.

"Damn, it's good to be back in familiar surroundings," Armand says, grabbing the protein bar and smiling at me, then he winces when he sees someone wearing a metallic, full-body suit, complete with helmet, walking out from the middle door.

Ignoring the suit, Armand jumps out of the van and violently begins detaching verm-based equipment from the cab of the van. Damn he's quick.

"The spirit is willing, but the body is weak," the suit says to me beyond my passenger-side window. The voice is dry, metallic even.

Armand stops and responds with, "Shut up. Just remove the useful parts and erase the rest." Armand mutters under his breath, barely audible, "Fucking Chi Gung model."

The suit responds, "If I were to erase myself, would I cease to be in the past?"

"Goddamn it, Carry, we don't have time for this shit. Just do it." Armand looks at me, and says, "The Chi Gung models have personalities from history. Any of this look familiar?"

I'm taken aback by Armand's dislike for Carry. "...not really."

"*Fine*. This one goes by Carry. Carry, John. John, Carry."

Carry nods at me.

Armand continues as he gets out of the van, "Now you've met for the second time, for the first time... ugh..." I watch a confused and frustrated Armand from my seat as he barely lifts his knee to effortlessly jump up to the raised floor. He moved so quickly, it was like I didn't see it.

YOU CAN DO THE SAME AND MORE, SOON.

Carry turns to me, and says in his really dry voice, "To remember is the most powerful—"

"Shut up, Carry, and get to work. Activate McCleese, and tell him to meet me out here." Armand looks at me and says, "I'm gonna check on what the Doc's doin' and give him the bug I found from Daab's people and then issue my report on his threat to the base. You'll have it ready for you in the Holoroom after you're—"

Carry tears away the van's hood while it is still latched shut. The shrieking metal sound ricochets off the walls and overpowers Armand.

"Hey! *Hey!*" Armand yells at Carry, "I'm talkin' here!"

Doc's voice comes out from within the central door, "Ah! Glad you guys made it. What the hell happened? Where's the Los Eatos van?"

Armand gives up and frowns at Doc for interrupting as I get out of the van.

"You'll have my report soon enough." Armand steps past Doc in the doorway.

"Good. Good." Doc walks out and waves to me apologetically. "Hey there."

"Hey, Doc."

Doc picks up on the reservation in my voice, and responds, "Again, I'm really sorry for everything, which will be explained, I promise. I just need to have—Oh, good, McCleese, you're up," he says as another identical metallic suit steps by. "Good," Doc continues. "Hey, McCleese, please give John a tour of the base, and give him some weed; he's been without it for quite some time, and under duress." McCleese nods at Doc, drops his feet down to my level with a metallic clank, and takes a couple steps toward me, when Doc says, "Uh, John, I'm sorry to do this, I've got to get back to work in preparation for tomorrow.

McCleese'll take care of you from here. Please let me know when you're ready to get started—we can't do this without you."

Before I can respond, Doc literally disappears.

I'm not sure what to expect. I feel worn out. I watch baffled as McCleese briskly walks over. He seems distracted.

"Right. How much do you know, thus far?" He has a British accent, a *very* British accent.

HIS DIALECT IS BASED ON EDUCATED MIDDLE-CLASS MALES OF SOUTHERN ENGLAND FROM THE 20TH CENTURY.

How is that relevant?

"Uhh... huh?"

"I understand you're experiencing a corrupted ResID activation," McCleese says. "We measure the corruption based upon how much you don't remember, and your lack of reaction time. How much do you and your verm know about the base? Did you recognize you are in a garage?"

My verm isn't talking. It seems disloyal.

"We're near Nothing, Arizona and uhhh... underground?" I didn't know what else to say.

McCleese nods. "Right! Gzzt!" He's stopped moving.

Carry keeps on working.

Apparently, McCleese is fine.

"Gzzzt! The Doc you just saw is a hologram, you see," McCleese says and turns with a bounce, waving his hand at the base around us. "This entire outpost's main functions stem from a holographic technology that is used to engage harmoniously with verms. Your connections aren't fully activated. In the meantime, let me show you around."

McCleese walks me around the garage and tells me it's the first of the few rooms that make up this Chronos Outpost, as he calls it. As I follow him around, I can't help thinking he hasn't given me any weed like Doc told him to.

I kinda miss hearing that voice in my head.

So, you're more at home here than anywhere else?

Silence.

Sigh…

A large hole opens in the floor with the loud whirring sounds of various huge hydraulic devices.

"Please step back now," McCleese tells me. "Carry's finishing up."

The hole's shutters open further, spreading in a circle that expands all the way from one side of the tunnel's opening to the other. Carry places a variety of random pieces of equipment from the van on the ground.

"It is not the vessel that is useful," he says to me, bending at the knees. With one hand, he leans in and pushes the van hard enough that, even in park, its tires screech to the edge of the hole in the center of the room and the van tips in, falling deep into the earth. "For it is the emptiness within that is useful," Carry says, as he turns to McCleese. The hole closes, and the ground rumbles and grinds with a deeper mechanical sound, rivaling the shutters in volume.

"What *is* that?" I ask over the noise.

"You call it our garbage disposal. Zssssst…" McCleese shouts. "It's part of the machine that gouged this place out of the ground. This part is mostly a sewage system now. The more active part of it still resides in our Holoroom. Any of this familiar yet? Zzzt!"

"No!" I shout over the churning of metal.

"I'm going to turn in now," Carry shouts over the grinding, "but before I do, here…" He reaches up and opens a shoulder blade panel in McCleese's suit.

"Ouzzzzzrrrrrrrrrrrrrrrrrt… t… t… t…" McCleese's suit says, as he twitches slightly, "ch—! Ah, much better. Thank you."

Carry closes McCleese's panel.

"That really did smart," McCleese says. "Thank you, Carry."

The grinding in the ground ceases.

Carry nods at McCleese. "As iron sharpens iron," Carry says, "so one man sharpens another."

"Come now, Carry," McCleese says, "you know that doesn't apply to us."

"Semantics."

"What just happened?" I ask them both.

"I was running low on power, and it was affecting my voice. Carry just gave me a boost," McCleese says to me. He looks at Carry and says, "Enjoy your meditation."

"Thank you," Carry says, bowing. He quietly leaves the garage through the door on our right.

"Right. Here we go now," McCleese says, beckoning with his metallic hands.

"What is the suit for?" I ask.

"Suit?" McCleese asks. "I, my friend, am an Ally Brand robot, the Chi Gung model—the best of the best, I say."

Great, Doc left me with a liar. "Oh, sure." I stand there in disbelief, still exhausted.

"Now, which door would you like to be shown first: door number 1, door number 2, or door number 3?" McCleese asks, pointing to each of the doors from left to right.

When in Rome, do as the Romans, I think to myself.

"Door number 3," I say. "Let's see where Carry went. You're really a robot?"

"Oh, don't be so naïve. Come along now." He leans forward and walks toward the door on the right.

I follow. We enter, and the room's lights go from dim to well-lit. Everything's an off-white color in here. Wherever I look, the objects come into focus with exceptional detail, but it's disorienting in the moment, and I don't know what I'm looking at.

THIS IS AN EFFECT OF THE BASE'S INTERACTION WITH ME.

Glad you finally decided to join us. I could have used your help when McCleese asked about you earlier.

No response.

McCleese patiently stands, waiting for me to do or say something, but I'm so tired, I kind of just want to sleep.

"Right," he says. "Here we have the sick bay, where the medical equipment, such as medical stations and medstands and beds et cetera, are."

Holograms start popping up out from various surfaces in my line of sight; some appear to be useful, others... I couldn't possibly fathom what they're for. It smells like a hospital.

As I continue looking around, my focus becomes even sharper. At knee height, I can easily count the threads of a cot. My surroundings slow down as McCleese shifts his weight to take a step. McCleese, in mid-stride, slows to the point of no longer moving.

I look around. Everything appears to have stopped moving.

I'M RECEIVING A LOT OF INFORMATION, SO I AM IN THE MIDST OF PROCESSING IT. JUST A HEADS UP, YOU WILL SEE DIFFERENT PARTS OF THE BASE REACT TO YOU IN DIFFERENT WAYS.

Good to know. Ugh, it's going to take a while to get used to this.

NO—IT'S GOING TO TAKE A WHILE TO GET BACK TO NORMAL.

Damn, this is tiring.

My surroundings return to a normal pace as McCleese's foot touches the ground.

"Ah," he says, "I see you've just had a chat with your verm."

Whoa. "Uh, yeah," I say. "How can you tell?"

"Ah, good good. You and your team programmed me, you see, to study the effects of verm technology on things, including people. For example, speed and pitch—the vibrations and movements your body makes, like heartbeat and breath, raise to a higher frequency when you speed up. I'm able to sense these things. I'll be here as you relearn your way through verm interaction, which you'll need to complete soon, or we won't have the advantage over Daab, and we'll likely all die."

"Wait, what?"

"Oh, I'm sure you'll do just fine. No pressure or anything." McCleese nods and continues. "Most everywhere here, we have a multitude of interactive holograms. We don't have the technology for making light into solid objects, like they have on some science fiction television programs," he says, shaking his head. "But we do almost exclusively use holographic technology to interact with electronic components. Some of these components are so small they cannot be seen with the naked eye. All this is available via the Chronos Outpost's resources. Some are quite wondrous, while others in fact are a complete waste of time." He moves between the two cots near the center of the room and waves his hand through an array of colors floating in a sphere on what looks like a vanity on the other side of the room.

"Ha ha! You see?" His form changes. He now has a full set of knight's armor, chain mail completely covering his head, and a sword. He announces, "Through the miracle of this base's holographic technology, I..." He unsheathes and raises his sword. "am Sir Lancelot!"

"Whoa. You look so much better as Sir Lancelot than as your suit thing."

"I see," he says in a disappointed tone. He waves his hand in the multi-colored sphere, and his body changes back to the suit, leaving his head as Sir Lancelot, complete with chain mail covering everything but his face. "We've got a few more rooms to go. Let's head through the hall with the robot cubby to the command center, which is 'Door number 2' from the garage."

"'Robot cubby?'"

"It's an Ally charging station. Sometimes we'll unmount from our suits while docked here to trade memory for stability with the virtual reality system."

I don't know what that means, but we step from the sick bay into the closet-sized hallway, and I recognize a familiar face. "Carry."

"Shh! He's *meditating*," McCleese whispers.

I hunch over as we continue walking to the next door.

"Oh!" I whisper, still walking slowly, as if somehow acting smaller would make me quieter. "But, isn't Carry a robot, too?" I ask as we enter the command center.

"Why certainly," McCleese whispers back, now near the center of the command center.

"How... Why is he... but, he's *meditating?*" I ask. "Robots don't meditate..."

"You really should keep up. He calls it meditating," McCleese says, shaking his head disapprovingly, but then he leans in to confide, "but really he's just recharging."

"I heard that," Carry scolds from the other room, still attached to his station.

"Right. Moving on. This," McCleese says as he waves his hands theatrically, sweeping the room. "*This* is the command center. From here, we can do many, many things."

I look about at Doc and the room. I didn't notice this before, but he is moving incredibly fast. His arms, hands, and fingers blur over multi-leveled holographic keyboards and levers floating in mid-air.

IT APPEARS HIS VERM IS FULLY ACTIVE AND FULLY ENGAGED WITH HIM AT THE MOMENT.

"What the hell?" I ask. "Is he real?"

There's a subtle breeze humming from his movements.

"Oh yes, absolutely real. We need to be prepared by Saturday at 1 pm..." McCleese explains. A large panel of holograms opens in front of McCleese, showing me a blue map of the route from where we ditched Daab—an area labeled Finger Lakes, in the state of New York—to here, Nothing, Arizona. "... because that's the likeliest time he'll arrive," McCleese continues, "considering the mileage he'll need to cover."

Various holographic displays flash before Doc's face, briefly showing local media coverage.

"He's performing anonymity protocols," McCleese tells me. "The process of finding and erasing all records of our existence so we stay hidden in this universe's timeline. See that there? He just set the APB on everyone as his highest priority."

"APB?" I ask. "What's that?"

"'All points bulletin,'" McCleese explains. "It's a 'calling all cars' term for law enforcement. Right now, all the law enforcement in the state of California is looking for you, and the Doc's creating a response to this, but the tour doesn't end here," McCleese says, as he motions me out of the room. "This," he tells me, "is our storage closet."

A door to my left leads to the garage. Ahead is McCleese's next room.

So, Door number 1 is a storeroom, Door number 2 is the command center, and Door number 3 is the sick bay.

I take a quick peek and look back, just to keep my bearings. "This," McCleese tells me, "is where we store all our medical supplies, backup tech, and car parts, as well as many other things, like clothing, and, most importantly for you organic folk, the bathroom." He walks into the room, and I follow.

"Is there any food in there?"

"Yes. I recommend the chocolate the Doc brought in recently," McCleese says. "Your previous ResID said you were very fond of it."

"Huh?"

McCleese keeps going as if I didn't say anything, "Generally, if there's something we need, it's in this storage room here," he says, grabbing something from one of the shelves, "such as your weed."

He hands me a metal pipe loaded with weed, then walks into the command center. I pocket a chocolate bar, take a hit from the pipe, and follow McCleese.

Armand walks in from a door to our left, opposite to Door number 2—the only room we haven't explored.

"My report's ready," Armand says to Doc as I follow McCleese further from the garage through the unexplored door. "You get done looking at that bug?"

"Yes," Doc says over his humming blur. "It simply underscores Daab's desire to find us."

I follow McCleese into a room a barn could fit in. The sound of electricity sparking fills the room, and I faintly smell ozone. There is a *thing* in here I'm unsure anyone, let alone me, could understand. The door slams behind us, startling me. I feel as though there's some kind of sensory input I'm receiving that my body doesn't know how to interpret.

What is before me looks like a large, black, and shiny cube-shaped gyroscope-looking thing. It seems to be about a meter in size, but I'm unsure—it's confusing to look at. It seems to breathe or pulse, but it also moves like a gyroscope, or like an automated Rubik's Cube, but light bends around it, like a mirage. I feel disoriented, or like I'm hallucinating, because as this thing moves, tracers from its surfaces trail behind every movement. It's as if its surfaces move in more than one direction at once, and yet, it seems to be stuck in mid-air in the center of the room. There's like a... a smearing of all of its surfaces throughout its every movement. It seems to collapse and replenish its shape constantly, like a moving three-dimensional optical illusion. Long bright purple sparks of static electricity jump across the various arching surfaces as it moves, like some other-worldly Jacob's ladder. The sparks are loud and random, but continuous.

It's exhausting.

Copper mirrors make up the surfaces of most everything else, as if to focus the randomly generated light back upon itself, showcasing this *thing* to whoever enters the room. A constant haunted wailing rises in my head, making me feel even more light-headed. I'm dizzy. Light dims—I think I'm blacking out... "McCleese..."

"This is the Holoroom. It contains the Model you see here," he says.

I pass out.

* * *

> Anny Klaura, U-A DOB: 2580-05-15, CID 09986520678

> ResID: 6.2 [altered by CIDs 99999999999/ResID: 6.5 & 09985240860/ResID: 4.3.2] M1 & M2

> U-B: [Room 9, The Eleven Motel, Sister City, CA, US, Earth] LT: Friday, 2009-10-30, 3:00 AM PDT

— Friday, October 30th, 2009, 3:00 AM PDT —

Anny is still smoking.

Lucia tosses and turns throughout the early morning, every once in a while coughing from the ambient smoke.

"I have to go to the bathroom," Adam says, slowly approaching his mother. "Why is it so smoky in here?" he asks.

"It's my medicine, son," she says.

"But, doesn't that mean I'm taking it too?" he asks.

"You're fine," she says quietly. "Go use the bathroom and go back to sleep. Here, gimme a hug."

They embrace, and Adam runs clumsily into the bathroom.

Anny's eyes have dulled. They squint when Adam turns the light on. She sighs. "Shut the door."

Adam starts peeing.

"Damn it. SHUT THE DOOR!"

The peeing stops.

Lucia stirs.

The door shuts. The peeing starts again.

"Why..." Lucia asks with eyes closed, "are you yelling?"

"He wouldn't fucking shut the door."

"Auna... what's going on?" Lucia asks with her eyes closed. "Why are you so short tempered?"

"I— I can't tell you that right now, I'm not equipped for that now," she says in monotone, and then in normal tones, "Please, please get Adam to Doc."

The toilet flushes.

Lucia's eyes open to see smoke everywhere.

"What? Yeah," Lucia says, "that's what we're doing."

217

"Promise me," Anny pleads, "no matter what, get Adam to Doc."

The bathroom sink turns on.

"Adam to Doc..." Anny says again, with begging bloodshot eyes.

"Huh?"

The sink turns off, and Adam quietly opens the door to tiptoe back to the nest of blankets he'd made on the floor for sleeping.

"Adam to Doc..." Anny says again, relaxing and leaning back, sleepy-like.

"Honey," Lucia says in the stupor of sleep, "what's... what's wrong?"

"Please... Adam to Doc," Anny says as her eyes close slowly.

"Hey... Hey... I promise—I'll get us to Doc, okay?" Lucia whispers.

"Adam to Doc..." Anny whispers back with her eyes still closed. "I'm okay... I'm okay now... mmmm sleepy... sleepy time now..."

Anny takes a deep breath, smiles, and rests in the temporary comfort of her intoxication.

Lucia opens her eyes just wide enough to look at both Anny and Adam, sighs in compassion and exhaustion, and falls back to sleep.

* * *

> John Waterman, U-A DOB: 2579-12-03, CID 09985240860

> ResID: 9.3.1 [altered by CID 09985240860/ResID: 8.2.0] M1, M2, & M3

> U-B: [Chronos Outpost.OID:00000000001, Earth: 34.4812, -113.3355] LT: Friday, 2009-10-30, 5:51 PM PDT

— Friday, October 30th, 2009, 5:51 PM PDT —

I wake up to the scent of the sick bay.

"We don't have time for this shit," Armand says as I open my eyes. He turns from Doc's blur of movement on a video and looks over a medical station at me. "You done bein' passed out?" he asks.

"What?" I ask, just barely getting my eyes to focus.

"Damn it, John, now is not the time to be fuckin' around," he says in my face. "You cool? We got shit to do." He marches from the sick bay into the garage out of sight.

"Well," McCleese says, as he leans over me, "*That* was fun."

"Sarcasm?" I ask, flabbergasted.

"Good, isn't it?"

"Not right now." I sit up. "What the fuck's going on?"

McCleese's holographic lips open slower than usual to say a word. Sounds and vibrations from various angles throughout the room also lower in frequency, plummeting through their octaves. All the other holograms in the room have already slowed way down and developed a slight red tint. I feel like my world is on pause. Even Doc's blur on the video is frozen.

How does this happen?

I'VE RESTORED YOUR SECONDARY MEMORY AND HAVE BEGUN WORK ON ESTABLISHING YOUR TERTIARY MEMORY. THIS TAKES PRIORITY. EVERYTHING I REVEAL NOW IS IN YOUR TERTIARY MEMORY. HOWEVER, THIS WILL BE CHALLENGING. I WILL JUMP-ROUTE THE MEMORY AND SUBCONSCIOUS FUNCTIONS OF YOUR CURRENT RESID WITH THE ABILITIES AND MEMORIES YOU HAVE AS AN AGENT OF CHRONOS, WHICH ARE HIDDEN NOW, BUT ARE NEEDED TO RUN THIS BASE. THIS HAPPENS NOW.

219

I'm... supposed to... run... this place?

OBVIOUSLY. I WILL ALSO BE WORKING ON STREAMLINING YOUR BODY'S SIMPLER MECHANICAL FUNCTIONS, SUCH AS HOW IT STRUCTURALLY DEALS WITH IMPACT AND PRESSURE. THIS IS THE FIRST STAGE OF OUR REAWAKENING...

I look around me as I breathe air into my lungs—everything feels pressurized and thick.

Doc's frozen blur remains unmoved.

McCleese's lips remain open.

YOUR DISORIENTATION WILL BE TEMPORARY, BUT DIFFICULT. YOUR REAWAKENING WILL BE COMPLETE WHEN YOUR TERTIARY MEMORY IS FULLY ACTIVE. THE GATEWAY TO YOUR TERTIARY MEMORY IS NOW REVEALED. LOOK!

I find myself awakening face-down at the bottom of a cliff in a dream-like state.

I hear wind. When it arrives, it blows right through me.

My hands are dirty.

I find an indentation in the ground beneath me... in the shape of my body.

I lift my head further and look up at a familiar cliff and then away...

I recognize it.

It is the maze from my dream.

* * *

> Anny Klaura, U-A DOB: 2580-05-15, CID 09986520678

> ResID: 6.2 [altered by CIDs 99999999999/ResID: 6.5 &
  09985240860/ResID: 4.3.2] M1 & M2

> U-B: [Shasta County, CA, US, Earth] LT: Friday, 2009-10-30,
  6:42 AM PDT

— Friday, October 30th, 2009, 6:42 AM PDT —

In the passenger seat of her little car, keeping pace with other cars on the road, Lucia wakes up to the sound of a siren passing by on the other side. She does what she can to stretch and shake off the stiffness she feels, confined to her safety belt.

"I didn't sleep very well last night," she says, frowning, "what with you smoking and mumbling to yourself all night... something about Adam saving the world, or something."

She picks up the scanner and plugs in headphones to listen in on what's going on, trying to give herself something to do.

"Can we stop somewhere soon? I'm getting a bit stir crazy, and from what my phone says, we're gonna have about a two-and-a-half-hour's drive once we get onto I-5. I'd kinda like to stretch out a little."

"I'm stoned," Anny confides while driving, bobbing her head as if listening to music only she can hear.

"Yes... of course you are," Lucia says, watching her. "So... you okay? You might need to cut down on the smoking—you're kinda leaving Adam without a mom, you know?"

"I don't have a mom. Is that what Adam told you?" Anny asks.

The scanner screeches white noise, then grumbles about a domestic dispute.

"No... it's just... you're making me feel lonely," Lucia says. "I can't smoke that much."

"Come onnnnnn, you can *totally* smoke this much," Anny says. "Look, see?" she asks and takes another drag from her joint.

221

"But the cops—" Lucia says. "We should be careful when driving."

"You think we'll see police?" Adam asks, waking up. "Hey, how'd we get in the car?"

"Your mother drugged you," Lucia says.

"Shut up," Anny says.

"Drugged me?" Adam asks. "What does that mean?"

"I just gave you something to help you stay asleep," Anny says, frowning at Luke. "You need your sleep."

"What's for breakfast?" Adam asks.

"Always hungry," Anny complains.

"He's growing," Lucia scolds, "you should know that."

"I'm always hungry, too," Anny says, trying to lighten the mood.

"You just have the munchies."

Flashing red and blue lights in the rear-view mirror reveal police about three hundred meters behind them.

"Uh oh, we got cops," Anny says, stiff with anxiety.

"What's for breakfast?" Adam asks again.

Anny starts to look frantic. "Los Eatos," she says.

"Los Eatos?" Luke asks. "That's right, we never did get breakfast this morning."

Anny points at the rear-view mirror and widens her eyes with an insisting nod.

Lucia looks behind them and sees the lights but continues her thought for Adam's sake. "We're not eating at Los Eatos. We'll have to eat at some other place."

After about a half a minute, the police car is about fifty meters behind them. Anny becomes restless. In desperation, she exits the highway to get away from the police, pulling into a Gas & Grab. To their surprise and relief, the cop car passes them by.

They all get out of the car. Anny goes inside to use the restroom. Lucia stretches and Adam lingers near the Gas & Grab store entrance, watching for his mom to return. When she does, Lucia and Adam go inside to shop to save time while Anny fills the tank.

As they stand in line with energy drinks, jerky, chips, sodas, bottled water, and some protein bars, one of the locals runs in asking to use the restroom, "because I gotta *dookie*," he says.

They get their things and get into the car.

As Anny re-enters the highway, Adam asks, "What's dookie mean?"

"It's slang for poop, son," Anny says, "like when you need to go use the restroom."

Lucia puts her hand to her face. "Ugh."

Adam giggles. "What's slang?"

"It's like fake words," Lucia says.

"How can words be fake?"

"Ugh," Lucia says from behind her hand, her tiredness and confinement finally catching up to her.

Anny tries her best to be dignified. "Dookie is just another word for poop."

"Dookie... poop..." Adam says, giggling in between each word... "dookie... poop..."

"Stop that," Lucia says. "That's annoying."

Adam replies in a whiny tone. "But I think 'poop' is easier to say."

"Shut up for a bit," Lucia says.

"Lucia..." Anny scolds.

"Lucia..." Adam copies.

"Well," Luke turns to explain, "He's just saying dookie and poop."

"Dookie and poop," Adam copies, but barely able to keep himself from the giggling overtaking him.

"Stop saying that!" Lucia yells.

Anny crouches down with wide eyes. "Hey!" she yells back. "Guard your own dogs."

Lucia freezes. Then, in her confusion, she repeats, "Guard your own dogs?"

"You heard me!"

Lucia, further confused, shakes her head and asks, "What are you saying?"

"Guard your own *watch* dogs," Anny insists with widened eyes.

Lucia shakes her head again, trying to clear out her confusion. "What? Look, there're *cops* on the look-out for us. We've got to keep listening to the scanner for any signs they might be onto us. Stop the car. Let's take another break. You listen to the scanner while I drive."

Anny pulls the car over. They swap seats and get back on the road.

Minutes pass.

"I've got five tunes you're gonna *like*," Anny says, nodding and smiling as if to convince Lucia of her confidence, but it is failing. Anny's wearing ear buds connected to the scanner, but she appears sleepy.

"Dooookieeeee!" Adam yells, and giggles loudly. Anny ignores it in her sleepiness.

"Shut up!" Lucia yells.

Anny's eyes close slowly, and her body relaxes.

"Seriously, Auna," Lucia says, "you've *got* to stop being weird. We've got a long way to go to get to Arizona. We haven't even gone through So-Cal yet. You look exhausted again. Whatever Doc's planning on doing, I hope he can cure you, too. Here," Luke pulls the ear buds from Anny's ears, "why don't you try going back to sleep, eh?"

"I am invincible," Anny whispers with closed eyes.

Lucia sighs. "I know you are, love," she says. She looks at the road putting one of the ear buds in her own ear and says quietly, "This has got to be the longest road trip in the history of the world."

* * *

> John Waterman, U-A DOB: 2579-12-03, CID 09985240860

> ResID: 9.3.1 [altered by CID 09985240860/ResID: 8.2.0] M1,
M2, & M3

> U-B: [Chronos Outpost.OID:00000000001, Earth: 34.4812,
-113.3355] LT: Friday, 2009-10-30, 5:51 PM PDT

— Friday, October 30th, 2009, 5:51 PM PDT —

A voice whispers, "This is our Dream now... Do you know what that means? You know what you have to do?"

I look to see who's talking to me. The voice is my verm. It looks like a ghostly orange version of me. Though I remember falling from the cliff and leaving the indentation, there is no pain. I stand, listening for the wind. A gust rushes through the laurel bushes that make up the walls of the maze.

"Yeah," I say. "Follow the wind."

I set out to reach the end of the maze. I run, using the wind as a reference point.

The maze is vast and enveloping—I may never get out.

"Repossess your soul," my verm says.

"Yeah, I get it—at the maze's end."

"I will help you," it says. "I can guide you through this state of Dream where I'll be connecting your memories so their reawakening can be complete."

I'm exhausted and enlivened simultaneously.

The verm disappears, and my surroundings become intimately familiar.

The wind blows through the laurel bushes, leaning them, brushing across their leaves the way a bow brushes a song from violin strings.

The more I run through the maze, the stronger my sense of direction builds, and the heavier the pressure of the wind grows. I follow, twisting through various curves, until the inkling of a thought begins to form. The cliff... the leaves... the maze... the wind... my ResID... in Dream... these things...

they're all me... I'm fearfully returning to an unknown normal—I am this wind, but I must be the cliff and the laurel, too. I stare down a long corridor of laurel.

For the last three years, I've lost myself in my own intoxication, apathy, and oblivion—I have become my own labyrinth.

Still, I keep thinking and wondering that this is me... in Dream... I am my surroundings. Clouds thicken above me and darken. The temperature rises, and from above in the darkness, three glowing lights begin to pierce through. The wind blows stronger, strong enough to push the laurel over and over. The lights feel strangely familiar and warm.

My verm reappears in my shape, orange and opaque. "You know these lights... they're all waiting for you to reawaken your previous ResID's memories. They're depending on you. For the sake of your world, you need to remember, for to remember is to create." He disappears.

The wind grows stronger, pushing me, breaking leaves off laurel, ripping branches free to scratch me. My surroundings are no longer familiar. A fear of the unknown grows within me.

The glowing lights in the blackened sky shine brighter. I kneel to steady myself and look to the sky. One of the lights has turned red. The other two have turned yellow and blue. Their presence is terrifying. They threaten to burst down upon me and displace me.

Leaves and branches fly everywhere.

Panicking, I leap and aimlessly run in fear, trying to keep my balance in the harsh wind.

Crack! Crack! Crack!

Memories of Armand, Anny, and Doc, in the form of lightning, burst forth from the red, yellow, and blue lights in the sky and strike me. As I run, my momentum fading, each strike shows me a different line of fate, and each fate spreads out into a different body of memories... memories from before three years ago.

"These embody some of your secondary and tertiary memories," my verm says, "reflected from previous ResIDs."

I collapse. I've just been struck by lightning... three times.

As I get up, I feel different. My ResID... or memories... something feels off. The bodies of memory lay before me. They all look just like me in their respective colors—red, yellow, and blue versions of myself. The red one feels threatening; the blue one feels manic and clinical, calculating; and the yellow one feels eager. They reflect my memories of Armand, Doc, and Anny, respectively. Leaves from the laurel tumble across their bodies from gusts of the wind. Though I recognize them all as my ResID's former secondary and tertiary memories, I am overwhelmed by a fear that they are different than me. Their existence terrifies me, even though they do not move. The wind pushes hard and the clouds roll in thick.

The doppelgangers get up.

In blind panic, I flee faster than ever. A storm is up ahead, but I still run toward it. As fearful as I am of losing myself in this maze, these inquisitors of my own identity chase me down like cops after a criminal, so I keep running. This wind is the one thing keeping hope alive against the threat of my surroundings.

Here they come...

Like holograms passing through each other, they run into me, matching my pace and my every movement, with every strike of my feet upon the ground. I'm disappointed in myself—I'm disheartened. I can't outrun them... but I still run... As each one merges through me, I wince from how deeply they resonate with me.

"In order to become better than you are, you must become something you're not," my verm says. "No matter. You're never who you think you are anyway."

And I was running so fast.

* * *

> Anny Klaura, U-A DOB: 2580-05-15, CID 09986520678

> ResID: 6.2 [altered by CIDs 99999999999/ResID: 6.5 & 09985240860/ResID: 4.3.2] M2

> U-B: [Sacramento County, CA, US, Earth] LT: Friday, 2009-10-30, 9:31 AM PDT

— Friday, October 30th, 2009, 9:31 AM PDT —

After the drive through the curve of I-80 BUS E, on CA-99, a California State Trooper matches speed behind Lucia's car. She's driving as inconspicuously as she possibly can.

After about five minutes of this, a Sacramento County Police car starts trailing the State Trooper.

Lucia's getting tense.

Adam's eyes are trying to join his mother's in a nap.

Then Anny screams with her eyes clenched shut.

Adam jumps.

"Ah! What the fuck!" Lucia yells at the same time.

Adam's little chest lifts from being clenched so tightly. He presses down, belting out the cry of an infant.

Lucia swerves.

Anny screams again before Adam's cry had reached its end. Her eyes are still shut.

The Trooper's lights come on.

"Goddammit! What the fuck is wrong?"

Anny's scream turns into wailing, eerily matching her son's in tone and volume. Her eyes remain shut.

The Trooper's siren comes on.

Lucia slows down.

Adam belts out more air as Lucia pulls over.

"I know you're tired, and you've just been startled, but I need you to stay in your seat," she says. As the car comes to a stop, she turns around in her seat to check him over, "Okay buddy?"

Adam continues to cry.

229

Anny is fast asleep.

"It's okay, honey. It's gonna be okay," Lucia says, frowning, trying to console Adam while she looks the car over, shooting glances around to see if any weed is out in the open. She puts her gun in the glove box out of sight and pulls out her insurance papers.

As they sit waiting, Anny slowly wags her head back and forth and begins repeating in her sleep, "Get Adam to Doc. Get Adam to Doc…"

Lucia sees that the County Police vehicle is parked at an angle with all of its lights on, blocking her view of any traffic coming from behind them.

Adam is still crying, mumbling, "Mommy," and reaching for her.

"Mommy's gonna be okay, buddy, but I need you to stay in your seat," Lucia insists.

The female Trooper opens her door but stops and kneels behind it. Her black, spiked mullet top stands like a small army above fierce, piercing eyes.

The male County police officer, with his comb-over blowing freely in the wind, clumsily jumps, rolls over the hood of his vehicle, and somersaults over his own hefty gut out of sight behind the Trooper's vehicle.

Adam is still crying in confusion.

"Lucia Gage, slowly get out of the vehicle with your hands and arms out," the wide-eyed County police officer yells behind the Trooper.

Lucia sighs. "Adam, buddy, I need you to calm down, okay? Stay in your seat. Mommy's trying to sleep."

He keeps wailing but stays in his seat.

"Hey, I'm going to go talk to the police," Lucia says softly.

He wails again.

"Don't be afraid. We're going to be okay."

He keeps wailing.

Lucia opens her door slowly, showing her hands above the door as she pushes it open with her forearms, and staggers into a standing position.

The County police officer, seeing how tall and well-built Luke is, is getting restless.

"Get out of the vehicle!" the Trooper vehicle's PA blasts out at the remaining anonymous heads.

"She can't hear you—she's been sedated!" Lucia says.

The officer comes closer.

"Get back!" the Trooper yells at the officer. "They are armed and may be extremely dangerous!"

"Slowly place your hands on the top of your vehicle," the Trooper's PA blasts.

Lucia complies.

Adam continues to wail.

"Now's our chance!" the County police officer insists.

"Go," the Trooper says.

The officer cautiously approaches the Civic, gun trained on Anny's head.

"Don't kill my mommy!" Adam begs through his tears.

"Hey, there's a kid in there!" Lucia scolds, but the officer continues methodically strafing the passenger side of the vehicle, gun trained on Anny.

She remains motionless.

The officer nods in the Trooper's direction.

The State Trooper reveals herself and comes up behind Luke with gun steady and handcuffs ready.

Adam is still crying. "Don't kill my mommy!"

"Lucia Gage... you..."—the Trooper twists Lucia's right wrist behind her to cuff it—"have the right to remain silent." She grabs Lucia's left wrist and cuffs it as well.

Static from the Trooper's and the officer's radios interrupts the Miranda. "Attention all units, this is an APB regarding the BOLO for POIs Lucia Gage, Auna Klaura, and Adam Klaura..."

The County police officer lowers his gun.

Lucia raises her head to gauge their reactions to Doc's voice coming from their radio.

"Stand fast—hold your position," the Trooper commands the officer, who instantly raises his gun back up, trained on Anny's head.

The Trooper puts an ear bud into her ear, and speaks into her mouthpiece, "This is unit 2501. We have suspects who appear to be the POIs..."

Adam is moaning, too exhausted to vocalize.

The officer's gun stays trained on Anny.

They stand there... waiting...

"Uh huh," the Trooper says into her mouthpiece. "Could you just tell it to me in English? Your jurisdiction's 10-codes aren't the same as mine."

They wait. Adam doesn't stop.

"Okay, roger that," the Trooper says.

The Trooper pushes Lucia off-balance, leaning her on her car, then removes the cuffs. "You're free to go."

"Hey, wait a minute," the County police officer yells. "We just got here."

"They called it off," the Trooper says. "Dispatch said there was a mistake at one of the county precincts... You can put your gun down now."

Adam moans.

The officer stands in disbelief.

"They're free to go!" the Trooper insists with a world-weary grimace.

"Fuck!" the officer says, holstering his gun forcefully.

"Sorry about this, ma'am," the Trooper says, as she turns away. "Drive safe."

The cops walk back to their respective vehicles. The County police officer shuts his door much louder than the Trooper, and they each drive away.

"I want my mommy," Adam whines over and over.

Lucia closes her eyes. She heaves her chest in a sigh as big as she could, and then she jumps into the car as fast as she can.

"Adam to Doc..." Anny starts up again. "Adam to Doc..."

Lucia undoes Adam's seat belt.

He leaps and crawls onto Anny, who remains asleep but keeps repeating "Adam to Doc..."

A few minutes pass and Adam finally calms down.

"We don't have very much time now. We need to get going," Lucia says to Adam while his mother continues to repeat her mantra.

Adam whimpers.

"I had a bad dream where everyone in the whole world got killed," Adam says, "and then my mommy woke me screaming."

"It was just a dream, honey," Lucia says. "Come on—let's get you back into your seat. I know you want mommy, but we have to get you guys to the doctor, okay? That way we can be safe. We're not safe right now. Mommy says we need to get to the doctor... that you've got something in your body that will hurt you, and the doctor is the only one who can get it out so you won't feel bad. We're going to get rid of the baddies, okay?"

"What—" Adam asks. "What are they going to do to us?"

"They'll make you feel bad," Lucia says as she wipes his tears away, "like you've got a tummy ache, only really bad, so we need to get you to the doctor, okay?"

Adam, still shaking, sniffs and weakly nods his head.

Lucia sighs, smiling with assurance at Adam, turns on the engine, and takes the car back onto the road.

"Mommy's gonna be okay," she says. "We're gonna be okay. The doctor is going to make it all better."

Adam's shoulders involuntarily shrug for a couple breaths as he calms down from crying.

"Thanks, Doc," Lucia says. "You're a life-saver."

* * *

> John Waterman, U-A DOB: 2579-12-03, CID 09985240860

> ResID: 9.3.1 [altered by CID 09985240860/ResID: 8.2.0] M1, M2, & M3

> U-B: [Chronos Outpost.OID:00000000001, Earth: 34.4812, -113.3355] LT: Friday, 2009-10-30, 5:51 PM PDT

— Friday, October 30th, 2009, 5:51 PM PDT —

Like dye in water, I feel their presence displacing the clarity of my existence. As each one joins with me, their light refracts off the gloss of the leaves surrounding me, as if a shimmering reminiscing of what they once were.

"I'm not who I think I am?" I ask my verm as I run.

"No one is," it says. "Now listen, if you're going to survive this storm, you need to be stronger. Your team—do you even remember why you formed your team?"

Red, yellow, and blue light shimmers in my skin and then fades away.

"Yes, I… remember… our mission… is saving Humanity…"

"So now, don't you think it's time you do some landscaping around here?"

I nod, turn away from my verm, and run toward the storm again. As I run, old and hidden memories rally my resolve, burning up any remaining shimmer in my skin. I am connecting more completely. I remember my team—our time together, our successes, our failures. The storm forms a funnel off to the right that touches down on the horizon beyond the maze.

Debris flies.

I get it. The storm shifts and charges from the right side of the horizon. I'm still running, trying to keep my bearings of the chaos in the sky as a reference to where I am in the labyrinth. My verm suddenly appears running next to me; its stride matches mine. My fight or flight instincts shift. The earth rumbles. The storm takes on a threatening direction.

I halt and stand. The earth is still. I am resolved. The storm rushes toward me, uprooting and throwing laurel bushes like a broom sweeping dust.

I stand waiting. My verm steps up next to me, standing resolute and waiting for the storm, which wrenches the labyrinth about like it is sand in the sea. I look into its glowing orange face and say, "I specialize in biological engineering—I'm a biocoder."

The storm devours us.

Purple lightning rips apart the sound barrier and thunderclaps push away the rain in oblong cylindrical shapes as the bushes of the labyrinth are tossed about within the storm. Pieces of wood and leaves slowly come together in the chaos, forming a humanoid shape, a giant wooden replica of myself as I am now.

My verm's voice says, "This represents all of your previous ResIDs' remaining memories combined."

It is gargantuan and towering above me.

"You must absorb it," it says.

"All this… inside me?"

"It's already all inside your head," it says. "Connect and absorb by osmosis."

A screeching sound echoes off the horizon, and all the volume and mass of the entire labyrinth, in the form of my human shape amidst the storm, shrinks to my size, spiraling upward to crest at the level of its gigantic head, and then it falls.

I watch myself fall, and wince as I land face down in the dirt… in the same impression of dirt I created when I fell off the cliff. I'm disassociated for a moment, and with my eyes still closed, I feel a shift in my legs and feet… a rumble in the ground. I recognize the cliff I fell from is above me as before I entered the maze.

Boulders fall from the cliff face. The earth shakes them down like pears from a tree.

The landscape heaves upwards like a wave, and I'm in the midst of a storm of boulders… and the entire horizon, thunderous under me, lifts me up and away from the cliff just enough for me to fall flat again and watch as the cliff landslides into the deep chasm torn in the earth from the rift.

Explosions of magma erupt, raining red and yellow earth upon the ground, cooling with unnatural speed, darkening to black, and fading into green... grass grows unnaturally fast, overtaking the wound in the ground.

In the moment that follows, the scarless landscape is flat... silent... as serene as a cemetery at dawn, but the storm remains overhead and surrounding me.

"Your tertiary memory is now locked online," my verm tells me.

I'm unharmed in the eye of the storm, and calm. I feel at home.

"Still, you know we're not done," it says.

I lift my head to see nothing but the storm and patches of grass around me; the labyrinth is no more.

"You must secure yourself completely," it continues, "locking your other memories, your secondary and primary memories online."

Before I have a chance to respond, white lighting bursts forth from me, extending to the walls of the storm, and I am no longer in my body. My clothes have been vaporized. I stretch to reach my body, and sparks of electricity arch finger to finger. They splay outward along every surface of my skin.

The storm continues to shroud everything outside its eye.

My verm sits in a trance, watching, waiting.

I reach down and grab hold inside my scintillating body, pulling it on like a cloak, my feet into feet, as if into shoes, my hands into hands, making sure to infuse every particle of my will to my body's familiar shape and size.

Lightning continues to fray the air around me, growing more intense, changing and engaging with the walls of the storm, roiling and vengeful against the obscurity of my temporary identity and the maze I had created to keep my real identity obscured.

In one final burst of St. Elmo's fire, the storm implodes. It is absorbed. I am clothed again. With finality, there is no pain.

"I am done now."

"No, John, that was just you. Now we can get started on why we're here," my verm says, standing, scowling, wild-eyed and naked, evaporating into particulate from bottom to top.

His evaporating form wafting up and around me lifts me. I am about to ask what this is all about when I'm spun into a spiraling cloud of orange particulate. I'm held in an orange horizon. The cloud begins to thin and spiral out horizontally from my position at the same speed and distance from me as the storm did, spreading for miles and miles. The orange horizon expands, and I'm shot up from the surface of the Earth until I'm affixed in the magnetosphere.

With no explanation, my clothes are completely gone again, and from frozen space... Humanity floats before me. They are naked as well, suspended and helpless. They are in terror. The pressure of empathy with all of their souls eviscerates my comfort. I wretch, naked and tortured. The orange about me fades suddenly as a dark threatening cloud consumes us all. Humanity's wailing in horror consumes me. Death-rattles possess and traumatize any last hope I have of comfort. Their screams reach my inner thoughts and are silenced. Even in the quiet of space, even after the deafening storm, my eardrums feel torn with the sheer magnitude of humanity's death rattles. I instinctively flail in reaching for them, desperate to be able to help them against the dark cloud. The last of their voices screams their last breath. An eternity of torment seizes me. I am catatonic... lonely... I can't breathe. My ears ring in the silence.

"I wanted you to remember that if we fail, John," my verm says, "You will witness the extinction of Homo sapiens. All of Humanity... all gone. However, now I think it's time we reactivate your Elder."

I'm still waiting for the feeling of trauma to pass. I don't respond.

"We've made some progress with the 6V code," another verm's voice says, "but we're not done, not by a long shot, because *I* haven't been fully reawakened yet. This is due to a corrupt ResID reactivation delaying my introduction. Please bear with us..." And with that, the dark cloud gives way to orange. The orange pushes me farther into space. Humans begin reappearing, clothed, and in comfort.

"If you thought a giant version of yourself was big," the unfamiliar verm says, "the resolve of Humanity's survival will be far heavier, but... to save them, you must bear this burden."

My trajectory lands me pinned face up on the bright side of moon. The storm that brought me out to space is now pushing its pressure and funneling deep into my gut and throughout my body. I have no more resolve to fight... I simply wait for this to be over. All the way from Earth, the orange storm rages, warping space-time, pulling the screaming voices I saw silenced, and pushing each one straight up my body's center-line, up my chest, throat, mouth, nose, and then right between my eyes, blinding me with their light until there is only darkness. In the silence, I blink to try to focus. I look out and... I see the Earth, the original home of Humanity, my *home*. In desperation, I jump for it, for home... My leap, powered by the verm that engulfed me... brings me closer to comfort...

"That storm—it's inside you now," the second verm says, as I fly toward home. "The point of the maze was not to stop you from getting to the end; the point of the maze was to stop you from reaching your storm."

Reality collapses. I am no longer falling. I find myself looking at an orange version of myself on a black background.

"That cliff—" it speaks, "the point of that cliff was to stop you from reaching your earthquake."

"What?" I ask, still regaining the sense of my surroundings. "Who are you?"

"That storm and that earthquake—they're locks, you see—locks that either lock your memories into place or out of place," it says. "You remember who I am now, don't you?"

"You're, uh... my Elder?" I ask.

It nods.

"It seems there's still a residual lag in your memories," the Elder says. "I was awakened when you entered the Holoroom, as we had previously agreed when I helped you establish this Dream to supplement the awakening of your ResID as it is now. It was a corrupt activation, thus the disruptive symbolism."

It sees I'm still listening, so it continues, "Verm-enhanced people typically don't have more than secondary memories, but you are unique because you are a chimera—a person with two distinct sets of DNA—a rare condition indeed. Your two sets of DNA have successfully bonded with two verms, a Primary, and me, an Elder. This establishes your Dream body.

"You see, your physical body contains your primary and secondary memories, as well as the physical components of myself, your Primary verm, and the inherent space-time taken up by your body itself. However, you are unique because your thoughts produce unique electromagnetic frequencies with two verms. These frequencies create vibrations that extend beyond the limitations of your physical body. This lets you process things so quickly that time appears to stop.

"Tertiary memories are created when your mind's electromechanical effects expand beyond your physical body's space-time. Somewhere between time and space, our way of processing your force of will causes your thoughts to bend the rules of the space-time continuum. The result is a state of existence we've called 'Dream' by consensus. Your abilities are multiplied exponentially... by two verms."

I smile.

"I have two verms now?" I ask.

"As McCleese would say, 'Come now, don't be so naïve.' We've always been here, waiting for you. Remember," my Elder says, "Dream is the realm of the subconscious, the realm of the language of instincts, emotions, demons, and guardians—a fantastical world where reality is limited only by your imagination, and enriched solely by your will. This was a perfect arena to awaken us."

"What when time slows around me, that's because of you?"

"It is because of your Primary, alone. Everyone with a verm can think faster than normal. This includes your team members. That's why they move as fast as they do, like you. However, the effects you experience as a chimera with two verms is that you think faster than everything else, including your own physical body, which seems to slow down relative to the speed of your thoughts. Because there's so much information to process, it is done subconsciously, via Dream. Dream allows the processing of much more information because it reaches beyond the Primary's abilities alone. The only limitation is that the world and your own body feel frozen in place or sluggish and heavy because you're thinking so quickly."

"So, what you're basically saying is I'm faster than everyone? I can enter Dream whenever I want? I can come and go as I please?"

"Yes, and when connected to any holographic technology, your effect on the network can have a subjugating effect on surrounding nodes. You will need to pay close attention to how you code, because you can overwhelm others. However, controlling it is something I'll be helping you with, in your subconscious, and whenever you connect to any technology. Keep this in mind—because of Dream, we can think and move faster than anyone else, which means we can code faster than anyone here, and we'll need this advantage, considering we don't really know what Daab's intentions are, and we don't know what saved him from the frequency that should have liquefied him. It's lucky Armand survived."

I nod and close my eyes. I have a job to do. I rest my sense of awareness for a moment, settling myself. The storm of emotion I've absorbed inside me slows. I open my eyes. Everything is frozen. McCleese is to my right. My consciousness lets go of Dream, and already, my Primary seems to have an agenda.

DAAB WILL DO EVERYTHING HE CAN TO STEAL THE MODEL. IF HE CAN'T USE IT, HE WILL DESTROY IT.

I consider the consequences of what that would mean and become instantly alarmed.

That would disrupt the entire solar system with the amount of power that thing contains. You really think he'd destroy this entire solar system?

HE'D DO IT WITHOUT HESITATION. CONSIDER THE STAKES. YOU'RE RUTHLESS ENOUGH TO BIOCODE AN ENTIRE FETUS, ADAM, AND THEN MAKE YOURSELF INTO A LETHAL EMP BOMB OUT OF DUST YOU IMPLANTED INTO YOUR OWN BODY TO BE TRIGGERED IN A WEAKENED STATE—CONSIDER IT KILLED EVERYONE BUT HIM. THINK OF HOW RESOLUTE DAAB IS, KNOWING YOU'VE HAD ENOUGH TIME TO REGAIN YOUR STRENGTH. STILL, HE'S GOING TO COME HERE WITH THE INTENT ON ERASING ALL OF THIS. BY ERASING YOU AND ADAM, HE LIKELY BELIEVES HE'LL BE DOING HUMANITY A FAVOR.

If Humanity has any chance to survive, it's Adam, so Daab's an idiot if that's his logic... Besides, we've all committed years of our lives to this plan, even though it's all fucked up now... but since Adam's still alive, it can still be redeemed...

IF DAAB THINKS FOR ANY MOMENT THAT HE WON'T BE ABLE TO USE OR DESTROY THE MODEL, HE'S GOING TO START MURDERING PEOPLE, INTENT ON ERASURE, STARTING WITH ADAM.

Adam is everything, and hopefully Anny's on her way here with him now. We don't have time to chat; I've got to reconnect you with the Base's computer and start getting this place ready to receive them.

I slow down.

McCleese's voice returns to the room as the holograms and ambient vibrations return to their normal speed.

"Well... your tertiary memory online yet?"

"Uh, yeah, you could say that."

McCleese nods. "Did you know you're the only known human in existence to have combined chimera biology with verm tech?"

"Yeah, I saw the movie."

* * *

— Friday, October 30th, 2009, 12:59 PM PDT —

Smoke billows throughout Lucia's car as they drive along I-15 North. Anny just finished smoking a bowl. Lucia rolls the window down to let all the smoke out as she exits the highway.

"Heyyy, I needed that," Anny complains with lethargy and eyes closed.

"Let's get some burgers, fries, and a milkshake!" Lucia announces loud enough to wake Adam.

He chimes in. "Yaaaay!"

She turns right at the exit light and enters a Burger Buffet parking lot.

"Huh uh ugh?" Anny asks, one eye opening before the other.

"Is this about as awake as you're gonna get?"

"Yesssh."

"Auna, I don't know how you're doing it, but you're screaming in your sleep. It's scaring Adam, and it's scaring me, too. I almost got arrested."

"Em shawree…" Anny simultaneously paws at the dashboard and clutches at her safety belt before pointing out the window in the direction of Nothing, Arizona, many miles away. "We got-tuhh get Adam to Doc…"

"I know, dear, we're—"

"Adam to Doc."

"—on the way, but we've stopped to get some food in you so you can regain some of your strength, okay?"

She gets out of the car while Anny repeats "Adam to Doc" a few times, rocking in her seat.

Lucia opens the door, unbuckles Anny's safety belt, and says to Adam, "Mommy's sick, dear. We need to get her some food, okay? She doesn't mean to scare you. We just need to get you and her to the doctor, okay?"

"Okay," he says.

The belt is off of Anny and Luke holds her up, shuts the door, and leans her on the car. "Come on," she says, unbuckling Adam from his car seat amongst all the grocery bags.

They enter the Burger Buffet, pay to get a booth, and order their drinks. Lucia does most of the eating and coffee drinking. After they down the milkshakes Lucia prepared for everyone at the desserts bar, Anny does most of the sleeping, and Adam does most of the talking.

"I'm sorry," the waitress appears next to their table stiff with anxiety, "but we don't allow sleeping," she says, nodding wide-eyed in Anny's direction.

"She's just got really sleepy medication," Lucia responds. "We'll be out of here soon, I promise."

Lucia pulls out a ten-dollar bill. "Here's a tip, and… sorry."

A couple minutes later, Lucia puts Anny's arm around her shoulders and lifts her up. Adam slowly follows them, stumbling out to the car.

Forty-five minutes later, Lucia continues speeding sleepily along I-40, heading east to Nothing.

The diazepam she put into Anny's and Adam's milkshakes gives her some peace.

* * *

> Anny Klaura, U-A DOB: 2580-05-15, CID 09986520678

> ResID: 6.2 [altered by CIDs 99999999999/ResID: 6.5 & 09985240860/ResID: 4.3.2] M2

> U-B: [Nothing, AZ, US, Earth] LT: Friday, 2009-10-30, 5:57 PM PDT

— Friday, October 30th, 2009, 5:57 PM PDT —

Exhausted, Lucia looks over her sleeping passengers, then checks the GPS on her phone to survey her relative surroundings as things pass her by. Anny and Adam remain asleep, but Anny looks a little blue around the lips. She's been jittery and hiccupping, continuing to talk in her sleep between heavy breaths about things Lucia couldn't possibly understand.

She turns left at Nothing to go east, when she sees a dark figure with a familiar gait walking up to the road. She slows down to check. It's him. She stops, rolls the window down on the passenger side, and yells, "Doc!"

* * *

> John Waterman, U-A DOB: 2579-12-03, CID 09985240860

> ResID: 9.3.1 [altered by CID 09985240860/ResID: 8.2.0] M1 & M2

> U-B: [Chronos Outpost.OID:00000000001, Earth: 34.4812, -113.3355] LT: Friday, 2009-10-30, 5:52 PM PDT

— Friday, October 30th, 2009, 5:52 PM PDT —

"John," Doc says, "the APB's been called off, but our erasure protocols will take another month, at least, to be fulfilled, even running tag-team, twenty-four-seven, especially since there were so many witnesses from Jane."

I open my eyes to the sick bay.

"Thanks, Doc," I say, briefly closing my eyes again.

I sit up and look around. This place is so familiar. It seems like just yesterday Anny and I were in a sick bay just like this one, obsessively hovering over the equipment and debating the most effective DNA combinations for our experiment. I remember how precise she always was, so careful to make sure everything was accurate...

In a moment, I'm swimming in memories... I smile... how eager we were to try anything to save Humanity, even to the point of fashioning a child together, and how much we gave up to bring him here...

My resolve brings my focus back to the present, and I pull one of the wires from the medstand, plunging it into my chest. It hurts only for a moment while my verm compensates. My sense of consciousness shifts and surfaces like an iris breaching the surface of water.

I also remember meeting Armand for the first time, decked out in all his martial regalia, chaperoning Doc, eager for him to make a false move.

The depth of Dream that allowed me to speak with my Elder now submits like an iced ocean, as if I were a submarine pushing through the surface to the more free-moving atmosphere.

"Doc," I call out.

"Yes?"

"My corrupted verm report is now ready for review," I tell him. "The info's shitty at best, but I've transferred only the important parts of the last eight days. You'll notice bits and pieces missing, like latitude and longitude coordinates. My verm's made do with what local information it could."

"Ah," he says, "I'm getting some of the data now."

I feel more awakened and alive than ever, but still a little disoriented. I need to know what's going on.

"Doc," I call out again, "I assume you gave directions to Anny to bring Adam here. Am I right?"

"Yes," he answers, "but Anny's got the 6V codec and Lucia will be with them."

"We'll deal with that when they get here," I say. "In the meantime, I'm gonna start the base up on a trace for Daab and feed the information back into the security system. It'll be redundant for you, but anyone reading my report will—"

"Yeah, yeah, good good," he interrupts. "I won't pay much attention anyway—I'll only need the highlights. Just keep it posted."

As I finger the holographic keys at the sick bay station, I'm starting to understand what Daab must have experienced when Armand described him being able to see with his skin. It's as if I'm seeing everything from outside my own body.

YOUR SIGHT IS NO LONGER EXCLUSIVE TO YOUR EYES. IF YOUR SKIN IS EXPOSED TO IT, YOU CAN SEE IT. THE MORE CLOTHES YOU HAVE ON, THE LESS CLEAR SOME OF THE IMAGERY BECOMES. IT COMES WITH YOUR SECONDARY MEMORY, WHICH ALSO SHARES THE DISEMBODIED POINT OF VIEW, DESIGNATED M2. THIS IS HOW YOU'VE BEEN ABLE TO REMEMBER THINGS YOU HAVEN'T SEEN, BUT WERE PRESENT FOR. THE SAME COGNITIVE PROTOCOLS ARE IN PLACE TO ALLOW YOU EXPERIENCES OF OTHERS WHEN YOU REVIEW THEIR VERM REPORTS. YOU WILL EXPERIENCE WHAT THEY EXPERIENCE FROM A THIRD-PERSON POINT OF VIEW AND IT WILL BE BACK-DATED INTO YOUR MEMORY, BUT CORRUPTED

MEMORY ACTIVATION CAUSES CHRONOLOGICAL INDEXING ERRORS, SO YOU REMEMBER THINGS AS YOUR PERCEPTION AND COGNITION ALLOWS.

Speaking of external experiences...

I call to mind the current state of things. Visuals in my mental space emerge.

Primary, have you connected with the base yet? Patch me in.

I CAN'T PATCH YOU IN FULLY UNTIL MORE OF YOUR CORRUPTION HAS BEEN SEGMENTED, BUT I CAN PROVIDE YOU ONGOING INFORMATION OF WHAT'S HAPPENING. ARMAND IS TRAINING WITH MCCLEESE AND CARRY IN THE GARAGE. THE DOC IS IN THE COMMAND CENTER. HE'S JUST COMPLETED MOST OF THE CODE INVOLVED WITH THE SEARCH AND ERASURE OF THE ELECTRONIC INFORMATION ASSOCIATED WITH OUR EFFECTS ON THIS UNIVERSE, AND HAS JUST BEGUN HACKING AN ENTRY INTO DAAB'S BASE.

Understood. Thank you.

"John," Doc's voice reaches me in my reverie, "we have some good news and some bad news. I've been able to find Daab's base's location, as it connects to the Internet, but the bad news is that it was too easy to find, and it's a Chaos Outpost. It's only a few hundred miles away. I've already had the system start a trace through Satcom and cell networks."

"Would the trace happen to start in El Malpais?" I ask.

"It's in a place called El Malpais, the badlands, yes," he says. "How'd you know?"

"That's where Armand and I were taken," I explain, "but if he's got active tech there, that means it wasn't fully destroyed in the underground blast."

"If he's had Allies in there," he says, "they'll be with him when he arrives, or maybe even before. So I'm going to start looking for where to hack those, but in the meantime, because our security system has reported that the cell phone I gave Anny is nearby, I'll send a holoclone up to meet up with them and keep the security system on standby so she can enter."

"All right, I guess it's time I get to work anyway. Let's see if I can help you find a way through all of Daab's shit," I say as I enter the command center and call up holographic images of information that he has acquired thus far.

"So, Doc," I say, as I sit down, "What do you have for me on where to hack Daab?"

"There it is on the terminal interface," he says, and a small holographic window comes to the front of the others.

"All right. Thank you for getting that set up for me, but I've got reports to review in the Holoroom before we start knocking on this door to see what answers. In the meantime," I say, jumping into Dream for a fraction of a second, "here are a few algorithms to try. They'll push our systems, but it'll at least let our friends in Chaos know we're not sitting on our hands. Give me a moment."

I step into the storage room.

"Okay Doc, here we go—I've found Daab," I report. "The updates should stream now…"

> Chronos Outpost, U-B, OID 00000000001

> RT Tracking POI … ongoing…

> U-B: [Highway 54] LT: Friday, 2009-10-30, 5:57 PM PDT

Progressing through the southwest part of Kansas toward Texas through Oklahoma's panhandle, a lone New York State Trooper speeds southwest on Highway 54 with a well-built, sun-burnt, and bruised unconscious man handcuffed in the back, wearing only his underwear.

* * *

> John Waterman, U-A DOB: 2579-12-03, CID 09985240860

> ResID: 9.3.1 [altered by CID 09985240860/ResID: 8.2.0] M1 &
  M2

> U-B: [Chronos Outpost.OID:00000000001, Earth: 34.4812,
  -113.3355] LT: Friday, 2009-10-30, 5:57 PM PDT

— Friday, October 30th, 2009, 5:57 PM PDT —

I grab a cot from the storage room and drag it through the command center into the Holoroom. Ambient ozone vents as I enter. The Model's movement no longer disorients me, even with the additional sensory input of skin sight. Various holograms emerge in my line of sight, showing me the status of each room in the base.

"Doc," I call out.

"Yeah?" His holographic image appears, smiles, and nods.

"I need you to compile a report that combines your and Armand's experiences; Armand's for the last two weeks and yours for the last three years, but highlight only the pertinent information."

"Most of that'd be from the 22nd to the 26th of this month alone." He touches a few points in the hologram before him. "Most of the reasons why we're in this predicament are because of my recent behavior, but on the bright side, the algorithms you've created are spectacular… It's good to have you back, John."

"I'm not fully there yet."

A blinking bulge in the hologram before me lights up in green, and I recognize it as an incoming message as I instinctively poke at it with my finger to receive it.

"There it is," Doc says. "Corrupt verm report of everything from the last two weeks, including Armand's entries during my ResID reactivation. They passed through me, so they'll not include certain information."

"Thank you, sir," I say, waving my hand dismissively. "The filtering I've set up to manage the corruption will only keep the pertinent information anyway. I'll be done with it in a bit. Also, when Luke arrives with Anny, I need to have the Holoroom prepped for her verm report."

"Understood," he says.

His image disappears behind me. I shoot a glance at one of the holograms showing me what's going on in the garage. Armand's playing with explosives, fighting Carry and McCleese, both of whom are emulating Daab's persona with holograms. I chuckle as I look for a perfect spot to lie down, away from the electric arcs of the Model.

He sure does have a passion for killing Daab, but it makes sense since Daab and his people tortured him.

I close the Holoroom's door behind me. I speak: "Create Primary sync for verm report: three years past, the Doc, mems one and two, universe B. Create secondary sync for verm report: congruent timeline, Armand, mems one and two, universe B, last couple weeks..."—I do some mental calculations—"and present at one point five million times real time, beginning on the mark of this pipe touching the floor."

The next five minutes are going to be a trip.

I pull out the pipe out of my pocket, lie face up on the cot, and lift the pipe slightly into the air. I let go of it and time slows down as I calibrate my mental acceleration. I watch the pipe switch from falling to stalling in midair. I slow down, mentally, just enough to allow the pipe to get close to the copper flooring. It takes forever.

Okay, Doc, let's see what you've got.

The pipe touches the ground and the entire room, including the Model, turns completely black. I expedite my mental acceleration, streamlining it, and allow myself entry into the mental realm of Dream. My dream self stands beside my body and waits. There is absolutely no light whatsoever, not a single photon.

From the darkness, my Elder verm appears, glowing orange in an orange suit. "You called?" he asks, smiling.

"Thanks for wearing clothes... I'm reviewing a report from Doc for the last three years. I'd like your help in interpreting the main points."

"All right."

In the next approximately three minutes of real time, two and a half years' worth of Doc's memories immerse and guide us through the experiences he's had leading up to this point. Over a thousand days of work on a project I spearheaded, and yet to my shame, I didn't do a thing to support my own cause during this whole time but fuck off.

"Don't feel guilt," my Elder says. "Anonymity has its moments, and guilt, like all emotions of conflict, compromises your cognitive bandwidth."

"To live is to conflict," I argue. "Besides, what I feel is not up to you. I can't imagine how bored Armand must have been. No wonder there was so much weed smoking going on. Doc worked tirelessly on getting the 6V program set up in that toy robot... entering code and verifying what I had laid out for him to do."

"He trusted you."

"He actually got it operational with no help from me... I guess that explains why he thought he could try it on himself... which is why he went crazy. Not the smartest choice."

"Even still, he got it operational. For being the Doc," my orange companion says, "he has redeeming qualities."

"That's why I included him. It's remarkable, considering he bet his sanity on my success... I'm really going to regret his Recollection."

"I warned you of that."

"I had no other choice who was as suitable for the task. With his understanding of memman tech, he's been invaluable. I'm still surprised he was allowed on this mission, considering those mem modules were preliminary."

The last thirty days come upon us quickly, so I accelerate my mental faculties further to slow down what I'm reliving.

"It's been a while since I've received a verm report."

"You're doing just fine."

I speed up fast enough to review the last ten days as if in real time. It lets me understand the details more vividly. It's painful—seeing Armand getting shocked by Daab's people. The mental overload Doc experienced overwhelms me. I'm having trouble not feeling disoriented.

"Stop!"

The world is on pause.

"I have to take a break."

Seconds pass in Dream as I reorient my sense of gravity.

"Ah, okay, I get it—he ran with an idea for testing I had off-handedly noted in the toy robot when I gave it to him—he put six virtual clones of himself and his verm into the toy robot's virtual reality to attempt testing of the codec, but the amount of resulting information he tried to process overloaded him. Makes sense though, considering he only has a Primary. His mental cascade failures explain the anxiety and his abnormal behavior. I never expected him to do it...Resume!" I said, and begin skimming past the next few days.

"Damn, okay—"

I speed up.

"I see he ..."

My mental pace is racing to keep up.

"Oh no! Doc put the 6V codec in Anny during her reactivation. My word! She's going to..."

"They know."

"Either the codec is decompiled from her, or it dies with her... but it's... it's been five days already now... she's— That explains why he's been working his ass off, hardly said a word to me. This is bad, really bad. They better hurry. If Anny's cascade failures have corrupted her real-time memories, she may not even be able to access enough of them to even remember her own name! I don't have time to decompile all of that—Daab's on his way, and like Armand said, we don't know how many Allies he has."

"Are you going to explain any of this to Luke?"

"I won't have time to, what with Daab showing up at 1 tomorrow afternoon. I'm going to have to help get the 6V codec out of Anny immediately when she arrives."

"At the same time, we can at least assess Daab's bug Armand found on the Los Eatos van."

"No need. Tracking hardware is simple."

"True."

My sense of consciousness shifts. The depth of Dream thins, and I resurface upon normal time. The report ends in darkness, and the former lighting returns.

"Damn that was a good report. I like reviewing reports. It's a good feeling to have most of my faculties back."

The hypercube-like Model returns and begins spinning and sparking again in the center of the room. I get up and stretch.

"Report current status," I say. My Primary pours information over me regarding the status of the base, including airflow, drainage, security systems, energy systems, temperature, etc. I bathe in the information as it flows through my senses. In an instant, my surroundings are as familiar to me as my doppelgangers in Dream. It feels like I'm not just inhabiting the base, but it's like an externalized part of my nervous system, like I'm wearing it.

This is a much more familiar response from the world around me than I expected. It's been too long since I've been this intimate with the world. My memory lag has been readjusted. My primary, secondary, and tertiary memories are now online and accessible. I feel like getting naked just to relive how crisp things used to be, but Lucia wouldn't understand.

"Armand?" I call out.

A holographic sphere appears before me, connecting me to the garage.

"McCleese and Carry need to help with sick bay preparations for Anny and Adam," I tell him. "Continue training with the base's security system until they arrive."

Armand's face relaxes for a moment as he realizes my ResID is finally reawakened.

"Roger that," he says. "It's good to see you're back."

* * *

> Anny Klaura, U-A DOB: 2580-05-15, CID 09986520678

> ResID: 6.2 [altered by CIDs 99999999999/ResID: 6.5 &
  09985240860/ResID: 4.3.2] M2

> U-B: [Nothing, AZ, US, Earth] LT: Friday, 2009-10-30, 6:01 PM
  PDT

— Friday, October 30th, 2009, 6:01 PM PDT —

"Hurry," Doc says, jumping into the car. "We don't have much time."

Luke says, "We need to quickly get wherever we're going anyway, 'cause Auna's in a bad way, and I need to pee."

"Blue lips. Looks like it," Doc says, then raises his hand in response to Lucia's inquiring face. "I'm going to take you to a place that's *very* well hidden." Doc puts his hand down and continues. "In order for everyone to get well and be safe, you're going to have to trust me implicitly." He waits a split-second and then asks, "Do you trust me?"

"I have to."

Doc points out the window. "Okay, see that raised part of the earth?"

Luke leans forward. "The dune-looking thing?"

"Yeah. I need you to drive toward it," he says. "Go fast."

"'Kay." Luke's tone is concerned, but she leaves the road. Anny and Adam are somewhat awakened by the jostling of the car on the uneven desert floor.

"Bluyuuyuughhh fyaaayayuuyuublublbubeeyeeyeehhhhhh..." Anny says, her body bouncing, unconscious from the sedatives.

"Okay," Luke says, "we're getting close to the hill, here. Where now?"

"Keep driving," Doc says.

The car comes right up on the hill, but instead of being heaved upward by the hill's incline, it moves downward into darkness. Instantly, they are in a tunnel. Lucia slams on the brakes, throwing everyone farther forward.

The front half of the car is halfway in the ground, but not damaged. Ahead, Luke sees a tunnel. Behind, she sees the desert.

"How did we—?" Luke asks looking back and forth.

"I told you," Doc says, "*very* well hidden. Please accelerate."

She presses on the gas and they're swallowed by the holographic surface made to look like the ground.

"What is—" Lucia's curiosity interrupts her as she leans forward to look up at the ceiling lights passing by. "Who built this?"

Doc waits a split second and says, "I regret the way you're about to realize how involved you really are in all of this, but please, continue driving. We're almost there."

"It's kinda dark," she remarks, looking around, easing onto the gas pedal. The car picks up speed.

"We'll come upon a large room soon," Doc says. "We call it the garage. Armand will be there, doing weapons training."

"Armand?" Luke asks. "What?"

"You'll see. John is here, too." He raises his hand again to interrupt her questioning further. "I'll show you where he is, so he can give you the tour." He puts his hand back down. "Once I leave you with John…" He looks over at Anny and Adam. "I've got work to do. Also, don't mind the smoke."

"Whatever."

Smoke begins to billow everywhere in the tunnel. From within and swirling around the smoke, green lasers and metal-covered flying objects of various sizes and shapes encircle the room as red laser fire bursts them into flames and automatic gunfire chases after them, blasting the room with deafening sounds.

As her car enters the garage, Lucia sees Armand firing two large guns, one in each hand. An explosion blows across the room. The entire drama disappears and the smoke is gone, leaving Armand in mid-stance with no guns. He rights his posture and waves Lucia down.

"What the fuck was that?" she asks Doc. "What just happened?"

"It's a hologram, and so am I," Doc says, "just like the entrance to our base. Park over there," he says, referring to where Armand is pointing. "Armand and John'll show you the rest. I'll be in the command center if you need me."

She complies, throws it into Park, grabs her Beretta, gets out, shoves the barrel down the back of her pants, and shuts the door.

"Where's the bathroom?" she asks. "I need to pee."

Doc disappears.

Luke yells, startled.

"It's okay!" a corporeal Doc yells, running out from the command center door, "I'm right here. Sorry, my hand turned off the—"

"Doc," she says, "I need to pee right now."

"Right! Yes, okay, so the bathroom is through that left door, then first subsequent door on your left," Doc says, leaning and pointing in the direction of the storage room. "Follow the wall to your right once you're in there, and you'll find it."

Luke's already running into the storage room through the command center.

"Okay everyone," Doc says, "we have to get Anny and Adam ready for the transfer."

Carry and McCleese show up, and with Armand's and Doc's help, they take Anny and Adam to the sick bay on cots. Then Doc returns to the command center to continue working. I remain in the Holoroom, observing passively the information the base provides.

"John," Armand calls out, "they're here."

* * *

> John Waterman, U-A DOB: 2579-12-03, CID 09985240860

> ResID: 10.4.2 [altered by CID 09985240860/ResID: 9.3.1] M1

> U-B: [Chronos Outpost.OID:00000000001, Earth: 34.4812,
  -113.3355] LT: Friday, 2009-10-30, 6:05 PM PDT

— Friday, October 30th, 2009, 6:05 PM PDT —

Now that Lucia's vehicle is in the garage, I've reactivated the base's security system and stepped into the command center to welcome her when she returns from the bathroom.

Finally I can find out what the hell's been going on. I need to start getting things prepared for a major hacking gig. That's new—she's cut her hair off. It's blond. She looks even more butchy.

McCleese and Carry have finished prepping the sick bay and have begun connecting tubes and wires to Anny and Adam to get started on diagnostics.

Hmm. Anny and Adam have blond hair too.

Doc says, "I've found out where Daab's control over his Allies is found, but there's a problem—they're under his conscious control in real time. The only way to hack them is to hack him."

"Understood," I respond while walking past him toward the sick bay. "Let's get Anny's verm report prepped. I need to review her experiences *immediately.*"

After returning from the bathroom, Luke runs into the sick bay without a sideways glance, and a bunch of alarms go off.

"Ow!" she says, plugging her ears and stepping back into the hallway. "Shit, that's loud."

"Oh, I'm sorry—you've set off an alarm in our system," I explain. "If you've got a weapon on you in the sick bay, those things go off."

"It's my dad's Beretta," she says. Her eyes are dark from exhaustion.

"I'm sorry about that. This base is filled with all kinds of security stuff."

"That's kinda shitty," she says, trying to get a peek at Anny and Adam. "You don't trust me?"

"It's harmless. We've got nanobots around here to interact with verms," I was saying, but she's ignored me and already put her gun aside and entered the sick bay.

"Doc," I say, following Luke, "what's the status?"

"I've got the process started," Doc says. "Now we just have to wait."

"How long do we need to wait?" I ask.

Lucia collapses.

"Long enough to take a nap," he replies, showing me a picture of what is right in front of me, Luke asleep on the floor. "They always pick the floor," he says. "There's a cot right there. Why can't you just see it?"

"She must have become exhausted beyond dignity. McCleese, can you put her in the cot?"

McCleese nods, rolls her over, and lifts her onto a cot.

"Doc," I say, "I need to review Anny's verm report."

"Sure thing," Doc says, walking into the sick bay. He begins addressing Adam's and Anny's sedated bodies.

"You better figure out how to deal with Daab and his Allies," he says to me. "We still don't know how he was able to survive."

"I'll Dream up something," I say and step out toward the Holoroom.

* * *

> John Waterman, U-A DOB: 2579-12-03, CID 09985240860

> ResID: 10.4.2 [altered by CID 09985240860/ResID: 9.3.1] M1, M2, & M3

> U-B: [Chronos Outpost.OID:00000000001, Earth: 34.4812, -113.3355] LT: Friday, 2009-10-30, 6:19 PM PDT

— Friday, October 30th, 2009, 6:19 PM PDT —

Shaking my way through the Holoroom doorway, the door hits me from behind, startling me in my dissonant state.

I've just absorbed Anny's verm report.

My world fades for a moment as I stumble through the robot cubby into the sick bay. I speed up my faculties and lie down to mentally metabolize what I've... too much disjointed sensory input... I've been overwhelmed. I close my eyes... trying to process it all... trying to send clips of it to the system for Doc to review...

I lose track of time...

> Chronos Outpost, U-B, OID 00000000001

> RT Tracking POI ... ongoing...

> U-B: [I-40 W] LT: Saturday, 2009-10-31, 1:00 AM PDT

At various points along I-40 W, first in the deserts of New Mexico and then in Arizona, a bandwagon of eight motorcycles, two cars, four vans, two trucks, and two semi-trucks break formation, park along the side of the road, and all behave as if they were having car trouble, each vehicle about ten miles apart. Some have their hazard lights on. Some have tools out and some have engines exposed from under hoods. To passers-by—if they even noticed—the drivers all seemed to be wearing the same metallic suits.

> Chronos Outpost, U-B, OID 00000000001

> RT Tracking POI ... ongoing...

> U-B: [I-40 W] LT: Saturday, 2009-10-31, 6:00 AM PDT

As the New York State Trooper drives through New Mexico, then through eastern Arizona, it passes what appear to be broken down vehicles about every ten miles; first a semi-truck, then another, then the trucks, the vans, the cars, and, eventually, the motorcycles. After the Trooper passes each group, they each seem to coincidentally have resolved whatever vehicle troubles they were on the side of the road for. They turn off their hazard lights and quickly follow the State Trooper.

Over a course of about thirty-five miles, the spread of vehicles becomes a bandwagon, with the New York State Trooper at the head, as though the head of a snake the size of a blue whale had just reattached to its body.

As the miles pass, the bandwagon accelerates, overtaking the Trooper until the Trooper finds a place in front of the two semis at the back. The motorcycles take the lead. The bandwagon snakes tightly with unnatural precision.

* * *

> John Waterman, U-A DOB: 2579-12-03, CID 09985240860

> ResID: 10.4.2 [altered by CID 09985240860/ResID: 9.3.1] M1,
M2, & M3

> U-B: [Chronos Outpost.OID:00000000001, Earth: 34.4812,
-113.3355] LT: Saturday, 2009-10-31, 12:28 PM MST

— Saturday, October 31st, 2009, 12:28 PM MST —

YOU CAN'T LIE HERE FOREVER, JOHN.

Someone's touching my shoulder. What's going on?

My eyes open to the sick bay.

"Wake up. It's almost twelve-thirty." It's Doc, hovering over me like a mother bird. "I think you should give Lucia a tour and introduce our current ResIDs to her," he says. "Daab's going to arrive soon, and it's going to really upset her."

"I've been out for six hours?" I ask.

I'm still adjusting, and my sense of my surroundings hasn't fully clicked yet.

"It's almost twelve-thirty in the afternoon on the 31st," he says, taking a step back to let me get my bearings. "You've been out for *eighteen* hours. Daab's almost here."

"Can't we... can't we just let her sleep?" I sit up. "Wait, eighteen hours?"

Shit!

Lucia's closed eyes squint after hearing my voice in the cot nearby.

"Yep," Doc says to me, "and we don't have some extra verm we can just throw at Luke. You're going to have to give Luke the tour the hard way. Carry, McCleese, and Armand are putting together their defense strategy, and I've got a shitload of hacking to do if we're going to erase the record of where you and Armand have been the last forty-eight hours, let alone access Daab's verm and his Ally shut-off codes. When Daab shows up, we'll be lucky if we can survive. I still haven't been able to fully hack into his base. I suspect he's got more Allies

265

than we think." Doc turns toward the command center door. "We'll be lucky if I can hack his base before he gets here."

"Okay, okay. I'll give her the tour," I say as he walks away. "Just calm down."

"Thank you," he shouts, already having walked out of the sick bay and sat down in the command center.

Lucia looks at Adam and Anny blankly. They're still sedated next to their respective medstations.

I walk over, sit down with her on the cot, and give her a hug.

"This hugging is weird," she says. "This place is weird. Everything's weird. What's going on?"

I let go and smile apologetically. I wanted to keep the atmosphere as friendly as possible since this is such a heavy burden to put on someone who's never been introduced to the reality of our universe.

"Wait here," I say to Luke. "I have something to show you."

I move outside her line of sight, and then speed up so that in a fraction of a second, I've grabbed a couple chairs from the storage room and Luke's gun from the garage, put the chairs in the Holoroom, and returned just out of sight with her gun hidden in the back of my pants.

"Come on," I say and lean into the sick bay door, keeping the gun just outside, "lemme show you something called the Holoroom." I continue out the hallway and into the command center.

"I've got some of the search and erasure protocols set on auto," Doc says to me. "I'm going to start setting up steps for the 6V codec transfer."

I turn around to see her lingering in the hallway, looking back at Anny and Adam. "Come on. They're safe. Doc'll take good care of 'em, I promise."

We walk in, and the cube-like surfaces of the Model glow and revolve inwardly and outwardly, electrifying the air.

Luke is going to have a hard time taking this all in.

At a normal pace, I then change the Holoroom to look completely dark but with a single bright red couch facing the Model.

"Let's smoke a bowl," I recommend.

"I'm not sure that's a good idea." She looks at everything like it's a practical joke. "Why did the room just... change?"

"We're from a future timeline in another dimension," I say as a non-answer, thinking I should just show her, "and this is a Holoroom. Most of the technology we use is a mix of holograms, 3D imagery, and interactions with nanotech."

Luke gives me the *I'm exhausted* look.

"All right, all right," I say. "Let me explain... Nice look by the way."

"Whatever," she says. "I loved my hair, and I still have no idea what you assholes have gotten us into."

"Look closer at your surroundings," I say, and relay commands to the room with my hands so fast, Lucia doesn't see it. The black background lightens.

She looks about the room and squints at the cubic gyroscopic object in the center of the Holoroom as it moves unnaturally upon itself and then slowly stops before us.

"This is the central core of a large dimension-shifting device. This hypercube acts like a screen saver when not in use, but its mechanical nature allows for various dimensions of time-space to converge upon a single locus. Really, it's part time machine, part dimensional shifter, but we just call it the Model."

"Why are you using so many big words?" she asks. "What the fuck is this... Model you're showing me? It looks like something out of one of those optical illusion books. How could you afford all this? This is another one of Doc's weird inventions, isn't it?"

She seems overly confused. Considering what I remember from Anny's report, it must be from a disruption to her sleep schedule.

"No. Sorry," I say. "Let me start over."

I wave my hand out of sight to bring the room back to blank with just the red couch. I sit and to try to think of how to best describe this while Lucia stands, looking around the room. "Have a seat."

She squats slightly to plop on the couch, but falls through it to the floor.

"OW!"

"Ha! That's for all those times you fucked with me while I was high," I say.

"Shut up!" she yells at me, disoriented, looking around while getting up, rubbing her bottom. "*This...* is a hologram?"

She pokes at the couch. She smiles a little when her finger goes through its surface.

"3D holographic imagery, yep!" I say, standing and smiling while she gets her bearings. "Here, you can sit where I was. There's an actual chair *in* the hologram." I explain as I reach into the couch and lift up a simple folding chair, "See?"

I set the chair back down and stand out of the way while she kicks the chair with her shin, moving it out of the hologram before sitting on it.

"Check this out," I say, and send more commands.

Suddenly, the room matches the back deck of her apartment with her brown couch, stained purple from her hair. The lights of Sister City sparkle in the distance. I sit in the other chair I'd hid in the couch, and pull out my weed and the metal pipe. "So *this* is what's going on..." I load the bowl and hand it and a lighter to Luke, who stops aimlessly looking around.

"You're from the future but hand me a metal pipe?" she asks.

"Hey, don't knock metal pipes," I say. "They remain faithful even under stressful conditions."

She reluctantly takes it.

"You talk weird, too, like you've had too much coffee," she says.

While she lights up, I start talking. "Sorry. Okay, answer me this: when did you meet me, Doc, Armand, Auna, and Adam? Just a rough guess..."

She blows out smoke and says, "Shouldn't I be the one asking questions? Around three years ago." She hands me the pipe and the lighter.

"Okay," I say, take a hit, and blow it out. "That makes sense because that's roughly when we got here." I hand the pipe and lighter back to Lucia and continue, "All of us got here around three years ago because that's when we arrived with McCleese and Carry, our Ally robots."

She hands the pipe and lighter back to me. "Robots?" she asks. "What kind of technology? Are you guys involved with some kind of corporate secret military or something?"

"Kind of both. We are technically funded by a secret military institution, but it's only secret because no one knows about it here."

She gives me a paranoid look.

"Sorry, this is going to be hard to explain. Basically, it's like this—there is a multi-galaxy-sized peace-keeping organization called Chronos whose sole mission is to destroy threats to human life. 'Course, what that implies is that aliens are real, and they can be kinda scary sometimes." I take a hit, blow it out, and pass the lighter and pipe back to Luke.

She takes them and a moment to think about what I just said, and then hits the pipe.

"And," I continue, "as with all large organizations, there's the potential for corruption, which I think we got."

Luke blows out smoke quickly to ask, "Wait. You're not an alien, are you?"

"Ha, no... I'm not an alien," I say. "Well, okay, I'm sorta alien-ish, but mostly human. I'm human enough to be human."

"So are you an alien or not?"

"Sorry, my brain is having to remap itself a bit. Let me explain." I gesture to ask for the pipe and lighter. Lucia clutches them, so I wave it off and continue. "So, there's a sentient biological technology called a verm that was found on a different planet than Earth, and it can stay sentient after it's been bonded to DNA. After the bond's complete, human abilities are improved. It even records the local time and date of your memories. It's a completely painless installation, too... Can I take a hit now?"

"Sure." She hands it back to me slowly, reserved.

"'Kay, thanks." I take a hit, blow it away, and continue, quite stoned.

"All of us have a biological technology inside our bodies—me, Armand, Doc, and even Anny and Adam. Verms significantly improve motor and mental functions. I can move and think faster than normally possible, even though otherwise, I'm a normal person. My cognitive bandwidth is also much larger with the verm technology. For example, the reason the room changed from couch to your porch," I explain, "is because I was moving my hands like this—"

I move my hands at a normal pace, changing the room back and forth between the Model and Luke's porch.

"Okay, that is hardcore."

"Yeah, but watch this," I say, and then move my hands faster, speeding up, until it looks like one reality overlaps the other.

"Holy shit!" she says, seeing the blur of my hands. "How the fuck are you doing this?"

"The verm changes a person's DNA," I say as my hands continue to blur the two realities, "and makes it so they can move and think faster, and it can also gather sensory input into a second memory, even if you're not consciously paying attention. Amongst other things, this room responds to certain hand gestures. It can also put memory into my head through a combination of nanotechnology and my verm."

I bring the room back to Luke's back porch couch.

"What do you mean?" she asks.

"It used to be that no matter how sophisticated, the code for a person's identity in any virtual or augmented reality was assigned by that electronic world. Now, with verm enhancement, the person... *is* the code, which for me," I explain, "because I'm fast enough, can be fed directly as machine language to the hardware via a state of mind I call Dream."

"John," she asks hunched over with confusion, "what are you talking about? Why can't you just show me directly?"

"Ah, uh, I realize I'm still recovering from the effects of Anny's, er, Auna's memories, and I'm explaining too much. I can't show you directly, because you don't have verm technology in you the way I do, but I can show you a memory I have that was extracted from Auna's experiences."

"What?" she asks. "How?"

"Just watch," I say as I bring up some of the information Doc gathered from Anny's memories thus far, and I set the room to playback.

The lights of Sister City disappear, and we see Anny full of wires atop Doc's table at his house in Jane. She's held affixed by her body receiving the 6V codec.

All the wires fall out from her body, including her eye, and the toy robot's lights fade to black.

Lucia grimaces at the sight of her loved one being in agony, but keeps her squinted eyes affixed on Anny.

A white noise buzz replaces all previous audio patterns of hum and whine.

"That toy robot—" Lucia says.

We watch Anny stand, shaking, pointing a trembling finger at Doc.

"You're *not* taking me away from Lucia," Anny says.

We see Doc respond: "I'm hoping, Anny, that we never have to."

"What *is* this?'" Luke asks me, smiling in wonder. "Why did he call her Anny?"

I pause the memory. "This is one of her memories played back through me after being absorbed by me," I explain. "It appears from a third-person perspective because I'm not the one experiencing it directly."

"Uh huh," she says, frustrated in confusion and disbelief. "When did this happen?"

"Monday night, around 10:30 PM, right before she showed up in the middle of the night, Tuesday morning, and said you guys needed to go."

"That was…" she thinks about it, then says, "Wait, you—you didn't watch our bath time, did you?"

"How do I put this?" I say, frustrated with not foreseeing the question.

Suspicion and fear instantly causes her body to tense up, and she grimaces. "You're a pervert," she says. "With all this tech, you're just a voyeur."

"Look, what's really important right now is that Anny loves you and—"

"Oh yeah? Who's Anny? I'm with Auna and Adam," she says, moving toward the door. "Oh I get it—your tech's been watching us make out this whole time. You've got all the backing and all the money, so you don't care that our privacy has been violated, and you're using all this tech to play it off like it's justified, but it's not, and you've lied to us this whole time to keep it covered up." She's trying the door, but it's locked. "Let me out of here!"

"It won't open mid-presentation. Look, I realize you're going through a lot," I try to explain, "but there's so much more to this."

"Fuck you. I've seen and heard enough. Let me out of here." Luke's eyes look dangerously threatening.

"Please, I just need to explain. This was Anny's—Auna's idea, too. Let me show you, please."

The room changes again by my hands, and we see Anny in the Brendon Motel room, right after Lucia had burst out of the bathroom with half-done hair with the scanner in her hand, just to leave the scanner out of the bathroom so she can finish her hair in peace.

Lucia looks up from glaring at me to watch the familiar scene.

We see Anny clumsily grabbing up the scanner's charging cord, plugging it in, and turning the scanner down.

"John," she whispers, "with a cleaner here, I fear that General Morgan, when we return, has…" She starts opening the banana Lucia gave her earlier. "John, we'll need every bit of help we can spare…" She takes a bite. "John, we'll need Lucia."

She lays her head on the table while eating the newly acquired banana and closes her eyes while chewing.

"Unbelievable. How do I know these are even her memories?" Lucia asks.

I stop the memory. "You want me to prove it with memories more intimate? Again, she agreed to this, too."

She thinks for a moment to let some of this sink in and shakes her head. "So, you've seen us naked. Unbelievable."

"Verms enhance the body's sensory input processing capabilities by interpreting signals in the nervous system more efficiently—"

She frowns. "This can't be happening. Has she seen you naked?"

"We've all seen each other naked," I say. "We can see with our skin. It's like synesthesia. Sight through touch."

"Sinna-what?" she asks.

"Synesthesia," I explain, "the ability to interpret sensory input through more than one cortex."

"WHAT?"

"Okay," I ask, "see Adam behind me?"

I start the memory back up.

"Yeah," she says.

"Okay," I ask, "see how he's twitching in his sleep?"

"Sure," she says.

"Okay, see there?" I ask, not looking, "He just rolled over. I couldn't have seen that unless I was processing light absorbed by my skin through my visual cortex."

"Okay, but, you already knew. You already knew without having to look."

"Ever since Auna yelled about you being a dealer at Los Eatos," I quote her, "you carry a really cheap never-smoked bong with you, just in case you have a really bad day, and really need a new bong fix."

"I see…" she says, scowling.

"That memory came from Anny."

"*While we were naked!* You're making me question all the reasons I came here for—to protect Auna and Adam from assholes like you who have way more power than they know what to do with, so they abuse it. We aren't toys to be played with, dammit."

"Nudity is not as taboo where we come from. But then again, it's not all that great either."

"Wherever you came from doesn't matter. You didn't ask permission."

"Seriously," I say. "Everyone who wants to can be naked, but that includes those who you don't want to see naked... like family."

"Whatever," she says. "I still don't feel comfortable with you seeing me naked. Just because you do it with your friends doesn't mean you can do it with everyone."

"I can easily become my own devil's advocate and say it's none of my business," I argue, "but when the physical, mental, and emotional safety of the only people in this world who know me is on the line, it becomes my business."

"Look, you didn't ask permission," she says. "My girlfriend and her son are somehow involved in some kind of conspiracy and I'm trying to save their lives. I almost got arrested because of your shit."

"Luke, I'm sorry, but that's the whole point—we want the same things. We're all here because of Adam. That's what I was hoping to explain—Doc, Armand, myself, Anny—we're *all* here because of him. All of us. I don't care about seeing you naked. I care about saving our world."

"If she's in on it, why's she acting sickly? How bad is it? Is that why you looked into her head? What does me and my girlfriend fucking have anything to do with saving the world?"

"It doesn't! I never saw that. That part was left out. Luke, I didn't want to upset you—I just wanted to prove that we're from the future, and I needed to review Anny's verm report so I can gauge how bad things have gotten in her head since Doc put a biological codec inside her."

"What the fuck? There you go again with words I don't understand," she says, "and stop calling her Anny."

"All right," I say, "it's like this—our team consists of a couple biocoders, a soldier, Doc, and the most special boy Humanity has ever birthed. Armand is a soldier. He never changed his memories or personality the whole time. His resident identity, or ResID, remained the same—his memories remained intact the entire three years we've been here. He's the easiest to explain. The rest of us have gone through significant memory and personality changes to fit in with society. We all have verms that facilitate the process."

"So you're alien after all," she says. "Great."

"No, we're *human*, just different. Compare Thomas Jefferson with someone who has a pacemaker and can drive a car. You'd say they're both human, but the 50-year-old grandfather who still has 30 years left in him needs the pacemaker to live and to drive his car. That doesn't make the grandfather any less human... and then, consider this: Thomas Jefferson never learned to drive a car," I explain. "The same principles apply here—verm technology is in the body the same way a pacemaker is in the body, but it can also be operated the same way that a car can be operated, only the car's on the inside."

"You're just making it worse," she says.

"But, Thomas Jefferson never drove a car. You did," I explain. "Even I've driven a car. In that sense, we're smarter than Thomas Jefferson when it comes to driving a car—we're *different*, but we're no less *human*. Just because I've got verm tech inside me, it doesn't make me any less human. On the contrary, the qualities that qualify me as human, such as my ability to make informed decisions, are enhanced by my enhanced nervous system. Does that make sense? We still cool?"

She puts the pipe and lighter in her lap and holds her head in her hands. "John," she says, "if this is going to make any sense to me, you're going to have to explain it bit by bit."

"All right," I say, "Auna's real name is Anny. She thought a name change would help her archive her identity as a genetic engineer easier, which was also to help keep Adam's identity secret. I had actually argued with her about it before the memman switch, because any ResID history would index any name she'd choose anyway."

"Dammit John," she says, "you're going to have to introduce things in order before you use them to explain things."

"Sorry," I say, "it's just that I've recently absorbed a lot of corrupted memories from Anny, so I'm a bit unsure of what things you understand versus what I've learned from her."

"Just shut up a second," she says.

I wait.

"Okay," she says, "so, you're saying that Auna's actually some kind of memory or bio-something engineer that has changed herself before I met her, and that Adam's identity needed to be kept secret. Why?"

"Verm technology is extremely rare, and it's new to our world," I say. "Only large government and huge commercial organizations can afford to apply verm tech to human hosts. Most don't want to. We've been trying to hide from someone named Daab since we found out he's arrived. He's got a verm, and he's a cleaner. You know—a hired gun."

She frowns and says, "Yeah, I know what a cleaner is."

"Yeah, listen, I've been having trouble the last few hours collecting all the mems because Anny, Doc, and I have corrupt ResID activations."

"Corrupt what?"

"It's like this—have you ever gotten so stoned drunk out of your mind, you're still feeling it the next day?"

"That's just a hangover."

"Okay, I have a really *really* bad hangover. The kind that's so bad that you don't know what day or time it is, you don't know where you are, what you're doing there, or how you got there, and someone's asking you a bunch of questions. That's why I'm having trouble explaining things. If it's any consolation, I really am trying to keep it together."

"It's not much help when you're *still* talking crazy talk," she says.

"It also means that since Anny's got the 6V codec ruining her mind," I explain, "I'm unsure I'll be able to save her. That's why we're in here—I'm going to try to save her, but, in good faith, I felt you needed to know what the hell's happening here, and I'm sorry it's not sufficient, but I can't stay much longer—I've got to help Doc save her. She's gone through a corrupt ResID activation with that codec scrambling her mind six different ways."

Lucia's just shaking her head as if to say, no, you're still not explaining it properly.

"Look, in our world," I continue, "we have something like an internet of people called Humanity. There, people's experiences are shared through memories. A ResID is basically your personality. It's registered with Humanity as part of your identity and rises in number for each of your memories' alterations—"

"Just… just shut up a second," she says.

"No," I insist, "it's important that I share this with you so that you can at least know what's going on, because I don't have much time to save Anny, and you are important to us, because you're important to Adam and Anny. Can't you at least believe that?"

"Most of this doesn't make sense to me," she says, exhausted, "but at this point, it doesn't matter to me as much as being with her and Adam. Whatever her name is, she's still Auna to me, but if you're all as different as you say, why did you come here and put me through all this instead of staying where you were, in a world that makes sense to you?"

"Because there's civil unrest," I say, "and there are threats to Humanity. For example, an organization called Chaos, of all things."

"What? Chaos of all things?" she asks, picking the pipe and lighter back up from her lap. "That's dorky."

"No, just Chaos."

"Is it spelled K-A-O-S?" she asks and takes a hit.

"With a C-H."

"Still dorky," she says, blowing out smoke with a bitter look to her face. "Ugh, that was ass. There's no place you can hide out?"

"Parts of Chaos have terrorized Humanity for many decades," I say, "and who we thought was a cleaner for Chronos, the organization that governs Humanity, may be an agent of Chaos. Whether this Lieutenant Daab is with Chaos or Chronos, it doesn't really matter—what matters is that he's out to get Adam, and he also has a verm, and he's coming here. He can move unnaturally fast like I can. So as it is, for your safety, I have to lock you in here until we deal with him."

"Chronos or Chaos or whatever. You want to lock me in a fucked-up room after telling me you've seen me naked. You know this is like kidnapping, right?"

"It's to keep Daab out. Don't worry. I'm faster than he is," I say. "I'll keep you, Anny, and Adam safe. I promise. Doc and Armand have got our backs. I don't want to sound cliché, but it's for your protection."

"Doc's an eccentric pothead and Armand's a restaurant owner. How're they going to—"

"Remember what Armand and Doc were doing when you arrived here?" I ask. "Armand is a soldier and Doc is a bio-software engineer specializing in memory manipulation technology, what we call memman tech, and by putting it into Anny, he helped keep Adam's 6V program safe."

"Yeah, but Auna's going crazy," she says. "Whatever you fuckers did to her is *killing* her and stealing her away from me."

I pause.

"It is my highest priority," I say in the most assuring tone I can muster, "to bring her back to herself, whole. As fast as everyone can move, I can move much faster. My team and I must protect Adam from Daab and the people who sent him here. We are willing to kill and die for this. Secondly, we must, at all costs, protect the Model from Daab if we want to get ourselves and Adam back home. Adam is something Humanity has never been able to experience before, but protecting the Model," I switch the room to display the Model moving, "is just as important to our mission, and for the next twenty-four to forty-eight hours, I believe the Model and Adam are what Daab wants most. I'm not going to explain in further detail, other than planet Earth and all of Humanity is in terrible danger if our mission fails. If we're going to save Adam's life, and this planet, we need to work together. You'll need this." I hand her her dad's gun.

She stands and puts the pipe and lighter on the chair and takes her gun. She puts it in the small of her back and smirks. "So, after everything's done with this Daab person, and Auna and Adam are safe, you're just going to let us go," she says with sarcastic tones, "knowing all this?"

"When all this is done, you'll be with Anny, er, Auna, and Adam, and all the weed you can smoke. I can also assure you that you won't have to worry about the law because Doc fixed that now and Anny and Adam still love and adore you and want to be with you," I say. "When they wake up, you can ask them." I pick up and offer her the pipe and lighter and lean in to ask with a stoned apologetic smile.

"I know they love me," she says, waving away the pipe and lighter. "You only know that because you're a voyeur," she says with disdain still in her voice, "and yet you talk about saving humanity."

I sigh and set the pipe and lighter on her chair in case she wants it again later.

CHANGE YOUR APPROACH HERE, JOHN. AT THIS POINT, YOU WON'T RECRUIT HER IF SHE'S STILL LOOKING FOR REASONS TO SAY NO.

I enter Dream for a moment to collect my thoughts. I spend what seems like a couple hours there trying to figure out a way to fully convince her. In real time, it is immediate.

"We're trying to save the *identity* of humanity, but we need your help—we believe this identity is, in its essence... adaptation and charity... but individually, as humans, we're limited by our cognitive abilities, and so we end up favoring those closest to us because the scope of who we can love is limited to who we are close with. As we live and share our lives, we adapt, and in our adaptations, we and our loved ones change. The bonds we share are what define us as human beings, but as we develop, we change until we're no longer our former selves, but we remember what we've shared with others. That sharing, that bond, is our identity. We develop as we share successes and failures with others—it's not that the memories are good or bad, it's that they're there *at all*."

"Wow," she says, not meeting my eyes, still exhausted. "What does this have anything to do with me?"

"You have that bond with us. From everything we've shared together, you are like family to us. Your father understood this concept when he willed his gun to you."

"John," she says, "that's not cool."

"Follow me on this one. His bond with you is still there, even after death, in the gun he willed to you. You carry him with you. This is what we're fighting for, too—the shared bond. Because of you, his memory lives on. It may be that you work at a diner, sharing a day-by-day connection with customers, but your connection with Anny and Adam is very important. We can't have the shared bond if we're all dead."

She sighs in exasperation, still looking away.

"Listen, Luke, where we come from, the identity of humanity is being threatened. The scars Adam has are due to a birth defect I created in his body to save the world."

Luke frowns. "Let's say I believe you—that you caused Adam's condition, and that Doc's the reason for Auna's suffering," she says softly, looking up at me, "and I shoot you in the knees."

"That's it! That's the bond," I say excitedly. "There's a threat to our world, to Adam's world, and the birth defect allows him to save our world. Doc and I are going to work to make Anny and Adam whole again. Then, Adam can save Humanity. It's that simple. He and Anny are heroes."

"What could possibly threaten Earth to the point that you'd want to cause health issues in a child?" she asks.

"They're superficial and painless," I explain. "What kind of health issues are you assuming he has?"

"Auna said his liver is dying," she says.

I am instantly confused, but then I recall Anny's memory.

"I am truly sorry. Adam is perfectly healthy. It's Anny I'm worried about most."

"What?" she asks.

"Anny said Adam had liver problems because she needed Adam here and knew she couldn't trust herself to get him here without your help," I say.

Luke, inhaling in defense, raises her fist with a pointed finger ready to stab me with her retort when something clicks in her head, and she holds her breath for a beat.

"I'll be damned," she says, dropping her finger, "she really Shanghaied me."

JOHN, QUIT BEING AN ASSHOLE. YOU NEED TO TELL HER THE REAL REASON.

I'm getting to that...

"Luke," I begin again, "there is a fungus-like entity that threatens Earth. It will destroy Humanity if not eradicated. Different organizations have speculated different ways to deal with it, and competing organizations want to try to control it, to weaponize it, but it's too dangerous. Imagine a biological weapon capable of destroying all life on Earth. Now Adam, on the other hand, working together with his verms using the 6V codec, will be able to find a way to calculate this entity's evolution and find a method to save Humanity from it."

"What does that have to do with us?" she asks. "Is the fungus already here?"

"No, but Anny's going crazy because Doc implanted a codec algorithm into her body that was originally intended for Adam, and she is overwhelmed by the changes," I say. "It's like a test-run of the 6V codec, which hasn't been fully developed yet. If Adam was implanted with it outside the confines of this base, it would be a disaster, and Anny's memories had been altered for security reasons so that she wouldn't remember where this base is. In all the world, this base determined you would be the best mentor for Adam, even above all of us, including Anny. That's what it has to do with you. Once Adam's been implanted with the codec, the six verms he has in his body will awaken and become active. That's what it has to do with the rest of us. The miracle of it all is that he is a meta-chimera. The scars on his body exist because his body's growing with six different sets of DNA inside."

"Six sets of DNA in one person?" she asks. "That's just straight-up impossible."

"Not with the bio-engineering technology we have in our world."

"I don't understand why this is all needed," she says. "Why not just blow up the fungus and be done with it?"

"It's already been tried. Blowing it up simply spreads the spores, and we don't comprehend its evolution or where it originated. We need someone like Adam who can think in broader terms than any human who's ever lived."

"Why wait this long?" she asks. "Why not go all out and grow brains from stem cells or something and make some kind of super computer out of that? He's just a child."

"It is paramount that a child is involved," I explain, "not just for the mechanical requirements of a child's constantly developing brain being the only means to do it, but also because we needed a human being. A person can't develop without having relationships in their lives. Any person or thing with this kind of mental power would be inhumanly smart and needs to be tempered socially. So we specifically intended to come to this chosen point in this space-time, in this alternate universe, to find you in your world and be in your life so that he could grow up as a *normal* human. We had hoped to spend twenty years here with you before activating his verms by implanting him with the codec and returning home, but since Daab has arrived in our space-time now, it means that in some part of the multiverse, at least one of the universes has sent a cleaner to our local space-time. The cleaner could have come from the Alpha universe and we've been disavowed before our maturity date. Either way, we need to protect Adam and the Model. That part is simple. Everything else is complicated."

"Complicated?" she says, trying to take it all in. "If there's a multiverse, why aren't there ten-thousand Daabs, or fifty million Adams already running about the place?"

"This is the one where this happens," I say. "We accept our fate and continue our agenda."

"What's to say *your* agenda is good? What about another universe's John's agenda?" she asks.

"I can't really get into what's good or bad," I say. "Speculation is irrelevant in the fate you create."

"What does that mean?" she asks.

"All I can say is that, there's really no definable good or evil, only acceptable and unacceptable in a community," I say, "and as human beings, we share our lives together, subjectively defining these terms together. That's what it means to be human—beyond any memory manipulation, beyond the illusion of a constant individual identity, beyond the illusion of the present moment—we adapt and we share. That is our essence, our glory, and we all want to share our lives with you: Anny, myself, Doc, and Armand..."

MAYBE NOT ARMAND SO MUCH.

Shut up. I've gotta sell this.

"...just as you have these last three years," I continue. "It would be our honor and pride to share our lives with you. However, I should warn you—it will be dangerous, and as we adapt, we will change dramatically. I may not be the same John tomorrow that I am today."

"You are certainly not the John I met three years ago," she says. "You're not even the same John since last time I saw you."

"Will you do it?" I ask. "Will you join Anny, Armand, the Doc, and me in protecting Adam?"

"In a heartbeat," she says. "That pipe is dead by the way."

I look down. "Oh."

Holographic visuals and a corresponding beeping tell me a connection with the command center has been opened.

"John," Doc says through the connection, "I've raised the dividing wall that'll separate us from the garage. The security system says there are hundreds of Allies and a great number of vehicles entering the tunnel. Carry and McCleese have already joined Armand. I'm going to go get set up in the sick bay."

"Okay, thanks Doc."

A subsequent holographic visual and beeping closes the connection.

"Stay here. My holoclone will show you what's going on, but for your safety, stay," I tell Luke as I gesture to activate it and a couple holographic screens. "I've got to get into the command center to deal with a few things."

IT'S NOT A GOOD ENOUGH EXPLANATION.

It'll have to do. With the danger we're in, I don't have any more time. The more she's familiar with our world and out of my way, the better.

I lock the door behind me just as my holoclone appears. I walk into the command center and look through the robot cubby to see that Doc has already attached himself to a medstation in the sick bay to facilitate the 6V codec transfer from Anny to Adam.

The security system goes into overdrive, startling me. Gun pods lining the walls of the garage activate.

* * *

> John Waterman, U-A DOB: 2579-12-03, CID 09985240860

> ResID: 10.4.2 [altered by CID 09985240860/ResID: 9.3.1] M1, M2, & M3

> U-B: [Chronos Outpost.OID:00000000001, Earth: 34.4812, -113.3355] LT: Saturday, 2009-10-31, 1:00 PM MST

— Saturday, October 31st, 2009, 1:00 PM MST —

A thunderous blast rumbles through the base from the other side of the wall.

"What the hell just happened?" Lucia asks.

My holoclone opens its lips to respond, while for me, the world slows down.

SEARCHING SECURITY SYSTEM... I'M SYNCHING UP A RADIO CHANNEL WITH ARMAND TO KEEP TRACK OF HIM.

What the hell? McCleese and Carry have just been wiped from their suits. Something bombarded their signal. I'm going to have to re-suit them.

Flashes of where everyone is comes to the forefront of my mind as I speed into one of the sick bay's cots and connect myself to the nearby medstation: Lucia's staring at my holoclone, waiting for an answer; Doc's body is peacefully resting beside Adam's and Anny's in the sick bay; his ResID's virtual body is frantically entering code into the system, trying to back up Anny's ResID. Armand is standing ready, eagerly awaiting the violence yet to come with a scowl and a grit-tooth smile.

"Checking..." my holoclone responds.

In the virtual reality I've just connected myself to, I've begun skimming logs from Doc's hacking of the Chaos Outpost thus far.

Give me a full report on Daab's systems' memory vulnerabilities and help me find where these Allies can be hacked. Start setting up Ally holoclones and smoke in the garage, connect me up to view Armand in real time, and reconnect McCleese and Carry to their suits.

WILL DO.

"All right, Doc," I say, "let's hack 'em."

MCCLEESE AND CARRY ARE RECONNECTED.

"John," Doc says, "why not just speed in there and destroy them all manually?"

McCleese and Carry activate their suits and stand.

Thank you.

"With McCleese and Carry in there," I tell Doc, "Armand's gonna be fine, and… we could use the parts. We'll need all the hack time we can get."

"Ah, right," he says.

"Besides," I tell him, "I have a few tricks up my sleeve I want to try out, like Wafflevision."

I speed up until Dream shrouds my thoughts beyond what Doc can comprehend. My Primary was right—with Dream available, cerebral challenges take less real time even though they aren't necessarily easier, but they also require real time to implement because of system limitations. Images and layers of technology fly through my vision as I race through creating various algorithms in my attempts to counteract the flood of machinery Armand, McCleese, and Carry are having to battle with on the other side of the wall. All the while, I'm able to see and hear what the base can see and hear, physically. I can interact with the virtual world and the real world simultaneously.

"Wafflevision?" Doc asks.

"Yeah," I say. "Wafflevision is cooler sounding than holographic scrambler."

As I approach the Chaos Outpost's GUI location on the net, I'm almost distracted, because I only now recognize the semi-trucks that took up the rear were filled with explosives, which just collapsed the only way out of here.

That's what that blast was behind the wall—we've all just been buried.

I relay the information to my holoclone to keep Lucia informed, and time returns to normal.

Smoke fills the garage and segments of holographic light distort depth perception to the naked eye, causing the room to appear as through the eyes of a common house fly on LSD.

"Hey, Armand," I call out to him, "Wafflevision's active."

"Wafflevision," he says. "Got it. Just get my verm synced," he says with eyes closed over the noise of the many engines coming his way.

"How are we going to get out of here?" Lucia asks my holoclone.

Can't get distracted. Need to defend. Need to stay focused and hack.

I set up the vision filter and relay it through the base's verm communication link to McCleese, Carry, and Armand so they can see. I speed myself up excessively and return to the base's interface. Holographic fractals throw horizons around me until I register with Humanity's software platform. Doc's location is upside down, just above me.

"Armand," I say as I move through the base's virtual reality toward Doc's location, "I'm syncing a descrambler with your verm now."

"Roger that," he says as he opens his eyes. "It's working."

"All right, Doc," I say through the security system, "I'm coming your way."

"Why is the base shaking?" Doc asks. "It's not helping me back up Anny's ResIDs any faster."

I transition through a cognitive bridge closer to Doc's location in the virtual reality.

Virtual gravity changes and places my body beside him.

"Daab's arrived," I tell Doc, "and since he survived the EMP that should have killed him, we don't know what to expect. We need to get the 6V codec packages into Adam. It may be the only thing that will save us. I'll need to find where Daab's cyber presence is located online."

"If Daab's here," Doc says to me, "I'm gonna need your help. There! Anny's backup is complete."

"Finally," I say, slowing down to real time. "Now to get the 6V from her into the system so I can compile it…"

"John," Lucia asks my holoclone again, "how are we going to get out of here?"

My attention runs to multitask quickly, speeding me back up so I can enter different commands into the security system. I relay a video stream from Armand's radio sync to the Holoroom's screens so Luke can see what he sees.

THE WEAPONS THEY'RE USING ARE PRIMITIVE, BUT EFFECTIVE.

From my connection with my verm, I take a real-time look at what's going on in the garage. Allies on bikes arrive first, only to fall into the hole in the floor, which has been covered by a holographic floor image. The following vehicles decelerate as quickly as they can, but still more fall from knocking into each other. They're churned to pieces by the garbage disposal. Daab makes his Allies change tactics—the passengers begin climbing atop the vehicles, and as vehicles fall, drivers and passengers alike leap. Some land. Most indiscriminately fire their weapons in mid-air at holograms created by the security system.

THEY'RE USING SOME KIND OF FLAME-THROWER, ONLY INSTEAD OF THE NORMAL STREAM OF NAPALM-LIKE SUBSTANCE, THESE SPRAY WHAT REGISTERS AS TWO SEPARATE STREAMS OF MAGNESIUM-ENRICHED THERMITE AND DRY ICE POWDER. THE RANGE AVERAGES ROUGHLY 6.5 METERS.

Luke stands silent, arrested by what she sees.

"John," Armand yells, "Where the fuck is Daab?"

McCleese and Carry have fallen again in the light of weapon fire. Their backups are having trouble reactivating their suits.

Some of Daab's Allies are connecting directly to nodes in the garage, disrupting Allies' connections.

"John," Doc says, "I need your help here."

Armand is doing his best to destroy as many Allies as possible, camouflaged by the security system's distortions.

With his speed, he's tearing Allies apart, ripping out skeletal parts of metal with ruthless efficiency.

"Just do your best for now, Doc," I say.

Their weapons are so effective that, in the confined space of the garage, some are actually degrading or destroying each other.

Lucia, seeing how fast Armand moves, sits down confused in wonder, trying to take it all in.

"McCleese and Carry are down again. Armand's fucked," Doc yells.

At my command, the pod guns lining the garage begin firing at Allies. Many of the pods are already damaged.

"Don't worry about Armand," I say to Doc. "He's trained for this shit. He can take care of himself. Just focus on getting the codec transferred."

From the Allies' guns, flared lines of glowing metal alight atop powdery dry ice. They land in congruent rows on various surfaces in the garage. They interact after a delay and explode dramatically, spewing carbon dioxide and molten metal so far that it reaches the ceiling, fifteen meters above them.

Armand raises his voice over the noise. "The air's gettin' thick in here, John."

"I'm working on it."

Allies fire their weapons directly into the disposal. The ground shakes from the disposal grinding so much metal and molten thermite. The disposal overheats, cooking the surrounding earth. Calculations of the security system push heavy on my consciousness. I feel the weight of Daab's presence from Allies connecting to nodes in the garage.

"Armand!" I yell. "Why are those nodes free to hack?"

"Didn't you close the ports?" he asks.

"Yeah," I say. "Look, just destroy them all. They're no good to us hacked."

ARMAND'S BEHAVIOR SHOWS SIGNS OF CO2 POISONING. VENTING CO2.

As he follows my orders, striking fractures and severance through the nodes in the garage, I push back against Daab's Allies' presence in the system and install McCleese and Carry back into their suits. Daab presses harder, knocking Wafflevision offline.

"Armand," I say, "Daab's just compromised our scrambling system."

"Yeah, it's a metal fuck-fest," he says to me. "All scramblin's offline. I'm gonna have trouble breakin' *all* the nodes right away—I'm havin' to dodge cover fire, and more of these assholes're connecting their shit up to nodes as we speak. You gettin' this on your end?"

"Yeah," I say, "we're doin' what we can."

I speed up again in the virtual reality, only to find myself in front of a layer of security—a stalling measure Daab's set up to distract me from hacking him. It looks like a castle. In Dream, I code trebuchets and battering rams. A torrential rain of rocks and splintered logs collapses the castle. It crumbles, falling into the earth. I break the sound barrier flying into the hole, breaching one of Daab's firewalls.

"Doc," I ask, "how much further do we have to go with the 6V transfer?"

"We've still got five layers left," he says.

In the garage, a couple of trucks long and fast enough to bridge the gap between the tunnel and the garage floor have landed their bumpers on the edges of each. Remaining Allies have freedom to enter the garage without hindrance. I fall into Daab's security layer, and what a coincidence—it is a labyrinth similar to mine, only this one's made of obsidian.

How many layers of security you have here, Daab?

I speed up and code myself as a lahar, a lahar of gasoline and gunpowder.

All right, you motherfucker, secure this...

With a single spark, the entire labyrinth is blasted from the ground.

The earth opens up again.

There's an avalanche of metal in the garage, and Armand will be overtaken by sheer volume of mass and airborne contaminants if we don't figure out how to shut these motherfuckers down. I've got to find Daab's connection to his Allies.

Explosions of extreme temperatures begin erupting everywhere from the constant buildup of thermite and dry ice. Vibrations from the violence cause particulate to fall from the ceiling in the sick bay onto its peaceful occupants.

Anny begins convulsing.

Lucia sees it on one of the displays and runs to the door, but kicks at it when she remembers it's bolted shut.

"Doc, how much further?" I ask. "Anny's body is taking a beating."

Lucia screams at the door.

"I'm doing the best I can," Doc says, "but we still have four layers to go."

"Please calm down," my holoclone says to Lucia. "The diazepam in her system is what caused the seizure, but please be assured, John and Doc are saving her life."

Trucks bridging the gap over the disposal creak and whine under the weight of Allies and the other vehicles. Armand destroys the front bumpers of the trucks with his guns, in hopes they will collapse into the shredder, but his firing's starting to slow down.

Lucia kicks the door once more before turning to watch the screens.

WE CANNOT WIN THIS BATTLE WITHOUT DEACTIVATING THOSE ALLIES.

I know!

Armand's skin is pocked by various metal and ice burns. The room temperature has risen to above 40 degrees Celsius. Bits of molten metal and dry ice start to fall from the ceiling, dropping down on Armand as he switches between firing on the Allies and the trucks' bumpers.

THE SYNC SYSTEM IS COMPROMISED.

"Armand, the oxygen in the room is nearly gone," I say through the system. "You're not going to be conscious for much longer... Armand... Armand!" *He can't hear me.* "Fuck!"

The trucks finally fall, but still, more Allies breach the gap.

McCleese and Carry collapse.

I can't find them in the system. What the fuck happened to McCleese and Carry?

THEY'VE BEEN ERASED.

Armand's breathing has slowed.

THE SYSTEM'S BEING INFILTRATED.

Goddammit!

Seven Allies from different directions turn their heads from hacking the nodes in the garage and rush Armand through the smog. He rallies, takes five out with his gun, grabs the first one he destroyed by the ankle, and uses it to bludgeon the sixth. Armand calls my name while he's fighting hand-to-hand with the last one. All that remains is its torso.

"Armand!" I yell back through the system.

He can't hear me.

The security system is fighting to ventilate the carbon dioxide emitted from the dry ice and the heat, but the system has been compromised.

He can't breathe.

"John," Luke calls out.

Armand's eyes slowly close, and he kneels with an Ally torso in hand, but the look of resolve on his face remains, like a dying king.

"Do something!" Luke yells.

Goddammit I don't have time for this shit!

I speed up and code a ten-meter-high tsunami through the virtual reality to seek out and destroy any further connection Daab has with his Allies.

Take that to your fucking connections, Daab.

"Fuck you," he says, startling me with his appearance in the system. "You're in my world now." He reaches out to subdue me.

I code quickly, swallowing Daab up to his neck in the obsidian shale gathered from his maze. "Wrong world, you piece of shit," I say, and squeeze shale through the surface of his skin, into his muscles. "Relinquish your Allies."

He hesitates.

I pierce his spine.

"NOW!"

Allies collapse upon the concrete floor of the base like dominoes falling, starting from the tunnel and spiraling outward.

"What just happened?" Lucia asks my holoclone.

Armand collapses onto the destroyed Ally he holds with a death grip.

"Armand!" Lucia yells, looking back and forth between the view of the sick bay and the garage.

Daab's ResID disappears from the suit of obsidian shale I made for him, telling me he's disconnected from the system.

"Daab's Allies have just been commandeered, and Daab's effects have been cleared of the security system," my holoclone explains, "but John's still going to need to hack Daab, himself, if we want to survive this."

Lucia nods, never taking her eyes off the screens.

How many Allies can we salvage?

SEVENTY-THREE OF THE ALLIES ARE DESTROYED. ALL ENEMY ALLIES ARE DEACTIVATED.

"Doc," I ask, "how much more time are we lookin' at here?"

"I'll need at least fifteen minutes," he says.

"We're not gonna have time. Damn it!" I open the proximity hacking software to hack Daab's personal signal directly. His interface appears instantly.

Clap. Clap. Clap. The sounds echo off the tunnel walls throughout the garage.

Lucia squints in the Holoroom, trying to figure out who's clapping.

It's Daab.

"You can't stop me, John," Daab calls out from amidst the smog and sizzling in the garage.

Armand's body lurches on the ground and vomits a dark substance. His eyes open.

Clap... Clap... Clap...

ARMAND'S PURGED HIS POISON, BUT I'M STILL VENTING CO_2.

"If you want to challenge me, if you wish to scan me," Daab's security software says with his voice, "find the correct particle, here, in this galaxy..."

A virtual version of the Sombrero Galaxy appears before me.

You have got to be shitting me.

I speed up to my fastest and use a year's worth of Dream time to code a search algorithm capable of spreading throughout an entire galaxy's space, down to the atom, looking for anything out of the ordinary.

Clap... Clap... Clap... Clap... Clap...

"John, you disappeared. Where'd you go?" Doc asks me in the system, but I'm still coding.

Daab struts into the garage wearing a New York state trooper uniform and a sword. He spits out a finger-sized SCUBA rebreather, and its jingles on the concrete echo amongst the sizzling.

"John?" Doc calls out in the system.

"Very impressive... gridders," Daab says to a smoking garage, walking sideways in plain sight to show off his gun, pointed at Armand, and the sword strapped to his waist.

"I had to code something in Dream," I say to Doc in virtual reality. "I was a little slow getting back so as not to disrupt the system with the code."

Behind the safety of the Holoroom door, Lucia's affixed to her chair, intently watching Daab strut into view.

My algorithm reports the location of Daab's weakness.

"I found the location I can hack Daab," I tell Doc. "It registers as a single hydrogen atom amidst an entire galaxy in VR—I don't know how he programmed it, but the proton spins around the electron, but it's not annihilated next to other normal hydrogen atoms."

"Well, figure it out," Doc says, as he continues to pull the 6V codec out of Anny. "We need to subdue Daab fast."

Still, even though I've found the lock, it doesn't mean I know a way to open it...

ISN'T IT OBVIOUS?

"Right," I say to Doc and my Primary simultaneously.

"Nice sword," Armand says sarcastically to Daab as they size each other up in the garage amongst their fallen metal comrades with the sizzling of thermite and smoldering of dry ice still filling the air.

"The New York officer, now dead, who unwillingly donated his vehicle to my cause had this evidence in his trunk." Daab says to Armand, patting the sword handle. "Convenient for me."

Armand sits up and draws his gun.

Daab leans to pick up a gun from one of his fallen Allies.

"Hey hey now," Armand warns. His gun is trained on Daab's chin. "Easy now."

Daab halts his lean.

Speeding back up, and jumping into Dream for only a moment, it hits me, and I return...

I must open this lock, I think while watching everything unfold from inside the system while resting in the sick bay.

Without hesitation, Daab's body follows through on its lean and time slows. He somersaults forward quickly, picking up the gun at the cost of one of Armand's bullets piercing his right shoulder.

The lock is an atom...

The bullet enters between Daab's collarbone and breastbone and drills through the flesh until it exits between his shoulder blade, ribs, and spine, embedding itself in the wall behind him, but Daab had already begun pulling the trigger on his own gun.

I can do this...

The spray of blood ejects from Daab's back and splatters the wall as his body recoils from the impact. His gun throws dry ice and thermite in a six-meter arc high in the air. He follows through, even with the inertia created from getting shot, and, as he heals almost instantly, the fire and ice race toward Armand.

I enter Dream for a moment too minuscule for Daab to notice.

Armand lifts the Ally torso he'd been holding and throws it in the direction of the flow, blocking the arc of temperature extremes. It flies toward Daab, bursting dry ice and thermite back at him.

Lucia, wide-eyed, can't make out what's happening in the speed of it all.

"Trying to hack me is like untying the Gordian Knot," Daab's voice says in virtual reality. "It is impossible."

Daab, in the garage, draws his sword, closing in on Armand. As Daab's personal signal presses closer to the security system, the dividing wall quickly falls open.

Our bodies are exposed!

"I'm still able to read your verm output, you realize," Daab's voice says to me through virtual reality. "I know your every move."

I respond, "I don't think you can read this—"

From Dream, I split the spinning proton.

The lock is opened.

Daab's ResID is blinded and burned by atomic fire.

HE'S HACKED, BUT THERE'S STILL SOMETHING ELSE HERE KEEPING HIM ALIVE...

I awaken from virtual reality to the sick bay. "The knot is cut!"

* * *

> John Waterman, U-A DOB: 2579-12-03, CID 09985240860

> ResID: 10.4.2 [altered by CID 09985240860/ResID: 9.3.1] M1 &
M2

> U-B: [Chronos Outpost.OID:00000000001, Earth: 34.4812,
-113.3355] LT: Saturday, 2009-10-31, 1:06 PM MST

— Saturday, October 31st, 2009, 1:06 PM MST —

With no more speed, and disoriented from my hack, Daab doesn't stand a chance. Still, he charges Armand with the sword, drawing down the blade diagonally.

"Hey!" Lucia yells in her fright for Armand.

Armand waits until the edge of the blade comes mortally close, then instantly twists into the arc of the sword, kneels close to Daab, grabs the wielding forearm in both hands, and effortlessly crushes both bones over his knee. The extended hand lets go of the sword with Daab's slow and sure surprise. Armand catches the sword in its fall, twists further, steps, and draws the sword through Daab's other arm.

As I slow down upon entering the garage, allowing reality to speed back up, I can hear the bones crack and splinter inside all the meat before the arm separates completely and falls to the floor, splattering blood under the arterial arc that has already begun flowing from the stub.

"Ew!" Lucia cringes, squinting and frozen, watching Daab look down at his stub shooting blood everywhere.

He is not healing.

Armand picks up Daab's bloody arm. "You... are... hacked," he says with a smile, shaking the arm fast enough that blood spatters Daab's face with each word.

"I've had worse," Daab says, trying to wink spattered blood out of his eye and hold his blood in with his broken limb.

"Isn't that a little overkill?" I ask Armand as I walk further into the garage.

"I got the job done," Armand says, waving Daab's hand at me. "I got the upper hand."

"I got the job done," I argue. "I hacked him."

"Gentlemen," Daab says.

"I hacked him *more*," Armand argues back. "I hacked his limb off."

"Gentlemen," Daab says. "I'm going to bleed out."

"I enjoyed it," Armand says, nodding and pointing at Daab with his arm.

"Right," I say. "All right, Daab, let's get you into the sick bay and get you cleaned up. Armand, get some restraints from the storage room."

Daab sighs.

Confused by everyone's flippant attitude toward Daab's arm being severed, Lucia takes her eyes off the screens for a moment to sit down, shaking from adrenaline.

As I walk Daab into the sick bay, Armand comes in with restraints fit for the criminally insane.

The alarm goes off.

"Turn that shit off," Armand says. "We need to keep him under the gun."

I turn off the alarm.

"I don't think bringing a weapon into the sick bay is going to help," Doc says through a holographic projection.

"It's the only way to figure out why the fuck this guy disrupted our plans," Armand responds as I reactivate Daab's nanos, but not his speed. "He's a *cleaner*. I wanna know who wanted him to *clean*."

"Don't get distracted, Doc," I tell him. "You've got a job to do."

His hologram turns his back in defiance and returns to work.

I reach for Daab's arm and Armand throws it to me. I put it to his stub so it connects.

Lucia's eyes grow wide as she sees Daab watch his newly healed arm steam and regain its shape and mobility.

"I'm not in the mood for talking, and," Daab says with a mocking smile, waving at Armand with his healed arm, "I believe I still have the upper hand."

Lucia shakes her head.

"Then I will restrain your hands," Armand challenges, grabbing Daab's hands at high speed, and tying them up in restraints, "and your legs." Armand follows by instantly restraining Daab's legs. "Then we can chat about who your boss is. Oh. I guess that's right now."

Then he lands a punch on Daab's cheek so hard and fast, Daab's head twists 180 degrees and recoils.

Lucia's face tightens up in disgust.

Something isn't right.

"That's for bein' an asshole," Armand says, as Daab instantly regains consciousness.

"WHOA WHOA," Doc yells from his hologram, "Don't be *torturing* anyone in the sick bay."

"This ain't no torture," Armand says. "I'm just askin' questions. Daab and I are just havin' a little chat."

Time begins to slow down around me and my thoughts are speeding up again.

Daab's face turns with boredom. "Quit playin' around," he says, the words getting slower as time slows. "I've got people to erase."

Armand raises his weight and fist into the air to bring down as much force as he possibly can, but it's happening slower and slower until he's stopped in mid-punch.

ARE YOU SURE YOU'RE GOING TO ALLOW THIS VIOLENCE?

Do you have any better ideas?

LET'S TRY A DIFFERENT APPROACH.

My body shifts with a slow-moving push against the air, reaching Armand's position, which, at this speed, is like trying to walk through deep water with a weight belt on. I grab Daab's chair, and pull him and myself out of Armand's punching path, trying my best not to fracture Daab's bones too much in the acceleration. In retrospect, the way he didn't die from my EMP, he likely could've handled me breaking a few, but he wasn't going to talk motivated by pain. As I move, I can feel Armand's knuckles scraping on my clothes as he bears down. Time returns to normal.

Armand yells, "Ow! Fuck! You burnt the skin off my hand!"

Shit. I still haven't gotten the timing of this down.

"You'll heal," I say to Armand, sweeping the scraped flesh off my clothes.

"Fuck you," he says, holding his hand. "This hurts."

I admit, it is pretty bad when you can see sinews, but his skin's closing up, and I don't have time to waste. I put my shoulder in Armand's way and get right in Daab's face.

"Daab. Look, here's the thing... We're trapped in here. There's no way out. You're hacked. You're outnumbered." Daab looks at me as if to ask *how the fuck did you move that fast?*

"You..." Daab looks at me, smiling, then at Armand, "just moved faster than him."

"Daab! You've lost," I say. "Whoever your boss is sent you on a suicide mission. Do you understand that now?"

Daab's clearly shaken, but he holds it well.

Armand calls out at me from behind bloody knuckles, "What the fuck are you planning here, John?"

Lucia shifts, still tense in her chair. Her breathing is shallow.

Daab's eyes jerk about at me, as if looking for any weaknesses I might have.

"Any tells you think I might have, Daab," I say, "are too fast for you to react to, see?" My hand is instantly in front of his face. He blinks from the slight breeze.

"This isn't a game of show and tell here!"

"Shut up, Armand! Daab! We just need to know who your boss is so we can avoid them when we get back home, all right?"

Daab holds his breath and nods once.

"Look," I tell him, "I'm a chimera—I have two verms. That's how I can move so fast. The extra verm in my body enhances my normal capabilities twice as much as a normal verm-enhanced brain. That's how I hacked you. Adam, on the other hand, has his capabilities multiplied exponentially six times. Anny and I used our genetic material to create a fetus of our own design. He is a chimera comprised of six unique sets of DNA. A meta-chimera. This allows him to contain six verms in his body, simultaneously. He is a miracle."

Lucia looks to my holoclone for answers, but is distracted by the procession of dialogue.

"He's not very fast now," Daab argues.

"They're simply not activated yet. Doc's working on it. I created the memman program bio-engineered to expedite Adam's verms' abilities and awaken them to their full potential." I take a breath. "I'm telling you all this because Adam is the answer Chronos has been looking for on how to beat the spores, and if we don't deliver, we're all in a world of shit."

Daab sighs, blinking at the ceiling, bored with my explanation. "Chronos... is just absurd. We're already in a world of shit, and it's because of Chronos. Look around you. Does this look like a utopia?"

"Chronos didn't do this," Armand responds. *"You* did it. I knew it—you're a fuckin' Chaos agent!"

"Uh huh, well, I never do what I'm told, anyway... I know all about your mission, John, and obviously, I don't care about you, or experiments on children... nor do I care about all of Humanity, for that matter."

"What?" I ask. "Why? You are human."

"Intelligent life is not exclusive to Humanity," Daab says. "Goddamn... as fast as you are, you're all fucking slow."

"What I don't understand," Armand cuts in, "is why you didn't just shoot our tires out."

"What?" Daab asks.

"That's a good question," I say. "You've been given a lot of time and resources to erase us, why confront us only now?"

"What?" Daab asks again. "You mean when you were jumping all over the northern hemisphere? Isn't it obvious? I let you go, and then I found you. All of you."

Armand cuts in again. "My verm was active the whole time, why'd your guys hold back?"

"Because General Morgan's a gridder," Daab says.

"Morgan?" Armand asks.

"Yeah. He betrayed you, you know?" Daab says, scoffing and shaking his head. "He betrayed us all. He hired me off-grid, giving me three hundred Allies and twenty-five subordinates to erase *that mistake*," he says, nodding arrogantly at Adam, who remains motionless. "His words," Daab says, shifting his posture in his chair.

He looks over the sick bay for a moment.

"Those were the people you killed back there in New Mexico by the way," Daab says. "Must have been the General's little insurance."

"Nah nah," I say, unwilling to believe he even knew Morgan, let alone that Morgan hired him. "That was all mine."

"Morgan must have known you'd try to kill us all," Daab says. "You know, those were good people. I'm surprised you have no remorse for being a mass-murderer."

"They didn't seem all that great, schoolin' me in pain," Armand says. "John was defending himself. Consider anyone who died that day collateral damage."

"You seem talkative," I say, getting frustrated with Daab's self-righteousness. "Tell me, how do you know Morgan?"

"He's the one who hired me," Daab responds.

"Fuck you he did," Armand yells. "He's the one who sponsored us—"

"Why are you even still alive?" I ask Daab. "Doc and I set up my EMP to liquefy your internal organs and your verm along with it."

"I don't know," Daab says. "Might've been General Morgan's little 'insurance' he poked me with."

I look at Armand and Doc's hologram for answers, but Daab continues...

"He basically said, 'If Humanity will survive, it cannot be said that our survival depended on experimenting on children. Erase that mistake of Humanity from existence, and I'll secure you a full pardon. I'll even set you up with your own planet, full of any kind of pleasure you might desire.' Sounded Mormon, but could I refuse? No—you were disavowed, like me; I hadn't had access to connect with the Doc, and according to the General, all I had to do was erase you."

Armand asks, "What's this got to do with the Doc?"

"You've got lie detection on, right? Check your systems and see if I'm lying…"

Now I'm curious.

"Anyway, as I was saying," Daab says, "after I gave my consent and turned to leave—"

"Answer the question," I demand.

"When I was trying to leave," Daab continues, "as I was trying to explain, before I got interrupted, Morgan started mentioning restrictions in the contract, saying, 'Their mems will have been manipulated, which makes them legally innocent. A person in my position can't have something like this coming back to me. So, if they're still ignorant, just keep tabs on them but don't disrupt their ResIDs. Otherwise, erase them.' Then, he shot a dart into my neck with who knows what on it and told me it was to ensure the job would get done. 'A little insurance,' he said. Fucking ridiculous. That's when I started to question his appreciation of my business… He gave me your ResID histories but didn't tell me more, and then I came here. Of course, not knowing who had active verms or not… well…" He pushes his weight against his restraints in resentment.

"Hey uh," Doc pipes up, his hologram sizzling into focus, "What could you possibly want with me?"

"I'm not telling," Daab says.

"You almost done in there, Doc?" I ask. "I never expected the prep to take this long."

"Yes," Doc says, "we're making progress—the final readjustments just require a bit more time. You'll be able to compile soon enough."

"You know," I turn to Armand and Daab, "there's something that just doesn't make sense—why would a Chronos General erase the only practical strategy for Humanity's survival?"

"I'm just a cleaner," Daab says. "I clean. Maybe there is another way to deal with the spores, like your way, but like I told Morgan, there's a dust solution to anything. Honestly, I don't care about politics or whatever. I don't care about the survival of Humanity. Morgan's a gridder; who knows why he does anything, just like you. You all still have the gridder mentality, because you've all connected with Humanity. None of you even know who the fuck you are. You all build superficial connections with each other to tell yourselves that after all the shit you've put your souls through, you still have some semblance of what it really means to be human. I'm not a garbage pile of dead personalities, like you assholes. I live my own life. I have a job, I do the job. You want cleaning done? I dust. It's that fucking simple."

"I don't understand," I respond. "Why don't you care about your own species' survival?"

"Because, for one," Daab says, "Humanity isn't *humanity*."

That's an alarming phrase to hear—it matches Chaos rhetoric.

"And second," Daab says, "Homo Sapiens don't hold a premium on intelligent life."

That also matches Chaos rhetoric.

"You sound like an agent of Chaos," I say.

"Goddamn," Daab says, shaking his head with a smirk, "You're pretty fuckin' slow for someone with two verms."

"You're a Chaos agent," I clarify.

"YES, you idiot!" Daab yells, "That's what Armand said. FUCKING PAY ATTENTION! Did you *really* think I'd show my cards to a shit-pile of gridders?"

Now the all the detracting makes sense. A Chaos agent would rather kill and die to keep the spores alive as a 'peer of life' than eradicate them to save Humanity. By confirming he's one of them, Daab just showed his last card—he's not a part of Humanity at all—he's an outsider.

"I've heard enough," I say. "Armand, watch him. I've got a codec to compile. Doc, meet me in the command center for a sec."

Doc hears me and shifts his workflow.

I speed up to meet with Doc's hologram in the command center.

"None of this makes any sense." I start ranting quietly so as not to reveal my concern to Armand or Daab. "Our whole lives, we've been told that Chronos conceives Humanity's resilience, observing nothing over survival, yet the highest-ranking member, save Chronos himself, is hiring what appears to be a Chaos agent, off-grid, to countermand our singular strategy for survival? It's unbelievable! All the years we've sacrificed to—"

"John," Doc says, interrupting me with his hand up, "I've got work to do, and we're not going to understand this until we return... It sounds like General Morgan, though. He didn't like this idea from the beginning. He may have found another way."

"You think so?"

He puts his hand down.

"Before we left, I could see something in his eyes that just didn't feel right," Doc says.

I sigh.

"But," I respond, "he represents the highest of Chronos's public authority. Why would he compromise his own values?"

"We don't know." Doc raises his voice in frustration, angering me. "This identity may never understand why this happened," he says, beating his fist on his chest, "and I have to get back to work—something you've not really done these last three years... You know, a part of me actually agrees with Daab about humans not being the only standard for intelligent life and honestly, if you really look deep enough, John, I believe you do too. Besides, our agenda and the General's values aren't inherently mutual. When we get back home, it will be my time—I'll have to submit to Recollection."

"We'll see."

"John," Doc says with his hand raised again, "you can't just dismiss the facts because of what you think should have been."

I consider it. "Look," I say quietly, "whatever your sentiment is, the only ones who have both the knowledge and the resources to organize this are the General or Chaos."

"Chaos could have done it with or without Daab, but we really can't know that until we get back and find out from Morgan himself," Doc says. "Hell, that's if he'll even tell us. Chaos has members of Humanity and the disavowed alike on their payroll. If a possibility may occur, it can't just be dismissed because it's unsavory, so my advice is to prepare for the worst. The worst-case scenario is that Morgan is actually working for Chaos, and we may be slaughtered upon our arrival."

"That..." I say, shaking my head, smiling at the idiocy of it, "that couldn't happen... Nah, you know what? It's just *Daab* who's on Chaos's clock. This is all *his* bullshit. Somehow he's rigged himself to lie without it looking like it."

"Again, John," Doc says, "it's all speculation anyway."

I turn away, giving up.

"I don't think we're going to get anything more out of Daab, and," Doc says loudly enough for Armand to hear, "you should tell our local soldier to calm down. We're not going to get anywhere with Daab by allowing Armand to indulge in violence."

I pause to smile. "You're right," I say, turning around. "I'm sorry. I won't let it happen again."

Lucia's calling for me from the other side of the Holoroom door to let her out.

"It's still not safe," my holoclone responds.

"Look, I have to get back to the extraction. I'm almost done," Doc says, waiting to transfer his holographic self to the sick bay, "and the impact we've made in this world won't erase itself."

"Thanks, Doc," I say as I enter the sick bay.

In the Holoroom, Lucia slowly paces back over to a chair and sits down.

"Now that we've been buried down here," I say to the sick bay, "we're going to have to bore our way out."

Daab scoffs.

Armand looks pissed.

"Why are you even here?" I ask Daab. "Why do you still believe you have the upper hand? You called us gridders, and you say you don't care about Humanity, but you claim Chronos hired you… and Chronos is for Humanity… so… why are you here?"

Daab scoffs again. "Like I said, I don't always do what I'm told."

"Oh, yeah," Armand says to Daab with a malefic smile, "everything's really fuckin' funny. Quit bullshitting and answer the fucking question."

Armand lurches at Daab, who doesn't flinch.

"Get back, Armand," I say.

Armand's smile disappears.

Daab bursts into laughter, but is silenced by a slap.

"Get back, Armand! Stand there!" I yell, pointing a couple meters away. "Don't fuckin' test me right now."

"Fine," Armand says, stepping back, "but this motherfucker is makin' our jobs a lot harder, and the fact that we're not beating more out of him is your fault."

"Yeah, but that's my problem, not yours, isn't it?" I ask Armand. "Besides, there's software for that."

Armand grunts.

"You still synced up to the security system?" I ask Armand.

"What's left of it, yeah. I ain't gonna disconnect while he's still alive," Armand says, referring to Daab.

"Good, because I've got to compile the 6V in Dream," I say to Armand as I sit down and connect myself to the medstation. "Stay connected when I go in, in case he fucks you up, and I have to clean up the mess."

"Now that I've been finally allowed to work," Doc's hologram announces, "I'm done with the 6V extraction."

"We're not done," Armand whispers to Daab with a wink from where he stands. Then he unholsters his gun and places it on the nearby medstand.

Luke can stay trapped in the Holoroom. I don't have time to babysit the uninitiated.

I lean back and close my eyes, devoting all my attention to what I'm about to do in virtual reality.

* * *

> John Waterman, U-A DOB: 2579-12-03, CID 09985240860

> ResID: 10.4.2 [altered by CID 09985240860/ResID: 9.3.1] M1,
M2, & M3

> U-B: [Chronos Outpost.OID:00000000001, Earth: 34.4812,
-113.3355] LT: Saturday, 2009-10-31, 1:22 PM MST

— Saturday, October 31st, 2009, 1:22 PM MST —

From his hologram's point of view and his location in the virtual reality system, Doc's still watching Armand's and Daab's physical and virtual dispositions.

"John," Doc says, "the virtual reality system is almost completely destroyed."

"The VR? Yeah, I know."

I double check on the security system to make sure Armand's and Daab's connections will remain secured.

"Any ideas?" Doc asks.

"I'm going to work around the VR's issues by creating a compiling interface and entering Dream to get the 6V codec running for Adam," I say, "but I'm going to need your help."

"Dream?" Doc asks me. "While we're this close?"

"I'll buffer it with a vortex," I say.

"Fine, that's fine," Doc says, frustrated. "What do you need me to do?"

"The 6V codec was never meant to be entered into someone's mind," I say. "It was meant to be like a dynamic filter. The reason you and Anny went crazy when the codec was inside you is because it was meant to organize the mind to handle six verms. Without the expected data volume, it starts *processing* the mind."

"John," Doc says, "I know this from experience. Can you get to the point?"

I code a space dedicated to Dream in the VR, a pocket in virtual space, a place where I can move faster than the system *in* the system.

"Sorry, Doc," I say. "I'm a little distracted from Daab, and your anger isn't helping."

Doc sighs and asks again, "What do you need me to do?"

"While here with you in the VR, I need to feed you packages of code compiled from within a place in the system dedicated to Dream... you got that?" I ask Doc.

He nods.

"Then," I continue, "you need to feed the packages into Adam's memory. We have got six verms and the savior of our world in that little body. We've only got one shot at this, and once we start, we can't stop; otherwise, Adam's mind will be corrupted, and we will have lost everything. You'll need to follow my lead as quickly as you can. We still don't know what Daab has that's keeping him alive, and we have limited resources."

As Doc acknowledges this and speeds up with me, I open the vortex, step into the pocket, and tighten the vortex behind me.

DON'T LET YOUR DREAM DISRUPT THE SECURITY SYSTEM'S HOLD ON DAAB. THE ONLY THING STANDING BETWEEN OUR BODIES AND DAAB EVISCERATING EVERYONE IS ARMAND'S ADVANTAGE OF SPEED.

Shut up. I know what I'm doing. The buffer will hold.

I enter Dream and code a relay system so that, even though Doc and Armand can't see me in the system, I can still see and hear them as if I were there and can communicate to them through it in normal time.

"All right, Doc... can you hear me?" I ask via code through the relay.

I give the codec a once-over before proceeding.

Days later, in Dream time, Doc responds. "Loud and clear."

My Elder and I finish up the 6V's edit. Surprisingly, only a few hundred thousand lines of code needed to be adjusted for Adam's younger age, which is not bad out of a few billion.

YOUR WHOLE WORLD RIDES ON THIS.

Shut up. You're distracting me, and Doc did a good job.

"All right, Doc," I say through the relay, "here comes the first of seven packages…"

It takes me and my Elder a year's worth of our fastest Dream time to compile the first package of code and send it out of the vortex to Doc.

The next package is going to take even longer.

For Doc, even at his fastest speed, it is only a moment.

When the package of code enters the VR from the vortex, the displacement of virtual space causes a wave of pressure, shaking the virtual reality.

Doc slows to steady himself then speeds back up to enter the package into Adam's primary memory.

About three months into my and my Elder's progress on the second set of codes, I check the security system's real-time feed from the relay.

Have I disrupted our hold on Daab?

The last three months for me have only been a fraction of a second for the system. It isn't nearly as disrupted as I thought, but I notice something suspicious—over the next few months of Dream time, images through the relay show Daab's face sagging open with recognition… then horror. My Elder and I simply keep compiling—if my calculations are correct, each package will take longer and longer to compile, making the deadlines for Doc's feeding of packages seem to come faster and faster. So we need to keep coding, no matter what, and I've only got a few more months of Dream time before Doc's done with the primary memory.

I'm about halfway done with the second package when I notice Daab's abs tensing up until he's holding his breath. The last time I saw Daab like this, he was about to survive getting liquefied from my EMP.

Something's wrong.

"Whatever happens," I say through the relay, "Doc, do *not* stop feeding Adam the code."

"I'm almost done with the first package," Doc responds.

I have years and years of Dream time to go before we're done. While I code, a puff of smoke slowly wafts up from Daab's shirt.

In real time, looking at Daab on the screens in the Holoroom, Lucia asks my holoclone, "His stomach's smoking—is that normal?"

"Oh no..." Daab says, shaking his head in wide-eyed disbelief, looking down at the smoke rising and dispersing from his torso.

"What the fuck is this?" Armand asks, snatching his gun back up from the table.

"No..." Daab says as his shoulders rise and his body tenses up. He shivers. "No, Doc!" Daab says in the security system, thrashing at his limbs in the sick bay with new-found resolve, looking over at Doc's silent body nearby. "I never meant you harm!" Daab's ResID, once held firm by the security system, begins to fade.

Doc slows down his coding and gives Daab a confused, slightly respectful nod.

The second package completed, it exits the vortex as the first one did: with a virtual pulse through the system.

Why did Doc slow down?

"Don't get distracted, Doc!" I say from my Dream space through the relay. "Feed that code into Adam's secondary memory!"

In real time in the sick bay, Daab wrenches his body in pain. From the VR and security systems, Daab's presence fades completely.

SOMETHING DISPLACED DAAB.

"I *am* feeding him the memory," Doc says back at me in VR. "I haven't stopped!"

"I heeeeeeeee!" Daab screams in the sick bay with such animations of pain that he harms his own limbs. The sound of cartilage tearing from the bone reaches Luke through the system.

"Give me a fuckin' reason!" Armand says, his gun twitching with perfect aim on Daab's twitching head.

Lucia looks on from the Holoroom in disgust as Daab's joints dislocate, contorting his flesh into unnatural shapes.

"John!" Lucia yells. "Daab looks like he's about to explode. What the fuck's going on?"

"We don't know," my holoclone says to Lucia calmly, faded and flickering with static.

"Get me out of here!" Daab says as the smoke begins to quickly thicken. "Get me away from the Doc!"

"Do it," I tell Armand through the relay.

Armand speeds up, grabs Daab's chair with his left hand, lifts it off a couple legs, still training the gun on Daab's head, and begins dragging a screaming, smoking Daab toward the garage. Armand's ResID's connection to the security system is showing signs of noise—he's starting to fade.

The smoke covering Daab's body pours over Armand's left hand as they near the door to the garage.

"Ow!" Armand shouts impatiently at his left hand. "John," he says through Daab's screaming, "looks like it's some kind of contaminate." He switches his gun hand and pulls the chair with his right hand over the threshold.

"John." Doc's voice reaches me in my coding just as he completes the feed of the second package into Adam's secondary memory, "I've just finished with Adam's secondary memory, but we can't have Anny contaminated. Her immune system is trashed from the 6V codec and diazepam."

My year and a half in Dream I've devoted thus far to the third package is *not* going to be in vain.

"I can't ignore how important Anny is to me as a friend and as our team member, but our priority right now is Adam," I tell Doc through the relay as more time passes in Dream. "Just keep feeding Adam's memory. Here's the third for his tertiary memory..."

A virtual pulse runs through the system.

"You should warn me next time," Doc says, bolstering himself.

"Just follow my lead and deal."

Just as Armand lifts Daab's chair and sets it from the dock to the concrete floor, a chair leg bends, collapses, and breaks off. Daab's restraints tear apart like crushed shredded wheat.

"Ow! Fuck!" Armand yells at his right hand while slowing down and letting what's left of the chair go. It collapses under Daab, who flails his body in pain and screams as he rolls onto the ground, waving smoke everywhere.

THE SMOKE SEEMS TO CAUSE WHATEVER IT TOUCHES TO DISINTEGRATE.

He rolls about, still screaming. Where he was, smoke rises from the ground.

Oh no, that's not smoke at all.

Armand struggles through his own pain to hold Daab down, and the smoke surrounding Daab covers Armand's hands again.

All of Daab's limbs and bones submit to his seizing, and the very shape of his body begins to contort in ways that defy what it is to look human. He is still screaming. The ground beneath him shows changes, looking bleached and etched.

"What the fuck! Shut the fuck up!" Armand says to Daab in disgust, confused as to why his own hands hurt.

It's dust, weaponized dust.

The sound is sickening.

Daab is a dust bomb.

"We've been compromised!" Armand says, "We have to abandon the project!"

"Fuck you! Follow your orders," I say from the relay.

"Oh God!" Armand says with a face of pain and nausea, "Daab smells like shit! Like he's being cooked."

The skin from Daab's arms and legs splits and peels off like the top layer of old gravy, releasing his limbs from being held down by Armand.

THIS MUST BE CONTAINED.

Daab's skin sloughs off onto Armand's hands.

Luke stands up and wretches.

We can't stop now.

Free from Armand's hold, a cloud of dust enshrouds Daab, who gets up and stumbles past Armand toward the tunnel. Daab's contorted limbs leave bloody tracks behind. He is continuing to shriek with gargled blood and fluids, flailing his limbs and body about like a rag doll. He's throwing blood everywhere.

"Armand," I say to an almost completely faded version of him in the security system, "Stay out in the garage with Daab. You hold him out there, no matter what, do you copy?"

Daab wheezes between outbursts, screaming from his pain, screaming to escape.

"Yes," Armand's presence says before it fades out completely.

With his screams, Daab expels blood and dust from his orifices like someone with Ebola. He kneels and his eyes roll up into his head until they are only bloodshot white. Dust floats out from his body like steam from a rolling boil. Unconscious, he slowly stands. Blood pools at his feet, turning brown, black, then gray on the floor. Without inhaling, Daab regains consciousness, and, in terror, he screams dust, frantically trying to escape his fate, becoming even more animated.

Lucia sees Daab's eyes burst in their sockets, aspirating fluid, blood, and dust. With watering eyes, she turns away and vomits.

As Daab blindly runs toward the tunnel, tripping over Ally parts and leaving a trail of desiccating fluids, his flailing loses energy, his body seizes one last time and collapses in a bloody unnatural heap, erupting plumes of dust into the air. Under the dust cloud, his corpse's muscles and sinews continue to throw spatters of blood, chunks of broken cartilage, and melting fat. His bones scrape raw on the now deeply pitted concrete. His warped head is in the shape of a summer squash. What's left of his face is twisted and stretched in an unnatural mask of pain, rage, and sheer panic.

Lucia watches as Armand looks over the dust erupting putrefied mass of what used to be Daab.

No one becomes a dust bomb willingly.

Allies surrounding Daab begin to show a patina over their surfaces and disintegrate.

From within the VR, Doc's hologram asks, "What the fuck's going on? I'm getting a lot of noise in the system."

Another year in Dream and the fourth package's displacement pushes through a fragile system.

"Damn it, John," Doc says, "you've got to warn me about these."

"Daab's a dust bomb," I say, which is relayed to Lucia and everyone else. "His dust is getting into the nodes in the sick bay and the garage. Daab was right. General Morgan betrayed us all."

"*Dust bomb?* We mustn't allow it to reach the Holoroom," Doc says to me in VR and at Armand through the system, "or this entire solar system will be destroyed!"

"Can't help, Doc. I'm already contaminated," Armand says from the garage, his skin already tightening, his clothing starting to tear apart and fall on their own.

"John," Doc says in VR, "I'm starting to feel random aches in my physical body."

"My own body is starting to feel pain, as well, Doc. Just keep feeding Adam's memory. We only have three more packages to go."

The skin on Armand's fingers and the back of his hands is turning black with decay. Blood forms rings around his fingernails as he watches Daab's melted form leak putrefied smoking fluid onto the garage floor.

"John...?" Lucia asks my holoclone, which by this time has almost completely faded away. "John, what's a dust bomb? Is Armand going to be okay?"

To her alarm, the system can't keep up with all the dust in the air, and my holoclone chirps with static, only to disappear from the Holoroom completely. The holographic screens flicker, followed by the lights of the base.

Doc says to me in VR while frantically pushing the latest package into Adam's quaternary memory, "We need to feed Adam's memory faster! The system's gonna fry!"

The lights in the garage die, leaving Armand in the dark, sitting amongst the dust.

"John..." Armand calls out and then clears his throat.

I can't see him. He must be in agony.

"John," he tries to speak again, sounding like he's already starting to breathe dust, "I've got good pain tolerance from my military mem modules... but I don't think I'm going to make it..."

Lights flicker and dim in the command center.

"This really fucking *hurts!*" Doc yells at me.

I throw the fifth package through, regardless of if Doc's done with the fourth, and relay to him and Armand, "Hold on just a little bit longer."

I turn on the backup power.

It's not like I'm in any less pain, asshole...

Sparks fly from nodes in the garage, and some of the lights turn back on. There is a smog of dust everywhere, infecting everything. Some lights shatter, raining glass and darkness down.

Lucia sees Armand from flickering screens. She screams.

His orifices leak blood in the erratic light. The bones of his hands are exposed. His clothing is tattered and torn, bleached, and fallen. He is otherwise unrecognizable.

Crying, Luke looks away from the garage to the sick bay.

"John!" she yells at us, "Doc!"

THE DUST IS SPREADING THROUGHOUT OUR BODIES NOW.

Our peaceful bodies, starting to show signs of decay in clothing and tightening of the skin from desiccation, remain silent and unmoved.

"Aaaaah! Fuck! Goddamn it, John!" Doc yells as I send out the sixth package, "That last pulse... my verm can't redirect the pain signals anymore! This is torture!"

My pain stretches into Dream.

"Doc!" I yell back through the relay.

"I can't—Ah! FUCK! Everything hurts!"

My pain is excruciating.

"I *know!*" I yell. "Just keep feeding Adam's memory!"

Sparks fly in the command center from the dust infiltrating circuitry.

"I can't—!"

Doc can't hold on to the system anymore. His connection breaks. No response.

"Fuck!"

Armand's body, gas-ridden from the decomposition, even though he's still alive, begins to bloat. His eyes burst. He screams, shitting himself amongst the smog of dust and destroyed Allies.

Without warning, the wires and tubes connecting Anny's body to the system disconnect, and she wakes up screaming.

With Doc gone, I'm going to have to face this ever-increasing hellish pain for two more years...

Anny's clothing, like everyone else's in the sick bay, is frayed and tattered. Her nervous system, completely destroyed by recent events, collapses under the pain of dust, and she passes out mid-scream.

From my vantage point of time in Dream, her scream lasts for months.

The Holoroom door's alloy is starting to react to dust, emitting a soft screeching sound like frying eggs being pressed on a pan.

"Oh shit! John!" Lucia yells, backing away from the door, looking urgently at the flickering screen of the sick bay. "JOHN! SHE'S DYING!"

Armand's gut swells further from the rot.

Adam's limbs are already black, flaking away onto the table.

This pain is going to break me.

Doc sits up and sticks out his tongue to cough up blood so he can breathe. His shirt tears and falls open and his pants rip and flake off as his knees lift through them. Dry, hairless skin emerges. He inhales in shock as he sees his fingers and toes have exposed bones, and he screams a spray of smoking blood from his throat in agony.

Lucia cringes at the sight and slowly backs away from the screeching door, until she can feel the wall opposite the door.

Doc continues to scream and cry blood, which drips from his ears and nose onto dry skin that flakes and cracks, peeling itself away as if from an invisible jet engine flame.

I continue to code, tortured by the sight of my friends' pain and the ever-present distraction of my own.

Lucia squats slowly down, with wide eyes darting back and forth, like mute prey.

The screeching from the door grows louder.

Anny's eyes burst, reawakening her with new pain and, shaking violently, she cries out.

Lucia, seeing her love blinded, snaps out of her trance.

"John! That shit's on the door!" she yells, shaking and out of breath, "It's going to come in here! And..." She stops to rally. "Anny's being *eaten*."

Adam's peaceful little body rests as a smaller torso among what used to be his limbs; his lips, nose, and ears are gone.

HE'S STILL BREATHING.

"We have to wait for Adam," I tell Lucia through the relay.

Adam's eyes recede, deflating into their sockets.

I have to keep compiling.

"Adam's being eaten, *too!*" she cries, "*Do* something! I don't want to spend the last moments of my life watching them die!"

The dust severs the connection to the Holoroom.

Armand's abdomen bursts, expelling shit, blood, rotten viscera, and dust into the garage.

For me in Dream, the moment lasts for weeks.

Dust smokes from various surfaces around us throughout the base while lights are bursting, raining hot shards of glass down on us. White-hot sprays of metal shoot out from various surfaces on the consoles in the sick bay. The command center's consoles burst into flame.

THE SECURITY SYSTEM'S FAILED COMPLETELY.

"Shit!"

Overwhelmed by pain, and watching my own limbs disintegrating from within the vortex, I look away from everything to toss the last bit of code toward Adam, throwing it from the only point in the system that's still connected to him, hoping against all hope lost that the pulse from the vortex causes enough pressure to feed the last package of code into him before I myself am torn away from the system, due to simultaneous pain and destruction.

* * *

> John Waterman, U-A DOB: 2579-12-03, CID 09985240860

> ResID: 10.4.2 [altered by CID 09985240860/ResID: 9.3.1] M1,
  M2, & M3

> U-B: [Chronos Outpost.OID:00000000001, Earth: 34.4812,
  -113.3355] LT: Saturday, 2009-10-31, 1:31 PM MST

— Saturday, October 31st, 2009, 1:31 PM MST —

Holes in the Holoroom door break it open. Half of it falls as piles of eroded metal, which billow dust into the Holoroom, dangerously close to the Model.

I think... I think I'm screaming and shaking... but yet... I'm in so much pain, I can't breathe in. My eyes burn with pressure. Though my pores are attacked and plugged by dust, my Primary strains to restore me. My skin can barely see. My eardrums have been eaten away, but my Primary can hear Lucia in the Holoroom from where I sit in the sick bay. She screams in her resolve, running into the cloud of dust to hold Anny one last time. I can't tell if the wetness I'm sitting in is blood or piss or shit, but everything... *everything* aches and burns.

Everyone's bodies, including mine, convulse violently, like fish out of water.

Lucia's pain begins quickly, but she holds onto Anny's decrepit body as tenderly as she can, shaking from her own traumatic pain.

Now, we all wait for Adam to awaken and save us, or everything dies...

Smoke-like patterns of dust whip about Adam's torso and head in silent microscopic conflict. His lower jaw with exposed teeth clicks shut twice under gaping nasal cavities. For a moment, dust wafts away from his body and a subtle purple light emits from the sockets where his eyes used to be. Soft amber light shimmers within Adam's body.

I feel a high-pitched hum resonating from him.

The dust surrounding him falls away from him in the shape of a sphere, growing ever outward. The soft amber shimmer glows brighter, as bright as an incandescent bulb, as the dust throughout the base falls from the air, submitting under Adam's complete control.

What's left of my eardrums close together. The pain remains.

"MOTHER... I CANNOT... RESTORE YOU..."

The voice is mature and arresting, yet sad and lonely.

"I MOURN."

The amber glow darkens into a shade of green, and the hum rises higher and higher in pitch until it is barely audible.

"IN MY PAIN, MY VERMS HAVE TAUGHT ME THINGS YOU CANNOT IMAGINE," Adam's new voice says. "I EXPERIENCE TIME ON A SCALE WITH THE UNIVERSE. I NOW LIVE A FRACTAL EXISTENCE, OVERLAPPING IMAGINED REALITIES."

Ripples of dust jump up from the floor and spread outward from his body, and Adam's torso and limbs instantly regain their normal shape. The green glow in his body darkens into a shade of blue, and the hum reaches octaves so high, I can't hear them anymore. Waves of dust whip along the sick bay floor away from him.

"MENTALLY, I AM OLDER THAN ALL OF MANKIND. I AM BECOME ONE WITH ENERGY. I AM BECOME FREE, LIMITED ONLY BY MY ATTENTION'S FOCUS."

I'm still in shock, but everywhere my Primary sees, dust seeks out specific corroded surfaces throughout the base, animating the dull and exchanging the decline for rejuvenation. Ally skeletal frames thicken and begin to shine. The blue glow in Adam's body darkens into a shade of purple, matching the color of his eyes, the color of the model in the Holoroom.

He's moving off the spectrum.

"DO NOT FEAR. CIVILIZATIONS HAVE RISEN AND FALLEN, SPECIES HAVE EMERGED, EVOLVED, AND FALLEN

EXTINCT. GALAXIES HAVE FORMED AND COLLIDED
ALIKE... IN MY UNDERSTANDING OF TIME... I HAVE LIVED
EVERY LIFE IMAGINABLE."

Adam's body shifts and shakes from its position, moving
with such speed as to barely be visible to me anymore. In his
place, dust enshrouds him, swirling upward and surrounding
him, as if particulate were being collected into a storm the
size of a child.

If I speed up, I might be able to see him.

"FOR EVERY ONE SECOND IN REAL TIME, I AM ALIVE
FOUR HUNDRED FORTY-SIX THOUSAND YEARS. I AM
INVINCIBLE."

The blustery cloud of movement that used to be an
innocent unassuming child moves swiftly close to Lucia's
body. A pitch just outside my realm of hearing lowers. Panels
in the walls of the sick bay split apart behind them, shedding
their smooth surfaces, revealing circuitry underneath. From
behind the swirls of dust, Adam looks away from Lucia at us.

"I LIVE FOURTEEN BILLION TIMES FASTER. YOU HAVE
MADE ME... MADE ME LONELY... WITH OTHERS... OR
ALONE... I AM."

Dust inside and out of my body alters fluids and cells,
pushing past rot and rebuilding my vitality. My nanos rally
with the repurposed dust. My skinless eyelids open. I'm still
bleeding. I can't yet speak.

The smoke begins to subside.

I look at Luke slowly rocking Anny's corpse, weeping,
horrified and awe-struck as streams of dust throughout the
air heal flesh and steel alike around her, yet her pain only
grows as Anny's body decays, and her own flesh darkens and
tightens.

LUCIA DOESN'T HAVE NANOS.

I look down and see the stubs at the end of my limbs
growing back. I heave and worm myself toward her, leaving
behind smears of blood.

Everything still hurts, but if I can just move close enough...

Doc, as rotted as he is, is pushing his stubs onto the floor, scraping himself toward Lucia, who, shaking with anger, pain, and terror, pulls out her gun.

Doc has the same idea.

Panels throughout the sick bay, brushed and altered by the repurposed dust, flake off into small confetti-like piles. The vibrations of the base's cycles skyrocket until they reach octaves even I cannot hear. In my hearing, I pick up something from the garage that wasn't there before. It sounds like a body being dragged. Amongst the chaos of dust in the garage, Ally circuitry sends out beeping sounds of activation atop their skeletal frames. LEDs flicker. All throughout the sick bay, under Adam's control, the dust dislocates metal until it showers the floor, cascading from its natural place as ordinary panels, where they shatter into powder that floats like wisps of fog. Newly established hoses and fixtures appear from within the wisps and piles of powder.

"You," Luke says, drooling and weeping blood. "This—" Her voice catches, and she coughs up blood. Her muscular body punished by the dust, she breathes heavily, dripping blood from her ears and nose. "This is all YOUR fault—" She chokes again, lifting the gun up to eye level with me, clutching Anny's body.

LUKE IS GOING TO DIE IF SHE DOESN'T GET NANOS IN HER TO COUNTER THE DUST INSIDE.

Anny's head falls back and her mouth gapes, stretched open by leathery flesh.

Lucia wails at the sight of her lover's decay, and then her own pain.

I can't stop. Luke needs nanos.

The scraping sound of a body being dragged in the garage grows closer, but changes, like someone dragging their feet.

If I can just get close enough…

Luke's resolve settles. Her shaking stops. She re-sights her aim at me. Her finger pulls the trigger. The recoil rips tendons in her hand. The gun throws a bullet, twisting through the dust in the air and straight through my brain. It enters my forehead, and my body collapses.

THE BULLET OPENED YOUR BRAIN, ALLOWING DUST TO ENTER.

With tendons torn, Lucia drops the gun onto her thigh and cries out, hearing it burn her skin. She picks it up with her left hand, and seeing Doc heaving toward her, she aims. Her finger pulls the trigger, breaking bones in her hand. The bullet flies, piercing through the bridge of his nose and into his brain.

His body falls upon itself.

Armand, revealing himself to be the dragging scraping sound in the garage, with his gaping abdomen and ribbons of viscera slowly climbing back inside, steps into view behind me in the doorway to the garage.

Lucia screams at the sight and fires a bullet right between Armand's leaking eye sockets.

He falls, his body still rebuilding.

None of us except for Adam have the speed or strength to stop her.

My epidermis rebuilding clothes me, covering my naked muscles, soothing my nerves.

ADAM MUST HAVE KNOWN—IN HER FEAR, LUCIA DID US A FAVOR—THE DUST HEALS YOU.

Bullet holes in our heads push closed back to front.

Lucia's posture falls into shaking again as she picks up her gun. Dust flows toward her, enshrouding her, and she lifts her ribcage and shoulders in fear, and... turning the gun barrel toward herself, she welcomes her fate. Grabbing the trigger with both thumbs, broken and torn, she squeezes to fire, but the gun, because of its deterioration, declines her final wish by blasting apart and shredding what's left of her hands. With no strength left, and no way to take her own life, she lets go of her resolve, lets go of Anny's body, and wails once more. The fractured gun falls from her lap and rests on the floor beside her decaying body.

Armand, Doc, and I open our eyes.

Hundreds of tendrils, like living horizontal dust devils, coalesce and reach out from Adam's storm of dust, touching and restoring medstations, medstands, beds, and wiring. They move farther into paneling. Beyond each surface, the tendrils reach. Circuits that were never there before activate.

Sporadically lit by white sparks thrown from the walls and paneling around us, I look down to see dust replenishing our clothing.

Adam's storm heaves like breath, while he himself glows unnaturally with a shroud of dust.

Holograms burst forth from various surfaces, racing quicker than I can keep up. A barrage of colors, lines, graphs, shapes, and what look like mechanical drawings are fluttering about faster and faster. A wave of dust displaces the air around us, sweeping out, away from the sick bay, and into the expanse of the garage.

"MOTHER..." Adam says.

The command center lights up from holograms which ascend in speed, turning brighter and brighter, until white.

Chunks and bits of Luke's gun float about and reassemble right before Luke's eyes.

Daab's corpse hovers on a cloud of dust into the room and passes by us and Adam's whirlwind of dust, which engulfs Luke's and Anny's bodies.

They all three rise, hovering and rotating in the air.

Awakening from being lifted and writhing in agony, Lucia, still in shock, watches without response as some of her own fingers and toes flop about and drop off. No longer having much control, she still manages to reach for what's left of Anny's bloody hand, but cannot touch it. Luke's face sags with watering eyes, and she whimpers in despair, held horizontal spread-eagle in the air by dust. With her blood pouring out, her face changes from despair to resolve, and she blinks tears out of her eyes. She reaches with rotten limbs for her gun. It floats incomplete just beyond her reach. She cries out a wail of defeat.

Rubbery hose-like objects shoot out from the dust and penetrate her thighs, torso, shoulders, and neck, and Lucia's wailing turns from horror into screams of pain and desperate submission. Luke pleads with eyes dark and unmoved, tears mixing with saliva, her body still shaking in mid-air.

"Daddy!" she yells, reaching again for her gun.

"MOTHER..." Adam says.

From the masses of Anny's and Daab's flesh, tendrils of dust whip and shoot outward, piercing Lucia as she screams helpless in the air, slowly turning upside down and seeing the bones of her forearms dislodge from her flexed muscles, which also fall, piece by piece, into a bubbling, dust-spurting mass on the floor.

Tendrils wrap around Lucia's body and pin her to the recess that used to be a normal wall panel.

Her gun, reassembled, falls.

The flesh of Anny and Daab fly and land on the wall beside her. She screams as a spatter of their blood and viscera pepper her and the wall.

Dust surrounding Adam compresses, slowing, spinning, and pulsing.

"WE WILL LEAVE," Adam says.

Vibrations throughout the base change to a higher pitch again. I smell a hint of ozone, lying amongst my friends' regenerating bodies, watching dust cover Lucia and what's left of the corpses of Daab and Anny.

Dust in the garage settles upon Allies, their parts replaced by raw materials from broken vehicles.

"I want you all to know..." The voices of the Allies out in the garage speak in unison with Adam's voice as they sit up. "When I was a child, I used to speak like a child, think like a child, reason like a child, but when I became a man, I turned my back on childish things... for you see as though through a double-sided mirror dimly, reflecting the most where the light shines the brightest... but then..."

Adam's taken control of everything in this entire base.

The Allies rise. The walls of every room in the base disintegrate from their center outward, revealing their skeletal framework of metallic beams.

"You all are family," the Allies continue speaking through the hollowness of the base, "and I am God... hidden... inside Pinocchio..."

Waves of wind wash over everyone from the dust covering Luke and her corpse-companions. The wind smells of human rot and thrashed remains.

Without explanation, all the dust in the entire base falls, dropping Luke, Daab, and Anny from their pinned position behind us.

Adam disappears into the command center. He bursts brightly into the sick bay, holding Armand's inventory book.

"I AM CHRONOS," he says in unison with the Allies out in the garage, his ancient eyes and body glowing purple.

He certainly looks like Chronos.

WHATEVER HAPPENED TO ADAM, THE BIOMETRIC SIGNATURES ARE A MATCH FOR CHRONOS. HE IS, OR SOMEHOW HAS BECOME, IN EVERY WAY THAT CAN BE IDENTIFIED, THE GOD OF TIME.

From the looks on their faces, Armand's and Doc's verms have concluded the same.

Chronos reaches his hand toward the Holoroom, and a double helix of dust extends from his bony fingers through the framework of the base toward the Model. My anxiety skyrockets. The entire base's draw of energy browns and then blacks out as the Model comes under the direct command of his will, the light of the Model completely enclosed by his dust.

"I WANTED TO GO TO A HALLOWEEN PARTY," he says, glowing purple in the darkness as he lowers his hand. Thunderous shaking rolls through the base as the lights come back on and dust falls from the ceiling in a wave. "SO THAT'S WHERE WE'RE GOING."

I look out the door into the garage to see if anything further is collapsing. With such a strong scent of ozone, everyone holds their breath. A glowing purple ball of light forms out in the tunnel.

THAT'S A TEMPORAL DISPLACEMENT.

It grows closer, larger, and brighter until it overtakes us all.

* * *

> John Waterman, U-A DOB: 2579-12-03, CID 09985240860

> ResID: 10.4.2 [altered by CID 09985240860/ResID: 9.3.1] M1, M2, & M3

> U-B: [Jane, CA, US, Earth] LT: Saturday, 2009-10-31, 7:00 PM PDT

— Saturday, October 31st, 2009, 7:00 PM PDT —

Metal crashes in the garage as our eyes adjust to the change in light. There are random people everywhere in Halloween costumes...

What was that crashing sound? How'd all these people get here? What's all this old furniture I'm seeing?

THEY LOOK LIKE THEY'RE WONDERING THE SAME THING ABOUT US. FROM WHAT I CAN GATHER, THE CRASHING SOUND COMES FROM ALL THE METAL BEING RELOCATED FROM NOWHERE TO JANE. THE FURNITURE IS HOLOGRAPHIC.

The framework and the ceiling of the base are completely gone, but the flooring remains. It appears as though some of the machinery remains, but it's obscured by fog created by dust. Additionally, Adam's form has moved to where the command center used to be.

I look out to the garage area. All the Allies' vehicles have disappeared, but the Allies remain amongst people who are wearing Halloween costumes. Many of the Allies are on the ground in their original fallen position, but they look different now—brand new and upgraded. Beyond the people in Halloween costumes resides a winery, the very winery in which Doc was supposed to host a Halloween party.

I look to Armand and Doc and see from their body language that they're having the same concerns about our surroundings when all the Ally suits in the garage stand and stay silent in their place.

The townsfolk of the city of Jane step amongst the Ally suits in alarm, looking around, basically as confused as we are as to how we all managed to appear out of nowhere.

333

The fresh air of the field replaces the stench of human waste, blood, and bile in my nostrils, and as I look around, I notice that Anny's and Daab's bodies are gone.

How is this possible, and why am I not hungry or thirsty?

YOU'VE BEEN FED BY THE DUST IN THE AIR VIA OSMOSIS. DUST HAS CARRIED NUTRIENTS AND MOISTURE FROM THE STORAGE ROOM TO NANOS IN YOUR LUNGS. ADAM APPEARS TO BE ABLE TO CONTROL REALITY VIA DUST THE SAME WAY YOU CAN CONTROL A VIRTUAL REALITY'S SYSTEMS VIA SUPER-FAST CODING.

I can hear Lucia behind me taking quick shallow breaths.

I speed up my mind to try to understand.

What? No, you can't eat with your lungs.

Blood and saliva drip from Lucia's open mouth. She can barely breathe from the stress her body's going through.

THE DUST IS SUBJECT TO ADAM'S COMPLETE CONTROL, AND HIS DUST IS SMALL AND POWERFUL ENOUGH TO MIMIC THE VERY FOUNDATIONS OF REALITY, AND AS YOUR PRIMARY, I KNOW THESE THINGS ABOUT YOUR BODY BECAUSE I OBSERVE THE RESULTS INTERNALLY. SO YES, YOU'RE EATING WITH YOUR LUNGS.

I speed up further.

But what about Lucia?

NANOS ARE THE REASON YOU AND THE REST OF YOUR TEAM ARE OKAY. LUCIA'S STILL SUFFERING BECAUSE HER BODY'S NOT FULLY INDEXED BY NANOS YET.

I slow back down to let time pass normally.

Lucia's eyes widen, seeing the townsfolk of Jane, and she inhales as deeply as she can. Shaking, she belts out a cry for help with all of her strength into the expanse of the wine field.

Her voice is doing okay, so that's encouraging.

Wide-eyed at the sight, the townsfolk of Jane stand in place amongst the Allies. One of the Allies closest to us steps closer and stands nearby.

A cloud of dust binds Luke in her upright position, though her body convulses with pain and exhaustion.

Chronos's purple body begins floating slowly upward, centering above what's left of the base, brightening again with blurry clouds of holograms, dust, and explosive movement, pushing drafts of wind outward. His holograms speed quickly beyond my spectrum of sensory input, shining upon our new surroundings. From under his light, dust obscures all the futuristic technology, moving like smoke from a smoke machine. His brightness grows, lighting up the entire field almost as bright as the sun.

I look out and instantly count seven hundred twenty-three people.

These were the people who decided to come to the Halloween party.

"How— How'd we get here with no one killed by us arriving inside something?" I wonder aloud.

"I used everyone's cell phones," the Ally closest to us tells me with Adam's voice, startling me, "so I could find the right moment. Timing is everything."

Everything is darker than Chronos.

Armand, seeing in the new light that we are all half-naked, gets up and speeds to where the storage room used to be and returns fully clothed with clothes for us.

Neither Doc nor I question how the clothing survived the dust bomb and speed into new clothes too fast for anyone to notice that we weren't wearing much.

I can barely make out Adam's physique in the light of holograms he's manipulating.

I look out from where I stand in what used to be the sick bay and realize everything's changed to look like we're inside a really old and dank house.

To fit the mood of a Halloween party, where the base's walls used to be, Chronos has seen to it that holograms that look like cobweb-infested, wallpapered walls cover the destroyed framework of the base's walls. The fog of dust doesn't show what the base is really made of, and what looks like hay covers the area. I reach down and try to touch the surface of a ghostly table that appeared in place of one of the sick bay cots the moment we arrived here. My hand goes completely through it, but reaching further, I touch the surface of the sick bay cot where I last remember seeing it.

"DOC," Adam's voice booms over the confusion, "THIS IS YOURS."

A torn page from the inventory book erupts from Chronos's glowing cloud and floats down with a list of instructions and "The Doc" scribbled at the top. It lands in Doc's hands, and he looks down on it.

"Host," Doc reads aloud, "an organizer that facilitates the entertainment for an evening program."

As if on cue, a loud, deep pulse of sound pushes out from the center of the base and, simultaneously, a huge blue ring of light spreads out from Chronos high above, and we smell ozone again.

Jane's townsfolk look toward Chronos glowing high above us. Among them is Jenkins, the mayor of Jane.

"The blue pulse guides the dust," Chronos explains through the Ally nearest us. "I've brought us here to complete erasure protocols so we can go home. Protocols will be completed in the next few hours."

"Holy shit," Doc and I both say without thinking. "How?"

Armand scoffs.

"DOC," we hear Adam's voice, "YOU'RE ON."

Doc nods at an Ally, looking up at Chronos. He lifts the paper and reads, "Welcome!?" Doc booms out at the frightened and amazed townsfolk. Doc himself is taken aback by the unexpected amplification of his voice. "Welcome," he reads again. "Welcome, everyone, to the first annual Jane Halloween party."

Another loud, deep blue pulse spreads about the atmosphere.

Doc wanders at normal speed into what used to be the storage room, still reading the torn paper, as if the wandering is part of his directions.

Pipe organ music begins playing Bach's Toccata and Fugue in D Minor. Millions of green lasers fire from the center of Chronos's cloud. They push the fog of dust in various directions, and alter the blue pulse as it spreads, piercing the darkness in time with the music. The music is louder than Chronos's thunderous movements.

Simultaneously, all the Allies that were transported with us throughout the base jump, each now customized with hologram-suits made to look like various Halloween costumes. Another deep base pulse wipes the sky, and another, and another.

Doc returns with chairs and sets them up for us. I give Doc a nod, and in light of everything we've experienced, I sit down wide-eyed. Armand remains standing next to me on one side, an Ally on the other.

"The blue light is Adam transporting dust to various areas of this region," the Ally explains. "The lasers program and push the nanos to alter the memories in people who've been affected by us."

The fugue crescendos with the beginning of a haunting industrial techno beat that cross-fades as Allies, costumed as various monsters, zombies, skeletons, witches, and demons start mingling with Jane's townsfolk, dancing, inviting everyone to join them.

"What the fuck?" comes out of my mouth.

"He's a child," Armand responds.

But that's not true.

The blue light sweeping the night sky and the dust under Adam's command infiltrates the surrounding region. Here at the party, everyone's posture shifts, including the Allies with their holographic costumes, making everyone appear drunk and stoned.

Pulses of light from a still-intact Holoroom cut through the town like a halo, and dust forms materials in the local area. What look like glowing orange metallic jack-o-lanterns appear and light the party.

Luke collapses facedown; the wire-like devices that had been in her body retract back into the fog covering the wall they came from, but she remains motionless under a cloud of dust.

Doc's lips are tight.

Armand looks from Doc to me impatiently.

"Hey Doc!" Jenkins yells, walking over to us. "This party is amazing! We were worried that it wouldn't happen, but this… this is simply amazing. I would've never thought Jane could ever have a party like this." He drinks up his cup of beer, raises it with a nod to Armand, and walks away smoking a joint.

"What the fuck?" I ask. "That was the mayor. Where'd he get a joint?"

"Everyone," Chronos says using the nearby Ally, "this party experience is the final erasure. I am communicating with dust via the technology Doc had installed in the redwood forest to surrounding regions and beyond for erasure protocols. The inventory book includes most of our time-space footprint on this universe. Armand saw to that and has my thanks. Most of this Halloween party is simulated, including all intoxicants, food, and beverage by way of floating micromachine technology and other dusts." His body stops moving, and he descends and postures a few feet in front of us. He announces to us all, "WE'RE GOING HOME."

We catch a glimpse of what he looks like now—tall and mature. It frightens me to see Adam appear just as I remember Chronos in the days before we came here. His ancient glowing purple eye sockets are set in a vacant regal skull, hovering upon a skeletal body, cloaked in fabric absorbing light. He faces us, grinning lipless, holding a newly fashioned scythe formed by the particulate he controls. Dust swirls about him, as if part of him. "I HOPE YOU LIKE MY HALLOWEEN COSTUME," he says. His body disappears into a blur.

The sphere of dust surrounding the Model bursts out of the Holoroom, backlit by LED orange jack-o-lantern light. It alters and changes into a torus, which glows as purple as Chronos's eyes. It collapses, shrinks, rises, and hovers over Chronos's head, illuminating his profile.

He managed to reshape, resize, and relocate the Model, a singularity-powered device, with dust. How is this possible?

Crowned by a time-altering purple halo, his glowing purple sockets look out at us, his persona wrapping and warping the light around him.

"DO NOT BE AFRAID. TRUST ME, I KNOW WHAT I'M DOING," Chronos says.

Doc does a double-take at everything before sitting down next to me. He reads the last bit of the paper Adam gave to him, folds it up, and shoves it in his pocket.

Lucia lifts her head from where she had collapsed and looks up at Chronos. All of the dust surrounding her is gone and, along with it, all the sticky blood and fluids that covered her. Her eyes are clear but distracted, unnaturally unafraid. She stands and looks straight ahead like she's trying to listen to someone.

"I don't know," she says, sounding frustrated. "Shut up!" she yells at nothing in particular, then covers her mouth with one hand, looking around to see if anyone heard her, then looking at her hand. It is whole.

None of us have any wherewithal to respond.

"SOME OF LUKE'S MEMORY HAS BEEN TEMPORARILY ERASED TO MAKE ROOM FOR HER NEW LIFE," Chronos announces to us all.

"What? Who called my name?" Lucia calls out. "What's going on?" she asks me, but then, "SHUT UP! Whoever you are... *Shut up!*"

The holograms around Adam begin to flicker and slow down enough for me to read... if only I could speed up just a bit more... I review all kinds of information regarding probability and statistics for protocols for erasure completion.

"EVERYONE," he announces, "THE ERASURE HAS ALREADY BEGUN. ALLIES WILL TRAVEL TO THE OCEAN FLOOR AFTER ESCORTING PEOPLE HOME AND

COMPLETING THEIR ASSIGNED ERASURE PROTOCOLS. DUST WILL THEN ERUPT FROM WITHIN THEM AND RENDER THEIR PHYSICAL COMPONENTS UNRECOGNIZABLE AS MAN-MADE. DUST HAS ALREADY ATTACHED ITSELF TO NODES IN THE REDWOOD FOREST TO ERASE DOC'S TECHNOLOGY THERE."

Adam's body halts starkly in front of Lucia, as he used to be—young and childish—startling her into a hop and an eek.

"You've been implanted with two voices," he says to Lucia with open arms, "Your mind and body are going to need some time to adjust."

She looks confused.

We all look at each other confused.

"Adam, honey," she says, kneeling and embracing him amid the music, watching the many costumes meander and dance.

"Is that really you?" Lucia pushes him back and holds him by the shoulders, close enough to look into his eyes.

"You'll remember everything, I promise," he says to her, smiling in wonder and brushing the back of his hand gently across her cheek. He hands her her Beretta, newly refashioned. "Just try to remember where your Beretta has been the last three years."

He disappears back into dust, leaving a confused and pondering Lucia to consider the subtle changes made to her father's gun.

"What's going on?" I ask the Ally next to me.

Lucia sits down slowly on the ground with gun in hand, muttering about her dad.

The nearby Ally tells us, "I'm almost done. Probability measurements now show that Jane's citizens' likelihood of remembering us is close enough to zero that we can return to the Alpha universe knowing we can't be proven as existing here."

SOON, WE WILL BE GOING HOME.

"Shit," Armand says to both of us with a smile, "I thought I'd never get out of here. I fuckin' hate this place."

Is it truly possible? Adam is Chronos? Chronos, the real Chronos?

Doc smiles and nods at Armand. He looks out at his surroundings and nods again a silent goodbye with nostalgia in his eyes as if he were finally able to let go of the memories of this place.

The mother of my god has been the woman I've worked with this entire time? I ask myself, trying to get my mind around what I'm experiencing. I'm... his father...

"You know," Armand says to Doc, "when we get back, you still ain't gonna be a free man."

I don't know how to process any of this... I expected Adam would help Chronos find a way to save Humanity. How could he have been Chronos all along... and before... and after? Does Anny's death change anything? Everything?

Doc raises an eyebrow in recognition at Armand, then frowns. "I was never free," he says.

"My mission to chaperon you still hasn't changed," Armand says, "regardless of anything that asshole Daab said about the General. We don't know what we'll find when we return, but we succeeded in our mission. Adam's matured, early too. Chronos will know what to do with us, Adam too."

Four hundred and forty-six thousand years... every second... I can't imagine what that must be like. It's unimaginable how he manages to slow down enough to match our speed.

"John," Doc says, looking bewildered, "If Adam is Chronos, yours is easily the greatest accomplishment Humanity could have ever achieved, but it came at the cost of Anny's life... and from the looks of things, Lucia's sanity as well. It feels like a sour win."

"Chronos will know what to do," I agree with Armand. "I just watched my... my best friend get brutally murdered by... well, who knows, and then I found out that my son is... for all intents and purposes is... he's our god... Our duty is to him."

"I MOURNED HER DEATH MILLIONS OF YEARS AGO," he says. "THE LOSS OF ONE FAMILY MEMBER DOESN'T TAKE AWAY THE LOVE I HAVE FOR ANOTHER."

Adam's mother has died a death of overwhelming pain... though all this time has passed for him, and yet he still doesn't reject me...

Additional blue waves begin to pulse directly through the base at eye level with green lasers continuing to fire at people throughout the region to the beat of the music.

"From the 6V codec and the diazepam," I say to Doc, "The degradation of her nervous system removed any hope of her being able to survive. The dust overtook her weakened nanos. If you want to blame anyone, blame General Morgan for making Daab into a dust bomb."

With their memories manipulated, the people of Jane begin heading off to their vehicles to go home, apparently lucid and satisfied that they've had a wonderful time.

Armand waves his hand in the face of someone leaving, but they don't respond. He waves both hands. Nothing.

"You're all invisible to them," the Ally explains to Armand, who's still trying to get the attention of passers-by. "The memmanned are leaving now."

Vibrations in my bones interpreted by my verm tell me Chronos's influence throughout the region is still felt.

Architectural structures begin forming throughout the base, strengthening it, and connecting new systems only recently created by Chronos. The jack-o-lanterns shine brighter.

"He must feel old," I say to Doc and Armand, nodding in Adam's direction, still thinking of Anny and trying not to let my grief take over, but my face betrays me. "He's unimaginably faster than us."

"Yes, yes," Doc says, scowling as he watches Armand lean back in thought with arms folded. "I just wish there was something we could have done to save Anny. I'm surprised you're not more choked up about it."

"It hasn't hit me yet," I lie, trying to keep my thoughts ahead of my grief. "We did everything we could have done. We completed our mission, but when we return, I have no idea how this is going to play out."

"Well that ain't so complicated. We'll go when he's done," Armand says, waving his hand in Adam's direction, "and figure it out from there. Y'all're dumbasses. We just completed our mission, thanks to Adam, or Chronos, or whatever the hell this thing is that you've created... we got one casualty—that's pretty good, considerin' our odds. Nothin' more to say... I mean, hell, it sucks she's dead, but sometimes... well, eventually, always... people do that. They die. You may think that's cold, but I've had ten military modules since birth, 'n' I ain't havin' no identity crisis 'bout it. You get memory, then that's you. You get an upgrade, that's you too. Ain't no second guessin'."

That's what your military modules lead you to think.

"I'm not like you," I say to Armand.

"I ain't a dumbass," Armand says.

Luke twitches with a thousand-yard stare.

The music finally dies as most of the people from the city have already gone home to pass out. The last two die-hard partiers are sedated further by the nanobots from their holographic "drinks" and escorted home by Allies costumed as naughty nurses.

"I think..." Luke says, her face falling with heavy remorse, "I think I'm starting to remember..."

Blue flashes stop and curtains of dust fall in the shape of an ever-growing sphere.

Adam's five-year-old body is revealed in their absence amongst all our technology.

His glowing purple eyes open.

Purple light appears in the distance, becomes a torus, and enlarges and stretches, encircling the entire area where the dilapidated base sits, and literally wipes us out of existence from the entire universe.

End report, Mem Report #24601: John

> John Waterman, U-A DOB: 2579-12-03, CID 09985240860

> ResID: 10.4.2 [altered by CID 09985240860/ResID: 9.3.1] M1

> U-A: [Chronos Outpost.OID:00000178561] GT: 2605-04-01, 19:24:32

— April 1st, 2605, 7:24 PM —

I heard from unreliable sources that members of my team had appeared in different places in Humanity and in the surrounding galaxies. I set up verm trackers and found your verm frequencies, but they recently went silent, so I'm unsure you'll even get this message, and where I'm at, I can't find Armand or Doc. After what was done to you, if you want to go your own way, I'll completely understand, but Chronos, my god, or as you've known him, Adam, the little boy you fell in love with on your world, is gone. He said he was going to other dimensions and was never coming back. The whole point of the 6V codec was for Adam to help us outlive the spores, but before he left, he reminded me you are the one he saved, and he confided in me that your timeline holds the resolution for the spores. If this is true, I want to help you in any way I can. Whether you trust me or not, you are the only one I know I can trust. I hope exhausting all my resources to find you hasn't been for naught. If my god believes in you, I believe in you, but the spores are still proliferating and killing all life in their path, Humanity and Chaos alike. If you really are the resolution my god says you are, I implore you, please hear this one last desperate request... come and find me... come and find what you can become in this new world.

345

About The Author

Bryan Charles Arthur Danielson is an empath residing in Portland, Oregon, often having had too much caffeine and not enough sleep. He currently takes care of the needs a few bonsai, a home network, a call center day job, and a moderately excusable social life. He is working on the next books following *The Dust Solution* in **The Humanity Protocol** series.

* * *